DAWN OF MAGIC

RISE OF THE GUARDIANS

FriesenPress

Suite 300 - 990 Fort St
Victoria, BC, V8V 3K2
Canada

www.friesenpress.com

Copyright © 2020 by Christopher Gorman
First Edition — 2020

Edited by Dan Varrette
Map illustrated by Christopher Johnstone

All rights reserved.

No part of this publication may be reproduced in any form, or by any means, electronic or mechanical, including photocopying, recording, or any information browsing, storage, or retrieval system, without permission in writing from FriesenPress.

ISBN
978-1-5255-6379-9 (Hardcover)
978-1-5255-6380-5 (Paperback)
978-1-5255-6381-2 (eBook)

1. FICTION, FANTASY, URBAN LIFE

Distributed to the trade by The Ingram Book Company

DAWN
OF
MAGIC

RISE OF THE GUARDIANS

CHRISTOPHER
GORMAN

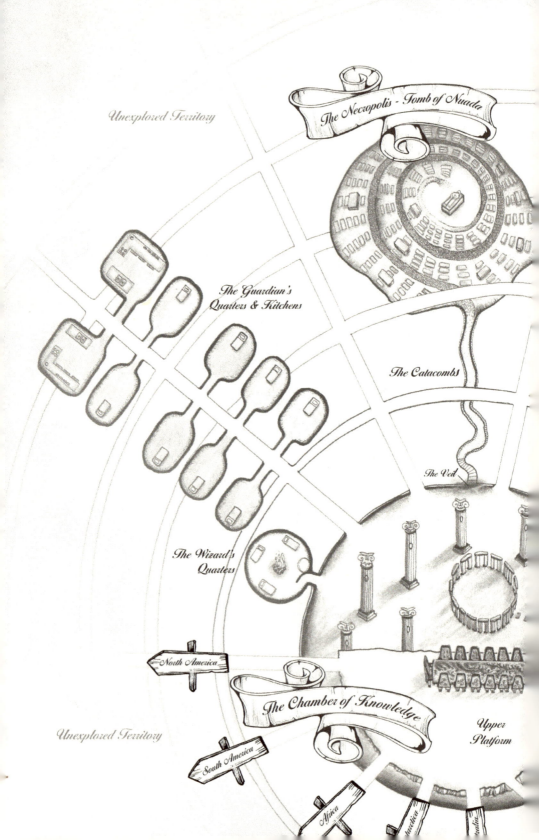

Chapter One

The piano man's fingers dance across the keys. His voice rings out loud and clear through the packed lounge, and at least fifty drunken university jocks sing along with him. Neil Diamond's "Sweet Caroline" is one of the few old bar tunes to have survived the collapse of the music industry in the mid-2070s. It was rediscovered on a dusty, beat-up karaoke machine in the early '90s, and ten years later it's once again a hit. Casually leaning against the bar, I feel a growing urge to sing along. I probably would have if I'd had more to drink, but I've never been fully myself in a crowd of strangers.

I take another sip and my wristband pulses. I glance down, rotating my wrist slightly, and a holographic image of James's head pops up from the device. His blue eyes are vibrant beneath his thick, bushy eyebrows, and his wavy, dirty-blond hair is sweaty and tousled from dancing. I bring my wristband closer so I can hear him through the singing crowd.

His eyes flick left and right, and he cranes his head around to look at my surroundings. "Are you still in the lounge? You said you were just going to grab a drink!"

"Yeah, but—"

"No buts. Get your ass back here. Third room, back corner." He grins as his head vanishes.

I cringe inwardly, wishing I'd avoided his call. I want to stay in the lounge the rest of the night to listen to the piano man, but I do feel somewhat beholden to James regardless of how much I dread the incessant crush of people on the dance floor. After all, he paid my cover to get in here and even topped up my account with enough money to buy a couple of drinks.

I stay for the rest of the song. When it transitions to a modern rendition of "Mr. Brightside," I make my way to the back of the lounge, to where a wide hallway leads to the second room of Surrender. Situated in the heart of Toronto's Port Lands, Surrender is arguably the city's cliquiest club, reserved for the elite and, in my case, their friends.

The kids filling this room are barely of legal age and full of the wide-eyed youthful innocence of being fresh out of high school. They're bouncing around to hits from the late twenty-first century—never my kind of music. I skirt around the room, leaving the class of 2103 to bop amongst themselves, and aim straight for the hallway that leads to the third room.

Once I get to the hallway, I tap my wristband against the bouncer's. He nods when he gets the green light indicating I'm at least twenty-one and have enough money in my account to buy something. This area is somewhat exclusive.

The bouncer ushers me through the sound curtain, and a wave of electro-pop pulses through me. The rapid beats sync perfectly with the synthesized waves of blue and white light that bathe the third and final room. Bodies bump and grind all around me. The people here are in their mid-twenties to mid-thirties—professionals early in their careers, here to unwind through alcohol, drugs, and sex.

This is the type of atmosphere that James thrives in. Since meeting Danielle, he hasn't indulged in anything more than alcohol and flirting, but submersing himself into this pit of preppy depravity serves as his relief. At first it was his reward to himself for staying glued to his books during the week and keeping his marks high enough to get into law school, but now that he's in law school, it's his reward for just surviving another week. Kudos to him. His father is a lawyer in the largest criminal law firm in the country, and his mother's a neurosurgeon, so they've set the bar for success pretty high. And I know they had to pull some pretty big strings to get him into university with his high school grades as poor as they were.

I scan the crowd, looking for the busiest cluster of people, as I know he'll be at the centre of it. But it's impossible to focus through the thick haze of chem-smoke filling the air. It diffuses the light and lends an ethereal quality to the writhing dancers. Clubs that cater to society's well-off developed chem-smoke years ago specifically to enhance the buzz of alcohol. This allows them to charge more for the experience as a way to offset an overall reduction in alcohol sales after water shortages drove the prices of drinks sky-high. Even after this short time, I can feel the chem-smoke's effects pulling at me, urging me to succumb to the lure of the music.

I hear James's voice in my head, telling me to let my guard down, to relax and live a little, and that no one will judge me in the overpriced shirt he lent me. No one will even know this club is so far out of my class that without him they would have laughed at me the second I walked up to the entrance. I look down at the shirt I'm wearing. He's probably right. It's a classy white button-up with a black strip running down the button placket. I'm wearing it untucked with the sleeves rolled up from the wrists to hide the fact that it's not long enough. Fortunately, I'm a little on the scrawny side for six foot four, as I've never been able to build much muscle. It means a shirt tailor-made for James's five foot ten lean and muscled frame almost looks intentionally formfitting on me.

I've hidden the tag on the black fitted dress pants I'm wearing so no one will know I borrowed them for the night from Dale's Clothing, the store I work at. In the hazy light, I catch a glimpse of myself in a mirror as I move through the crowd, and I have to admit, I do look like I belong. However, everyone around me in their short skirts and tight dress shirts is so into their own little circles that I shuffle past them unnoticed.

I take another sip of my beer, noticing that it's almost empty. I should conserve it. Beer is a luxury that Riley's, the local pub in my part of the city, and all the other bars I can afford with my meagre salary, stopped offering long ago. They switched to a condensed vapour essence when the price of water made alcohol unaffordable to the masses, but it makes a poor substitute. Beer's flavour, mouthfeel, and aftertaste are something you miss. But with the average pint now topping two hundred dollars, this is now an experience that only the rich (and their not-so-rich friends) can typically afford. Since James and I are at different places on the economic spectrum, we usually do things that are cheap or free whenever we hang out. When he insists on taking me to a place like this, he also insists on paying.

If he hadn't transferred enough money into my account to cover several drinks and the cover charge, I wouldn't be in here with him now. But I really do hate spending his money. I've tracked every cent he's lent me since we first met five years ago. I record it in an antique ledger that belonged to my grandfather. James doesn't expect it back. He doesn't want it back. He made that quite clear the first time I tried to make a repayment. He belongs to one of those very wealthy old-money families, and he's quite generous and relatively modest. Although he's occasionally guilty of taking his wealth for granted, he never rubs it in anyone's face. Still, I'm adamant I'll pay it all back to him one day. I take a small sip before continuing my way through the crowd, determined to make this drink last.

The song changes, and bodies surge to the increased tempo. A bead of sweat breaks out on my forehead. It's the third Saturday of July—ladies' night—and as fancy as this club is, its air conditioning has failed to hold off the relentless heat with this many people packed inside. I make a mental note to give James a hard time tomorrow. He promised me I'd love it here, but he knows from previous experience that this isn't my scene. Still, as the saying goes, when in Rome . . .

I inhale deeply, feeling the chem-smoke enter my lungs, and my resolve to conserve the last of my beer crumbles. I tilt it backward, draining the glass. Dancing my way through the crowd toward the bar, I scan the sweaty, swirling faces for James. I think I catch a glimpse of his face in the distance, but he disappears before I can tell it's him for sure. I slip through a small gap in the crowd as I reach the bar and come to an abrupt stop as two women effortlessly appear in my path.

The woman on the left has dark brown hair that flows down to her shoulders. Her friend's hair is hot pink and cut in a tight bob. They're dancing together, but they turn as I approach to include me in their dance. Instantly, the high I've started riding recedes and I feel my guard starting to come up. It takes every ounce of effort I have to keep dancing. It's been four months since I separated from Jenn, my fiancée of three years. Since then, James has tried to entice me to a club at least half a dozen times. Until tonight, I couldn't bring myself out of my depression for long enough to do anything fun, let alone go out to a club where I might meet another woman. But James had shown up at my place earlier this evening, his customary charm on full blast, determined to get me out of the house. I succumbed but was fully planning on avoiding any intimate contact.

The brunette smiles at me. Her smile is disarming. I smile back. She looks maybe mid-twenties—my age. Her lipstick is ruby red. It looks like a finishing touch to makeup that's there only to enhance natural beauty. She moves closer, sliding her fingertips down my shirt, and pulls me into the rhythm of their dance. I feel some of the alcohol-induced bravado returning, and I smile again, my nervousness ebbing. They look at each other and giggle.

The one with pink hair asks me a question, but it disappears into the pounding music.

"What?" I yell.

She reaches up and pulls me to her so my ear is almost level with her luscious lips. She isn't wearing any lipstick or any other makeup. She's beautiful just the way she is. "I said you're super cute! What's a guy like you doing dancing alone?" She leans in closer so she can hear my response, her arms still wrapped around my neck.

In the back of my mind, I hear James shouting encouragement. I swallow the bitter retort I have at the ready. Instead, I try to soften my eyes, and I force a grin. "I was just dancing in the piano bar," I lie. "Now I'm on my way to meet up with a friend."

"A girlfriend?"

I shake my head, and the two of them share a look. They pull me into their dance again.

As we dance, their light touches on my body begin to break through my reticence and boost my self-esteem.

"I'm Aiden!" I shout over the music.

They smile, but don't offer their names in return. I guess I didn't shout loud enough. I'm about to lean over and repeat myself when the brunette casts a glance in the direction of the bar. It's almost subtle enough to still be discreet. It's enough to bring to my attention that none of us has a drink. I do some quick mental math. I can afford two more drinks with the money James lent me. I won't be able to buy for the three of us, however, without digging substantially into this week's budget.

As though I were thinking out loud, the woman with the pink hair stretches up and kisses me on the cheek. I feel her lips hovering just above my skin as she weaves her hand through my hair. I turn, my body responding automatically to her invitation, but she pulls away. I must be more starved for attention than I thought, because animal instinct overrides reason and the decision is made for me. I might have to fast for the next week if I still want to pay rent, but it's going to be worth it.

"Drinks?" I ask loudly. I mime taking a drink, expecting the music to wash away my words.

Their faces light up, and they each take one of my arms. They seductively draw me toward the bar. I grin at the sight of the two women pulling me along behind them, thinking of how proud James will be when he realizes I didn't need a wingman to pick up.

We get to the bar and they order their drinks. The bartender slides two martinis and a beer over. When I pass the martinis to the women, they smirk at each other. I can't help but think of how sexy they look. This time the brunette leans in and gives me a kiss on the cheek.

It takes a moment for me to realize the bartender has repeated what I owe for a third time and longer still for the amount to fully penetrate my thick skull. I've never ordered a martini before. I actually thought they existed only in twentieth-century period films. When I shake off the sheer astonishment, I reach out my arm. It feels numb. The bartender impatiently slides his wristband over mine. Even through the din of the club I can hear the chirp of my account draining and putting me in the red for the month. More than a grand for three drinks—without a tip! The worst part? If I tell James about this, he'll feel personally responsible and will force me to accept even more of his money. I glance around at the throng of people sipping on cocktails and tossing back shots. What the hell do these people do for a living that they can afford this kind of frivolous luxury? I close my eyes, swallow the moment, and turn to flash a fake smile at the two women.

They're both gone.

I glance around for a few seconds, thinking maybe they just made room for other people to order, but they've completely disappeared into the crowd. My empty bank account is the only proof they existed at all. The bright, elated cloud I'd been riding collapses as anger swells, transporting me instantly to the open doorway of my old apartment.

I'd decided to surprise Jenn with a flower and a kiss before she left for her bachelorette party the week before our wedding. I'd quietly climbed the stairs to our apartment, stopping dead as I opened the door. There was Jenn on her knees in the kitchen. Her co-worker, Adam's, fingers were threaded through her hair, and he had an expression of ecstasy on his face. I shudder at the memory, just as strong now as the day it happened.

I toss back my beer, slamming the empty glass down on the bar. The noise of the glass striking the countertop jolts me from my nightmare. A bubble of space opens up around me as if the people near me can sense the darkness roiling inside me. I should never have let James talk me into coming to this fucking place.

There's a light touch on my arm, and I turn a fierce glare upon a woman around my age with dark brown hair pulled into a tight ponytail.

She winces at the anger in my eyes but doesn't back away. "Excuse me. Are you okay? Your aura seems off."

My what? *My aura?* I shrug her hand off my arm and head to the other end of the bar. "What a nut," I mumble.

I order another beer. I won't be able to afford rent this month now, anyway.

One of the lesser-known features of chem-smoke is that it's designed to suppress the dark, angry thoughts some people get when drinking. But I've plummeted too quickly. It will take a while for the chem-smoke to catch up. I sip my beer and glance around darkly, looking for James. I'm going to tell him I'm heading out. I'm no good to anyone like this, least of all myself.

The crowd parts for just a moment, and I see him in the centre of it all, dry ice flowing around him, multicoloured spotlights bouncing off him. It's as if he's not moving to the music but rather letting the music move through him. He moves with the confidence of someone who has never wanted for anything in his life and has never looked like anything less than Adonis.

His bright white shirt clings to his sweaty body and showcases his perfect runner's physique, and his eyes are locked on one of the hottest women in the club like she's the only woman in the world. She tries to pry his shirt off his body, revealing glistening abs. He smiles at her and takes a small step backward, letting his shirt fall back down again.

Back when I first met him, James would have let the woman take his shirt off. He would have wound up with her and her friends back at his house. But then he'd met Danielle. She'd never come to a place like this, but she trusts him enough that she doesn't mind when he does, and he's never betrayed that trust.

He's the focus of attention of every woman on that part of the dance floor, but he doesn't let it get to him. He doesn't even seem to notice that most of the guys nearby are watching him with envy. They try in vain to imitate him, but they all fall short of achieving that special alchemy of calmness, strength, confidence, and good humour.

I sigh and take another sip of my beer. My desire to leave is still strong, but I don't want to interrupt James's enjoyment.

While the music continues to pump and the dancers continue to grind, I look around on the off chance that I might know someone else in the crowd.

Suddenly, James is at my side. He leans in close and shouts over the music. "Here, I got you this!"

I take the beer from him and hold up my half-full one. "I haven't even finished this one yet!"

"I noticed! Drink up!" He drapes his arm around me and leans in close enough for me to hear. "And this whole emo thing you've got going on doesn't suit you." He waves his hand, looking at me as he does. "There! Negativity dispelled!" He smiles conspiratorially. "Those two swindled me once too, so don't feel too bad. And don't give me that surprised look. You're my best friend! Of course I'm keeping my eye on you." His fingers fly over the face of his wristband for a moment and then he glances back up at me with a smirk. "There. Two margaritas and a beer just magically reappeared in your account. I can't have you starving or having to crash on my couch when you get evicted."

"They were martinis," I say bitterly. I force a smile, trying my best to make it real. My mood does lift a little bit, which surprises me. "But thanks."

James pushes my glass up toward my mouth. I take the hint and chug the rest of my beer. He grins as I take a giant swig of the next one.

"Better?" I ask him sarcastically.

"Much! Now listen. This beautiful lady thinks you're cute!" James grins his "I'm more than half drunk" grin as a young blond woman materializes from behind him. Her red dress glitters in the spotlights and her heels are easily four inches high. Her bare legs flow up to where her too-short dress ends just low enough to tease and tantalize the imagination. Her eyes are big with beautiful long eyelashes.

I blink and smile at her, hoping she didn't notice my eyes lingering. She smiles knowingly while James grins even wider, punches my shoulder, and disappears into the crowd.

"Hi! I'm Sara!" she yells, leaning in close.

"Aiden!" I pause, searching for a way to continue the conversation. "So . . . you think I'm cute?" I grimace at how lame that sounds, but she laughs and her face lights up.

"You're hot, actually! Your friend tells me you're a good dancer." She doesn't wait for a reply, but grabs my hand and drags me into the crowd.

I hesitate for half a heartbeat, trying to overcome a bout of guilty feelings about Jenn. Then my feet begin moving of their own accord, following this beauty in the red dress. She's like a goddess, a siren. But she doesn't stop when we reach the centre of the crowd. We continue past everyone, aiming toward a door on the far side; only now do I realize it's there. She looks at me as she rests her hand on the panel of the palm reader. There's a twinkle in her eyes. "The real party's out here!"

When the door opens, she pulls me through behind her.

Fresh air hits my face. Outside, there's another pulsating throng of bodies dancing to a live band on the pier—with one major difference from inside. I freeze. My eyes widen, and my mouth falls open in amazement. The music, Sara, the crowd—all of it fades to the background. Less than ten feet from me is the harbour. Calm waves shimmer in the moonlight. We're so close that I can almost hear the water splash against the pier through the music.

Sara places a soft hand on the side of my face. When I finally focus on her, I see that she's staring at me intently.

"Haven't you ever been on the lake?" she asks.

I shake my head, unable to speak, overwhelmed by the beauty. I slowly find my words. "It's so beautiful. I've seen it through the Waterfront Gates, but that's the closest I've been."

She stares at me for a moment and then guides me to the pier. We stand at the edge, and I feel her eyes on me, burning with curiosity, as I stand there, surrounded yet alone. I long to hear the waves, to feel them wash over my feet. If only this music would stop for a minute; it won't, of course. I glance back at the crowd of wealthy dancers. They're so caught up in enjoying what they have that they don't realize what they're missing out on.

Sara then turns me toward her, this time cupping my face with both hands, and I find myself looking into her eyes. "James said you were special." She guides my hand to her waist. "He says you see the world differently from everyone else. I see what he means." She starts dancing, pulling me closer. I cannot resist.

Although I can't keep my eyes from the water, I open my mind to the music. I feel it moving through me, and I relax and stop thinking. My body moves to the music. Slowly, I turn my gaze from the water to what's right in front of me. Sara's smile lights up her face, and I move closer.

I lose track of time as we dance under the moonlight, the waters of Lake Ontario rippling beneath us. Our hips pulse to the music as we grind into each other. My lips move first to her neck and then to her soft, luscious lips, while my hands slide down her sides and back, caressing every inch of her body.

I don't know how long we danced like that, nor do I know how we managed to get back home, but I do know that at some point after dawn, I wake just long enough to see her zipping up her dress on the way out of my apartment. As the door closes behind her, sleep claims me once again.

Chapter Two

I'm running. Fast. My life depends on it. I don't know where I'm going. I don't know what I'm running from. It's dark—so dark I can't see more than half a metre in front of me. I have no hope of avoiding the many branches and leaves reaching out to strike at me as I run. They cover my face and arms in tiny, painful cuts, while gnarled tree roots grab at my ankles.

Tree roots: I must be in a forest.

But how did I get here, and *why* I am running? There's a knot of fear deep in the pit of my stomach. I feel like a deer pursued by relentless wolves, all of my senses on full alert.

The sky lights up. A blinding blue-white light morphs the dark shadows of the forest into hideous monsters reaching out for me. Seconds later, thunder crashes through the forest so loud it almost deafens me.

The sky lights up again. And again. Three lightning strikes in quick succession. Three blasts of thunder so close together they become one cascading explosion. And then a deep, oppressive silence fills the forest. Only my ragged gasps for air and the sound of my footsteps crunching the twigs on the forest floor pierce the cloud of silence.

A wind picks up out of nowhere. Branches rattle against each other, sounding almost alive. The wind grows stronger, colder. I hear hooves pounding the ground behind me, and I glance over my shoulder to see a massive set of antlers through the trees, gaining rapidly. Lightning blazes through the sky again, and the dark antlers become a giant stag, with eyes full of knowing and intent. I run faster, trying desperately not to stumble as the cold turns to an icy chill.

"*Aiden . . .*" My name flows with the wind. Ghostly and no more than a faint, masculine whisper, it wraps itself around me. Something deep inside me responds to the whisper, awakening, calling to the wind, beckoning it. I smother that part of me that seeks to welcome this darkness, embracing instead the terror.

"*Aiden . . .*" A new voice calls. Feminine and commanding, cold and icy, it's so powerful that tentacles of fear sink into my heart. The pounding hooves stop, and I glance behind me instinctively. There's nothing there but blackness.

"*Aiden . . .*" Another voice, full of ancient feminine power unrestrained, cuts through all of my walls and barriers and reduces me to utter panic.

Lightning lights up the forest again. Massive, primordial vines stretch out all around me, reaching for me.

"*Come to me . . .*" The voice has changed subtly, sounding almost welcoming.

The fingers of fear tighten. Beads of cold sweat run down my face. The welcoming quality of the darkness spurs me to run faster, my muscles straining.

Lightning flashes again. Thunder crashes. I'm out of the forest, but I don't stop running. Behind me, the vines twist and stretch their tentacle-like fingers toward me. Lightning illuminates the sky again and my heart sinks. I've reached a cliff. The edge isn't even ten feet away. I spin around to face the churning mass of vines as fear courses through my body.

Now that I've stopped, the vines slow. There's a sinister quality to them. I back slowly toward the edge.

The tangled mass of vines opens, revealing a green-tinged darkness. It's as if I can feel the heart of the forest itself within the vines, beating strong and welcoming. The shadow of a woman emerges from the darkness, ancient and terrifying. As it moves toward me, the age of centuries seems to fall away from it.

"*Come to me . . .*" Her voice echoes from the heart of the forest.

My heels reach the edge. The vines loom ever larger.

"*Embrace my power as it flows through you.*"

I feel myself contract, folding in on myself, as something deep inside my being reacts to the voice. As I edge backward, I get dizzy at the thought of falling off the cliff.

"*Aiden.*" This is a new voice—not exactly sweet, but the sound of a hundred voices in one. It sounds like the forest itself, as though the trees of the forest and the soil between my toes were somehow beckoning me to join them. It comes from over the cliff.

I look behind me. Somehow, Toronto lies right below me.

From here, the CN Tower gleams like a jewel, the heart of downtown. Although it lost the distinction of being the tallest building in the city about fifty years ago, the newer, taller buildings surround it in a ring and radiate out from it instead of obstruct it from view.

The lights of the city illuminate the night sky, bathing it in an unnatural daylight. Even at this hour, countless vehicles snake through the core. The thick, pervasive smell of exhaust assaults my senses, contrasting harshly with the rich smell of life and decay in the forest.

I've never seen the city from this viewpoint before, and it takes me a moment to realize that the densely populated bloom of lights in the north part of the city marks the Downsview Refugee Park. In the outer areas of the city, rough, dry vegetation slowly swallows up the abandoned industrial and commercial buildings as nature reclaims the land.

Mist rides in and shrouds the city in its depths.

Air rushes past, and an intense vertigo fills me. When it stops, I look out over the cliff again. There's nothing but air.

"*Aiden,*" comes the sweet voice, "*be strong. Don't give in to fear. Trust. Believe in yourself. Step over the edge and come alive.*"

It makes no sense. None of this makes any sense. I know nothing but death awaits if I step over the edge, but the dark mass of vines fills the entire cliffside now, and there is such an intense power emanating from it that any attempt at resisting it will likely mean death too.

"*Believe, Aiden. Believe in yourself, and believe in the world.*"

A black tendril detaches itself from the vines and stretches toward me. Closer. Closer.

And then the whole world begins to shake.

"Goddamnit, Aiden! Would you stop screaming?"

I open my eyes with a loud gasp. For an instant, I don't know where I am. When I reorient myself, I realize I'm lying naked on the floor next to the bed, staring up at the ceiling.

James is looming over me with a firm grip on both of my arms, pinning me.

"Um, what are you doing?"

James stands up and looks at me incredulously. "What am I doing? I'm keeping you from killing yourself is what I'm doing! I could hear you yelling from the living room."

"Really?" I rub my eyes and take a deep breath.

"Yeah, and I figured I'd better check on you when I heard you falling out of bed. Do you have any idea how much you were flailing and banging around?"

"What do you mean?"

"At first I thought you were having a seizure, but then you started screaming at me that you didn't want to die. You wouldn't wake up no matter what I did. Must've been one hell of a nightmare. What the hell were you dreaming?"

I sit up and pull the sheet off the bed, using it to cover my waist. "I—I don't know. There was an ancient forest. I think it wanted to kill me. Then something else was trying to save me—sort of. That's basically all it was." I look around the room again. My back is sore from where I fell, my head is throbbing, and I can't remember anything from last night. I groan. "Can I get up, or do you like me on the floor like this?"

James shakes his head and laughs. "Better put some clothes on, bud. Danielle's almost here. She wants us to go to church with her today."

I groan again. Danielle is from a Roman Catholic family and is by far the most religious person in our social circle. She goes to church without fail every Sunday and is always trying to drag James and me along with her. Knowing how intensely skeptical James is of anything spiritual or religious, I was amazed when their relationship made it past that first Sunday. It amazed me even more the first time he dragged me to Christmas Mass with them. But James is the kind of person who would help absolutely anyone. Danielle has known how truly good he is—despite his lack of religious conviction—ever since they first met while volunteering at a homeless shelter in the east end.

They've made it three years like this, respecting their differences, celebrating their similarities, and engaging in the occasional spirited (and spiritual) debate—and every so often she convinces him to go to church with her.

I drag a hand through my hair as I slowly stand up. I give James a sidelong look. "Do we *have* to go? I've got a headache like you wouldn't believe."

"Sure do. Apparently, the Archbishop of Boston is in town and leading the mass today at St. Michael's Cathedral, so that's where we're going. Danielle's more excited than she's been in weeks. You know how she gets when she's like that. I need support with me so I don't say something I'll regret."

Sighing heavily in resignation, I look to my clothes where they lie strewn next to the bed.

"Besides," James says with a smirk, "I figure you owe me for making me sleep on the couch last night."

"Wait..."

I stare at him blankly for a moment and then look around the room in confusion: the queen-sized bed; the matching black wood nightstands on either side with modern-looking square lamps; the large black armoire in the corner; the antique mahogany dresser with hanging brass handles and matching mahogany-framed mirror on top; the pale grey walls... Slowly, the fact that I spent the night in his bed finally sinks in.

I've spent many nights at James's loft, but I've always woken up on the couch.

My eyes scan the room and settle on the red lipstick on the nightstand. Not once have I seen Danielle wear lipstick. She belongs firmly to the anti-makeup, natural beauty camp. I think back. A face pops into my head, smiling. She dances before me; her lips press against mine; our bodies entwine on the bed—James's bed.

"Oh my God."

James chuckles. "Did you have a good time?"

"I, uh, don't really remember."

James grins widely. "Then I guess you had a good time."

"But, um, about your bed...?"

His grin turns into a boisterous laugh. "Don't worry about it. It's seen worse, believe me. Much worse." He winks, and I just roll my eyes at him. "Besides, I couldn't very well let you use the couch. I don't think she would have liked that very much, and since you live way out in the middle of nowhere, you taking the bed seemed like the best option."

I ignore his jab about living in Riverside, but he's right. No woman who goes to Surrender would be caught dead on the east side of the Don River. "Do you remember what her name is?"

"No idea." He stops, seeing the expression on my face. "And it's not important. You'll never see her again anyway. Sometimes, my friend, you need to be spontaneous like that. Besides, if she were after more than what she got, she would have told you how to reach her or at least waited for you to wake up before sneaking out."

I shake my head, but the throbbing there makes me immediately regret it. "Not used to beer," I say quietly.

James chuckles. "Yeah, the real stuff hits hard. I'll grab you something that'll help."

When James leaves, I step up to the mirror. My green eyes are inflamed with blood-red veins, and the skin around them is puffy and dark. My normally lightly tanned skin looks pasty, and the five o'clock shadow I had yesterday is now making its way toward an actual beard. I try to pat down my finger-length jet-black hair, but it's no use. It's sticking up all over the place in a greasy mess. Small wonder she disappeared, waking up to this beside her. I look like I haven't slept in weeks.

It's not far from the truth. The nightmare I had last night is the latest in a series of connected dreams. The first one occurred on the night of my eighteenth birthday. The entire dream took place in absolute silence, and everything was black, but a powerful force filled me, called to me wordlessly, and struck fear so deep into my being that when I finally woke up, I was convinced that the waking world was the dream. I've had one of these dreams a year since then.

On the night of my twenty-fourth birthday, I opened my eyes to that now familiar darkness to watch it fade into a rich, ancient forest. Crude stone structures lay all around me in various states of disrepair. That was when she first spoke to me. I don't know who she is, but her voice is deep and powerful. She calls me by name, and it makes my entire body shudder with a strange combination of terror and excitement. That particular dream was when the chase first started. Whenever I run, her energy follows. The dreams are becoming more frequent—first monthly, and now weekly. I'm actually considering seeing a doctor about them. My only reservation is that most doctors try to put you on medication for this kind of thing, and I don't want that. My mother and grandmother both had difficulties sleeping. Their doctors started them on sleeping pills first before progressing to antidepressants and finally antipsychotics; none of it helped.

That's what I'm afraid of, really. My mother has never explicitly said she suffers from nightmares, but I've been visiting her much more often since she developed a brain tumour. I've seen her stare at her bed in fear; I've also sat beside her and calmed her while she sleeps. Why wouldn't I be terrified? Between the night terrors, some major money issues, and worries about my mother's health, I can't remember the last time I had a good night's sleep.

I squeeze my eyes shut to block out the headache as I grab my clothes from the floor. Holding them in front of me in case Danielle has already arrived, I step into the living room.

"Don't worry. She's not here yet," James says, holding up a large glass. "Here, drink this. It's a protein shake with electrolyte powder. It should help ease your headache."

I take it from him, nodding my thanks. He then throws himself down onto his large couch and swipes his hand through the channels on the holo-screen.

James's place makes me jealous. He has a corner suite on the eleventh floor of the Merchandise Lofts building at Dundas and Church, right in the heart of downtown. It's open-concept, with twelve-foot ceilings and a brick feature wall. The other walls are painted a crisp white and are adorned with brightly coloured abstract and geometric art. The only furniture he has in the living room is an antique Victorian armchair and a huge black leather couch that makes even me look small. They both face the wall where the holo-screen is. A large white island with a polished black marble countertop separates the living room from the kitchen. The kitchen is equipped with black glass appliances, including a fridge, an oven, and a dishwasher. They gleam in the large pot lights.

A while back, James converted the second bedroom into an office with an old-fashioned desk made of solid oak and a faux fireplace to add to the ambiance. On either side of the fireplace is an oak bookshelf with books on law and history. James particularly prides himself on his antique *Encyclopædia Britannica* set from the late twentieth century.

He can't afford the place on his own, of course. His father has paid for it since James got into law school. They made a deal when he first agreed to follow in his father's footsteps: James would pay for his own day-to-day expenses by working as a waiter at Carmen's Steakhouse, and his parents would pay for all home-related expenses. I think it was his father's way of compensating for feelings of guilt about not being around a lot when he was young.

I set the empty glass down on the marble countertop and make my way to the washroom.

I look at myself in the mirror again and shudder. I hope James's protein shake will help make some of the pounding in my head disappear.

I turn the water on and step into the shower, sighing with relief as the hot water hits me and steam billows around me. I stand there, the showerhead set to massage, and let the water run down my back. This is going to be a long shower.

My landlord and I have had long conversations about the environment and are in complete agreement that something urgently needs to change to prevent the world from plummeting into chaos. This is why I fully supported him when he installed water limiters. If you run any tap in the building for longer than five minutes, the water to your whole apartment is cut off for ten. I remember the first time it happened to me. I stood there, hair full of shampoo suds, for the full ten minutes. The government has since mandated the installation of paid showers. On every shower is a small chip scanner that you run your wristband across to activate the water. This has made it too expensive for me to shower for longer than five minutes anyway.

Thankfully, James's parents firmly believe that money can fix anything. I usually find their excess slightly off-putting, but this morning I'm perfectly fine with placing James's family card against the chip reader and standing under the shower for as long as I want, even if it's costing them a small fortune.

The lights go out, and the steady hum of electricity flowing through the apartment goes quiet. Only the sound of rapidly cooling water echoes through the washroom. The timer on the chip scanner informs me I've been in the shower for thirteen minutes. *Shit*. I'm usually better at keeping track of time, but today I completely forgot that brownouts in this part of the city are scheduled for between eight and eleven in the morning. Regular rolling brownouts were confined to July and August when I was young, but these days they go from May to September. There is simply too much demand on the province's power grid with the intensifying heat.

Pressed against the wall of the shower, I stick my head under the cold water and rinse off the shampoo. I thumb the water off and feel around for my towel in the darkness.

As I towel myself dry, I hear Danielle's voice coming from the living room. She's always been a loud speaker, but today she's excited about the interview she had on Friday morning. She's been the top salesperson for two and a half years running, and the regional manager called her to offer her the position of district manager for South Central Ontario. His hope is that she'll pass on her skills at building accounts to up-and-coming salespeople at Linwood Apparel.

"So does that mean you'll be making more trips to Buffalo?" James asks her.

"Well, yes . . ." The excitement in her voice softens, and I cringe as their voices get too quiet for me to hear.

Linwood Apparel is based in Buffalo, and Danielle already makes trips across the border two or three times a week. James hates it, but I've never been sure whether it's because she's gone so often or because he has to listen to her complain about the long wait times at the border crossing. I do know he often tries to be out when she gets home so he doesn't have to listen to her rant about how President Massie and Prime Minister Tremblay should do more to solve the "border crisis."

With a whir, the power returns and the lights flicker on. I glance in the mirror. I almost look human again. I start styling my hair, and Danielle's voice drifts through the door again.

"And then he told me how he's looking forward to working with me more closely. And you know Ben. He's the best in the business! I could learn so much from him if I get this. It's such an exciting opportunity, and—"

I open the door and poke my head out. "Hey, Danielle! Didn't you tell me last week that Ben's a slimy, inconsiderate prick and you couldn't wait to get out from under him?"

She turns to me mid-sentence, her brow furrowed, a scowl etched into her features. James laughs, and she simply sticks her tongue out at me. I wink at them as I close the door again and get dressed.

The paleness has disappeared from my face, and my usual healthy tone is returning. I run a hand through my hair, giving it a slightly messy look, and glance at myself one last time. I'm almost ready to take on the world. If only the throbbing in the back of my head would stop, I'd be good to go.

When I put my hand on the door handle, however, a searing pain arcs through my skull. I drop to my knees, holding my head in my hands as images from my nightmares flash by: cold black clouds all around me, devoid of feeling. I stand alone amidst a storm, thunder and lightning crashing. The ground disappears and I am falling.

Stop it! I shout in my head.

The images disappear, the pain returns to the usual dull throb, and I realize that my eyes are clenched tightly shut. I keep my eyes closed and count to ten, visualizing a peaceful meadow, trying to relax my tensed muscles. I feel the pressure start to ease, and I slowly stand and try to compose myself.

There's a knock at the door.

"Just a minute!" My voice is shaky, and I look at my hands. They're trembling violently. I take several deep breaths and wipe the tears away from my red eyes.

Why is this happening to me? I wish I knew. When my mother wasn't listening, my father used to lean in close to me and whisper in my ear, "You're going to wind up just like your grandmother!" It was especially hurtful—and I eventually realized it was why he did it—because I loved my grandmother dearly and yet was also incredibly frightened that he was right.

In her early fifties, she was diagnosed with delusional disorder after years of tests and psychiatrist visits failed to pinpoint any other cause for her increasingly paranoid claims that she was being stalked and spied on. My grandfather struggled to get her to take her medication, and eventually he and my mother moved her to a permanent care facility when the police politely informed us that they couldn't keep coming for false alarms. My mother used to take us to visit her once a month, but those visits dwindled as her condition got worse.

I'd read that the disorder is hereditary. Could this be the first signs?

My mother refuses to talk about my grandmother anymore, and I briefly wish I hadn't cut ties with my father. I'd be able to call him up and ask him about it, but I haven't spoken to him in six years, and I wouldn't even know where to begin looking for him.

I take another deep breath, willing myself to be calm. The knock comes again. Taking a deep breath, I open the door.

Danielle is there. Her piercing amber eyes, framed by dark brown hair that spills over her shoulder and down the small of her back, stare at me questioningly. Her hand is on her hip, and her lips are squeezed together tightly. She taps her foot impatiently. Her mother was a model from Venezuela, and Danielle had inherited every ounce of her good looks. Even with her agitated look, it's easy to see what first attracted James to her.

"Lord help us all! You take more time to get ready than I do! Are you ready?"

"Ready for what?" I ask innocently, hoping she'll give me an out.

She rolls her eyes. "James told me you wanted to come to St. Michael's with us this morning."

"He lied."

"James wouldn't lie to me."

I look past her at James, who is still lying on the couch. He just lies there and smiles up at the ceiling. "You're going to come keep me company, right?" he says.

"To be honest, I'm not feeling the greatest, but I'll come." I figure that if he can stretch the truth, I can too. "Especially since you promised to buy me a coffee later. I'm desperately hoping it will make my head feel better!"

Chapter Three

St. Michael's Cathedral Basilica was clearly designed to impress. Ten huge stone pillars support a high vaulted ceiling painted sky blue. The pale grey walls are adorned with statuettes of Jesus and Mary. Sunlight streams through gorgeous stained glass windows all around us. In the centre of the nave, at the top of the north wall, the light from a large blue rose window devoted to the "Immaculate Heart of Mary" shines down on us. Directly across from it is a red rose window devoted to the "Sacred Heart of Jesus." Danielle has seated us directly beneath the Heart of Mary, facing a gold shrine dedicated to her. From here, we have a perfect view of the proceedings.

"'People of Galatia! After you have had a clear picture of Christ crucified, right in front of your eyes, who has put a spell on you?'" Cardinal Gallagher speaks loudly, firmly, with just a hint of a Boston accent. He holds his gold-plated crozier out before him with his left hand as if warding off an unspeakable evil. He is in his early forties, which, according to Danielle, is very young for a cardinal, let alone an archbishop, and his wavy black hair swoops out of his red zucchetto and down over his forehead. His white rochet with scarlet vestments and sash are impeccably tailored, and even through the layers of cloth, it's obvious in his posture and movement that he has a muscular frame. He stands in the centre of the sanctuary, energized and engaging, sweeping the crowd with hawkish brown eyes and making eye contact with as many people as he can.

He makes for an impressive sight. In contrast, Toronto's own archbishop, Cardinal Manzanedo, is approaching seventy and emanates the peace and calm I've always associated with priests and ministers.

I stopped going to church after my grandfather passed away and there was no one else who cared if I went. I've never experienced anything as full of ritual and meaning as today's High Mass. It started with the first chime of the sound bowl ringing through the air. Then, as the voices of the visiting Boston choir filled the grand cathedral, a minister slowly carried a large gold cross down the central aisle. Cardinal Manzanedo followed with his simple hooked crozier, and another minister trailed him with a large gold-covered Bible. Taking it all in, I was struck by the sheer majesty of this church. When the smell of the burning frankincense used to anoint the altar reached us and all of my senses were engaged in the ritual, I began to rethink my earlier reluctance to join Danielle and James. By the time we reached the homily and Cardinal Manzanedo stepped aside for his guest from Boston, I was enthralled.

"So wrote Paul the Apostle to the Galatians," Cardinal Gallagher continues, his deep voice snapping me back from my reverie.

Danielle glances at me, and I smile at her. She seems genuinely happy that I appear to be enjoying myself. She focuses on the homily again, and I lose myself in the Cardinal's deep drone. And then I feel it: the increasing tempo of the throbbing inside my head.

Oh, God, not here. Please, not here.

At the front, the choir from the Cathedral of the Holy Cross in Boston stands and begins to sing a hymn praising God Almighty.

My headache erupts into a full-on migraine. I close my eyes as the music fills the cathedral and the pain fills my head.

What the hell is wrong with me?

Beads of sweat run down my face and I take a breath, confronting the pain. *You cannot happen now!* The pain vanishes.

I open my eyes, but the glory of the cathedral has vanished. Where a moment ago tall pillars laced with gold rose to a gold-embossed ceiling, there is now a dark and ancient tunnel of well-trodden stone. The air is thick with age and disuse, and it feels like it's been years—centuries, maybe—since the last visitor graced these halls. I can still hear the choir around me, but the voices are distant. It sounds as if they're trying and failing to penetrate the tunnel.

Where am I?

"*Lannóg Eolas. You will be safe here.*"

The answer comes as a silent whisper filling the air. It makes my skin tingle with its energy. It's the same silent whisper that offered me refuge from the dark storm of my nightmare if I would only place my trust in it.

Why have you brought me here?

"*To deny the truth is painful. To accept, liberating.*"

I have no idea what that's supposed to mean, but this is clearly not the time to explore my own madness. I might be lost in a musty tunnel of my mind, but my friends are beside me, and they're sure to notice that something is amiss sooner rather than later. With any luck, they're too focused on the choir to have noticed anything wrong with me.

Now that I think about it, the voices of the choir are getting louder, and there's a very real sense that they're actually assailing the tunnel.

I must go.

"*Stay.*"

Now's not the time.

"*If not now, when?*"

I can't think of a good answer to that question, so I instead squash the image of the tunnel in my mind and step back into reality.

A heavy silence has filled the church, and it's broken only by the hushed whispers of fellow parishioners. I look around, wondering what I missed. Anxious murmurs rise from the congregation, and several people have their arms outstretched, pointing.

I follow the gaze of a couple in the pew next to us, and I catch bits and pieces of the whispers.

"It's so dark . . ."

"The candles—every one of them just blew out . . ."

"Look at the windows . . . !"

When we entered the church earlier, the sun was shining brightly and there wasn't a cloud in the sky, but now the stained glass windows are dark and a storm rages outside.

James nudges me while he and Danielle whisper to one another, but I'm too absorbed in what's happening around me to pay him any heed.

Outside, the wind howls, and the stained glass windows start to rattle.

Seated in the sanctuary, Cardinal Manzanedo makes the sign of the cross, his eyes flitting nervously from window to window. Around him, the other priests and ministers whisper to each other in wonder.

All except for Cardinal Gallagher and his choir. They stand there silently and are focused on . . . me. Terror grips me, utterly and completely. Despite the Cardinal's calm face, his eyes are ice cold and locked with mine, a malicious hatred in them.

Panic wells up inside me. Trembling, I grab James's arm. "We have to go," I hiss quietly.

"What? With that storm?"

"*Now.*"

"You're as white as a ghost, Aiden. What the hell's the matter with you?"

"I don't know, and I don't want to find out right this second. Please, can we get out of here?"

James doesn't respond right away, but he's finally followed my gaze. "My God, he's looking at you like you're Satan himself." His eyes dart between Gallagher and me.

I don't feel like the Lord of the Flies, but after everything that's happened, I say nothing. I don't know what to say.

James turns to Danielle and whispers, "Baby, we've got to go. I think Aiden's going to be sick."

Danielle looks at me, and her eyes go wide, making me wonder what sort of hell I must look like. She nods once before quickly grabbing her purse and standing up.

James steps out in front of me and makes his way toward the exit. I follow him, hoping to be as discreet as possible amongst a congregation already whispering about strange occurrences. Danielle puts her hand on the small of my back and guides me through the crowd. She casts a long look at Gallagher on our way out. I feel his eyes boring into my back the entire time. I can't tell whether it's the strength of Danielle's gaze that holds him there or something else, but the Archbishop of Boston remains firmly rooted to the centre of the sanctuary as we leave.

The big double doors of St. Michael's Cathedral close with a resounding thud. There is a sense of finality to it, as it's punctuated by a peal of thunder that rumbles through the city the same instant. The rain is coming down in sheets.

The city's rain-catcher system will be working overtime to divert the precious water to its aeroponic vertical greenhouses, and outside the city, the government's storm chasers are probably out in droves.

We stand in the tiny alcove just outside, our backs to the cathedral, our faces to the rain. Judging by the looks on James's and Danielle's faces, I know they have no desire to venture out into the storm, but there's a terrifying tightness gripping my chest, and every hair on the back of my neck is screaming at me to flee this place.

I turn to them. They look at me, and I see both fear and concern in their eyes.

"I feel terrible," I begin, wishing I could keep my voice from trembling. "I'm just going to go home. You stay here until the storm passes."

James turns to Danielle, and then slowly back to me. He swallows before speaking. When he speaks, his voice is soft and full of compassion. "Aiden, I'm not exactly sure what just went down in there, but I've known you for a long time. Wherever you're going, I'm with you."

"Thanks, James, but—"

Danielle steps forward and takes my arm. "No buts about it, Aiden. James is right. You need us. Besides, the storm seems to be letting up, and some of your normal colour is back. There's a wonderful little cafe closer to the water if you'd like to go grab a coffee and relax. How about it?"

I shake my head slowly. Coffee is a rich man's drink, and after last night's fiasco, I can't be splurging. "I can't afford coffee this week, but thanks anyway." Also, the last thing I want right now is to be surrounded by a bunch of chattering wealthy people pretending to be happy. However, as the rain soaks through my clothes, I realize I'm actually craving the company of someone who's privy to my madness.

Danielle's brow furrows with concern. "My treat today," she says. It's as though she can sense my wavering.

"You know what?" James says. "I'll get it. Uh, remember how I said we'd grab one today?"

I smirk at him. "All right. We can do a coffee, I guess. A small one."

Danielle's worried expression softens into a smile, and she releases my arm. "You'll love this place," she says. She then takes James by the hand, and they step past me.

As I begin to follow them, I notice that the heaviness in my chest eases with every step I take away from the cathedral. What's even stranger is that the rain stops soon after we leave the property. The sun emerges as we cross Shuter Street, mere steps away from St. Michael's.

We pick our way through the homeless people crowding the sidewalk and the edges of Bond Street. I look over at James as he falls into step beside me.

"Strange weather," he mumbles, looking at the sky with eyes full of unease.

Danielle's little cafe is on the corner of Church and Front. It's one of those holdovers from the independent cafes that thrived for decades during the age of the hipster. Somehow, this one has withstood the onslaught of corporate chains, and it's full of character and coziness as a result.

Three small groups of people also thought this would be the perfect place to while away a Sunday morning, but they're all situated close to the window. We decide to take our coffees to a round table next to the darkened fireplace instead, where we'll have some privacy.

After a few moments of us sitting and quietly sipping at our cups, Danielle's eyebrows raise, and she draws our attention to the holo-screen embedded into the table. "See this?" She points to a news headline. "The States have beefed up their patrols along our border *again*. All this talk about the drought on both sides of the border leading to higher crime rates and increased drug smuggling has them caving to pressure from the far right."

I silently curse whoever thought people coming to relax at a coffee shop would want to be constantly aware of the news. Politics always sets Danielle off, especially American politics. Granted, given her regular work trips to Buffalo, she's also very much affected by it.

"Won't that make it even harder for you to go there?" James asks with concern. "I thought encouraging cross-border travel was one of President Massie's key election pitches to the northern states?"

"It's going to make it near impossible to travel!" Danielle says. "Even with my NEXUS card. It was actually starting to get better before the Tea Party took control of the House this year." She shakes her head before taking a sip of her coffee. "I never thought I'd see an extremist faction of the Christian right get so close to governing America. With the Liberals poised to overthrow Tremblay's Conservatives here, Massie's just trying to quell the rumblings in the Republican Party and show the Tea Party that he's willing to stand up for American interests."

American interests, I think, are mostly responsible for our country being in the plight it's in right now. For more than a decade, Prime Minister Tremblay has led Canada calmly and quietly, being careful not to raise the ire of our American neighbours. At the same time, he's gently aligned our policies so they won't run counter to American interests. The gradual assimilation of Canada by America that started in the twentieth century has accelerated greatly as a result. It's a situation that most Canadians oppose, which is one of the key reasons the Conservatives are falling rapidly in the polls. In contrast, the Liberal Party leader, Olivia Peterson, has been campaigning very successfully on reaffirming our national identity, even though she's relatively new to politics.

In the past, what happened here in Canada would hardly be more than a blip on America's political radar, but when the United Nations officially declared a worldwide drought in 2073, Canada's status as the world's largest source of fresh water made it a concern for many countries—but none as much as the United States.

The rapid escalation of natural disasters drove most of the world to invest heavily into research and development for solutions. In the United States, the Democrats and the moderates within the Republican Party enacted several laws to limit the impact of population growth on the environment. Their actions drew the wrath of the Christian right, who loudly challenged the government's right to increase taxes and force people away from using fossil fuels for good. The more the scientists blamed human activity for the widespread droughts, rising temperatures, and surging sea levels, the more the deniers sought refuge in religious scripture, especially the parts where God gives humans dominion over the Earth. Religious extremists have long felt their cries have fallen on deaf ears, and they've only become louder and more extreme. For the better part of a year, they've been promising to march across the country to take back control of the nation in the name of God if their leaders keep refusing to listen.

That President Massie is a moderate and his mother is Canadian are likely the only reasons relations haven't deteriorated sooner, but his victory in the election was very shaky, and most of my friends believe that, Republican or not, his time in power will be short. There is widespread speculation that he could be pressured into resigning. It seems to me that whatever comes after Massie's time in office won't likely be good for Canada.

Danielle sighs as she continues to read the news.

James leans forward. "That's terrible, babe." He takes her hand, and she stops scanning the holo-screen and looks up at him. "But as terrible as it is, we'll work through it. Right now, we're here for another reason."

Danielle looks over at me. "Yes, you're right, James. Sorry. This is a problem for another time."

James turns to me, staring deeply into my eyes, seeking the truth. "What the hell happened back there, Aiden?"

I swallow once and then stare into my mug, seeking for a way to describe the past twenty-four hours. It's easier to look into the mug than it is to look into my friends' eyes. "It's hard to explain. I've been having these dreams, like the one you rescued me from one this morning. They are, well, they're almost more than dreams."

"What do you mean?" James asks. "Like, long-forgotten memories? Dreams can do that sometimes."

"No. Nothing like that."

"What then?"

"Dark clouds. A forest. The city. I don't know what's driving them." I glance up into his eyes. "But if I didn't know it was impossible, I'd swear I was actually visiting these places."

"Stress? Work, maybe?"

I shrug. "Working in commissioned suit sales in Toronto's financial district is about as far from urban forestry as you can get."

I've loved trees since I was old enough to know what loving something meant, and since high school, my dream job has been to grow urban tree canopies to help save our planet. I even went to university to pursue it. I never would have been able to afford it without my grandfather's help. He was so proud that his only grandson was doing something to help the environment that he gave up most of his remaining pension to help me achieve my dream.

He died when I was in my second year at university, and I had no choice but to get a job. My current job was the first one available. It helped me pay for school for another year, but then my mother got sick and couldn't work anymore. With my father being a deadbeat abuser who she'd kicked out years ago, I had to start supporting her. Before I knew it, I was trapped in a cycle of all work, no school, and none of it getting me any closer to my dream.

James and Danielle know all about it. The summer I quit school, I started volunteering for Tree Canada, helping them plant new trees and care for existing ones. This is how I met James. We bonded high in the boughs of High Park, pruning the ancient black oaks. That was when I told him my sob story.

"The dreams are similar," I explain, "but something new happens each time. They mostly involve me being chased through the forest by primordial beasts, or me being lost in subterranean passages. When I wake up, I can still smell the earth and the decay of the forest, or the dust and the dampness of the tunnels. Sometimes, in those moments, just after I regain consciousness, it feels like some monstrous thing in the dark clouds is still staring at me . . ."

My voice fades as an old man slowly approaches our table with an ambling gait. His limp is pronounced, but he uses an ebony cane with a white handle to help him along. Despite his white handlebar mustache and well-trimmed beard—as well as a deep scar running down the side of his face—his eyes twinkle, and there is a gentleness about his features that I find disarming. His tweed jacket and matching bow tie stand out in the cafe but look well suited on him.

James glances over his shoulder to see what I'm looking at and shakes his head slowly. "Beggars are everywhere now," he says under his breath. He flinches when Danielle pinches his arm.

There are ten other empty tables, but he walks right up to ours. Danielle smiles at him as he comes to a stop beside us. He grips the head of the cane in both hands and returns her smile, and the twinkle in his eyes comes to life.

He sits down at the table beside us and pivots his body until he's facing me. When he speaks, he sounds scholarly. "Quite the storm we had earlier, wouldn't you say?"

"Um, yeah, it was, wasn't it?" A small sense of relief fills me. Until now, I'd actually thought the storm was only over St. Michael's—that it was *meant* for me.

"Yes, sir. I don't recall ever seeing such a nasty-looking storm come and go so quickly."

I shrug nonchalantly and take a sip of coffee. I don't want to encourage the guy, and the silence from James and Danielle suggests they don't want to, either.

The man leans back into his chair in a relaxed manner and changes the topic. "You know, when I was younger, I used to come down to this shop and people-watch. I found it soothing, and it brings me back to my youth to do it now."

"You don't really look all that old," James says quietly.

The old man laughs and turns to James as if seeing him for the first time. "Turning seventy-six next week, son. At this point, I've seen many more days like this than I'm likely to see in the future. It's why I value days like today, where the weather is so beautiful. So many people out and about enjoying it. See this?" He gestures at the people streaming past the front of the cafe, shopping in the outdoor market, lounging by the fountain in the centre median. "All of these people—most of them strangers—and yet they are all here having a good time. For some reason, a scene like this reminds me that we all have our place in this world."

"There are some," I say quietly, perhaps against my better judgement, "that don't belong. Square pegs trying to fit into a round hole, if you will."

His gaze leaves the windows, coming to rest on me. It's intense, thoughtful, and oddly calculating. "You'd be speaking about yourself, I suspect, but you'd be wrong, my young friend. In this world, there is a place for everyone. *Everyone*. Some of us take a long time to find our place, as it happens, but you will find your place, or your place will find you. One way or the other. This world takes care of its own. This I believe and have always found to be true. It will give you a chance to find your way on your own, but it won't leave you adrift forever."

I chuckle. "You speak as if the world is a sentient thing."

The man's eyes widen slightly. "And so it is, young man . . . so it is. Put your trust in it when all else fails, and it will take care of you."

I'm silent for a moment—a long moment. He says nothing more to interrupt my thoughts, which are running rampant in every direction at once.

The man then stands up and leans on his cane, his eyes now filled with sadness. "The question is . . . who will take care of the world? Who indeed?" He turns and ambles toward the exit, muttering under his breath the whole way, leaving Danielle, James, and I staring at each other in disbelief.

The door to the cafe opens as he approaches it, and at least a dozen more people file in. Soon, all the tables are full. Rambunctious teenagers take the tables closest to us, making further conversation virtually impossible. Realizing the moment to talk about what happened to me this morning has passed, we take the rest of our coffees to go.

And so it is that I find myself standing at the Waterfront Gates, my face pressed through the steel spires. I wish they'd part just enough to let me in. The steel fence stretches the entire length of the waterfront, from Cherry Street in the east to the Billy Bishop Toronto City Airport in the west. Situated just south of Queens Quay, it lets the public get close enough to Lake Ontario to hear the waves lapping at the water's edge, while keeping us far enough away that there's no chance of any stray garbage making it into the lake. On this side of the gates, hundreds of people stroll through the artificial grass and run, jog, and cycle along the cracked pavement. Twenty years ago, I'm sure the design was beautiful, but now it's all faded, crumbling, and overrun by the city's most unfortunate. Dozens of homeless people sit in makeshift homes and cardboard boxes on both sides of the street.

In sharp contrast, many of Toronto's richest citizens lie on the sandy beach just on the other side of the fence, soaking up the sun in their bathing suits. Still others stroll casually along the boardwalk, watching the sailboats from the Royal Canadian Yacht Club cut through the gentle waves.

Past them, across the harbour, I can see Surrender, the nightclub that provided me my first direct access to the water since moving to the city six years ago. My memories of most of last night are still hazy, but the sight of Lake Ontario's gentle moonlit waves, close enough that I could have leaned over and touched them, will stay with me forever.

I look over to the old ferry terminal. Seeing it sends me spiralling back in time to when I first told my grandfather I was moving to Toronto. The moment he found out, my grandfather got very excited, and he started telling me how beautiful the harbour was. The pictures he painted of people lying in lush green grass while others happily played Frisbee, picnicked, or just read a book quietly on one of the benches with the lake as a backdrop seemed surreal to me. He raved about standing in line with his friends, coolers full of beer in hand, for a packed five-minute ferry ride to Toronto Islands and the beaches there.

"Toronto has some of the world's cleanest beaches, Aiden!" he'd say with childlike excitement. "Blue Flag beaches!" he'd add, though he could never explain just what a Blue Flag beach was—something about sustainability.

It was a picture made all the more powerful because the climate had begun shifting radically when I was still a child. At first we thought we were going to be spared the droughts of the nations along the equator. In Canada, record-setting rainfall came in deluges, and snowfalls regularly shut entire cities down. If it had continued, we would likely have rainforests by now. But as the rains and snows increased, winter and spring seemed to shorten, ultimately giving way to unbearably hot and dry summers.

By the time I was ten, the small town of Brooklin, Ontario, was nothing like the lush green world my grandfather described, except in the carefully controlled "green zones" that only the town's wealthiest were allowed to enter. Even before we had to sell my grandmother's family farm north of town, grass grew only by the riverbanks, ponds, and springs, and even there it was sparse. The grass in the roadside ditches had long ago withered and died, replaced by patches of crabgrass, dandelions, and other drought-resistant vegetation.

I should have known that his memory of the lush and beautiful waterfront wouldn't be my reality, but his enthusiasm was so compelling. I couldn't wait to get to Toronto's waterfront to experience a world where plants grew freely and everyone lived in harmony with nature.

I was, however, crushed when I showed up with my swim trunks and towel only to find the ferry terminal locked and chained behind the Waterfront Gates, decades-old graffiti and weeds covering the entrance. The rusting derelict ferries sat keeled over into one another, their trestles having long since collapsed from the violent storms as the waters of Lake Ontario receded.

The city eventually sold the ferries to Singapore for an unbelievable price given their condition. That same year, Shanghai was declared a loss. Thirty four million residents had been displaced, forced to uproot and flee the rising ocean levels caused by the melting polar ice caps. Ten years before that, Miami had suffered the same fate. Singapore was one of many affected countries that continued to do whatever it could to avoid losing everything.

Toronto needed the money desperately. When war erupted throughout Europe and the Middle East fifteen years ago, refugees flooded to Canada. Free-flowing water and ample land to cultivate had long ago caused the Canadian Dream to usurp the American Dream.

We welcomed them, eager to grow stronger as a nation against the backdrop of global catastrophe. In school, they taught that taking in refugees and helping them thrive was a shining example of true Canadian values, and it was what had always set us apart from the rest of the world. My family agreed, because with the huge influx of people working on farms, there was cheaper food and more people to pay taxes, which made life better for everybody. According to my grandfather, Canada was built by immigrants. "Without them," he'd say, "you and I wouldn't be here. It's our duty to welcome others with open arms and love in our hearts."

That all changed seven years ago following the Great Crop Failure. As world temperatures skyrocketed and relentless human consumption strained food and clean water supplies, disease and famine in the world's poorest countries spiralled out of control. In particular, a bacterial pandemic swept through large parts of Africa, Asia, and South America. When the disease began to spread to Europe, scientists rushed to perfect a genetically modified organism that would specifically target the bacteria causing it. However, in their haste, they had miscoded the genome of the organism and inadvertently made it highly adaptable.

The defective designer organism made its way across the Atlantic in a shipping container destined for the American Midwest and landed in summer amidst of one of the most intense droughts in modern history. Within weeks, the organism had mutated and started attacking the pesticides Europe had long since banned, killing the plants they were meant to protect in the process. With the dry wind, it spread rapidly, destroying crops all across the continent, leaving desert-like conditions across much of Western Canada and the United States. Crops failed, albeit to a lesser degree, even in places such as Ontario, Quebec, and the Maritimes. In a single season, more than 80 percent of North American crops withered and died. Millions turned to cities for help, and within six months, Toronto's already dense population had swelled by another three million.

As the temperatures continued to soar, so too did the cost of maintaining the city and ensuring that everyone had access to the basic necessities of life. The sale of the ferries was just one of the many measures the city took to prop itself up. But now, strapped for cash, the city is unable to fund public transit and the social assistance that the province cut off years ago. This has hit the city's poor hard, and a clear rift is forming between those with money and those who have to resort to desperate measures just to feed their families.

A burgeoning underground has risen, and with it violence and lawlessness. My grandfather had been able to stroll the waterfront fearlessly at night, even alone. Today, I wouldn't consider coming anywhere near this place after dusk, even with an army of friends. I find some comfort in knowing he died before he could see the ruined husk of what had brought him such joy.

After thinking about my grandfather, my thoughts return to the strange old man in the cafe. His parting question is stuck in my mind. Who would take care of the world? As I stroll along the rusty old fence separating me from the lake, picking my way through hundreds of people from all walks of life and a myriad of nationalities, it strikes me as a particularly pertinent question.

I try to forget about it. After all, even my teachers eventually started talking about the future as something to survive and stopped pushing students to pursue our dreams and change the world. "Our course is set, and now we just have to try to survive what comes," my grade ten geography teacher once said. "It doesn't matter what we do now," my grade twelve history teacher said almost weekly. "The world as we know it is over." A fatalistic worldview? Perhaps. But it helps explain why church attendance is soaring.

A child runs around me in circles, and I smile at him. His parents call him away when they see me smile. They don't know I'm harmless. They don't know I won't sweep him away and sell him to slavers in South America if they blink at the wrong time. When I was a child, my mother used to send me to the corner store by myself, and my friends and I used to spend from sunup to sundown running through the park on our own. Sure, that was small-town Brooklin, but how much the world has changed!

I continue walking, and I feel myself getting calmer. The calmer I get, the more the throbbing in my head fades. Could the headaches and dreams all just be from stress? I know stress can affect your body in strange ways, and I really haven't given myself much recuperation time. It's been three years since

I could afford to take anything more than two days in a row off at work, and it's been more than a year since I've had time to lose myself in tree planting.

That used to be my escape: feeling the dark soil wrap around my fingers as I lower the tiny seedling into its new home, watering it, wishing it well on its new life. That volunteer work helped me feel like I was still being at least partly true to myself. Maybe everything that's happened recently is just my body's way of saying, "Hey, Aiden, how about some me time?" I smile wistfully. As much as I'd like to believe that, I doubt stress can get bad enough to cause a thunderstorm to chase you out of church. Even James and Danielle know something is off.

As if on cue, my wristband chirps. A message from James scrolls along my wrist. He wants to know where I am, and if I'm okay. I rotate my wrist slightly, and the holo-keyboard comes to life below the band.

"I'm fine," I type.

The reply comes almost instantly. "Liar. Danielle just left. Meet you at Coventry's for a beer?"

I'm not really in the mood for a beer, but I could definitely use his company. James always makes me feel better.

There are already two beers at the table when I arrive, and I can tell James is itching to tell me something.

"What the hell took you so long?" he says. "Things are about to get very interesting!"

"Why? What's going on?" I slide into the chair across from him.

"The Tea Party merged with the Christian Evangelical Party early this morning and are making a bid to overthrow the government. They think if they can motivate enough people to support them, Massie will have to resign or at the very least start acting on their demands."

"Damn..." I mumble, sinking back into my chair and taking a sip of beer. "This is what Danielle was talking about this morning, isn't it?"

James nods. "Nearly thirty thousand Christian extremists took to the streets of Louisiana this morning to head for the I20. The CBC is reporting that they're going to completely shut down all the interstates between Louisiana and Washington and that by the time they get to the White House, there'll be enough of them that the tail end will still be in Tennessee. They're calling on similar marches to start from Salt Lake City, Sacramento, and Spokane."

I take a couple more gulps. "It's finally happened then. The US is going to be led by extremists! That many people will grind their economy to a halt, and Massie will have to do whatever they want . . . which, of course, will involve us."

"That's what I'm saying, and it's even worse than you think. The leader of the march is this old white guy named Glen Davis, a retired minister who looks like he's in his eighties. He made a proclamation this morning that there's no shortage of drinking water and that it's all just fearmongering by Canadian scientists in the pocket of drug cartels trying to drive up the price of water. He's calling for an immediate lift of the rationing of drinking water."

I nearly spit out my beer. "*What?* They can't seriously believe him!"

When we were young, the Great Lakes were declared national treasures by both the United States and Canada. These lakes alone can't supply the entire continent's demand forever, though. Seven months ago, America's water consumption taxed its freshwater lakes and rivers to the point where the ecosystems could no longer support it. Combined with the already high levels of pollution making much of the water unsafe to drink, people across the country started getting sick. They declared a national state of emergency. We've been shipping water to them for free ever since, hoping it would help keep their political climate stable and that the weather would one day shift for the better.

James shakes his head and raises his glass. "To stupidity!"

We snicker as we clink our glasses and each take a drink.

"You learned about the Great American Experiment in high school, didn't you?" James continues. "That era of politics around the turn of the last century, when President Trump proved that people will believe anything, no matter how outrageous, as long as they don't have to question their beliefs? We almost didn't make it through that experiment, and now it's starting again!"

I curse quietly in that sage way of young people everywhere when no other words will do.

We drink the rest of our beers in silence, staring at the crowd of people walking by the patio. After the waitress drops off our next drink, James clears his throat.

"So, um, I know you keep a lot to yourself Aiden, but what happened to you today? I'm your best friend, and you know I've got your back no matter what."

I take another sip and say nothing. I know he's right, but that doesn't make it any easier to tell him. How do you confide in someone that you think you're crazy—or worse, possessed—especially when that someone doesn't believe in anything he can't experience with his own senses?

"Well," I say, unsure of where this is going to go, "you know that nightmare I had this morning?"

He nods. "Sure."

"Well, like I told you this morning, I've been having the same dream—or at least an iteration of the same dream—for a while. Actually, I had the first one when I turned eighteen. At first, they happened once a year, but then it started happening every few months. Ever since my twenty-fourth birthday, it's been almost daily."

"Really? The same dream every day?" James sounds a bit incredulous. No surprise there.

"No. Not exactly the same dream, but it's always the same theme. In the one from this morning, this menacing blackness approached me. Somehow, I knew I'd be dead if it caught me. And maybe not just in the dream . . . but in real life too. I don't know."

"You know, people die in their sleep all the time. It doesn't mean a *nightmare* killed them . . ."

I roll my eyes at him. "James . . ."

"Sorry, Aiden." He splays his hands in a gesture of peace. "Go on."

"It felt so real, though . . . so I ran from it toward the sound of someone who was calling my name. I ran until I came to a cliff that overlooked the city. It seemed different somehow, like something was off, but the blackness wouldn't stop coming after me. The voice told me to jump off the edge. What's weird about it is I had the strangest sense I'd be okay if I did."

"So did you jump?"

"I was about to, I think, but then you came in and manhandled me."

James laughs, but it's not his usual deep belly laugh. "Okay, then, what the hell happened at St. Michael's?"

I sigh. "I wish I could tell you. One moment I was zoning out to Cardinal Gallagher's voice, and the next moment the choir starts up and there's this horrible pulse of pain in my head. It made the world shift, and I was suddenly walking down this ancient tunnel. And I know this sounds weird, but if I hadn't been there with you in the church, I'd swear it really happened."

James looks into his beer for a few seconds. It's like I can almost hear his ever-rational mind racing to come up with a logical explanation for everything I've just told him. "If I hadn't seen the way Gallagher was glaring at you, I'd be telling you that you should see a doctor or a shrink or something, but what happened today wasn't normal at all." He takes a long sip of beer, the whole time staring at something only he can see.

His eyes focus on me, and he leans forward. "Seriously, Aiden, I don't care if you're the Antichrist. You're still my Aiden, and there's not an evil bone in your body. I don't want you to sideline me in this, either. I'll understand if you want to be alone and figure it out, but with you falling out of beds and blacking out or whatever in public, I think maybe it's best I stay close to you." He reaches out and squeezes my arm. "We're going to figure out what's going on." He smiles. "And if it does turn out that you're the Antichrist, you better save me a place next to you at your table!" James chuckles at this, but in his laugh I can hear that maybe he's not quite sure whether or not he's joking.

I want to run, to flee this conversation about my insanity. Instead, I sink deeper into my chair and take a swig of beer. "I'm pretty sure I'm not," I say with a dismissive wave of my hand. "I don't know what's going on, but I'm pretty sure I'm not evil incarnate, or the bringer of the Apocalypse or anything."

James throws me a look steeped in mock suspicion and then breaks into a grin. "It's too bad you can't afford to take a holiday. Maybe you're just overworking yourself." He pauses, and his faraway expression that always worries me clouds his face. "Have you ever been to a psychic or medium?"

My eyes go wide in surprise. Not in a million years would I suspect James would suggest I see a psychic. He's more likely to suggest I see a psychologist or a psychiatrist. James simply doesn't do woo-woo. "Never. I've always been scared they'd actually see something."

He laughs. "You know they give me the creeps! But I have this friend named Keegan who lives in the east end, in Leslieville. He's just down the street from you, actually. I go to him pretty regularly for acupuncture treatments and massage. He's a good guy. Anyway, we got to talking one day, and he does psychic readings. It's not my cup of tea, but I thought at the time that it might be something you'd find interesting." He pauses, leaning forward intently.

"Well, after hearing about your nightmares and seeing you at St. Michael's today, do you think it would help?"

I shift in my seat, feeling anxious at the thought.

James smiles reassuringly. "He's the gentlest person I know. Wouldn't hurt a fly."

"I don't know..."

"Hey, get this. In his free time, he wanders through the forests in the Don Valley, exploring and nature watching. I've gone on a few hikes with him now, and he's awesome! You're going to love him."

This guy's apparent love of forests strikes a chord in me. Regardless, I know I'll need to get out of my comfort zone if I'm ever going to get any help with my problem. I finally smile, and James takes this as his cue.

"Perfect! I'll give him a call now and make an appointment!"

Chapter Four

I slowly open my eyes. I glance at the wall above me, and the image of an upside down clock brightens the dark room. The clock senses I'm lying down and reorients itself so I can read it clearly. It is 2:30 a.m. I groan, pulling the sheets tighter around me. I lie there, staring at the ceiling.

Please, don't let sleep elude me again.

I close my eyes, and strange shadows play over my eyelids. The effect is so reminiscent of last night's dream that a shiver runs down my spine. My thoughts racing, I crack open an eyelid, suddenly afraid that I'm still dreaming. It's nothing but moonlight dancing magically through the only window in my basement bachelor apartment. Someone must have walked by the window.

I sigh when I realize I'm covered in a cold sweat. Again. Every night, it's the same thing. I lie awake for hours, my thoughts drifting between how I squandered my grandfather's money and his faith in me, to how I messed things up with Jenn to drive her into Adam's waiting arms, to how I'm going to handle my mother's failing health—how I'm going to handle whatever version of nightmare will hit me next. After that, I wake up in a panic, the nightmare having driven me from my slumber. It would be enough for these thoughts to plague me during day, but it's been months since I've had a good sleep.

James is right; I do need help. But a psychic?

Movement flutters past my window again, and my heart thumps loudly in my ears. I live at the end of a dead-end street with nothing but a small parkette across from me. Sure, it's a favourite haunt of transients, but they shouldn't be this close to the house. It happens again, and this time I see it's just a raccoon.

I throw the covers aside, disgusted with myself. I'm not the type to run headlong into a fight, but I've never been afraid of harmless shadows either. Tonight, I'm going to change the tide. Instead of lying in bed and dreading falling back to sleep, I'm going to do something constructive, like clean my apartment.

"Half-light," I say, and a strip of pipe lighting running around the walls bathes the apartment in a dim light somewhat akin to dusk.

My feet hit the floor, and I feel a violent pulse in my head as my senses come alive. It's like a set of inner eyelids I didn't know I had have suddenly opened. I'm standing in the middle of the same tunnel from the episode at St. Michael's yesterday. The stone floor is rough on my bare feet. All is quiet now, though. The voices of the choir are no longer assailing the walls.

The air feels dusty, and a dank smell speaks of a deep network of underground tunnels. Light from a nearby torch flickers on the wall opposite me, illuminating rubble that wasn't there last time. A section of the ancient tunnel has crumbled, perhaps from whatever odd power the choral voices had. Granted, most of the rubble appears to be caused by the passing of centuries. It looks like I'm the first being to step foot along this path in a millennium—even if I'm not actually here.

I look up as I hear shuffling from down the corridor. Two robed figures round the corner, approaching slowly, quietly, staring at the torch in a mixture of awe, fear, and suspicion, as if they've never seen one before. The first one is a woman in her early thirties. Her dark brown hair flows just past her shoulders. She has a large nose with a slight hook in it, as though it's been broken before. Her close-set brown eyes are framed with soft laugh lines, making her look like someone who smiles easily and is quick to laugh. I stifle a gasp when I notice the second one is the old man from the cafe. I can see the tweed jacket and bow tie underneath his robe. He looks more serious than he did yesterday, but the twinkle in his eye is almost aglow in the torchlight.

I want to say something, but somehow I've forgotten how to speak. Regardless, they don't even seem to see me. I find this odd at first, but then I remember this is just a dream. With that realization, I smile and decide to push the dream's boundaries. Knowledge, after all, is power. If I'm going to be stuck having these dreams for the rest of my life, I should start learning how to make the most of them.

I focus on the torch and will it to go dark, fully expecting nothing to occur.

A gust of wind rushes down the tunnel and swirls around the torch, snuffing it out. The woman gasps, and there is such panic in that sound that I feel deeply ashamed at having frightened her. I focus on the torch again, willing the light to return, but nothing happens.

In the darkness that envelops us, I hear the rustling of robes as the two figures spin about, seeking the source of the disturbance. I hear one of them slowly approach the position of the torch. "*Bheith ag lonrú*," the woman murmurs quietly. I can almost feel the longing in her voice, but the torch remains dark. She sighs in response, a deep and heartfelt sigh of disappointment.

Of course my dreams would invent a secret language to complicate things.

The woman turns to the old man. "Sometimes the energy here is so intense that I think it will actually respond to me."

He smiles gently and places a hand on her arm. "I think we all have those moments."

I stare at the torch, rolling the odd phrase through my head. Did she think that speaking those words could have lit it? I offer my best imitation of the same phrase, sure that I'd butcher it. The torch remains dark, but something stirs deep within me, urging me to try again. I speak the words again, nearly shouting them, concentrating on mimicking the emphasis the woman used, and the torch bursts into blinding flames. I curse, jumping back, and I see the two strangers retreat from the light, glancing every which way for whoever is in the space with them. I quickly whisper the phrase again, focusing carefully on getting the words right, and the torchlight ebbs back to normal.

In the flickering light, the woman's eyes are bright and full of fear. The man's eyes are alert, and his nostrils flare as if he's trying to sniff out where I'm hiding. For a long moment, the woman stares directly at the spot where I'm standing, as if she senses my presence. Then the old man gently places a hand on her arm. They both turn away and continue down the passage until they disappear from sight.

I listen until I can no longer hear their shuffling footsteps. I take a tentative step in the direction from which they came.

"*Aiden* . . ." comes the voice from my dreams, echoing down the corridor.

I pause. There's a part of me that doesn't want to continue, that's too frightened to learn what the voice wants. Another part of me—quieter, and yet somehow more insistent—tells me that now's the time to find out what's going on. The usual panic and urgency I feel in my dreams is gone tonight; tonight, all is calm. Something tells me that the answer to all of my questions—the reason behind my insanity—lies at the end of this tunnel.

"*Not all,*" the soothing voice says with a hypnotic calmness, "*but many things will soon be revealed to you.*"

I slowly descend a stone staircase further down the tunnel. The torches along the wall roar to life as I pass them, responding to my presence. With each step, I become more comfortable with my surroundings. As I go deeper, it begins to feel as if I belong here, as if this ancient place has been waiting for me to venture into its depths. I notice that my steps have become much more confident. It's the same feeling I get when I hop out of the truck after a day of working in the trees: energized, as if I actually have a purpose greater than selling suits to a bunch of Bay Street posers.

I glance down and see that the black boxers I arrived in have morphed into a billowing black robe. I look around me once again, and it's as if the walls are alive. With each step I take, they grow brighter. Strewn rubble rises and forms into brilliant archways and gilded columns. The walls change from dark and gloomy to bright and clean. It's as if my being here is healing this place.

I round a corner, and the tunnel widens. I stop, my eyes wide and mouth slack. Never have I beheld such beauty. I've come into a vast chamber with a vaulted ceiling that towers several stories above me. It's supported by grand columns with strange engravings that seem to glow with power. Near the top of each column, a dark red crystal orb is mounted. The crystals gleam in the bright flames roaring from massive sconces that line the walls all around the chamber. However, it's the massive stone table before me that ultimately draws me in.

It's a table you would expect to see in a hall of kings. It's easily twenty feet long, five feet wide, and three feet tall. Thirteen massive stone thrones sit around it, six down one side, six down the other, and one at the closest end. Their backs are ornately carved with swirling triskelions, and the seats are wide and deep. On the right arm of each throne a large torch blazes, illuminating the table before it.

The vast tabletop thrums with an energy like none I've felt before. In the centre is carved a map of a mountain range. Rivulets of quartz run through it, radiating brilliantly. As my eyes trace one of the veins of quartz, I am drawn deeper into the chamber. I reach the far end of the table and gasp. Water cascades from the mouth of the quartz river, flowing freely over several small boulders and down a wide spiral staircase. I am awed.

I step down the stairs to the lower level of the chamber. In the centre stands a circle of giant sarsen stones, much like what Stonehenge looked like before it collapsed in the 2070s from widespread tunnelling beneath it. The stones tower above me, and for a moment, that's all I can see. And then I hear the beautiful music of water tumbling over rocks again. Between the stone circle and me, I notice that the waterfall feeds a large pool of glittering, clear water. It takes my breath away.

I step up to the pool as reverently as I imagine a pilgrim would have approached the Holy Grail.

"*Behold* . . ." the voice whispers from all around me.

The pool, the stone circle, all of it, recedes into mist. In the centre, a small orb appears, growing rapidly until I can see the surface of the world within it. The orb rushes toward me and I fall into it. Lights appear, and soon I see they are cities. Buildings seem to rise. I'm only a few metres from the surface when I stop falling. The world starts spinning below me as I hover. I soar past people. There are happy people and sad people. People singing. People shouting. People laughing. People crying. People playing. People toiling. People are being rescued. People are being killed. I'm orbiting the world like a flash, and all around the Earth is life as I know it. Nothing is pure. Nothing is evil. Everything is somewhere in between.

And then something changes. It's barely discernible at first, as if the atmosphere of the world has become darker. Entire cities then go dark. There are widespread power outages. Parents fight with their children. Friends become strangers. Lovers separate. Brothers take up arms against brothers. Fires light up throughout the world.

The orb spins and focuses on Canada as explosions erupt, rocking the country. It spins again, and more explosions rock the United States. As it continues to spin, a sense of impending doom fills the world as the turmoil intensifies and spreads. Fires rage through cities. Great fissures appear, swallowing the fracking and surface mining operations that governments have allowed to proliferate. Sadness, anger, and fear are everywhere. Everywhere, people are dying. It's a horrifying sight that stabs deep into my soul.

"*All of this must come to pass, Aiden . . .*"

"*But why? And why show me?*"

The scene before me fades into darkness. It remains black and heavy for a long time before I call out to the voice. I hear nothing, and it stays like this for what feels like hours until finally my eyes open to the sun shining through the window of my apartment.

I stretch my arms out and shift my feet, trying to loosen the stiffness in my limbs and drive the dream from my mind. It was so real that I can still smell the smoke of the torches. I sit back down on my bed and glance at the clock: 8:00 a.m. Five hours have passed. I've been standing beside the bed this whole time, and I feel every minute of it.

Sighing, I lie down with the intention of resting for the fifteen minutes before my alarm goes off, but my blood goes cold. My feet are black with dust, and beside me lies a two-foot-long stave. It looks old—pine, perhaps. The top is wrapped in a charred rag so ancient that it's threadbare. A wisp of smoke swirls from the end. I literally can still smell the smoke from the dream, but how is any of this possible?

I sit up. A lump rises in my throat. I pick up the torch, holding it at arm's length. I stare at it for a long time, wrestling with whether I should run it outside and throw it as far away as I can or hide it in the deepest recess of my closet. In the end, I do neither. I set it with what is almost a sense of reverence on the bookshelf at the end of my bed.

The torch looks out of place in my apartment. I stare at it for another moment before the anticipation starts to eat at me.

I whisper, "*Bheith ag lonrú.*"

When I realize my eyes are clenched shut, I crack one open just a slit. The torch remains unchanged.

Sighing, I force both the dream and the torch from my mind. This is too much to process this early in the morning. Blocking the strangeness as best I can from my mind, I get ready for another day of selling suits.

Chapter Five

"What do you mean you dreamed it into existence? You know that makes no sense, right?"

James stands in my bedroom, staring with obvious disbelief at the torch on my bookshelf. He arrived after his lunch shift at the restaurant, ostensibly to make sure I was still doing okay, but I suspect his real motive is to make sure I'm not going to bail on visiting the psychic with him tonight. He found me sitting cross-legged in the centre of my bed, staring at the torch.

I'm torn between trying to light the torch with James here and trying to forget it's even sitting there. I told him about most of the dream and about waking up with the smoking torch next to me. I decided to leave out the vision of the world going up in flames. It's probably for the best, judging by his reaction so far.

"Okay, okay!" I say. "You know that old widow up the street? I found it in her backyard while taking a shortcut to work."

For several more moments, James says nothing. I see his eyes flick between the torch and the only three books on the shelf: *High Magic: Theory & Practice* by Frater U∴D∴ and *The Middle Pillar: The Balance Between Mind and Magic* and *The Tree of Life: An Illustrated Study in Magic* by Israel Regardie. When I was in high school, I'd had an intense interest in scholarly magic. I haven't indulged in it in years, but each book had cost me almost a week's pay, print books being as rare as they are, so I've been loath to part with them.

When James's gaze finally meets mine, the worry in them is undisguised. He sits on the bed beside me, his hand resting lightly on my shoulder. "Aiden, I know you had an interest in this sort of thing before. I can't say I've ever understood it. But seeing these"—he gestures to the books on the shelf—"it's a little more understandable why you're having these dreams. Have you considered that maybe the dreams are completely unrelated to the headaches? I know you haven't been to see a doctor. Maybe you're getting headaches because of some sort of nutritional imbalance. It's also been forever since you've taken a day off of work."

I look away. I understand what he's saying, and on some level I know he's coming from a good place. It also hurts to hear him rationalize my deepest nightmares into something his logical brain can understand.

He squeezes my shoulder. "I know it's been hard since your mother got cancer, man. Having to pay for rent and food for yourself on top of buying her medications would be a lot for anyone. And I won't pretend to know what you're going through, but I am concerned about how it's affecting you. It's an incredible burden, Aiden, and I respect you so much for taking it on, but this much stress isn't good for you. To be honest, I'm surprised that headaches are the only way it's manifesting."

"So . . . what? I'm just supposed to put up with this for the rest of my life?" Anger creeps into my voice. "Or should I just stop buying her medication and watch her die? Is that what you're suggesting?"

James pulls back, and his eyes go wide. "No! I didn't mean that. I just mean that what you're doing *has* to affect you. It's impossible to handle as much as you are without it affecting you. I just think that maybe you should see an actual doctor . . ." He trails off, looking away for a moment. "There are medications that could help, if that's what it is."

I glare at him, aghast. We've had many conversations about how I feel about doctors and prescription drugs. Seeing how they treated my mother—repeated misdiagnoses, various trials with different pills, each one affecting her worse than the one before it—affected me very deeply. They finally discovered the tumour in her brain, but it has grown to the point that all they can do now is treat the symptoms. One of her doctors suggested an experimental procedure that could potentially cure the cancer, but the surgery isn't covered following the deep cutbacks to the healthcare system.

When I finally speak, it's with a deep bitterness. "If you're just going to tell me I should be on meds, why bother trying to hook me up with a psychic?"

"Aiden, with these nightmares and headaches you've been getting, have you considered it could be your subconscious trying to tell you something? Maybe it's time to slow down a bit. If it's your subconscious, Keegan can help you with that."

Irrational anger bubbles just below the surface. I can hear him talking, but his words are barely registering. "And what about that thing?" I look over at the torch on the shelf.

James doesn't even look at it, and the realization hits me that he's not simply helping me explore my options. He truly doesn't believe a word I'm saying. "Is it a stretch to suggest that maybe you blacked out from one of your headaches and found the torch somewhere?"

I uncross my legs and push off the bed. I begin pacing because I've started to hyperventilate. He doesn't take the hint.

"Hell, you could even have made it yourself." James crouches down and jabs a finger at the light scorch marks on my floor. "To be honest, I'm a bit surprised you're not more concerned that you dropped a lit torch in your bedroom!" His voice is full of recrimination.

I stop pacing and stare ahead, refusing to meet his eyes. It's been years since I've been as angry as I am right now. I close my eyes and attempt to centre myself, to regain peace. I can feel my temples throbbing. Several moments pass in awkward silence.

"I think you should leave," I say, my eyes still closed.

After five years of friendship, this is our first major disagreement.

I hear him stand up. He steps next to me and takes a deep breath. "Aiden, I'm just—"

"I said get out!"

"I hope you go see Keegan," he murmurs. He sounds hurt and frustrated.

James leaves, closing the door slightly louder than usual. My hands are at my sides, balled up into fists. I breathe deeply for a minute, and they gradually unclench.

I glance over at the torch again. I think of the ancient stone hallway. I think of the old man with the handlebar mustache and pronounced limp. In my dream, he had that same black cane he'd had in the coffee shop. He was even wearing the same tweed jacket and bow tie. Is it possible I invented it all?

The truth is, nothing James said is a stretch. I've been hearing voices, seeing things, *feeling* things, and my dreams have started merging with reality. This is what my grandmother was medicated for—and my mother too before the cancer.

I sit down on my bed, cradling my head in my hands, massaging my temples with my thumbs. It's all too much to comprehend.

My wristband buzzes. I glance at it. James has sent me an address: 993 Queen Street East. Along with it, he texts, "I let him know I can't make it but said you'll be there."

He was right. Keegan's practice is close to my house; at a nice relaxed pace, it will take me about fifteen minutes to walk there. He's situated on this side of the river in the heart of Leslieville, an area that has managed to retain a sort of rustic charm as the general east side declined. It's not as well off as the Beach with its upscale clientele, but it's a substantial improvement from Riverside itself.

I have half an hour before my appointment, which gives me just enough time to eat some of the dried river trout and dehydrated vegetables I've been eating for the past three days. I eat quickly and then leave. I don't like feeling rushed. I prefer to be a few minutes early for all of my appointments, even if it's an appointment with a psychic.

Leaving my basement apartment feels like leaving behind a horrible nightmare. I feel lighter with each step I take away from my door. I suspect it has something to do with the torch in my bedroom. Its presence seems to take up my entire apartment. In a way, it has become a symbol, either of the onset of some serious psychotic disorder, or of the fact that something really freaky is happening to me, for the lack of a better term.

By the time I reach the corner, I'm practically floating with a sense of lightness and freedom. I can still feel the sense of dark foreboding deep down in the centre of my gut, but for the first time in weeks, it's not a giant pit of fear. Even the guilt I had started to feel about kicking James out of my apartment has disappeared.

I step onto Queen Street East. I've rounded this same corner thousands of times in the past five years, but it feels like I'm actually seeing it for the first time. It's a corner stuck in the last century. Multiple depressions from that time hit it hard, and now it's full of abandoned storefronts and rundown buildings. Several of the windows are cracked wide open. Still others are boarded up. Signs of a darker kind of life are obvious from glimpses of candles behind the boards and discarded needles around the entrances. They're prime examples of the state of disrepute the area east of the Don River descended into over the past thirty years or so.

The sun begins to set slowly. I was terrified to go out at night when I first moved here. I'm still afraid to, but those of us who live here understand that no one comes here at night willingly. The city's upper classes have it partly wrong. This area may be a cesspit of criminals, but the crime rate here is actually relatively low. There's no point in stealing from those who are almost as unfortunate as you. Everyone here is just trying to get by.

Like all July nights, tonight is hot, so I'm wearing a dark blue T-shirt that's only slightly faded, shorts, and sandals I've had to restitch three times now. It's still hot, even though the sun is setting. The temperature today hit above forty degrees without the humidex, which is the sixty-seventh time this year and the twentieth day in a row. After the shortest, warmest winter we've ever had, it's no wonder there's a water crisis. The sweat beading on my forehead and running down my back is doing a good job of hiding my growing nervousness about seeing Keegan.

As I get to Leslieville, the number of dilapidated buildings decreases, and I pass several stores that are actually open for business. It's not Yorkville, but it's an improvement.

I hear James's voice echoing through my head as I walk: "If it's your subconscious, Keegan can help you with that."

Maybe I shouldn't have kicked him out. I'd feel a lot more comfortable right now if he were here with me. If I'm going to be honest with myself, I'm actually a bit scared. Meeting new people has never been something I've been very comfortable with. Going to my first-ever psychic by myself is a whole new experience for me.

I occasionally check the street numbers on the buildings, keeping an eye out for Keegan's address. I don't recall if I've ever been this way. When I look up at a rundown (for Leslieville) building, I stop dead in my tracks. This is 993 Queen Street East. There's a hand-painted wooden sign hanging above the window that reads "K's Bookshop" in gold letters. In the window I can see a few actual books stacked on the sill, and looking deeper, my eyes go wide with wonder. There are shelves and shelves of books, with more books towering in stacks beside each shelf. It's like a booklover's antique shop, considering the last of the traditional book publishers went out of business before I was born, having finally succumbed to the pressures of digital publishing. The typical reader now simply uses a wristband to access digital versions of virtually every book ever published.

There's no neon sign proclaiming that a psychic is in residence. Besides being a treasure trove of print books, there's nothing remarkable about the place at all. I glance again at the address on my wristband just to make sure I'm at the right place.

The door is propped open, and the distinctive smell of old books lures me in. Just inside is a man around my age, sitting at a giant oak desk that appears far older than many of the books lining the shelves. His brown hair is brushed over his eyes. He doesn't see me at first because he's engrossed in a book he has set open on the desk. His tight black V-neck shirt perfectly accentuates his swimmer's build. On his right calf, below the hem of his beige shorts, is the Eye of Providence tattooed above a crescent moon. He's definitely not what one would expect to see sitting at an oak desk in an old bookshop. The shop is otherwise empty. When I walk over to him, he looks up from the book he's reading. His eyes linger on me a moment before he stands.

I have the better part of a foot on him, but James was right. His whole energy is that of peace and calm. His pale blue eyes and the intensity of his gaze strike me immediately. It's like he can see into me, though it feels comforting rather than invasive. It's like that moment when first meeting someone and an instant connection flares to life, regardless of gender or age or physical attraction. It's like one soul recognizing the other, and there's a magnetic pull so strong that it tethers the two together.

That's what I feel in this moment with his eyes locked onto mine. His eyes are like refreshing pools of cool water on an oppressively hot day.

"You must be Aiden," he says. His voice is velvety, and it calms and disarms me completely.

I blink away our gaze. "That's me." I reach out to shake his hand, but he steps around the desk and envelops me in a hug instead.

"Nothing but hugs in this building!" He releases me and takes a step back.

"Nice to finally meet you, Aiden. I'm Keegan. James has told me so much about you. I'm glad you could make it!"

I grin. I feel at ease by his welcome. "Pleasure to meet you too. Your shop is beautiful." I look around at the vast selection of books.

"Thank you so much. I've poured my entire soul into it. Feel free to look around a bit after our appointment."

This genuinely excites me. "Definitely!" I pick up a tattered copy of Mark Twain's *Adventures of Huckleberry Finn*. It feels like a priceless relic in my hands. "So is the alternative healing just a side business for you?"

"Actually, the books are the side business." Keegan walks to the front of the store and locks the door. He flips an old sign from "open" to "closed" before turning off the front lights. "I come from a traditional Catholic family. It took them years to accept I'm gay. Considering how long it took even in today's society, I figured they'd disown me if they knew I also make a living doing energy work such as reiki, crystal healing, and psychic readings."

I carefully set the book down.

"Twain," Keegan says. "Have you read it?"

"Not on paper!"

We share a laugh. I'm glad that James suggested I come here. Everything about Keegan says he's open and trustworthy.

Keegan heads to the back of the store. "Right this way."

There's not much in the way of sunlight coming through the front windows, so with the lights off, the bookshelves seem like a maze, stretching up tall and twisting and turning in several directions. The light from the front of the store shines through gaps in the bookshelves, creating eerie shadows. It all serves to add to a growing magical ambiance. I wasn't sure what to expect from a psychic, but the setting definitely makes this one feel real, and it fills me with a strange sense of unease.

Keegan leads me between rows of books down the central corridor of the store. We round a corner into a tight hallway lined with overfilled bookshelves on both sides. At the end of the hall is another shelf loaded with books much the same way. I'm not sure where he's bringing me. When we reach the end of the hall, Keegan turns to me and grins. "This right here is what convinced me to spend every penny I'd saved to buy this place."

Keegan rests a hand on a book on the middle shelf. It's a copy of *The Oxford*

Shakespeare, but it's too dark for me to see which edition it is. He pulls the book out, reaches his other hand into the gap, and twists something. He then returns the book to its spot on the shelf. Seconds later, I hear a click and a whir, and the bookshelf recedes slightly before sliding into the wall like an automatic door at a shopping mall. Keegan chuckles upon seeing the amazement on my face.

We pass through the opening into the next room, and I swear I feel a difference in energy. It's definitely colder back here, but there's something else—something deeper. I can sense it instinctually. It's like a wellspring of positive energy that wraps me in the confidence of knowing that coming here was the right decision. It definitely strengthens the feeling I have that there's more to this bookseller than his good looks.

The two windows at the back of the room have an excellent and close-up view of a brick wall that probably wasn't there when the windows were originally installed. The building blocks out most of the remaining light of the setting sun, but the soft glow of three antique lamps otherwise light the room. Beneath the windows is an ivory Victorian-style fainting couch with a mahogany side table. In the corner to my left is a tall antique grandfather clock. Its loud ticking echoes through the room. On the other side of the couch is a shelf lined with various candles, Tibetan brass bowls, chimes, and crystals. Beside the shelf are a massage table and several bottles of essential oils.

Keegan ushers me past the couch to two comfortable-looking black leather armchairs that frame a fireplace with a beautiful marble mantel. Upon the mantel are titles such as Carl Jung's *Undiscovered Self* and Dante Alighieri's *Divine Comedy*. Between the armchairs is a small round table. Resting upon the table are a notebook, a fountain pen, and an inkwell.

"Take a seat, Aiden."

I sit in one of the armchairs as Keegan moves around the room, dimming each lamp in turn. He then takes a candle from the shelf before sitting in the armchair across from me. He places the candle at the centre of the table beside us and reaches into his pocket. He pulls out a pack of matches and lights the candle. Matches are about as rare as books these days. By the time the sulphur hits my senses, I am entranced.

Keegan smiles at my expression. "Beautiful process, isn't it? My grandmother collected matches and left them to me when she died. Candles and matches and the like make everything so much more magical."

A few moments pass as we both gaze at the single flame.

Keegan eventually sinks back into the armchair and throws a foot up onto his knee. "So, James tells me you've never been to a psychic."

I nod.

His eyes narrow a bit, but his voice softens. "You're troubled by dreams." He reaches across the table and takes my hand. "You have one of the strongest, most vibrant auras of anyone I've met, but the edges are faded and fractured. It's like you're approaching utter exhaustion."

I nod again and meet his gaze directly. "I am. I've been having very intense dreams, and they're causing me terrible headaches."

Keegan sets my hand back onto the arm of my chair. "I think perhaps we should just talk today. We can go deeper on your next visit. First I'd like you to tell me a little bit about yourself and how you've come to be here."

I take a deep breath and release it slowly. I hadn't really planned on telling my life story to a stranger today, but I instinctively trust Keegan. Maybe it will help. "What would you like to know?"

"Why don't we start with what happened to you when you were a boy to cast such a long shadow over your soul?"

Oh, is that all? This guy wants to get straight to the source, and I don't know if I'm ready for that. "I thought you said we were going to get deeper on the next visit . . ."

Keegan rests a hand on mine. "Aiden, psychic exploration has untold depths. Beginning with childhood is a great entry point into the work we do."

I'm quiet for a long time, and when I do finally look up, there are tears in my eyes. "My father wasn't always a drunkard and a deadbeat. He didn't always beat us . . ." I notice Keegan doesn't even blink. "It was losing his third job in the span of four years that drove him to drink."

"What do you remember of that time?"

"I still remember the day he came home, staggering up the driveway. I was eleven. It was three years before my grandmother died and about six years before my grandfather moved in with us. My mother was doing the dishes when she looked out the window and saw him standing in the driveway."

"What did she do?"

"She told me to go to my room. She said, 'Your father's lost his job again.

He'll need some time alone.' Then she went outside to meet him. It didn't take long, and I didn't go to my room right away. I heard them arguing about money and how alcohol was a luxury we couldn't afford. Then I heard him hit her in the face. I poked my head around the door just in time to see her reel backward and land on her side in the grass . . .'"

"How did you respond to that?"

"I panicked. I could barely take my eyes off my mother. When I did, he was staring at me . . . Only it wasn't my father anymore. It was some monster. The second he started up the path to the front door, I took off up the stairs to my room and hid underneath my bed. I heard his footsteps, heavy on each stair. He came into my room and yanked me out from under the bed. I got eleven spanks with his belt that first time, one for every year of my life . . .'"

I continued when Keegan didn't say anything. "That was the day everything changed. My mother withdrew into herself then, and my sister Suzanne and I went from playing around the house without a care in the world to whispering and tiptoeing whenever he was home, afraid he'd hear us. He'd beat us whenever we disturbed him. The only time we were safe was after our grandfather moved in, and even then only when he was home."

Keegan leans forward in his chair. "How long did this go on for?"

"It stopped after I moved to Toronto when I was eighteen, so seven very long years. My father never did get another job. He'd sold our car and used the money to buy alcohol and purchase stocks in a start-up that he was sure would make him millions. It never did. My mother had to get three jobs to keep food on the table while he sat at home and drank his unemployment cheques away."

"Did your leaving help put a stop to it?"

"No. About a year after I left, something happened that drove my mother to finally kick him out. I've never found out what that was, but I'm thankful for it. She had started drinking by that time, too, but she hid it better."

I fall silent for a couple of minutes before speaking again. "Deep down, I'm ashamed of myself."

"Ashamed? Why?"

"I left my mother, my grandfather, and my younger sister with a monster."

"You did what you had to do survive, Aiden. Staying in that environment wasn't healthy. And perhaps fear for your safety is what kept your mother from doing anything earlier."

"Maybe you're right; maybe you're wrong..."

After a pause, Keegan says, "What's your relationship with your family like now?"

I wince. "My sister and I haven't really spoken since. We met again at our grandfather's funeral two and a half years ago. It was first time I'd seen any of them since I moved out." My voice chokes as I continue. "In that time, my mother had developed a brain tumour, but it took too long to diagnose it. She looked so sickly at the funeral. It broke my heart because she couldn't afford the medication she needed. That was the last time my sister and I spoke. We agreed to split the monthly drug costs. I sometimes think about contacting her, but..." My voice fades, and my shoulders begin to shake as tears run down my face.

I don't hear Keegan stand, but I feel the heat from his hands hovering above my head and then brushing slowly down past my shoulders.

"I've been afraid ever since that I'll turn into him," I say. "He's part of me. If it could happen to him, it could happen to me."

"And that fear touches everything." Keegan's voice is so soft that I barely hear him.

"I've never really thought of it that way, but, yeah, it really does."

"It makes you live your life in the middle, where it's safe."

"Safe?" I'm not sure what he means.

"You have so much love inside you, but you're afraid to fully commit yourself to anything. You're afraid that at your deepest core lies a being as cruel as the one your father became when pushed beyond his limits. This prevents you from venturing anywhere near that core."

I don't say anything. The weight of sharing something so intimate with someone I've just met is pressing down on me.

Keegan returns to his seat and smiles disarmingly. "I'm sorry. I may have gone too far, but I can only tell you what I see and feel. After all, isn't this why you've come?"

I nod and wipe the tears away with the back of my hand. "It's true."

"Maybe we should end here for today."

I once again notice the intensity of Keegan's pale blue eyes, and I find myself falling into them.

"Today's session is free of charge," he says. "Think of what I've said. If you feel that any of it resonates, we'll come up with some sort of fee structure tailored to you."

Keegan stands and turns all the lamps on full. "Please feel free to look around the store." He smiles.

I murmur my thanks, but I'm too unnerved to stay.

Chapter Six

For the first time in what feels like forever, I had a dreamless sleep. There was no thrashing wildly through a deep, dark forest; there was no mysterious voice filtering into my subconscious; there was no worry about my mother. There was just pure, untroubled sleep. I think back to yesterday evening and the warmth emanating from Keegan's hands as they hovered above me. Was it that? Or was it that I'd actually spoken with someone about all of my issues for the first time in my life? Either way, I have him to thank for my good night's sleep. I'll be going back to see him for sure.

As I arrange my necktie into a Windsor knot, I think back to what Keegan had to say. I've never felt like I had a fear of commitment. I mean, I proposed to Jenn. Sure, it had taken two years of her hinting about it, but I still did it. And if I could have afforded something more romantic than getting down on one knee after a homemade candlelit dinner, I would have.

My hands falter, and I mess up the knot.

Or would I have? That was before I'd reconnected with my family, so I wasn't sending money to my mother every month at that time. Back then, I could have afforded dinner out. Actually, I'm pretty sure I took her out for her birthday a few weeks later.

I did love her. I doted on her. I was there for her when her brother was gunned down in a spate of senseless violence. I cheered her on when she was nominated for valedictorian at her college. But maybe Keegan's right. The closer Jenn and I got, the more I simultaneously withdrew. By the time we started planning our wedding, we had essentially stopped sleeping together. I would come up with excuse after excuse for why we couldn't. I actually believed those excuses at the time, but looking back through this new lens, I now see that I was afraid—afraid I'd eventually subject Jenn to the same abuse my father inflicted on my mother. Did that fear drive me to sabotage our relationship? I've blamed Jenn this whole time, but could it actually have been me who drove her into her co-worker's arms?

I don't want Keegan to be right, but at the same time I can't shake the feeling that he is.

I fix my tie and finish getting dressed, doing my best to stop thinking about Keegan's words. I didn't know what to expect last night, but I definitely didn't expect him to see right through the self-delusions I've been unknowingly building for years. I also didn't expect to leave his bookstore feeling like a giant weight was lifted from my shoulders. As I climb up the stairs to leave my apartment, I roll my shoulders, amazed at how relaxed they feel.

When I get outside, I glance at my wristband. There's a message from James: "How'd it go?"

"Great," I reply. "I'm definitely going back."

I step onto the thickly treed path leading to Eastern Avenue. Squeezed between the train tracks and an abandoned self-storage building, it's a great shortcut to East Harbour Station—if you make friends with the people who call the path home.

Only once have I been roughed up a little, but it was my own fault. I was out late with James one night and ignored his advice to spend the night at his place. When I got off the subway at East Harbour, I used the path without thinking. It was much darker at night than I thought it would be, and someone jumped me from behind. The guy threw me down, punched me twice in the face, and held a knife to my throat while he rummaged around in my pockets. While I was both stunned and shocked, he had enough time to find my wallet.

I'm not a fighter, but you don't grow up the poor kid in the suburbs and not learn how to throw a punch. As soon as my mugger tried to get up, I brought my knee up hard. He fell forward on top of me, flinging the knife and my wallet away as he planted his arms. I then grabbed his right arm and rolled him over until I was on top of him. I work hard for every cent I own, and when that asshole tried to take my money from me, it triggered my primal instincts. Seizing the element of surprise, I landed three solid blows to his face. His body went limp.

When I stood up to retrieve my wallet, the five guys who have lived on the path since before I moved into the area were peering at me through the darkness. Not one of them moved or said anything as I staggered down the path, blood dripping from my knuckles and from my already fattening lip.

I avoided the path for a few weeks after that, and I haven't taken it after dark since, but the people who live there have treated me with grudging respect ever since.

When I get to Eastern and Broadview, I check my wristband and type, "Sorry about last night. Maybe next time you can come with?"

"Love to," comes James's response almost immediately.

I smile as I enter the subway station.

When I get to the store, my manager, Debbie, is busy with a customer. I smile at her as I walk past to put my lunch in the back room. She smiles back, and it's not hard to see why she almost always makes her sale. She has a smile that lights up her face. It seems to make most customers trust her immediately. When she focuses her large brown eyes on you, you feel like you're the only one in the world she has time for.

Debbie's two daughters are close to my age, and her husband, Ron, is easily sixty. She's probably in her early fifties, but today she's wearing a beautiful royal blue dress that perfectly complements her dark brown skin and makes her look at least ten years younger.

When I return to the sales floor, I notice that something seems off with Debbie. Most people probably wouldn't notice it, but she and I have been the only two employees at the store since I started here three years ago. It's her hands. Her arms are normally open and expressive, as if she's perpetually looking to give you a hug. Today they're clasped in front of her, and she's twitching her thumb as though she's nervous about something.

It's not her customer. He seems cheerful enough. He's a clean-shaven middle-aged man with neatly trimmed hair. He's nothing out of the ordinary amongst our clientele. Yet, a moment later, he walks out empty-handed.

I look around. Suits are out of place on four different stands, and several shirts lie open, draped haphazardly across the shoe display. It's very unlike

Debbie. She always reprimands me if I try to engage a new customer without first cleaning up after the previous one, no matter how busy we are. My concern grows when I hear her sigh and see her shoulders slump. I've never seen her like this.

"Hey, Debbie."

She looks over at me smiles again, but it seems forced. "Oh, hi, Aiden."

"Are you okay?"

She doesn't answer at first. She draws in a deep breath that seems to fill her up with life again. She stands up straight, but her smile is muted. "Not really, Aiden. I'm really sorry, but I'm going to have to leave for the day, and I'm not really sure when I'll be back."

I blink. "What?" Mondays are usually one of our busiest days of the week. We never work alone on Mondays.

"I know. I'm sorry. But Ron got arrested in the US last night. I have to go get him."

Now I'm doubly shocked. Debbie's husband is an investigative journalist, but I have never heard of him landing in that kind of trouble before. "*Arrested?*"

I follow her to the back room, where she picks up her purse. "He was on an undercover assignment with Channel One News, getting a scoop on this Glen Davis fellow and the inner workings of the Christian march when they got started. He decided to follow them to get an inside view of the whole journey."

"Wow, really?"

"Yes, and last night a section of the march turned violent. A bunch of people set fire to an effigy of the president, and fighting broke out. Ron was close enough that when state troopers swooped in and threw the whole bunch of them in prison, he got taken in too."

"No way!"

She ignores me. She frantically packs her purse and then runs around the store, trying to clean up after herself.

"Debbie, don't worry. I'll get that."

"Oh, thanks! Sorry!"

"You don't owe me any apology. You're obviously not in the right state of mind to work."

"Well, thanks anyway. And, um, I'm going to need you to work a little bit extra."

"No worries, Deb. I get it. Take as long as you need." I take the shirt out of her hands that she is trying unsuccessfully to refold. "Here, I'll take that. Deb, you should go. When do you leave for the States?"

"I've booked a flight for this afternoon. If you have any errands you need to run before I leave, you can. You weren't expecting this."

"No, no. You go. Get Ron back."

"Thanks, Aiden. And Aiden . . . ?"

"Yes?"

"You look better today than you have in a while. Whatever you're doing, keep it up."

I give a noncommittal nod. "I will. So you don't know how long you'll be gone?"

"No idea at all. If we're lucky, we'll be able to get it sorted out in a couple of days. His editor is flying down with me to make our case, but she warned me that it could take at a week or longer if things get complicated."

She falls silent, and I see a storm of tears beginning to brew in her eyes. I step forward, pulling her close and giving her a tight hug, wordlessly praying that Ron will be all right. I'm sure she is doing the same as she steps away from me, rubs her eyes quickly, and runs out the front door.

I quickly tidy up the store a bit before more customers arrive. I then pause to look around at the racks of prim and proper suits and the walls of shirts all neatly folded and tucked into their cubbies. Just outside the large front window, I see the crush of suits and skirts marching by. I sigh. This is so far from my dream of being an arborist. I can usually convince myself that my situation here is just temporary, that as soon as I've got the money saved I'll go back for my last year of school and then I can really start making a difference. Today, I am having trouble conjuring that illusion.

I can't stop thinking about how horrible the next couple of weeks are going to be: working open to close, seven days a week. I miss Debbie already. I suppose there's an upshot: I'll be able to pay rent this month with all the overtime. I'll also set aside whatever's left over to pay for my mother's medication. It'll ease the burden on my regular paycheques.

Fortunately, the door opens and a customer walks in, interrupting my anxious concerns. After that, the rest of the afternoon is as busy as I expected it to be. In many ways, I'm glad. Running from customer to customer limits the time I can reflect on how much I dislike where I am in my life right now.

Just before dinner, there's a gap with no customers. Grabbing my lunch bag, I slap a sign on the door saying I'll be back in thirty minutes and rush out before anyone can try to keep me from leaving. Stepping out, I close the door to the store and hold my wristband up to the lock. It reads my data and validates that I'm authorized, and the locking mechanism engages with a whir and a click. I run across the street to where the sculpture garden in the courtyard at Bay and Richmond gives me just enough privacy.

I stop at the crosswalk for a minute and scan the news that's scrolling down the screen on the lamppost. I stare at today's top headline for a few moments, trying to decide whether to believe it or not. In big bold letters, the screen declares: "Water shortages in States pushes water rationing throughout Canada." I hold my wristband near the headline, and a small chirp signifies that the article has downloaded. A holographic screen comes to life above my wrist, and I scroll through the article, eyes wide in disbelief, as I slide seamlessly into the horde of speed walkers. In order to continue supplying the American people with the water they need, our government has ordered stricter water rationing across the country.

When I get to the sculpture garden, I pop my last two-dollar coin into the water fountain. It sputters, and a single drop forms at the spout and falls with an echo into the drain. The tap is dry. Oh, yes, I'll definitely be voting for Peterson's Liberals tomorrow. Tremblay and the rest of his Conservatives might as well have resigned from office when they allowed this to happen.

The rest of the week passes much the way Monday did, and by the time Saturday afternoon arrives, I'm exhausted but also excited. James and I had apologized to each other earlier in the week, and I'd told him all about my session with Keegan. He was almost as excited as me that I haven't had any nightmares since my last appointment, and he'd made a follow-up appointment with Keegan for this evening. It's just in time too, because this morning I woke up with an all-too-familiar headache, and I know it's only a matter of a day or two before the dreams begin again.

I lock up the store and head north toward the subway station where I'm meeting James. However, I don't get more than five steps before he appears, his face breaking into a big grin when he sees me. He's carrying two small paper bags, and he holds one out to me.

"The subway was quick today, so I ran and got us some fried rainbow trout from the fish truck!" he says excitedly.

I grin back at him as I take the bag. My grin widens when I open it. The fish sits on a bed of roasted barley. It's the ultimate fast food these days, since the droughts have made most land-based agriculture unsustainable.

"Thanks, James! I'm starving!"

"I figured you wouldn't have had time for lunch today. Is Debbie having any luck with Ron?"

"None. She called two days ago to say it would be at least two more weeks before they could even get a hearing."

James shakes his head. "That's terrible. I can't believe your office can't find anyone to cover for her to make it easier for you."

I shrug. "It sucks, but it keeps me busy. Besides, I need the cash right now."

He nods, and I follow him down into the subway.

"So you still haven't had any issues since your last appointment?" he asks.

"Well, this morning I woke up with my temples throbbing. That usually accompanies the dreams, so I'm assuming another one is close. But I've woken up feeling refreshed all week!"

"That's awesome, Aiden." James smiles brightly as we squeeze into the crowded subway car on our way to Carlaw Station. "Stress can do so many things to our bodies. Sometimes you just have to talk about everything to get it all off your chest."

"It's true. And the reiki he performed took all the tension out of my shoulders and neck. That alone was worth it!"

"Absolutely. I'm so glad it's all working out." James stares at me and lowers his voice so the other riders can't hear. "Any luck finding out where that torch came from?"

"Not really." The torch appearing in my bedroom is the one thing that can't easily be attributed to stress. "But you were right. Being as stressed as I've been, it's entirely possible I sleepwalked. Maybe I made the damn thing in my sleep. My feet *were* dusty, like I'd been wandering outside."

"That cloth does look like it's from one of those canvas drops the homeless use to protect themselves from the rain along that shortcut you always take."

"Anything's possible."

James and I shuffle farther into the subway car at one of the stops as people jostle each other getting on and off.

"So did Danielle hear back from her interview?" I ask once the train continues on its way.

"Yeah, they called her last night finally, but she didn't get it, so she's in a bit of a mood right now."

"Sorry to hear that. About the job and mood both!"

He punches me in the arm as the speaker on the train announces that we're arriving at Carlaw Station.

At street level, we stop at a small pod of picnic tables to eat our fish. From where we're sitting, we can just make out the corner of K's Bookshop a couple of streets down.

"Nervous?" James asks.

I nod. "Not as much as I was last week, but yes."

He squeezes my arm. "It'll be just as good this time. Let's go."

It's half past six by the time we step up to the shop. The sign on the door says the store closed at six, but we can see through the window that Keegan is still helping a woman with a purchase. We check the door and find it's unlocked, and we quietly step inside so we don't interrupt them.

The woman stands at Keegan's desk with a loose, almost airy manner to her pose, her shoulder-length dark brown hair flowing freely. Her loose cream-coloured blouse, dark brown leggings, and knee-high tan boots are perfect on her, even if they look like she didn't buy them this decade. Her skin has the golden glow of someone who loves the outdoors, and as she speaks to Keegan, her smile lights up her face. We can't hear what they're talking about, but I sense a happiness in her voice that entrances me. She laughs, and her fingers linger on an open book. Its pages are yellowed and crinkled with age, and it teeters on top of a stack of equally ancient looking books.

I feel myself drawn to her, and I try to remain inconspicuous as I circle around the shop to get a better look at her face, but James sidles up to me and pokes an elbow into my ribs.

"Stop staring!" he hisses in my ear.

I glower at him and glance back just in time to see the woman look away from me.

She says something to Keegan and laughs quietly. It's a silky laugh that fills the room with joy. She then closes the book and tucks it into a cloth bag before I can read the title.

Keegan walks her to the door. "See you next time you're in town." He locks the door behind her and then turns to James and me with a smile stretching from ear to ear. "Sorry, she's my accountant, and one of my best customers. We normally do business remotely, but she always buys something from my rare books collection when she comes to Toronto. Anyway, enough of that. James, it's so great to see you again! I didn't expect you today."

James laughs. "Aiden said you worked some magic on him last week, so I had to come and watch this time."

"You're always more than welcome." Keegan envelopes James in a hug that is returned in equal measure. He turns to me and welcomes me with a hug of my own. "Welcome back, Aiden!"

"Thanks! I've been looking forward to it."

He smiles. "I have to be honest, when we last met, I wasn't sure what we were dealing with. Some people just need to talk; some people need energy healing. James here just needs massages. But since then, I've decided that today we should dive right into your psyche and work on your energies."

"Why's that, K?" James asks.

I simply nod, unsure of what any of that means.

A shadow crosses over Keegan's face. "Well, when I worked on you, Aiden, I thought I noticed something strange about your aura. I didn't have the room properly set up for viewing auras, though, so I wasn't quite sure what I was seeing. Today, we're going to get to the heart of that."

James and I glance at each other, our eyebrows raised, before following Keegan down the towering columns of books toward his back room.

Keegan rests his hand on *The Oxford Shakespeare*, and he looks back at me. "Ready?"

I nod, and he pulls the large volume out and twists the door opener. The bookshelf slides open. As we enter the room, I feel that same welcoming energy wrap itself around me.

This time, the antique lamps are dimmed, and the massage table rests in the centre of the room. James throws himself onto the fainting couch beneath the two windows, and Keegan gestures to the massage table.

"Aiden, if you'll make yourself comfortable on the table, please."

I lie down, casting my eyes about the room as I do. The two black leather armchairs sit against the wall, leaving room for a large circle of unlit candles to surround the massage table.

Keegan places his hands on either side of my head and speaks quietly—too quietly for me to distinguish his words. Moments later, he steps away and lights the candle on my immediate right. He looks at James. "Could you please get the light, James?"

The room darkens, illuminated only by the single candle to my right and the slight trickle of light squeezing through the window.

Keegan lights another candle a few feet away, and then the one after that. He walks slowly and methodically from candle to candle, studying me intently as he journeys around the circle. As he lights another candle, he leans close to me. "You look much more relaxed than the last time we met. Your dreams no longer trouble you?"

"I haven't had one since I last came here. It's one of the reasons I'm back."

He lights another candle, then another. From where I'm lying, I can see that I'll be in the centre of a circle of thirteen candles once they're all lit.

"Even my headaches have stopped," I say, "though I did have one this morning."

Keegan hushes me. "Please don't tell me anything else. Today is about visions and second sight. I don't want anything you say to taint any visions I might have."

He lights the second last candle without taking his eyes off me. "Last week, I mentioned that your aura is really strong and vibrant, but the edges of it are faded and... fractured. But there is something else as well."

He places a match to the last candle. All around me I feel energy thrum and then the fireplace roars to life with a whoosh.

I look from the fireplace to Keegan to James and then back to Keegan.

Keegan's eyes flick from me to the fireplace and back again, which is as much surprise as he registers. He looks at me intently, but I see him glance a couple more times at the fireplace. When he speaks, his voice is soft. "That's never happened before. And the circle I just cast is much stronger than any circle I've ever cast before." He looks at James. "You've brought me a very interesting subject."

James doesn't speak. He just stands there and nods with a look shrouded in disbelief.

Keegan stares at me, but not directly at me; it's like he's looking at something just above my shoulder, or just slightly away from my body. "It's strange. You simultaneously have the strongest and weakest energy field of anyone I've ever looked at. It's almost as if something's blocking it."

"You can see that?" I ask.

He smiles. "Part of the process of generating the circle was opening up my third eye, my inner vision, allowing me to see your energy field, as well as the energy flowing through the world around you. Close your eyes, please."

I close my eyes obediently, but somehow I can sense the movement of Keegan's hands. They move down the length of my left arm, never touching, hovering just a hair above my skin. He goes all the way down to my left foot and then up my right leg. When he reaches my right arm, he moves one hand to my left side and brings his hands slowly up the length of my body until they join just above my head. It takes every ounce of control I have not to shiver. I know he's not actually touching me, but my skin feels like it's on fire everywhere his hands have gone.

"Aiden . . ." James whispers.

I hear fear and uncertainty in his voice. "What is it, James?" I ask.

"You're actually glowing. Do people always glow when you do this, Keegan?"

"No. Can you feel anything, Aiden?"

"Yeah, it feels like an ice-cold fire everywhere your hands are going."

"Interesting," Keegan says quietly, and the room falls back to silence.

I feel the warmth of his hands hovering around the top of my head.

"I can see why you have headaches," he says. "Most people's energy is spread fairly evenly around them, flowing in a nice concentric circle that radiates from their heart out to the aura's edge. I was just now trying to find the source of your energy. Yours starts from the ground and flows up. It feels like it wants to flow down into your arms, but something is blocking it. Instead, it's flowing straight up to your head, where it ties itself into a huge energetic knot. I've seen the knot on a much smaller scale in people who've suffered traumatic events as a child, but you're the first person I've seen that seems to be drawing their energy from their feet."

Well, my childhood may not have been rosy, but I know people who have suffered far worse. Maybe James is right in blaming my headaches on how I internalize the stress in my life. As to my aura being centred in my feet, I definitely believe that every human has a unique energy field, but I've always been skeptical of auras and those who claim to read them. I don't want to say that to Keegan though, so I settle with a generic, "Oh."

I flinch as an intense stab of pain shoots through my head like a hyper-focused migraine.

"Sorry," Keegan says. "I'm trying to find an end to the knot so I can unravel it. If I can unravel it, I can probably reset the flow, and . . ."

His voice fades to nothing, and I sense that his hands have come to a complete halt. It seems like hours pass like this.

"Keegan?" James asks, his voice strangely distant.

I try to open my eyes, but they don't respond. It's like I'm present in my body, but it's no longer listening to my mental commands.

"Aiden?"

It's James again. I'm powerless to reply, but I *feel* him stand. I can feel everything in the room: James cautiously approaching Keegan and me, concern emanating from him; the flames of the candles flickering; the fire in the fireplace as it dances in the slight draft coming through the window cracked open an inch; the spider weaving its web in the corner; the cockroach scuttling under the desk that hasn't been moved in years; Keegan frozen, his eyes wide, in front of me. My eyes are closed, but I can feel everything with such intensity that I can actually see it.

I feel James reaching his hand out to touch Keegan, and I know instinctively that whatever is happening here, James isn't supposed to be a part of it, but I'm powerless to stop him. As his hand touches Keegan, there is a brilliant flash.

The flash lasts only an instant. James, Keegan, and I stand atop a cliff overlooking the city. It's the same one from my dream. Our faces and clothes are smudged black with ash and soot. Smoke billows from below, fires roar, and the sound of explosions fill the air. There is a loud boom, and a black fighter jet screams past us. A moment later, buildings below us collapse.

I feel anger building inside me, deep and powerful, and a rush of energy cresting. The anger builds into an unstoppable force, and I throw back my head and issue a deep, primal scream. A pulse of energy vibrates with me at its epicentre, and the vision vanishes. A gush of wind erupts, and James, Keegan, and I fly apart.

My whole body aches. It feels like I've been stretched out on a rack from medieval times. I open my eyes, but the room is black. I hear Keegan grunting as he stands. He curses when I hear him kick something while stumbling toward the light switch. He fumbles with the switch, but the room stays dark.

"Aiden? The matches should be beside you. Can you find them?"

I reach toward the table that was beside the massage table and discover three things: the table is on its side, I'm no longer on the massage table, and there's an intense pain shooting through my right leg and the side of my face. I feel around the floor near the table and find the matches. "Got them."

A few very long seconds later, I feel Keegan's hand brush against mine, and he takes the matches. In the silence, the sound of the match being struck fills the room. One of the candles flickers to life, and Keegan shines it around the room.

The massage table is shattered. Splinters of it lie around the room. James is slumped against the far wall beside the fainting couch. He holds his head in his hands and groans quietly. Glass from the now broken windows is scattered around him. Blood oozes from several cuts on his arms, and a deep bruise is forming on his leg. Keegan, standing in the light of the candle, looks almost like he did in the vision. He obviously took the brunt of whatever energy exploded when James touched him because his skin is black with ash from the fireplace, and his shirt hangs off his body in tattered shreds. He cradles his right arm as if he injured it, and I can see a large cut running down his face.

"What was that?" I ask him when I can speak again.

"I have no idea."

"I saw this vivid vision when James touched us. It—"

"I saw it too. I'm pretty sure we all saw the same thing." He grimaces as he squats down beside James. "James, are you all right?"

James groans again and looks up. His eyes are bloodshot. He looks like hell. "I'm alive. I don't know if I'm all right." He stretches his bruised leg out and kicks the piece of table that looks to have caused the bruise, sending it skidding across the room. "You guys were both frozen. I didn't know touching you would feel like an atomic bomb."

Keegan puts a hand on his shoulder to reassure him. "No one could have known, James. I have no idea what any of that was." He pulls James into a gentle embrace, holding him, caring yet hesitant.

It's obvious that Keegan cares deeply for James. I do too, but something about Keegan's posture and the way his eyes have softened makes me wonder if there's something more.

I feel shaky as I get to my feet. I shuffle across the room to take a closer look at everyone's injuries, but exhaustion and stabbing pain overwhelm me. I grab the wall for support before slumping to the floor. It feels like the perfect place for a short nap.

"Keegan?" I pat the floor. "Sit, bud. You must feel as bad as I do right now."

Keegan forces a smile. As he sits, I see a tear in the corner of his eye, and something else that's there only for a second. It's just long enough to make me absolutely certain that he saw a whole lot more than he's letting on.

With that thought playing through my head, I drift off to sleep.

When I wake, it feels like I've run a marathon up the side of a mountain, but the headache that started returning last night is completely absent.

The candle that Keegan lit after the explosion still flickers, but it's substantially lower now. I look to my right and smile. James and Keegan are sleeping deeply still, Keegan with his head nestled into James, and James with his arm wrapped around Keegan in a comforting embrace. Keegan's expression is content and happy, which is completely at odds with the black soot and dark streaks of blood that cake his face.

Still smiling, I glance at my wristband to see what time it is. Its small display is dark. I tap it, but nothing happens. I shake my head in irritation. The band is only two months old, and I've hardly looked at it the past couple of days. The battery shouldn't be dead yet. It was fully charged yesterday morning.

I look up at the corner by the door, but the old analog clock lies in pieces on the floor. All the broken windows can tell me is that it's dark outside.

I'm too awake at the moment to go back to sleep, and leaning against the wall has become too uncomfortable. I quietly pull myself up. I pick up the candle and survey the room. Whatever happened last night definitely wasn't a dream. Splatters of dried wax mark the floors and walls like an abstract artist gone wild.

The two black leather chairs are ruined. They're blown apart. Even the stuffing looks burned. Springs from the seats are scattered around the room.

Pictures and books lie scattered all over the floor. The only piece of furniture relatively intact is the antique fainting couch.

I cringe at the destruction, knowing that Keegan has poured his whole life into this place. I wonder how it's possible that the three of us aren't hurt more than we are. I think back to all the dreams I've been having. Did the same energy that caused all of this somehow also protect us? I can't think of any other explanation.

Not wanting to wake the other two, I pick my way through the mess toward the door, favouring my right hip. I must have landed on it when the massage table imploded. I quietly head back to the front of the bookshop. A quick glance reveals that only the bookshelves closest to the wall between the two rooms were damaged by whatever energies were unleashed during our session.

The antique light on the giant oak desk is still on from last night, which sparks the thought that maybe Keegan has a charger I can use to recharge my wristband.

On the desk is the stack of ancient books that were there when James and I arrived. Some have bookmarks, some have dog-eared corners, all are on the occult. I flip through the top one, but its flowing script is in a language I don't recognize. To the left of the books are some handwritten notes that appear to be a combination of Latin and the strange language from the book. I hesitate over the notes just long enough for a burning curiosity to develop, but I force my eyes to keep moving.

There are several other stacks of books on the desk. Next to one of them, I finally find Keegan's charging pad. I remove my wristband and rest it on the lightning symbol. I wait patiently for it to charge, resisting the urge to peruse the notes. A few minutes later, there's still no sign of life on the band. "Shit." I'm out of options. I decide that maybe it needs more time. Sighing, I leave it on the charger and return to the back room to try to get a little more sleep.

Chapter Seven

When I wake up again, James and Keegan are sitting on the fainting couch. My body aches, but my head feels clearer than it has in years.

A faint trickle of daylight comes through the broken window, but the brick building outside it makes it impossible to tell how long I've slept. I groan and sit up. Keegan stands and brings over a washcloth and a bucket full of soapy water.

"It's not much," he says, "but it will make you presentable enough to get home."

I rinse off and immediately feel better. James and Keegan are clean, but both have bruises and cuts in several places.

"Any idea what time it is?" I ask. "I'm supposed to open the store at noon."

"Neither of us is very good at telling the time by the sun," James says, "but we think it's around ten. Hard to tell for sure, though. Both of our bands are dead, and Keegan's computer is fried."

"I tried mine last night, and it's dead too."

"Yeah, we saw it on the charger," Keegan says. "The energy pulse must have had some kind of electromagnetic impact. It fried all the modern electronics in the building."

Well, there goes the five months of overtime it cost me to get the wristband in the first place. I'll never be able to afford the mid-contract replacement cost. Of course, in the grand scheme of things, the band should probably be the least of my worries right now.

I shift my focus back to the matter at hand. "So, um . . . what are we gonna do about what happened last night?"

James answers after a few seconds of quiet deliberation. "Keegan and I have been talking about that since we woke up. We're thinking we shouldn't tell anyone yet, not even Danielle—in fact, especially not Danielle. None of us has any idea what happened, and until we do, it needs to remain our secret. Agreed?"

I nod emphatically. "You know I'm not going to tell anyone. Look how long it took for me to confide in you, and you're pretty much the one person in the world I'd tell anything."

James laughs quietly and reaches his hand out, palm down. "Let's swear."

Keegan and I each put a hand on his.

"Brothers bound together in secret." James smirks. "I always thought it would be cool to swear a pact like that."

We all laugh, but it's restrained and somewhat nervous.

I sit cross-legged on the floor, facing James and Keegan on the couch. "That vision we saw . . . I've had one just like it, only it's just me standing in the flames. It's always been just me until last night."

Keegan leans forward. "Energy work is sensitive and delicate. It's possible that I tied myself into your energy somehow by working with it like I did last night. Then, when James touched us, all three of our energies wove together in a"—he gestures around the room—"rather explosive reaction."

"Yeah, but that doesn't explain the visions."

Keegan remains quiet for a moment before speaking. "No. No, it doesn't. This might be hard to believe given my profession, but I've never believed in visions and gods and spiritual beings. For me, energy work is a science. I add a magical element to the process to draw people in because people are drawn to mystery like moths are drawn to a flame, but I always think of it as channelling human energies. From that angle, you could have projected your dream to James with me as the energy bridge."

James is clearly thinking about that. I've known him a long time, and I've never known him to be anything but confident, but this is the second time in the past couple of weeks I've seen him shaken, if not downright scared. The expression on his face is the same as it was at the church when he saw Cardinal Gallagher trying to slay me with his eyes. It's that look he gets when facing something he'd like to pretend isn't happening.

"That makes sense, Keegan," he says quietly. "If Aiden has a bit of ESP or something, then, like you said, he could have projected it to us."

Keegan stares at me for a second, and then makes a decision. "Let's leave it at that for now. I'll see if there's anything I can dig up in the books on telepathy and energy flow that might help us explain things. Maybe we should meet regularly until we figure this out."

"I think that's a good idea." I'm glad Keegan suggested this. At this point, I don't know what else to do.

"And, Aiden, while you were sleeping, I had another look at your energy field. There's definitely something happening with it. I managed to soothe it a little bit by drawing some of the energy away from you. It didn't settle your aura down completely, but it did dampen the sparks flying off it." He extends his hand. In it is a tiny wooden vial with a cork. "Here, this is for you. It's what I drew out. I usually give these to people whose sicknesses I heal, but it seemed appropriate to do it for this too."

I hesitate at first, but I reach out and take the vial. It's as wide as my baby finger and shorter than my index finger, so it sits easily in my palm. I close my fingers around the pale wood as though it's something either sacred or evil. I'm not sure which this is, and judging by Keegan's expression, I don't think he is either. "Why would you give these to sick people?"

He laughs lightly. "The first time I ever healed anyone, it was this guy I was madly in love with. He was so sick he couldn't even get out of bed. As I lay there beside him on the second night, I realized I would rather be sick than have him suffer. So I visualized the sickness flowing through him, imagined what it looked like and made it real to me. Then I drew it out and into me and fell asleep. The next morning, he was bouncing with excitement because he felt like he'd never been sick a day in his life. I, meanwhile, was bedbound for the next three days and was sicker than I've ever been before or since.

"After that, I kept trying to heal people because it felt right to use my gifts for something. I eventually realized that instead of drawing their sicknesses and energy into myself, I had to send it into something else. That's why I came up with these vials. I use wood because it's such a great insulator—and because it looks old and magical. Birch in particular has long been associated with protection, healing, and new beginnings. I give them to the person afterward because, frankly, I have no desire to have that many illnesses near me. No thank you!"

"That makes sense." I stare down at the birch vial that is supposedly full of my energy. It doesn't look all that remarkable, but it definitely feels magical. "Well, thanks, Keegan. Should I do anything special with it?"

"Nope. Just don't open it until we figure out what's happening to you!"

"I definitely won't be opening it. So how much do I owe you?"

Keegan scoffs. "Don't be insulting. You paid me for a year's worth of sessions when you knocked James so flat on his ass that he had no choice but to spend the night cuddling with me instead of his girlfriend!" He laughs when James elbows him. "Okay, I'm kidding about that—mostly. Seriously, though, you don't owe me anything. I've never experienced anything remotely close to what we just went through, and I'm pretty sure that if anyone else had, I would know about it. What happened last night might be something completely new in human experience. To me, that's worth exploring more deeply." He pauses, and his gaze becomes more intense. "What I'm trying to say is, if you're both willing to work with me, I'd be more comfortable considering these sessions as case studies instead of paid sessions since we're all learning together."

James looks at me, and then back at Keegan. "You want me to join in too?" James asks.

"Absolutely," Keegan replies. "Whatever it was that happened here last night . . . you were the catalyst."

James stares at me. His expression is a blend of willingness and disbelief. He waits for me to make the decision. I nod, and he looks back at Keegan.

"Well," he says, his voice lacking its usual confidence. "Looks like we'll be back." He stands. "All right, Aiden, we better leave if you're going to get to work, and I have to get this wristband fixed so I can message Danielle. She *hates* it when I don't message her before getting out of bed. This late into the morning, I might as well consider myself a dead man."

It's half past twelve when I literally stagger into work. I was hoping that the universal payment chip in my wristband would still function, but it didn't work for the subway, taxi, or bank machine, so I had to make the trip by foot. I couldn't even shower when I got home because the chip wouldn't activate the water. Instead, I used a towel to wipe off as much of the soot from the fireplace as I could. I don't look very professional, but at least I've managed to look a bit more presentable. I might have made it on time were my hip not throbbing, and if I didn't have to stop twice to put a new bandage on the deepest cut on my left leg.

I'm three steps into the store when it registers that I didn't have to unlock the door and the lights are already on. I notice too that almost all the suits are gone and there are shirts scattered everywhere. I spin to the sound of heels clicking on the tile floor. A businesswoman with blond hair, white blouse, black windowpane suit jacket and matching miniskirt, and far too much makeup looks me up and down distastefully.

"It's Aiden, I believe?"

"Um, yes, ma'am. And you would be?"

"Janice Rainer," she says without a hint of warmth. "I'm the district manager for Toronto Central District."

"Oh! Nice to meet you."

Something's wrong here, but my brain isn't moving fast enough for me to comprehend what it is. I put my lunch bag on the corner of the checkout counter, because Janice's body language is making it rather clear that I'm not allowed into the back room at the moment. I set the wooden vial down beside it.

"Do you know why I'm here, Aiden?"

"To be honest? No, I don't, though I suspect it has something to do with this mess." I wave my hand around the store.

"Quite right, quite right. Debbie did say she thought you were smarter than average." Janice makes no attempt to disguise her contempt. She takes three steps toward me and wags a finger in my face. "The only reason you aren't behind bars right now, young man, is that the surveillance footage clearly shows you placing your wristband in the correct location to lock the door."

My eyebrows shoot up. Behind bars? Clearly I'm missing something.

"Nonetheless," she continues, "it can't be a coincidence that the one day you *forget* to lock the door happens to be the same day thieves decide to load up on designer suits and clean out the safe they conveniently knew how to access. All of this while your manager is off on emergency leave."

"Thieves?" Is she seriously blaming me? I'm incredulous.

"Oh, don't get smart with me. I know you had a part in this, and I'll find out what it was. The police said they'll be contacting you as well before they left. In the meantime, your employment here at Dale's Clothing is suspended pending an investigation. Hand over your wristband, please. I've been authorized to revoke your access to the store in the interim."

I'm frozen in place. I stare at her for several seconds. There's not a single thought going through my head. It's all just empty.

"Well, what are you waiting for?" Janice thrusts her hand out.

I meet her unflinching glare, unstrap my wristband, and toss it to her. My own anger at being treated so unfairly is building. "Be my guest. It quit last night."

Janice runs her own wristband over mine. If mine were still functional, this would have deprogrammed the lock sequence of the store, but instead nothing happens. She frowns. "No matter. I'll do it manually."

A strange noise draws my attention from Janice. I stare in shock at the wooden vial next to my lunch bag. It vibrates violently and starts to roll toward the edge of the counter. My body finally snaps into action. I lunge for the vial, scooping it up and shoving it into my pocket. I can still feel it pulsating against my leg, but now that I can't see it or hear it, it's easier to pretend nothing is happening.

"What's that?" Janice demands. Her voice shifts toward the frantic.

"None of your damned business," I snap.

Rage fills her eyes. "Out!" she screams. "Out! Out! Out!"

I grab my lunch bag, my wristband, and stomp out the door.

Chapter Eight

It's been four days since Janice essentially fired me from Dale's—four days spent cycling between despair that I won't be able to afford rent or my mother's medication and anger at Janice and at myself for letting her catch me off guard. I have nothing to hide and am guilty of nothing. Why didn't I even try to defend myself? I've been trying to keep the anger in check though, because the stronger it gets, the more I feel Keegan's wooden vial vibrating in my pocket. The vial terrifies me. If I weren't so worried about someone else getting hold of it, I wouldn't carry it with me at all times.

On Monday, James brought me one of his old wristbands. It's three generations old and slow, but, as he pointed out, it's difficult to receive callbacks for job interviews without one. It's Friday now, and so far I haven't received any.

James, however, has called several times, trying to get me to go back to St. Michael's. Ever since that night in Keegan's shop, he's been insatiable in his search for answers. On Tuesday, he had picked up the torch to bring to Keegan so he could examine it. When he called me yesterday, he was going back and forth between *The Tree of Life* by Israel Regardie and three physics textbooks dealing with string theory. I'm not sure what taking me back to St. Michael's will do, but he's convinced it will help him prove that there's a very scientific explanation for what happened to us. I've been able to put him off so far by telling him I'm out pounding the pavement looking for jobs, even though I've been too depressed to even get out of bed.

Today, though, I have to get out of the house, mostly because I opened the cupboard to grab lunch only to find it empty. Even after I discovered I'm out of food, the urge to just bury my face in a pillow almost won out. Only by promising myself a trip to the waterfront was I able to overcome the self-deprecating pity I've been wallowing in.

I decide to walk, saving my subway trips for when I actually get an interview. I picked the right day. We've gotten an uncharacteristic break from the heat. The day is simply hot instead of borderline unbearable. The breeze actually doesn't feel like a convection oven for a change.

I get to Yonge and Dundas and find the square filled with people. That's not unusual, but the relative silence of the place piques my curiosity. I look up at the large screen to see Olivia Peterson, our new prime minister, in her trademark emerald-green suit jacket. Her voice echoes throughout the square.

"My friends and fellow Canadians! Canada has always been known as a giving nation, as a nation that has the best interests of others at heart. Today is no different. Some have accused me of being inhuman and cruel for wanting to cut off our neighbours, the United States of America, from our water supply. This could not be further from the truth.

"Water is a basic necessity of life, and it is the duty of the Government of Canada to ensure that every Canadian has access to fresh drinking water, especially in these times of need. Until now, this hasn't been an issue. Having the world's largest reserves of fresh water, we have always had enough. Sixty years ago, our predecessors deemed that the water flowing through our country's veins needed more protection. They bestowed personhood to the rivers and lakes of this nation, with all the privileges and rights therein. Since then, we haven't treated the water as if it is ours to do with as we will.

"This foresight is why we still have the best access to clean drinking water out of all the nations of the world: We treat it as our brother, sister, mother. For the past five years, however, we have allowed our humanitarianism to trump our respect for the Earth. As a result, our lakes and rivers are being depleted at record speed. Even in this great country, drinking water is becoming scarce. In our efforts to keep everybody healthy, safe, and happy, we have instead made it worse for everybody.

"Today, that ends. The great aquatic ecosystems of our nation have been seriously damaged, and it is no longer possible to end the conservation measures put in place already, but neither will we continue to fulfill the water demands of a neighbour who has no respect for these ecosystems. Regardless, we cannot in good conscience cut them off completely. Effective immediately, we will ship only enough for basic drinking water and irrigation. We need to let the ecosystems of our Mother Earth replenish and repair themselves.

"Does this mean the United States will have to change their ways? Absolutely. It means that the majority of the states will have to follow the leadership of such states as California, Vermont, and New York, who long ago implemented strict water conservation policies. It is our belief that we can restore the water systems of both nations if we all show the respect to the Earth that she deserves, if we all use water for irrigating essential crops to feed our people rather than use it to feed the lawns and pools of the wealthy. Until then, our austerity must continue.

"At the end of last week, a team of scientists reported to the previous government that if we stop all non-humanitarian shipments of water and continue our own strict conservation efforts, our aquatic ecosystems will return to sustainable levels within the next ten to fifteen years."

The Prime Minister pauses, holding up a hand for calm, but the crowd she is speaking to on location is just as unnerved as the crowd here at Yonge and Dundas. I take the pause as my cue to leave. These days, environmental policy is almost as big a target of violence as environmental activism. The way my luck has been lately, I'll get caught up in a riot if I stay too long.

I wander down Yonge Street, my thoughts miles away. My life is nothing like I thought it would be. I've always known the world favours the wealthy and that I'd face challenges, but I still always thought I'd at least have a chance. My mother getting sick was the beginning of the end of that belief. I had never considered life without my mother before. Watching her spiral from someone who cherished the joys of life and carried her happiness wrapped around her even despite my abusive father to someone who winces in pain with even a hint of a smile was the hardest thing I've had to do in my life.

The next hardest was facing the decision between paying for her drugs to hopefully keep her alive long enough for a cure to be found or finishing school for my dream profession. It wasn't really a choice. I was obviously going to choose my mother's immediate health over an uncertain future career, but I still can't help but think how different my life would be if I weren't trapped in a job that gave me no satisfaction, if I had a job where I could make a difference.

I scoff at the irony. My job is no longer trapping me, and even as I work to keep my mother's health in check, my own spirals out of control. What other possibility can there be for the constant headaches, the dreams that make it almost impossible for me to function? I laugh at myself, barely aware of the passers-by taking extra space to step around me. I can't sleep, I have no job, and my fiancée found the love of her life the day before our wedding. Hell, even God thinks me unworthy of sitting in his place of worship. And as though my own life spiralling out of control weren't enough, with Peterson's announcement that it will be ten to fifteen years before the water supply returns normal, violence in and around the city will likely skyrocket.

I absentmindedly step into the crowd of people milling about the waterfront. I wonder how many of them have had their dreams snuffed out at every turn. I pause to allow a group of young street kids to run by. As I stand there, I'm taken by the unsettling feeling of a set of eyes burning into me.

I look around slowly, and my eyes meet those of a woman sitting on the patio of a coffee shop on the north side of the street. An almost electric spark runs down my spine. Something about her is familiar. When she smiles, it hits me. It's the same woman who was in Keegan's shop on Saturday. I return her smile shyly and glance up and down the street, trying to find something to distract me. When I look back at the coffee shop, she's still looking at me. She now looks amused. I blush, but I find myself crossing the street as though my feet have minds of their own.

When I step onto the patio, she looks up from her coffee.

"Would you like a seat?" she asks.

The trouble is, now that I'm here, I'm terrified to actually speak to her. I could just say hi and leave, but there's something familiar about her that goes beyond seeing her a few days ago in a bookshop. I feel like I know her from somewhere, and that feeling makes it impossible for me to leave.

"Beautiful day today, isn't it? It's nice to get a break from the oppressive heat." Her brown eyes have an intensity that's almost startling. "Please, sit." Her voice is sweet, welcoming, and so familiar that it breaks me from my silent reflection.

I sit across from her. "It's the nicest day we've had in weeks," I say finally. "I figured I should enjoy it while I can." I carefully omit the fact that I've been spiralling into depression and only came out for food. "Do you come here often?"

She takes a sip of her coffee. "To the waterfront? No. This is the first time I've been here in a long time, actually. I used to come here a lot with my cousin when I was younger, but it's been years. Nowadays, I come to Toronto only when business demands it and leave as soon as I can. The hectic pace is a little difficult to adapt to when you're used to small-town life. This time, I'm stuck here for a few days, so I thought I might come here to get away from it all for a bit."

"I see. So, where are you from then?"

"Oh, it's just some small nowhere place. You probably haven't heard of it." She pauses and looks pointedly at my hands fidgeting on the table in front of me. "Do you want a coffee? I'm Caitlin, by the way."

I smile awkwardly. There's still something about her that I can't place, but my reticence to meet new people is fading, and I'm glad for the opportunity to explore it further. "I'm Aiden. It's a pleasure to meet you. And I'm fine. I'm not much of a coffee drinker." It's a lie, but coffee is definitely too rich for me right now. "I'll keep you company while you finish yours, though." I place my hands into my lap to prevent them from revealing my nervousness.

Caitlin smiles back, but doesn't say anything.

"I know what you mean by getting away from the hectic pace!" I continue. "I was covering a bunch of extra shifts at work and had the privilege of experiencing both the morning and afternoon rush every day."

She grimaces. "That sounds like a handful. Where do you work?"

"Well, until recently, I worked at Dale's Clothing at Bay and Richmond. Now I'm ... how do you say it these days ... searching for new opportunities." I kick myself mentally. A fine way to get into her good graces—telling her I'm unemployed right at the start.

She doesn't dig into why I'm unemployed. "Oh, really? My father was a tailor when he was younger. He still does it from time to time, on the side. What kind of opportunities are you looking for?"

I feel myself opening up to Caitlin's warmth. "I've always wanted to be an arborist. I just have to finish the schooling for it. In the meantime, I'm looking into a number of environmentally friendly agencies."

A wide grin full of sparkling white teeth spreads across Caitlin's face. She grabs my arm excitedly. "That's wonderful! And much needed in today's world."

"Thanks." I smile genuinely. "So, I'm sorry, but I have to ask. Were you at K's Bookshop on Queen East on Saturday, right?"

"I was! You were one of the guys who came in just at closing time." She leans forward. "I specialize in small business accounting. Heh. *Exciting*, I know . . . What can I say? I've always liked numbers. I look after Keegan's accounts. Plus, I've always had an interest in literature."

She pauses, taking a sip of coffee. "So, you looked like you were a million miles away strolling down the street just now. Besides getting away from everything, what brings you to the water?"

"I'm that easy to read, eh? One of my friends really wanted to take me to St. Michael's Cathedral, but, well, let's just say it turns out that church isn't my cup of tea, so I came down here where he'll never look."

Caitlin laughs. "Good," she says lightly. "I hate stuffy religious types."

She drinks the remains of her coffee and then leans back, looking decisive. "Well, Aiden, this might seem a bit presumptuous, but I feel like you're someone worth getting to know better."

Those intense eyes of hers meet mine, and a gentle breeze blows her perfume past me. I feel the world shift underneath me. I now realize why her voice sounds so familiar. It's not only sweet and welcoming, but it somehow sounds like the flowers of a garden, all the trees of the forest, the wind blowing through the trees. It's a voice I've heard every night of my life for the past year. I struggle to keep the alarm off my face.

Caitlin stands. "Would you care to join me for a walk to Union Station? I have to deliver some files to a client, but I'd appreciate the company."

A moment ago, I probably would have said yes—but now? Not a chance in hell. I force a smile, wishing I had a drink I could hide my face behind. What if this is just another step along the path of going mad? Caitlin's just an accountant—an accountant who likes books. I'm probably just letting recent events get the better of me. What would James or Keegan say? How could a woman I've just met be the same woman who's been haunting my dreams?

Caitlin raises an eyebrow. Her entire posture is relaxed, at ease, not at all that of a dream-chasing . . . being . . . ? Witch . . . ? Sorceress . . . ?

"Aiden?"

"Oh. Uh. Sorry." I force another smile, hoping she doesn't see through it. At the same time, I force myself to think that she's just a normal woman, and that these are otherwise the thoughts of a man for whom life has obviously become too much. "I just remembered something I have to do this evening, but sure. I'll go as far as Union."

The setting sun, though still hot, allows the breeze off the lake to offer a refreshing respite. It would explain why the boardwalk is busier than usual. A big red streetcar pulls to a stop in front of us. It's overcapacity when it arrives, with everyone inside pressed tightly together from the back window to the front door. When it pulls away from the stop, there are enough seats for everyone, and about fifty more people are standing with us at the crosswalk.

I glance over at Caitlin and see that she's holding her satchel tightly against her. Her lips are pinched together. She looks up the street as though she's expecting another streetcar to disgorge another fifty people in our midst. Seeing her like this, I feel less wary of her.

"Does the crowd bother you?" I ask.

She tosses me an awkward smile. "There are crowds, and then there's this." She looks up the busy street again.

"Let's make our way to the station."

We match our pace with the people in front of us and join the mindless stroll up the street.

"So . . . literature . . . That's not a popular pastime these days."

Caitlin chuckles. "Perhaps I should remind you that you were in the same store?" She smirks at me as she continues. "Actually, I find that a surprising number of people seem to enjoy it, but it depends on what you're reading. There's nothing like the power of words being able to move you. Plus, books are very good at offering excellent interpretations of the past, and if we don't fully understand the lessons of the past, how can we ever hope to survive the challenges of the future?"

"I think I get what you're saying. I remember reading a lot when I was younger, and I still have a few books of my own. But it's like I stopped mostly because it was never encouraged. Our culture obviously doesn't care about books. It's really sad, actually. I love books. I used to dream of having a library in my home with wall-to-wall books, a sliding ladder, a fireplace, and a comfy chair to curl up in."

"Is that what brought you to Keegan's shop the other day?"

"Oh, for sure." I'm reluctant to even hint at what actually brought me there. "My friend James knows I love books and thought I'd find it fascinating. But it's money that stops me. It always comes down to money, and we never had a lot of it growing up. My mother did the best she could, but it was difficult because my father hardly ever worked and spent most of his unemployment cheques on beer. My mother worked three jobs just to keep us going, and now all of that work and stress have caught up with her."

Caitlin looks at me, intently focused on what I'm saying.

"She was diagnosed with a form of grade three brain cancer two and a half years ago—anaplastic oligodendroglioma," I continue, "and she can't work anymore. So I took as many shifts as I could to pay for her medications and hopefully save up enough for school." I shrug. "That's the only reason I came to the city. I've never been attracted to the hustle and bustle. I came only because I wanted to turn my passion for trees into a career, and there are college programs here that can help me do that."

Caitlin remains quiet for a few seconds, and then she says, "I don't remember you saying you were in school."

I sigh. "I'm not. I'm trapped in an endless cycle where I work, pay for my mother's medication, and pay for rent. If it weren't for my friend James's generosity and his determination to lend me money and have me tag along with him, I'd be a hermit."

Caitlin's eyes are wide and filled with sadness. She stops us there on the sidewalk, and gives me a hug. "I'm so sorry to hear all of that, Aiden. Your story is truly remarkable, though. I know of too many people who would have allowed what you've experienced to defeat them, and too many others who would have abandoned their family and just looked after themselves. How you've prioritized your mother in your life speaks volumes to who you are as a person. Like your friend James, you are a giver. Those are rare these days."

She flashes a quick smile, and we continue walking. I can't help but feel like a jackass for even thinking she isn't trustworthy.

"What about your family?" I ask after a few minutes of silence. We're getting close to Union Station now, and I realize I've talked an awful lot about myself and haven't let her give me much in return.

"Mine?" She seems shocked that I'd ask such a thing. "I'm one of those people I just told you about." Her voice is tinged with sadness. "I've never been particularly close to my mother. As for my father, after the family tailoring business folded, he decided to indulge in his interest in diplomacy. He's an attaché for the Canadian Ambassador to Brazil, so he travels around South America a lot. When I was young, we moved often, and I rebelled against that.

It's been at least seven years since I last saw him."

Before I can reply, a strange sensation washes through me. I try to hide it, but I know it will be impossible. The little wooden vial in my pocket is vibrating again. Caitlin doesn't seem to notice my discomfort. Her head is turned, as she's looking up the street again. I discreetly reach into my pocket. I wrap my fingers around the vial and pull it partway out so I can take a peek at it. My fingers freeze, however, and the vial slips free. With a light clatter, it bounces off the sidewalk and the cork pops out. My headache roars back to life with a vengeance ten times as strong as ever before.

Caitlin turns away from the street and looks at me inquisitively as I gasp and clutch the sides of my head.

"Are you okay?" she asks, lightly resting a hand on my arm.

I take a long, slow breath, trying to ease the pain. I'm not ready to answer yet. Through the haze of pain, I catch a glimpse of two people standing in front of the entrance to the subway station across the street. I focus on them and realize with a jolt of shock that the one on the right is the old man from the cafe on the day of the St. Michael's incident—the man from my dream of the tunnel. Beside him is the woman who accompanied him in that same dream. Caitlin's eyes narrow as recognition flashes across my face. I instinctively turn to head back the way we came, but Caitlin takes hold of my arm before I can go.

"Aiden," she says, "are you sure you're okay? The station is this way." She says it as though nothing's wrong. Does she not sense something's off?

I pull away from her, taking a couple of steps backward. "Yes, I know. It's just . . . I forgot to do something." I wipe a bead of cold sweat from my brow and try to focus on something other than the pain shooting through my head and the fever that starts racking my body.

Caitlin stares at me, confusion and compassion clear on her face. "We're almost there," she says quietly, reaching out and grasping my arm again. "Let's cross here. It'll be quicker."

I look up and down the street. The traffic isn't heavy, but it's busy enough to cause me some concern, especially in my condition. "But the crosswalk . . ." My head hurts so much I can barely speak. I want to leave, but there's something compelling in Caitlin's voice. Still, I try to pull my arm away from her grasp.

And then I hear it, echoing through my head: *"Be strong. Don't give in to fear. Trust. Believe in yourself."* It's the voice from my dreams. It's Caitlin's voice, but her mouth hasn't moved. I'm not losing it. I've already lost it. "*Your body is imploding. Step over the edge and come alive.*"

Without saying a word, Caitlin releases my arm, steps out into the street, and doesn't look back.

A feeling of . . . wrongness . . . hits me as I step off the curb and follow her without another thought; it's something so incredibly wrong that someone whose head weren't pounding and who was actually getting regular sleep might recognize it as impending disaster.

That realization hits me a heartbeat later when I spin my head to the sound of squealing tires. A car barrels toward us well above the speed limit, and my senses go into full alert. Time seems to slow to a crawl, and it's like I can see everything. The man and woman from my dreams are staring directly at me from across the street, horror etched into their features. I see the driver of the car about to hit us, and I can tell from his bloodshot eyes and slack jaw that he's drunk. Or is it because I can smell the alcohol?

I've never considered myself the hero type, but without even thinking, I grab Caitlin and propel her out of the way. It all happens in slow motion, which is probably a good thing, because I doubt I'd have time to get her to safety otherwise. Her jaw is set tightly, but her face shows no sign of surprise or fear. Her eyes are focused on me like lasers.

Somewhere deep within me, I feel something click. I'm now standing where I stand in my dreams, facing out over an endless abyss while the gentle but urgent voice tells me once again to step over the edge. This time, I am certain it's Caitlin's voice. This time, without question, without hesitation, I step over the edge and feel a warmth and comfort surround me. At the very core of my being, a wellspring of power blossoms.

I spin around to face the car. My hands reach down and make contact with the hood as a surge of raw power from deep within me arcs out of my fingertips and slams the front bumper into the ground.

Pieces of asphalt fly and sparks erupt as the metal of the car grinds against the road. I somehow fly away from the car instead of being crushed beneath it. But I'm not flying fast enough, and the car isn't slowing fast enough. I let go of my thoughts and let my instincts take over.

My hands dig into the air like a shovel, and I feel another surge of energy fly out of them. The earth below my feet buckles and thrusts upward, slowing the car immediately. More and more earth piles until the car shudders to a stop.

I stare at it for a moment, slightly amazed that I'm not dead. At the same time, I'm certain that I am and that this is my dying dream. Through a haze of confusion, I see people running toward me. I feel Caitlin's gaze upon me, but when I look for her, I can't see her in the crowd. *Who is she?*

I hear sirens blaring loudly as they approach. I catch a glimpse of the man and woman from my dream as they make their way toward me. Do they mean to help me? Do they know what's happened?

The world goes dark as I collapse into a heap on the ground.

Chapter Nine

When I awaken, every bone in my body is aching and every muscle is on fire. An earthy smell permeates the air, and an odd feeling of ancientness fills me. The throbbing in my temples that has been my constant companion for the past several years is completely gone; if only it were the same for the rest of my body.

I crack my eyes open and see that I'm in a dimly lit room. Several massive torches, disturbingly similar to the one lying on my bookshelf at home, line the walls. I lie there quietly for a few moments. The cold of the stone floor seeps into me. Shadows flit through my vision in the flickering torchlight. I stifle a sharp intake of breath. Strange black-robed figures, each with a staff, march in a circle clockwise around me, chanting slowly and rhythmically. Afraid to draw attention to the fact that I'm awake, I flick my eyes around. I'm lying inside a circle of sarsen stones—stones I've seen before. I flick my eyes to the right and see the opening to a wide spiral staircase—right where I knew it would be. Grand columns stretch into the darkness above me, supporting a high vaulted ceiling. I look up at the nearest column and see a crystal mounted near its top. I can't see the colour in the dim light of the torches, but I have no doubt that it's a deep ruby red.

I could cry. I'm lying in the room from the vision of Armageddon or whatever the hell it was I dreamed, but this time it feels too real. The only difference is that it seems far older. There is a layer of dust and ancientness coating everything. The massive wall sconces are there but dark now, and there's no water cascading down the side of the spiral staircase. This place is otherwise like the one in the dreams I've had for the past six years.

I try to flex my arm, and a spasm of pain arcs through it. I groan involuntarily, my eyes clench shut, and the chanting stops. I hear the rustling of robes, and several torches shine over my face. This has never happened in the dream before. A tiny part of my brain is ringing an alarm. I shut it down because the thought that this isn't a dream is too terrifying to consider.

"Aleksandar, he lives," I hear a woman whisper in a raspy voice with English accent.

"Was there ever any doubt?" The man's voice has a thick Russian accent.

"I shared Elizabeth's concern," another man says. "None of us knew how expending that much magic in his first try would affect him."

I feel a shiver run down my spine. The third voice is strong but gentle, trustworthy. I've heard it before. I see in my mind's eye the handlebar mustache, the tweed bow tie, the ebony cane. It's the old man from the cafe, the one I've been seeing both in real life and in my dreams.

"What are you saying?"

"I'm saying death was a very real possibility."

Magic? Death? Did I just fall down the rabbit hole?

I flash back to Caitlin's face. Her eyes are fixed on me as the car slams into me. The realization that this isn't a dream hits me like a punch to the gut. My eyes burst open, and I sit straight up, thrusting the pain aside.

"Caitlin!" I cry. "Where's Caitlin?"

There's a bustle of activity as everyone flinches or scrambles at my sudden outburst. The hooded figure closest to me pulls back his hood. I see the gentle face of the old man. In place of his ebony cane is an ancient-looking staff slightly taller than he is. He passes the staff to the hooded figure next to him. He then kneels next to me and grips my arms firmly. He looks me square in the eyes.

"Caitlin is fine. We brought you here because you need to rest, to heal."

I squirm, but the pain is too much for me. "*Where—is—she?*" I'm not sure where it's coming from, but there's a very real anger blazing within me, and it comes out with each punctuated word. To his credit, he is unmoved.

"She accompanied you the entire trip here." He raises his eyebrows. "You are concerned for her. That's good. She's resting in the next chamber. She has given us much to talk about since arriving here."

That Caitlin is here too at once relieves and terrifies me. I'm thrilled that she's close by, and now I can stop worrying about whether she got hit by the car. At the same time, I can't help but remember the sound of her voice echoing through my head, urging me to step over the edge. Was that real? What is the truth? The only thing I'm now convinced of is that I really and truly am here in this . . . this cavern with strange people wearing robes skulking about. Wherever *here* is. I struggle to sit up.

"Where are we?" I mutter with a wince.

"We are in the caverns deep below Skellig Michael, at the intersection of the St. Michael and Apollo ley lines off the southwestern coast of Ireland. It is a place of great power, though the monks who live on the island above us have long ago forgotten us." The old man smiles and gestures around the grand chamber. "This is the central chamber of Lannóg Eolas—or the Citadel, as we often call it. For over five thousand years, the chambers in this ancient citadel have been home to all that remains of the knowledge of magic. These secrets have been passed down from generation to generation to us, the Guardians of Knowledge." He pauses, staring at me intently. "We've brought you here because you need our help."

Since almost none of that makes sense, I ignore everything except his last comment. "I was getting along perfectly fine before I noticed you following me around the city."

"Really?" He raises his eyebrow again. "No strange dreams? No splitting headaches?"

I don't say anything, but he searches my eyes. Apparently, my college friends were right when they told me I shouldn't play poker, as he smiles consolingly and pats my knee very much like a grandfather might when offering life advice.

"I thought as much. Do you have any idea what's causing your headaches?"

"No," I say as I stand up slowly. I still don't trust him, but it's obvious to me that he genuinely believes what he's been telling me. I decide that indulging him a little won't do any harm. "But they've always been accompanied by the dreams, and I've always kind of felt they were connected somehow."

"They are. Probably more than you could imagine." He offers me his hand. "I'm David, the Citadel's historian."

I stare at his hand for a moment, knowing that taking it might very well be like entering an agreement tighter than any contract. But if any of what he's saying is true, then David offers the first real hope I've had of understanding what's happening to me. My eyes meet his, and I reach out, my fingers closing firmly around his. "I'm Aiden."

David smiles and steps to the side gracefully. "Allow me to introduce the rest of the Guardians." He extends a hand.

The figure holding David's staff steps forward. She lowers her hood, and I see that I was right. I did see her in my dream. Her face lights up with a smile so radiant that it draws you away from her disproportionate eyes and nose. Her brown eyes almost glow in the dancing light of the torch. "My name is Jennifer." There's no trace of the uncertainty that was in her voice in the dream. "I am the Guardian of Illusion."

A woman closer to my age steps forward. She walks lithely, athletically, despite the heavy robe. Her face is sharp-featured. Her skin is ivory white and dotted with freckles, and her frizzy fire-red hair is pulled into a loosely controlled ponytail. She looks confident and sure of herself. "I'm Elizabeth. I serve as the Guardian of Conjuration, and I am the Citadel's resident expert on the power of faith." She nods as she steps back.

The next robed figure is clearly male. His muscular bulk is barely concealed beneath the robe. He approaches with his back straight and shoulders squared, his entire being filling the space he's in. When he lowers his hood, his jaw is wide and chiselled, and his lips are pressed together in what appears to be a permanent frown. Short-trimmed sideburns frame his square face, and he sports a buzz cut. "I am Aleksandar, Guardian of Destruction." He looks as though he fits his role perfectly.

Beside him is a young man, barely out of his teens. His five o'clock shadow glistens on his dark brown skin in the torchlight. He wears small square glasses that look very old-fashioned. He looks the most ill at ease of the so-called Guardians, but at the same time he seems full of youthful exuberance. His voice is deep and quiet, and he speaks quickly, making his nervousness more apparent. "Sean." He waves. "I'm Sean. Guardian of Alteration, and the Citadel's science adviser."

The next Guardian to speak does so from my right shoulder, and it actually makes me jump. I didn't hear her stepping up. She speaks quietly, yet confidently, and stands with an air of command that only Aleksandar beats. Faint lines trace her face, and her black curly hair is touched with grey. "I'm Mary,

Guardian of Magic Fundamentals." As she speaks, she squeezes my shoulder in the manner of a long-lost friend, though I'm sure I've never met her before.

"And this," David says as he gently puts his arm around the final hooded figure, "is our Speaker."

The woman lowers her hood, and her stark white hair cascades to the small of her back. I find myself staring into the face of someone who is without a doubt the oldest person I've ever seen. She remains hunched as she comes forward, and dark eyes set within a face papery with age wince with each step as she pushes her staff along. Yet when she speaks, her creaking voice somehow manages to spark with resolve and power. "I am Evelyn," she says. "I provide guidance and insight from the Goddess herself, Mother Nature."

I stare at them all in turn. I have no idea what any of them meant when they introduced themselves as Guardians of this and that, or a woman who speaks for Mother Nature. Each of them clearly believes in what they're saying, but how can any of it be real? The silence goes unbroken.

Finally, I clear my throat enough to speak again. "It seems a bit shady, all of you hiding out in caves, wearing these robes like you're in some kind of cult. And how did you get me to Ireland, anyway? I don't even have a passport."

No one says anything. The look on David's face is that of someone struggling to explain something to someone who has no frame of reference to understand the answer. In the end, it's Evelyn who saves him the trouble.

"We know this will be difficult for you to understand, but time is short. In days of old, the power of nature allowed humanity access to its strength and gave us the ability to control parts of it for the betterment of the world. But long ago, there was a great battle between the world's last two wizards, one in service to nature, one in service to faith. The wizard serving nature lost that battle then, but this battle is about to be fought again. This time, the power of nature must prevail if the world is to survive. Our whole lives—and for the whole lives of those who came before us, and those who came before them, stretching back to long before the first books of the Bible were written—we have been waiting for you."

It's a hard statement to accept at face value.

"You've been waiting for *me*? Why me?"

Evelyn smiles, but there's no warmth in those thin lips. "Someone like you, then—someone who can channel the powers of nature and has the capacity to understand them."

"I don't understand any of this."

"Understandable," she says, which earns a quiet chuckle from the rest of the group. "Your life, Aiden, is about to change. I wish I could tell you that you stand at a crossroads and have a choice before you, but the reality is that this is more like choosing between jumping off a cliff willingly or being pushed off the edge unwillingly, the latter of which would more than likely kill you."

A chill runs down my back at her words, and I laugh uneasily. "Funny you should say that, because that's exactly the choice I was given in my dreams—and in real life, it seems."

"And you chose to jump, I believe, did you not?" This sounds more like an acknowledgement than a question.

"It wasn't really a fair choice. I didn't know that car was coming."

"The choices we face in life are seldom fair," Aleksandar says, "but life will not ask more of us than we are able to bear. The truth is, Aiden, you've been chosen for this by a great entity that chooses very carefully."

"An entity?" I ask, trying to keep the incredulity out of my voice. "You mean God?"

Elizabeth speaks this time. "More like several gods. When the world was first formed, there were many places of power where the energetic eddies from the birth of the planet swirled into conscious beings that early humans knew as gods and goddesses. They make up the body of those with whom our earliest ancestors coexisted."

"You mean like Apollo and Demeter? They're real?"

Ignoring my undisguised disbelief, she continues. "Many people are familiar with references to such beings from classical Greece and ancient Rome, but these gods predate even those cultures, of course. We speak of the primordial gods and goddesses of the land itself. These gods and goddesses gave dominion to the power of nature to ensure the continued balance and cycle of all things. Over time, humanity has come to know this power by many names: Mother Nature, Gaia, Durga, Asase Yaa, Yemaya, Coatlicue, Danu, Mother Earth. It is she, in all her forms, whom we serve. By stepping over that cliff, you have chosen to serve alongside us."

"I haven't chosen anything!" I feel my anger rising again. This is too much for me to handle. I very much dislike feeling I'm not in control of my life. "Look at you all! You're nothing but a cult that has cajoled me with lies and deceit into thinking I have no other choice but to do what you say." I glare at David and Jennifer. "You two! I know you've been following me around. How long have you been following me? Have the rest of you been spying on me? What if you were wrong about me? Caitlin and I could be dead right now." At this point, my blood is boiling. "I have responsibilities! I have to take care of my mother!"

"You're right," Jennifer says, stepping forward. "David and I were assigned to protect you when it became obvious that you might be the one we've been waiting for, and you and Caitlin could have died if we were wrong about your abilities." She pauses briefly. "When you stopped the car, however, you found magic inside yourself to do it. Do you remember that?"

I glare at her, my jaw clenching and unclenching. I've never been an angry person. I've never wanted to yell and scream and shout at somebody as much as I want to yell and scream and shout at her right now. But I don't. The expression on her face is genuine and concerned. I close my eyes and slowly allow my memories to flow. At first, there's just the sound of screeching tires and shouts of warning. And then . . .

"I remember reaching into myself and finding a pool of power that wasn't there before." My voice is barely even a whisper, as though saying it too loudly will make it real.

"It's been there your entire life. You've just never noticed it before." Jennifer holds up her hand, warding off my skeptical rebuttal. "Up until shortly after the birth of civilization as we know it, the world was governed by the power of nature. It ruled fairly and justly as Elizabeth told you, and it shared its secrets with all of humanity so that there were humans who knew how to harness its powers. The greatest of these came to be known as wizards, and though their stories have faded with time, they were once so powerful that we still tell folktales of wizards and witches, men and women with the ability to influence the elements.

"As civilization grew, people had less time for nature. They found new magic in things such as astronomy and rudimentary mechanics, giving birth to the power of science. And then one day, a small group began worshipping the gods, perhaps reasoning that worship was a valid alternative to living in harmony with nature. This worship grew slowly, but a small part of the universal ether grew to like it and coalesced into the power of faith. This new consciousness called itself El and actively sought out worshippers. It didn't care who worshipped it, or how they worshipped, so long as the worship came.

"As El's strength continued to grow, it became multifaceted, becoming different gods to different tribes and pitting tribe against tribe in an attempt to gain more worshippers. The stronger El got, the less influence Mother Nature had on our development. Powerful wizards became rare, and those who still lived were hunted and exterminated.

"The power of faith really came into its own with the advent of the Abrahamic traditions, when El in its various forms became the cornerstones of Judaism, Christianity, and Islam. The influence of these religions spread like wildfire and eliminated any ties to the old gods, forcing the power of nature to go deep underground to survive. But the stronger faith got, the more questions humans asked, for faith without magic is blind. There is magic in nature. We can see it and feel it flowing all around us.

"Slowly, the power of science grew from its beginning as collective human ingenuity into attempts to answer the questions that arose from the void left behind by magic. And though the religions of the world tried throughout the Dark Ages and beyond to smother science and to answer these questions on their own terms, human will is a difficult thing to crush. As we desperately searched for answers that faith could not provide, science grew in strength and faith began to lose its hold on the world."

Sean takes up where Jennifer leaves off. "And thus the circle reaches its close, for science answered many questions about how the world works, but it could not and cannot answer any of the questions about *why* the world works this way. It left people feeling empty and . . . cold. We're born as social creatures that interact with the earth, the sea, and the sky in such a way that fosters harmony between all creatures.

"We were created by the power of nature as a bridge between the elements: a creature equally at home in all elements, designed to help keep the world in balance. That we have turned away from that purpose has set the world dangerously askew."

Thoughts of the state of the world today and images from my dreams swirl through my head. "You're saying that we've reached a tipping point? If humanity doesn't wake up and embrace nature soon, it will be too late?"

Evelyn steps forward and places a wrinkled hand on mine. "We're saying that the world reached that tipping point half a century ago. The days when we could have saved the planet without a major disruption to the ways of humanity have passed." She looks into my eyes with absolute conviction. "With you, Aiden, the power of nature is making its final play. It has entrusted you with the ability to harness the elements, to wield its power as once the wizards of old did. If magic does not return to the world soon, there will be no world left to save. *You* are its chosen vessel to return magic, balance, and harmony to the world, and we are your guides."

I stare at the old woman standing before me. Slowly, my gaze sweeps over the others. The cavern is eerily silent. None of this makes sense. Yet, now that I've heard it, I can *feel* something: a steady thrum of power emanating from the walls themselves.

I look at the walls and see that the stone is *alive*. It pulses with a heartbeat. The air between the walls and me seems almost electrified, and the hair on my arms stands on end. I look around the chamber at the standing stones that tower over us like living giants. I look to the dried-up quartz riverbed that sparkled with rushing water in my dreams, the vaulted ceiling supported by crumbling columns inlaid with dusty red orbs. Beneath the thick layer of centuries-old dust, the chamber *feels* like it longs to be the sparkling wonder from my dreams.

My eyes pass along the gloomy walls, coming to rest on each of the massive sconces. I look again at Evelyn for a long moment. Holding her eyes, I raise my hand toward the torch closest to us. The rest of the Guardians turn to see what my hand is pointed at, but Evelyn's gaze never leaves mine.

"*Go on.*" She seems to whisper it into my mind. "*Do it.*"

And so I whisper it, the phrase I heard Jennifer mutter in my dream: "*Bheith ag lonrú.*" I watch as she and David turn as white as ghosts. As the last breath escapes my lips, the flame atop the torch roars higher and higher until it alone could light the cavern. I feel the very cavern itself respond. It warms as new life breathes into it and the gloom falls away.

I slump to the floor and draw my knees up to my chest, the awareness of my pain nearly forgotten. I don't know what I expected—surely not for something to actually happen. I can't help it. I hug my knees tightly. A single tear runs down my face. They're telling the truth—and my life is over. I'll never escape this place now that they've seen this. I'm some sort of freak. Will I ever see my mother again? James? My sister? Home? Countless thoughts and feelings rush through me in an instant.

For a long moment, the Guardians stare down at me as though unsure how to treat someone whose life has just ended. Perhaps they expected me to be happy?

Evelyn lowers herself to one knee with David's assistance, and she draws close to me. She again places her hand on mine. I want to withdraw, to run, but I don't. Her hand is warm and, after a moment, calming. She takes hold of my chin and gently raises it until our eyes meet. She smiles. It's a genuine smile that lights up her whole face and seems to erase a century of age.

"Aiden, you have made me as happy as I was as a little girl getting her first Christmas present from St. Nicholas. I had nearly given up hope that this day would come in my lifetime, and now that it has, I am so happy that I would dance if I thought my old bones could take it! Welcome, Aiden, to Lannóg Eolas."

I say nothing. I just rock back and forth, allowing her words to sink in. I gently squeeze her fragile hand. In the depths of my being, something is responding. Some quiet voice within is whispering that this is where I belong, that here I can make a difference, that I'm not getting anywhere in Toronto anyway.

I take Evelyn's hand. "Thank you for the welcome." I kiss her hand as one would kiss the hand of a queen. No one stops me, and no one seems surprised, but Evelyn smiles and gently withdraws her hand as David helps her to her feet.

"None of that now, Aiden," she says. "We are but Guardians of Knowledge, and it is we who serve you. True, we have been waiting a long time, but for a few of us, our time to share our secrets with you is short."

"What are the Guardians, exactly?" I ask.

Mary speaks next. "Long ago, the last wizard, Wizard Nuada, gathered thirteen of his most trusted advisers before his final battle. He spent years sharing with them his secrets right here in this chamber. He chose these thirteen advisers because they showed talent in the core magic disciplines but did not have the strength necessary to actually work the magic. They could only access Nuada's magic through special staffs he created." She looks pointedly at the staff in her own hand. "And since they lacked the ability to create their own magic, it would be much harder for the agents of faith to hunt them down should Nuada lose his battle.

"Those thirteen advisers were the first Guardians of Knowledge. They met in absolute secrecy here in this chamber once every month to make sure no part of the knowledge that Nuada shared with them was lost. They spent their lives training their firstborn children in the knowledge they'd been granted so someone could take their place upon their death. We seven today are the last of the line."

I stare at them in silence, unsure of what to say. I remember the resigned disappointment on Jennifer's face the night she tried to light the torch in my dream. These people have spent their entire lives waiting for me so they can teach me to use something they've longed to use their entire lives; that's sacrifice. I shake my head and recall that David said we're in Ireland.

I jump up to my feet, ignoring the pain that shoots through my body. "Are we actually in *Ireland*? How the hell did you get me here, *unconscious* . . . without a *passport*?"

"No one really knows how we get to the Citadel," David says. "There are portal stones and burrows near each of our homes. Some are nearly as large as Stonehenge and Newgrange. Others are buried in caves. With these on our person"—he reaches into his robe and pulls out a small gem that appears to be moonstone or something similar—"we step between the portal stones. After a brief wave of nausea, the air swims and we step onto paths that lead to these tunnels. Between two and three hours later, we emerge into this chamber.

"The tunnels are a magical network of paths created by the wizards of old that shortens the distances between here and other places. Jennifer journeys from Victoria, British Columbia, and I from Peterborough, Ontario, and we meet along a path about an hour from here. Evelyn travels from Wales; Aleksandar from Russia, south of St. Petersburg; Sean and Elizabeth from England; and Mary from North Carolina. We all walk different speeds and distances, yet it takes us all about the same time to journey here."

My panic rises as it becomes more obvious that he's not lying. I pace frantically, alternating between wringing my hands, pulling at my hair, and looking past the Guardians for any sign of an exit. "I just lost my job," I say to no one in particular, "and desperately need to find a new one. Maybe you can all afford to just pick up and travel across the world every month, but my mother is sick and needs me to support her."

David looks at Jennifer and the rest before he answers. "I'm afraid it isn't safe for you to go home right now."

I stop to glare at him. "What do you mean?"

"A lot has happened since we brought you here. Your body was already weakened because your power desperately wanted to be used, but since you didn't know it existed, let alone how to use it, it could only bash against your mind over and over, hoping you would discover it. That's what caused you such headaches and lack of sleep. And when you were forced to tap into your power with no training, you dug so deep into your energy reserves that you were almost completely depleted. If we hadn't been trying to find you and weren't nearby at the time of the accident, you probably wouldn't have survived. It's taken three weeks of constant care and daily healing rituals within the circle for you to wake up, Aiden."

My eyebrows shoot up. "Three weeks! How is that possible?"

My brain scrambles to retrace how much medication my mother had left and when it will run out. Too many things are happening for me to think clearly, but my quick guess is she's been out for a least a week. I need to call her. Right now. I look at my wristband, but all that's there is a scar. I glare at David.

"Where's my wristband?" I ask coldly.

"You fried it when you stopped that car with your magic," comes a familiar voice.

I spin around. "Caitlin!"

"The Guardians had to delicately remove it from your wrist without taking too much skin along with it. You shouldn't have modern technology so close to you."

Excitement fills me at the sight of her. Who is this woman? On the day of the accident, I could have sworn she was the woman from my dreams, but that can't be true, can it? Then again, so many impossible things have happened since I woke up that I don't know what's possible and what's not anymore. She holds up a blackened wristband, her posture defensive. I stare at her warily, unsure of what to say.

Frowning, she thrusts the wristband into my hand. "It looks worse for wear, but I had it fixed. You won't likely get any reception this far underground, and I doubt your data plan extends to Ireland anyway. I almost regret getting it fixed, though, since you're yelling at those who dedicate their lives to serving you."

David raises a hand. "It's not his fault, Caitlin. He has absorbed a lot of information in a short while. His world is shifting radically."

I stare at the wristband. It looks like someone tried to light it on fire. I press my thumb against the backplate and it chirps, recognizing me. I look up at Caitlin. She's standing there, oddly defensive and cold for someone who was so friendly to me on our first meeting. I should thank her for fixing it. Instead: "Are you her?" My eyes go wide. I didn't intend to just come out and ask her that. I swallow as she stares at me. "Are you the voice that's been guiding me in my dreams?"

"I am." She says it quietly, and she visibly relaxes a bit. "I'm sorry. This must be a lot to take in all at once. The rest of us have had a long time to prepare for this." She flashes an apologetic smile at me.

I try not to let her smile disarm me, to undermine how betrayed I feel.

"Thanks for saving me," she continues, "and for not dying. We've gone through a lot of trouble to find you."

I roll the wristband between my fingers for a moment. "Wow," I say quietly. I look up, and her smile fades. "My judgement of character must be worse than I thought. When we spoke that day, I spilled my soul to you. I trusted you with some of my most personal secrets. You were a complete stranger, but you seemed so trustworthy. And how do you repay me? You break my trust and betray me." At this point, I'm just short of yelling. "That whole thing with the car . . . Was that even an accident?"

Caitlin doesn't answer. She doesn't have to. I can see it written all over her face. Disgusted, I turn to take my anger out on the others, but I'm stopped by the looks of surprise and confusion on their faces. Perhaps they didn't know she had planned to risk both of our lives.

I look back at Caitlin. "Why?" I ask, my voice tremulous.

She straightens her back and faces me directly. "We've known for some time that a powerful wizard was awakening in the world, and a wizard *must* be guided through their awakening. Without guidance, the result is often rather chaotic and volatile. It can lead to a gruesome death that can easily be a danger to others. Your presence has been rippling through the natural world with growing intensity."

"How do you know all of this? Are you a Guardian too?"

"No. I'm something the Guardians call a Seeker. I'm very sensitive to magic, with a very low-grade telepathic ability. Over the past year, you've cried out often enough in your dreams for me to connect with you that way. I could feel your power building, so I tried to guide you through your dreams while frantically trying to find you in the real world."

It's again too much to take in. I turn away from her, cradling my head in my hands, hoping beyond hope that if I rub my eyes hard enough with the palms of my hands I'll wake up from this nightmare.

I think back to our conversation at the cafe. "Were you really at Keegan's to do his accounting?"

Caitlin frowns. "I positioned myself as Keegan's accountant several years ago because he has some power of his own that I've been monitoring. I was at the bookstore that day because I was drawn to some residual energy I sensed there, but I couldn't figure out what it was, as there was nothing obvious beyond a handful of occult texts. When you walked through the door, however, I knew instantly why I was there."

"You knew about me just like that?"

"Not exactly. A couple of weeks before that, some family business took me to Toronto, and my cousin convinced me much against my will to go to this nightclub called Surrender." Her voice drops to almost a whisper. "I believe you're acquainted with it?"

My mouth falls open. "You *followed* me to Surrender?" I'm incredulous.

"Followed you? No. I didn't even know who you were at that point. I don't do clubs normally, so imagine my surprise when I saw you standing by the bar, whole rainbows of magic sparking out of you uncontrollably. I'd never seen anything like it—so much magic trapped inside and struggling to get out. That's when I knew I was there for a reason. I tried to reach you then, but after you rather rudely brushed me aside, all I could do was contact David to let him know I might have found you."

I think of how awestruck I was by her both in Keegan's shop and at the waterfront cafe. "I don't remember you trying to talk to me at the club."

She looks at me, and with the barest hint of a smirk, she holds her long hair in a ponytail with one hand and puts her other hand lightly on my arm. "'Excuse me. Are you okay? Your aura seems off.' Perhaps not the best pickup line."

Oh my God. I blush, and she laughs quietly.

"Don't worry," she says. "It's not the first time I've been brushed off at a bar. Anyway, I was very glad I had contacted David when I saw the sheer amount of power building in St. Michael's the next morning."

"You were at the church too?"

"No." She shakes her head. "I followed you to it, but I wasn't lying when I told you I hate stuffy religious types. I can't stand churches. I just saw the after-effects, which was almost enough to make me wish I'd gone inside. David arrived just after you left for the cafe, and I told him about everything I'd seen."

"So you knew what I was going though . . ."

Caitlin takes me by the hand and gazes into my eyes. "Aiden, who knows how long your magic had been trying to manifest? The dreams coming more and more often, the headaches getting more and more intense—you were getting ready to explode. I was planning something much less dramatic and thought I had more time when we met for coffee, but when your magic started exploding out of you on the street corner, I couldn't risk losing the planet's only hope. I just acted without thinking, hoping you'd do the same."

I stare at her for several seconds. "You threw yourself in front of a car without knowing for sure I would, or could, save you?"

She squeezes my hand and smiles. "I knew you could. I hoped you would."

I look away at the stone floor in silence. I can't decide whether I hate her or respect her, but I finally look up at her again. "Well, I guess you played me perfectly. If you had told me I'd be walking with you to Ireland through a network of magical tunnels with two mysterious people from my dreams, I never would have agreed to go with you to the station."

Caitlin smiles sadly. "Thanks for that. I know you don't trust me yet. Truth be told, I wouldn't either if I were in your shoes, but I hope you will come to in time." She looks around, gesturing at the Guardians around us. "Don't worry. You're in good hands here."

"Except I'm broke. You're all telling me I have to stay here and embrace some destiny that until an hour ago I didn't even know I had. You say I can't go home, but I can't stay. I can't shirk my responsibilities. My mother is very ill, and her medication is expensive." I run a hand through my hair in frustration. "My rent is due. I also owe my friend James a lot of money. As it is, I'm going to have to ask him for help to pay rent this month—if he'll even talk to me. It's been weeks. He's probably worried sick, and I have no idea how I'm going to explain all of this to him."

David places a hand on my shoulder. "We can take care of your mother from here and can also help you close your lease, but it is simply not safe for you to leave here yet."

I shrug his hand off and draw myself up to my full height. My mind is made up. "I don't care how much I hurt. I have to leave. I have to get a job and get my life back." I look at Caitlin. "You got me here. You can take me back."

David shakes his head. "That's not what I mean, Aiden. The world is not the same as it was three weeks ago. El senses that its aged foe is making a move on a chessboard dusty with disuse, and it is stirring angrily."

I look from Caitlin to David and back again. "What is he talking about?"

"When you stopped that car, we weren't exactly in a quiet neighbourhood. Hundreds of people saw that mountain thrust up out of the ground, saw *you* with your arms outstretched and some sort of mystical power flowing from them to the ground." Caitlin glances at David and Jennifer. "They saw how you and I were rushed away by two non-descript people seemingly skilled at disappearing into thin air."

I stare at the torch, whose flame has resumed burning normally. "They saw magic..."

"Thankfully, there are no videos or pictures. Your magic is a very strong form of energy that can't coexist with today's electronics. It destroyed every computer and wristband for two blocks, and the authorities aren't able to get a clear picture from the nearest surveillance feeds."

Part of me is in awe that I have that kind of power. Another part of me is terrified. A very large part of me is saying that this is all impossible. But I *feel* different, like something has awakened within me.

When I don't say anything, Caitlin continues. "People are scared—terrified, actually. Some think aliens and sorcerers are among us, and some think someone set off an EMP device in the heart of downtown Toronto. They all think that someone is you. Artist sketches and renditions of the accident are still playing over all the news feeds, and the rift that was slowly forming between Canada and the United States finally erupted when Canada's parliament unanimously denounced the attacks but chose to keep the borders open."

"What's happened?"

"It gave enough strength to the so-called Christian March that they were able to overthrow the American government," David explains. "The mainstream media is currying favour with the new government by claiming that Canada is a nation of devil worshippers, with 'He Who Used the Power of Satan' as the main culprit. Tensions between the two countries have never been as high as they are right now, and on both sides of the border, there's a manhunt on for you."

It takes me a moment to digest this information. When I do, a word comes to mind, but it seems too crude to say in front of Evelyn.

Caitlin smiles knowingly. "Most of the sketches don't look anything like us, but there's a handful of you that are amazingly accurate. It seems that everyone has overlooked my role in the incident. Nobody has paid much attention to what I might look like."

David rests his hand on my shoulder again, trying to calm my anxiousness. "Do you see why you must stay here?"

I search for a way around their argument. I can't find one. "How will you take care of my mother?" I ask morosely.

"There are some advantages to being the oldest secret society in the world. Paying for your mother's medication won't be a problem. We can make sure she doesn't want for anything."

"I see." I try to maintain my composure. "But I can't stay here forever. You said it yourself. The power of nature has chosen me to bring it back into the world. I can't do that from a cavern in Ireland. And while I appreciate the offer to pay for my mother's medication, I have to be able to see her. She's *dying*. I need to spend as much time with her as possible."

"We understand your concerns, but—"

"And there's something else you should know," I blurt. "I gave James the torch from the tunnel to study with our psychic friend Keegan, so if this power of faith you're talking about is after me, then my friends are most likely in danger now too."

The Guardians huddle together, and worried murmurs pass between them.

"Torch?" David asks, his voice hushed. "What torch?"

"The one I took back with me from my dream when you and Jennifer passed by me in the tunnel." I say it nonchalantly, knowing they're unnerved by this revelation. Nice or not, good purpose or not, it's what they deserve after what they've put me through.

More hushed debate fills the chamber while Caitlin and I look on silently.

"You have made some good points," David says finally. "You won't be here forever, but you cannot return home before we teach you enough about your abilities that you can keep yourself safe. As a Seeker, Caitlin is far more skilled than we are at navigating the world and its people. She can bring letters to your mother until we feel it's safe for you to venture forth with supervision."

"*Letters?*" I exclaim. "I have to be able to—"

David raises his hand. "Letters," he replies in a tone that brooks no more argument. "As in handwritten letters that your great-great-grandfather would have written and sent by post. We want you to become a wizard, and we are willing to train you as such, but you cannot leave before you're trained, not even to see your mother. On this we are unbending. We cannot take the risk that our enemies will find you when so much is at stake."

The air is tense as the Guardians await my response. I've already lost my job this month; I'll probably lose my apartment too. Right now is probably the best possible time for me to leave the city, but it's painful to think of not being able to see my mother. To think of losing contact for . . .

"How long are we talking?"

David's posture is unwavering, but his expression is compassionate. "It could be months. It's difficult to say."

Months. With her health the way it is, my mother may not even have months left. How can I justify staying away? Yet, how can I return to Toronto knowing what I now know and let the headaches claim me?

"Aiden?" Caitlin says. "Once the immediate danger has passed somewhat, I could bring you far enough out of the Citadel that you could call her. Would that help?"

I nod. I don't trust my voice at the moment.

David clears his throat and continues. "As for James and Keegan, you cannot afford the distraction at this point in your training. But if what you say is true, the danger for them is just as real as it is for the rest of us. Caitlin will ensure that they remain safe until you have demonstrated your magic to your first teacher. She will then collect them."

I shake my head. "I get that you had to 'collect' me for various reasons, but it's not fair to just pluck them willy-nilly out of their lives. Let me call James first. He's trustworthy."

Several of the Guardians start to protest, but Evelyn holds her hand up.

"When the time comes, you may contact your friend," she says.

I smile and bow my head in her direction. "At least one of you listens to what I say."

David raises his eyebrows, and I see Sean cover up a smirk.

Chapter Ten

It's been a few days since I woke up at the Citadel. I've spent them recovering in rudimentary living quarters in a smaller chamber adjoining the one with the stone circle I woke up in. Of course, size is relative. My new home is nearly twice the size of my apartment in Toronto.

There's a short, curved tunnel separating the two chambers, ensuring at least a modicum of privacy. Just inside the entrance is a long slab of white stone that makes a nice bench, if not quite a sofa. The room is more or less a circle, and about fifteen feet to the left of the bench is a small pile of hay flattened into a sleeping pad and covered with a thick grey wool blanket. Mine is the only "bed" here, but at a quick glance, I'd say you could easily fit five others. In the centre of the room is a fire pit just large enough to heat the room nicely.

The floor is rough and unfinished stone, but the walls are highly polished and broken only by six torches evenly spaced around the room. To the right of the entrance is a large column of natural stone that juts out from the wall. Built into the base of the column are two small closet spaces. The one is full of preserved food and basic supplies. The other has a small assortment of my clothes that Caitlin had collected from my apartment. Embedded in the stone above the closet are several hooks. On one of them hangs a white linen robe.

On the far side of the chamber is a small stream of spring water. It pours from a small opening near the ceiling and pools into a natural basin before draining back into the earth. It's the perfect location for me to bathe privately.

This is to be my home until I can prove I'm worthy enough to leave. When I pressed the Guardians to give me a better idea of how long I'd be here, Mary was quite adamant that it will take me at least six months to grasp the rudimentary skills of magic. That seems like forever, but then I remember they've spent their entire lives learning what they're going to teach me. From that perspective, six months will probably just be scratching the surface. Nonetheless, I'm determined to change those months I can't see my friends and family into weeks.

As I lie staring at the dark expanse of stone above me, my first day of consciousness at the Citadel seems almost like a dream. I stretch, and my muscles groan in protest, reminding me that I'm definitely not dreaming. My bed is reasonably comfortable, all things considered, but I'm still sleeping in a cave. At least it's warm this morning. On the first two nights here, I was hesitant to light a fire, afraid the smoke would fill the chamber and suffocate me, but the damp cold finally drove me to light one last night. I was relieved to see the smoke rise lazily to the ceiling and curl its way up and out to who knows where.

As the embers of last night's fire burn out, I reluctantly push myself to my feet and light one of the torches. I use the torch to light the other five until the room is bright enough to see comfortably. I walk over to the basin and stick my head under the gently falling spring water, giving my hair a quick rinse. The water is icy cold, but I don't have a choice. I jump into the basin just long enough to splash myself a bit and then run over to the remaining warmth of the fire before towelling dry. The number one reason so far this morning for wanting to get back to civilization: I despise cold showers.

With a resigned sigh, I stare at the white robe hanging on the column. I told the Guardians that I refuse to walk around the streets of Toronto in a robe, but they insist on my wearing the garb of a wizard in training while I learn about magic. None of them actually remembers the part of the ancient lore where it specifies why a wizard must wear a robe, but they're quite insistent. I pull the robe over my head and set it around me nicely. It's actually not as bad as I thought it would be. Plus, it's thick and heavy enough to keep me warm down here.

As I tighten the rope around my waist, David appears at the door. He coughs quietly to let me know he's arrived. I smile at him and turn slowly, showing off my new robe.

"What do you think?"

He smiles, and I see the same twinkle in his eye that I saw in the coffee shop. "It's very fetching."

"What are we getting up to this morning?"

"Evelyn wishes to show you something. If you'll follow me, please."

We exit my quarters and David leads me through the vast chamber toward the spiral staircase. We ascend the stairs to the massive stone table from my vision. It's just as impressive in real life. Evelyn sits on the stone throne at the head of the table. The torch slotted in the arm of the great chair casts a flickering light on her face.

David guides me to the throne on her right, and as I sit on the wide seat, the torch in the arm of my chair springs to life.

As I expected, engraved on the table is the map of the mountain range. I lean forward to inspect it closer, but it's not anything I've seen on any map before. The rivulets of quartz meander through it, thrumming with an ancient energy.

"Thank you, David," Evelyn says in her creaky voice.

After David leaves, she turns her wrinkly eyes on me. "My sight in this world is limited now, but last night I received a vision of terrifying intensity. With you coming into your power, Aiden, the time our ancestors and we have long awaited is finally at hand. Although our ancient enemies have not pursued us in thousands of years, they are still watching closely. If we let down our guard, they will snatch victory from our grasp." She pauses, holding her hands open before the table. "Some of this may not make sense to you right now, but it's important that you see it. Come close and see what I have seen."

I follow her example, leaning in closer until my face hovers over the giant stone tabletop. Evelyn's finger swirls around the pool of quartz in the centre of the mountain range, and it shimmers, transforming into water. On its surface, an image takes form.

"Our history," says the Speaker.

Within the pool a sky forms, black and stormy. The world it creates enthralls me. Lightning arcs across this sky, illuminating gnarled trees barren of leaves. The bony branches of the ancient trees overlook a massive grey mountain.

At the base of the mountain is a village, but the people there are tired, joyless, loveless. There are monuments in the village dedicated to great warriors and explorers—relics of a long-dead time.

The ancient highways that once led there only lead away now. None of the residents ever leave the village, and no visitor ever comes. Once, long ago, this village was a mighty city—or so the old folk had said. They are long gone, however, and their tales are no longer told. Even the buildings they spoke of have collapsed into heaps of dust under the weight of ages.

In days long past, a castle stood atop the mountain. Once tall and strong, overlooking the whole of its mighty kingdom, its towers and ramparts crumble as we watch. Huge sections of wall occasionally collapse into the village below. If the tumbling stone were to crush someone, no one would even notice. With lifeless eyes staring straight ahead, the remnants of humanity in the village would walk on by as though nothing had happened, wandering toward the day their own calamity will claim them. Yet, within this dying castle is the only true life remaining in this once great kingdom.

In the castle's depths, a blacksmith labours to forge the perfect sword. In the only tower that still stands, two wizards are locked in a struggle for power over the hearts and minds of the people below. One wears robes of white, his normally serene face contorted in pain. The other wears robes of black, concentration and anger etched onto his face. Waves of energy envelope the two, crackling with the ferocity of their masters.

The white wizard fights to restore the power of nature to her once great stature. The black wizard has given his strength to El, and his only goal is to topple the white wizard, the last bastion of magic in the world.

The two wizards have been locked in battle like this for well over a thousand years. The strength for their continued battle over control of a kingdom that died long ago comes from the few people still left in what remains. The wizards' power has been slowly draining all life from the surrounding area, and now only the pitiful village remains.

Had the white wizard known what was happening, he would have died of shame, but so focused was he on preventing the black wizard from taking over his dominion that when he reached out for a source of energy to support his own failing life, he hadn't noticed where it had come from. And so the warriors and the merchants and the lords and the peasants had all given their lives unwittingly, their essences absorbed by the magic of he who had once been the kingdom's only hope.

As I watch, powerless to change the outcome, the blacksmith puts the finishing touches on the sword that the black wizard had imbued with a power as bright as the sun itself. One thousand years after he started his work, the blacksmith strikes his hammer upon the steel one last time.

The eyes of the black wizard light up with excitement. This sword will give him dominion over all living things and instantly convert those whom it touches. The blacksmith presents the sword to his master. The black wizard's mouth turns up in a prideful sneer, and he prepares to embrace his victory.

The white wizard, sensing his end is near and accepting that nature will not prevail this day, does the last thing he can do, the last thing the black wizard expects, the only thing the black wizard isn't prepared for.

The white wizard draws on all of his remaining strength, and far below in the village, the last of the villagers and buildings collapse into dust. He then thrusts his mortal enemy's power away for just a heartbeat. In that moment of distraction, nature's champion throws himself upon the sword as it crackles with the energy of pure faith. As the blade plunges through his adversary, the black wizard looks down in both shock and anger. The white wizard, in a voice raspy with old age and disuse, speaks the first words to be heard in the kingdom in centuries: "This sword shall never fully be yours."

And as the white wizard's final breath passes through his lips, as the sword pulses with electric green energy, as the last tower of the castle falls to dust around them, the black wizard angrily withdraws the sword from the white's torso and pushes his adversary off the wall, sending him plummeting to the earth. Then he turns and vanishes into the annals of time while a stone rises in the heart of the forest. Engraved upon the stone are these words:

> Here stood Dunadin, mightiest of all kingdoms. It fell to deception of the highest magnitude but will rise again when one who is full of truth and justice holds the Sword of Dunadin.

A dense fog billows out and swirls around the stone, and as the stone disappears from sight, the image fades away.

I look at Evelyn. Her eyes are closed, and her body trembles lightly.

"What does it mean?" I ask softly.

Her eyes don't open, but her face turns to me. "We learn three lessons from this. First, when the Wizard Nuada lost to El's champion, he sowed the seeds of nature's return in the power of faith itself. Second, the Lost Kingdom of Dunadin is a necessary part of nature's return. Third, as a wizard, you have the ability to access great power, but you must constantly guard its source, lest you use too much and wind up hurting those you love."

She turns back to the table and dips her finger into the pool of water again. The surface ripples, and the image changes to a giant circle divided into three equal portions. The first portion is green, with images of people interacting with animals. A feeling of warmth, belonging, and yearning emanates from it. The next portion is white, with images of armies marching and fighting. A feeling of cold and a strange mixture of hatred and love emanates from it. The last portion is blue, with images of outer space, laboratories, disease, and tombstones. Huge swaths of forest are clear-cut in the name of human progress. A feeling of emptiness and loneliness emanates from this section of the circle.

"The present," says the Speaker, "where all has been equalized. We spoke of this at your awakening. Faith, which has held sway for so long, has been under siege by science. Over the centuries, the power of faith has spread itself too thin and has had too many factions. In the beginning, this helped. It didn't matter which creed you believed in, as all belief strengthened the one called El. But as faction fights faction, more and more become disillusioned. And now science, which has been trying to undermine faith, almost since El first came into being, is gaining followers.

"But the power of science has no room for the very real concept of the human soul, and so its followers end up feeling adrift and alone, full of emptiness. Even though their lives are full of people, there is no real meaning in any of their connections. And while the power of science erodes the power of faith, our Goddess, Mother Nature, has slowly been sowing her seeds. Now she has a strong and vibrant community following the old ways that honour her."

Evelyn swirls her finger around once more, and the image descends into chaos, death, and destruction. Oceans swallow cities, storms ravage the world, smog chokes populations, and disease runs rampant as temperatures climb. It's very similar to the one James, Keegan, and I shared. It fades away slowly, and a still image takes its place. One half depicts light and life, and the other half depicts darkness and death.

"The future is a cleansing. Faith and science will fight furiously for what they think is theirs, but nature must prevail or the world is doomed." Evelyn leans forward, gripping my hand with a strength I wouldn't have thought possible in one of her advanced age. "It is only through nature's triu harmony can be achieved."

She releases my hand and folds her hands in her lap. "You, Aiden, are her champion. You must return the world to balance. I know your reluctance is strong, but you have now seen how the world got to this point and have seen what will happen if we fail."

I take a deep breath. "I have seen the ending of this vision before, Evelyn, only I was with James and Keegan. The three of us stood over the world as it burned."

She looks at me, her expression soft and gentle. "That the Goddess, Mother Nature, called to you herself must mean we are very close indeed to the time of reckoning. I am curious. How did you receive this vision?"

"Keegan is an energy healer. He was attempting to find the source of my headaches. While it was happening, James touched us both, causing a violent spark of energy that blew the room apart. The vision occurred at the same time."

Evelyn remains silent for a long moment before speaking. "Thank you for sharing this. We have no concrete knowledge on this particular subject, but it sounds to me like the three of you bonded and your magical charge flowed into them." She stares at the pool on the table as the vision dissipates. "We briefly discussed James and Keegan when you first awoke after your arrival. Are you close?"

"James and I are close friends. I met Keegan through James only recently, but I guess you can say we connected pretty quickly." I smile.

Evelyn smiles back. "Ah, yes. Our Seeker is already watching Keegan, but I shall ask her to keep a closer watch on James now as well. If you charged both of them, it's possible they will manifest as wizards as well."

The next morning, I wake early in a cold sweat. Nightmares filled my sleep with dreams of floods, fires, and famines, as if invited by Evelyn's vision.

The fire has died down completely, and a damp chill has settled into the chamber. I climb out of bed and use a match Caitlin provided to light the torch closest to me and then use the torch to relight the fire. I recall how I struggled to strike my first-ever match at the Citadel; even though they're rare nowadays, the Guardians fortunately have a stockpile of them. At the time,

I asked David if I could use a lighter instead. He just smiled and said, "You should keep practicing with the matches." They clearly share Keegan's belief that a match is more magical than a lighter.

As I poke at the fire, I again see the vision James, Keegan, and I shared. Our soot-covered faces stand in the middle of a warzone. I also see the vision of water sweeping cities away. I then wonder what being nature's champion will entail.

I pull a grill over the fire pit and put a pot of water on it to make myself some oatmeal for breakfast. It's standard fare here, probably because it's easy to make, it's filling, and it has a long shelf life.

I'm nearly finished my breakfast when I hear footsteps in the tunnel outside my quarters. I look up to see Aleksandar's hulking shape fill the entranceway. In contrast to David's warm approach yesterday, Aleksandar appears cold and unemotional. His squared shoulders and permanent frown, coupled with his military haircut and rigid stance, say today is going to be much different from yesterday. When he speaks, he is all business.

"Are you ready for your first lesson?"

I bow my head. It seems to fit his ceremonial mood. He turns silently and begins to make his way back to the main chamber. I follow in his wake.

We stand looking around the large central chamber. It's just Aleksandar and me. With just the two of us, the chamber feels especially vast. I look to the large circle of sarsen stones. In the centre of the stones, a circle is mapped out with thirteen torches burning brightly.

Aleksandar puts his arm out in a sweeping arc. "We have come to know this space as the Chamber of Knowledge because it is where all of our learning begins and ends. Your education will start here before it expands to the other chambers." His sweeping gesture ends with him pointing at the stone circle. "This," he says, his voice grave, "is a sacred circle. Do you know what makes it sacred?"

I peer at the circle, hoping to decipher a secret. I can feel a subtle energy glowing around it, but I can't determine what the cause of the energy is. I take a stab at it. "Because we are in a sacred place?"

He shakes his head slowly and frowns. "It is neither the place we are in nor the fact that it is lit by fire that makes it sacred. I don't have enough power to make it significantly magical, but it is sacred because I poured my soul's energy into it as I created it. Any circle can be sacred if we create it with that intent. The creation of the circle is part of a ritual that joins us to the flow of the world, to the cycle of energy that spirals endlessly throughout everything in the world."

"Intent..."

"Yes, that is your first lesson. When you spoke the phrase '*bheith ag lonrú*,' you caused the flame of the torch to grow, but you didn't have to use those words. Magic has nothing to do with saying fancy words or waving a wand a certain way, although sometimes such acts can help magnify and focus. Magic is *intention*. It is the act of using your will to influence the energy flowing around you and through you to cause it to respond to you. Without intention, magic is nothing. Does this make sense?"

I nod. In a very strange sort of way, it does.

"Good. This stone marks due west. In the beginning, we will focus on clearly setting your intention on rising, growing energy. There will be times when you will want to change this, but for now you will start charging your circle from the west, while facing the rising sun, and walk the perimeter of your circle sunwise."

"Sunwise? Is that like clockwise?"

Aleksandar gives me a look. I'm not sure if it's angry or amused. "Not exactly. Clockwise refers to man-made timekeeping. What we want to do is walk our circle in the direction the sun travels so that our magical energy grows like the brilliant light of day. In the northern hemisphere, this happens to be clockwise. If we were in the southern hemisphere, we would have to walk counterclockwise to follow the sun."

Aleksandar continues. "Giving a blessing to each direction can help significantly increase your intent of creating a sacred circle. I have already charged this circle to help guide you, but I want it to be magnified by your intention, so we are going to walk the circle together and overlay your circle onto mine. That way it will be sacred to both of us. Are you ready?"

I'm actually terrified, but he didn't ask me about that. I can't otherwise think of any reason to say no. "I am."

Together, we step forward to the pillar that he indicated as the west stone. He stops, raising his eyes to the heavens as if he can see them through the rocky ceiling.

"Remember," he says, "it is wise to set the mood for your intention from the very start. I always pause at the entrance and allow myself to relax, to forget about all of my concerns from the outside world. None of that matters here. Feel the earth beneath your feet, and feel the sky above you, grounding and centring you."

It seems odd, this big brute of a man talking about something so meditative. Nevertheless, I do as he says, thrusting all of my worries aside and focusing on the sensation of the stone floor. I feel the bits of grit between my toes and then extend my focus up through my being into the sky, which I know is beyond the rock somewhere. It takes me several moments, but I eventually begin to feel at once both calm and energized, as if nothing can touch me.

"Now, we move sunwise around the circle. With each step, feel the ground beneath your feet being charged by your energy."

I follow him as we head in a circle around the flaming torches. With each step, I envision the ground beneath me charging with my essence. When we reach the north stone, Aleksandar stops again and faces outward.

"Picture yourself deep in a forest, in a clearing beneath a sky full of stars."

"Okay."

"Now repeat after me."

He speaks slowly, his voice low and powerful, and I imitate him, putting my whole being behind my words: "With the blessing of the great wolf of the forest, I call upon the powers of the north."

For several minutes we stand there in silence, facing the north. I try to imagine what the energy of a powerful wolf would feel like and then imagine that flowing into us. We then slowly turn and continue along the circle to the east.

Aleksandar pauses again. "Picture the sky above us as clear and blue for as far as you can see. The sun begins to rise, and through the radiant beams, a hawk soars toward us."

I picture it, and it comes clearer and faster than the image of the forest.

"With the blessing of the great hawk flying through the dawn, I call upon the powers of the east."

From the east, I can almost hear the cry of the hawk and feel its wings beating.

We continue along the circle to the south, and behind me I can feel a charged line following us.

At the south stone, Aleksandar turns and thrusts his arms out. "The hot midday sun warms the lands before us. Smoke rises from a blacksmith's forge, and the great stallion of the south stands free and strong, ready to offer us his power."

He pauses to let me fully feel the scene, and then we say, "With the blessing of the great stallion in the heat of the sprint, I call upon the powers of the south."

I feel the temperature of the chamber ratchet up several degrees, and there is so much energy flowing through me that my hair is literally standing on end. I glance at Aleksandar. He's looking at his arms, as the hair on them is also standing on end. He looks up at me in both awe and apprehension.

It occurs to me that with the Guardian's limited power, he could have done this same ritual a thousand times and never felt anything remotely like this. Does he normally feel anything at all? Or do his rituals hold power for him and no one else? I wonder how much power the Guardians can draw on through their staffs. I make a mental note to ask Aleksandar later.

The circle flickers, and I feel Aleksandar's eyes burn into the side of my face.

"Focus!" he barks. "Distraction can ruin all intention!"

I force my stray thoughts out of my mind, envisioning the circle in my mind again.

Aleksandar nods and seems satisfied. Together, we step onward to the west.

"Picture the sun setting over a calm and peaceful ocean. The water ripples lightly, and the ever tenacious salmon swims against the current."

After another pause to let this vision fill my thoughts: "With the blessing of the great salmon, I call upon the powers of the west."

I repeat the words and feel the power of the salmon flow out of the water and into the circle. We then turn to the centre. I can feel the ocean currents pull the energy of the earth up into us and the energy of the sky down into us, connecting us to earth, sea, and sky.

Aleksandar stands beside me, looking a bit agitated. Perhaps he's struggling to come to terms with a power he could only theorize until now. He swallows and takes my hand in his. "Now with all of your intention focused behind your words, repeat after me." He says each phrase slowly, giving me time to repeat and feel the full power of each. "This is sacred time. This is sacred space. I am fully present, here and now."

With a rush of air, the energy of my circle joins his. The air itself ripples around us, and the flames on the torches stretch toward the tops of the sarsen stones. Aleksandar turns to me, and a smile is on his face for the first time.

Without releasing my hand, he walks us to the centre of the circle. We sit cross-legged in the centre, and his smile disappears as he becomes all teacher once again.

"Welcome, Aiden, to your first sacred circle. From now on, you are to have your circle formed before your Guardian arrives each day. I will light the torches each morning if they are not already lit. This is one of the most basic magical skills, so it draws little energy from my staff. You've already demonstrated to us that you can make a flame stronger; now you must demonstrate that you can light one. Use what you learn each day to prove our faith in you is well founded. When you can light these torches on your own, this stage of your training will be complete, and the next Guardian will come."

"What other training will I receive?"

"Once you reveal your power to all of us, we'll know which discipline your strength lies in. If it is destruction magic, I will return to teach you everything I know, and eventually you'll be able to throw fireballs, unleash earthquakes, and wreak havoc with tornadoes should you so choose."

The look of incredulity on my face grows as he speaks. "Why would I ever need to learn that?"

Aleksandar says nothing for a moment. For just a heartbeat, I think I see a haunted look pass over his face. It's gone as quick as it came. "Not all magic is meant to calm, soothe, or put one at ease. Also, the magic that flows through your veins could be very different from that of another. We have to try all of the disciplines so we know which one your blood responds to the strongest."

"What are all the disciplines again?"

"When the Wizard Nuada created the Guardians of Knowledge, he divided his craft into separate schools. Six of these schools have been lost forever with their respective Guardians, but four remain. I am the Guardian of Destruction, Sean is the Guardian of Alteration, Jennifer is the Guardian of Illusion, and Elizabeth is the Guardian of Conjuration. Each of us is a specialist in our school."

"What happened to the other six schools? What are they?"

Aleksandar sighs. "That is a question best left to David."

"So I'll be learning from him and the others as well?"

"Learning the history of our ways, of the human race, is just as important as learning how to light a torch. With David, you will learn of these histories. Mary will bring order to our teachings and weave them together, and Evelyn will speak to you more of the future. Their teachings will reinforce and add depth to your training."

"Well, what do you think so far? What do you see in me?"

"Since your magic manifested when you used the power of the earth to destroy a car that was a threat to you, we've decided that destruction magic is a good place to start."

"Destruction magic sounds kind of dark."

"It is only so if you choose to use it to such ends. In stories, there is black magic and white magic. In reality, there is no such thing. There are only dark or light *wizards*. It is how the person behind the magic chooses to use the energy flowing through them that influences its colour. Which path you choose is not for me to decide."

I try to imagine a situation where I would choose darkness. I can't.

Aleksandar seems to read where my thoughts are. "Remember, the world is seldom black and white. It is shaded in greys that get lighter or darker with the choices we make. Regardless, we are a long way off from having to worry about that. If you are ever going to learn how to light the thirteen torches of the circle with magic, you will first need to learn how to light one on demand and under controlled circumstances. But this is tomorrow's task. For now, we sit in silence and meditate on how the circle feels."

This is how we spend the remainder of the day. By the time the torches have almost burned out, I feel fully at one with the circle that Aleksandar and I made.

Chapter Eleven

My brow is knotted in frustration. Aleksandar's face reveals that he is just as frustrated as I am.

It's been almost a full month since that first day in the circle, and I haven't been able to make even a wisp of smoke. I'm starting to think the Guardians have the wrong guy.

For three weeks, Aleksandar's has been the only face I've seen. Each day, I cast the circle and sit in darkness until Aleksandar finally arrives bearing a torch, which he uses to light the torches of the circle. Each day starts with a lesson and ends with him staring at me for hours while I stare at an unlit torch in frustration.

For what seems like the hundredth time, Aleksandar says slowly, "Remember, magic is just the physical manifestation of intention and will. If you have a torch that you want lit, what do you really want?"

"I want the torch to be on fire."

I stare at him for a moment, hoping the do-it-yourself part of the lesson is finally over, but he remains completely silent and impassive. We've had a battle of the wills each day for several days now, and I always lose.

Grumbling, I focus on the torch, willing fire into existence. Nothing happens. I concentrate harder until beads of sweat run down my face, but the torch remains as cold as the stone surrounding us. I look up at Aleksandar in exasperation.

He reaches out and picks up the torch. "What is your intention?" He holds up the torch mere inches from my face.

"To make the torch catch on fire."

"And how are you expressing your intention?"

"By focusing on fire."

He frowns. "You must learn to change the way you think. You told me you did well in school. Use your knowledge of science. Think about what causes fire."

"Heat."

"And what causes heat? Think deeply, Aiden."

I think back to high school science. "Friction and the movement of atoms."

"And what is magic?"

"The intention of my will on nature."

"So if you want the torch to cast light, what is your true intention?"

I stare at the torch in his hands for a few moments, and my understanding slowly begins to dawn. "To create enough heat at the centre of the torch that it catches on fire!"

Aleksandar passes the torch back to me. I hold it in my hands, focusing intently on the end of it. Nothing happens, but I feel like it wants to.

I change the way I hold it so it feels less like a stick of wood and more like a torch. I aim my free hand where I want the fire to ignite. I let my intention travel down my arm and into my fingers, gathering focus as it goes. I want the atoms at the end of the torch to move faster, to generate heat, to cause the torch to burst into flame. I want it desperately. I focus on this and nothing else.

The slightest scent of burning wood reaches my nose. Slowly, a tendril of smoke rises from the torch, and then, all at once, the end explodes into flame.

The stone-faced Aleksandar actually grins—if only for a second. He then stands and leaves without a word.

Drained and exhausted, I retire to my chambers. Magic, it turns out, takes a heavy toll on the body.

It's another several days before I can do it consistently. On the third day of the fourth week of my training, Aleksandar arrives to find the thirteen torches of the circle already blazing brightly and the circle alive with energy. I sit in the centre in quiet meditation. He stops just outside the circle and meets my eyes. Then he bows low, turns, and walks back the way he came.

I can't contain my happiness. I grin and then muffle a whoop of excitement. Joy expands within me, radiates beyond the circle, and echoes through the Chamber of Knowledge. With a whoosh of energy, the chamber responds.

All around me, massive wall sconces roar to life, the flames reaching high. I approach one slowly, but there is no visible source of the flame. It's as if the fire is fuelled by the magic of the chamber itself. I look around in wonder and notice that the sconces have illuminated a flowing script engraved on each of the grand columns that seems to glow with energy of its own. The ruby crystals at the top of the columns sparkle in the light of the sconces. With amazement, I turn to the sound of water. At first, it's just a trickle, but it swells rapidly, becoming the beautiful waterfall of my dreams as it cascades down the side of the spiral staircase. Entranced, I approach its base. Fresh misty water hits my face, cool and refreshing. I've never been this close to a waterfall.

The floor of the chamber here is staggered somewhat, and the water disappears into a small crack where the floor juts up slightly. It flows through a natural tunnel like a culvert and emerges on the other side of me, transforming a small depression in the chamber floor into a beautiful shallow pool that wraps around one of the columns and reaches toward the stone circle. I'm left standing on a narrow path leading from the circle to the spiral staircase.

Almost reverently, I squat and dip my hands into the water. It's as icy cold as the water in my quarters, but somehow it's so much more satisfying. It's been so long since I've been this close to fresh water, and deep down I know it's cleaner than any lakes or rivers I've seen.

My eyes follow the waterfall to its source on the upper level of the chamber. I can't see over the edge, but I know where it's coming from. I slowly climb the spiral stairs, feeling the magic of this place growing. When I reach the top, my mouth drops open. Just as it did in my dream, the mouth of the quartz river on the table has awakened and water rushes out of it. I reach out once more, cupping my hand, and I slowly raise the precious liquid to my lips. It's so fresh, so full of life.

My dreams continue to come true when the walls of the chamber brighten and layers of ancient dust fall away. Lannóg Eolas has felt magic within its walls once again and is coming alive.

I lower myself to the floor and dangle my feet off the edge. For what seems like hours, I sit like this, letting the magic of the place wash over me as I gaze out at the inscriptions on the columns, wondering what they mean.

Finally, hunger gets the better of me. Smiling, I descend the stairs, close my circle, and stroll to my quarters. My joy is tarnished only slightly by the sadness I feel that there's no one I can share this beautiful moment with.

When I enter my quarters, the flickering flame of a torch is bouncing off the walls. I halt in surprise, and then notice a dark figure huddled in front of my cupboard. With lightning-like speed, the figure springs and spins around to face me.

Instincts I didn't know I had flare to life. I crouch slightly, and my hands come up before me, glowing with brilliant flaming energy. Caitlin's face appears in the light cast by the uncontrolled flames churning around my hands. Her eyes go wide in surprise, and she takes two quick steps back, very slowly raising her hands defensively.

"It's me!" she yells. She continues her retreat until she's partially hidden behind the column. "It's me, damn it!"

My panic dissipates, and I focus on calming the fire that flows through my veins. I can feel as much as see the glow surrounding my hands fade away.

"Caitlin?" I call out quietly when the last of the fire is gone. I can barely see her behind the column. "It's safe. I'm sorry."

Several seconds pass before she reappears. My heart falls as I see the hesitation in her eyes, but she puts on a smile.

"I guess wizards don't like to be surprised by unexpected guests," she mumbles.

"I'm so sorry." For a second, I see the same Caitlin I saw that day at the waterfront—sweet, innocent, open—and I want to console her. And then I remember how skillfully she manipulated me, so I settle for a meek and unconvincing, "I would never hurt you."

She grimaces, seeing right through me. "I know, Aiden." She steps closer and places a hand on my shoulder. "Although what your magic might do before you realize it could be a different story. This is why the Guardians insist that you be alone during this part of your training."

She glances down at my hands. "That was impressive. You appear to be learning much quicker than the Guardian's thought you might."

I shake my head. "Thanks, but I have no idea what happened just now, or how to do it again. That was purely instinct." I walk over to the darkened fire pit and prod at the remains of some charred logs. Her being here now feels too uncomfortable. "What are you doing here?"

She raises her eyebrows. "Haven't you wondered how your clothes got here? Or where all of these supplies come from?"

I blink at her. I don't want to admit that I haven't thought about it.

She shakes her head. "Men," she mutters as she returns to the cupboard. "I have to finish stocking you up."

"I can do that myself if it will help."

"It won't," she says dryly.

I sit quietly while she restocks my cupboard with some food, as well as fresh towels, bedding, and clothes.

After a while, I decide that even the company of someone who betrayed my trust is better than no company at all. "Try to be careful when you leave." I wait for her to respond, but she doesn't react. "There's now a rather large waterfall and a pool that you'll have to pass on your way out," I say with a grin. I'm excited to see her response, but she doesn't even blink. She just continues emptying her bag into the cupboard. My grin fades and my voice goes dry. "Wouldn't want you to fall in because you didn't know about it."

"I've been by it already," Caitlin says finally. Her voice contains none of the excitement I thought would be there. She glances at me. "You know, you should be more alert when you sit high on a ledge in the open like that. If I'd been an enemy, you'd be dead."

"You walked past me?"

"I had to," she says briskly. "There's only one way in."

She says nothing else, but it's been so long since I've had company other than Aleksandar.

"Do you know what happens next?" I press. "I think I've passed the first of the Guardians' tests."

She doesn't reply. Moments later, she stands up. She appears to have recovered from the initial shock of our meeting. Any vestiges of the Caitlin I met at the waterfront are now gone, replaced by the dutiful aloofness of a Seeker. She zips up her dark-red leather jacket and slings her black leather backpack over her shoulder. She looks at me. "How the Guardians choose to train you is not my responsibility, wizard. My job was to find you and keep you safe until they could get you here."

She leaves without saying another word, and I'm left staring after her. Which Caitlin is the real one? The open and carefree one I met at the cafe? Or the no-nonsense one that just walked out of here without so much as a goodbye? I think of the alarm on her face when she saw the power I'm capable of, as well as the caring look in her eyes, the touch of her hand on my shoulder . . . They seemed instinctual and genuine. Yet, there's a side of her that seems impassive, or stoic. Perhaps these are the means by which she operates as one charged with the task of detecting, locating, and protecting wizards.

A darker thought enters my mind: What if the reason she says so little is because she's actively reading my mind? Earlier, she said she has low-level telepathic abilities, but she didn't explain what that means. Maybe she doesn't need to speak. After all, she's able to speak with me in my dreams.

I sigh, shaking my head. It's impossible for me to know the answer. I'll have to confront her about that the next time she's here. For now, I need to distract myself. David promised he would bring some books for me to read, but he hasn't come by yet, so I decide that a nap is the perfect way to restart the day. I change out of my robe, flop down onto my mattress, and close my eyes.

For the next several days, I begin each morning by diligently creating a circle in the Chamber of Knowledge and sitting in its centre to wait for a Guardian to approach. None have so far. On the third day, however, I got lazy and decided not to wear my robe. Not only did I manage to set fire to all the torches in the circle, but I also singed the sleeves of my shirt. Intrigued, I ran back to my quarters. After much practice, I concluded that, as unfashionable as they are, the robes are blessedly immune to—or at least resistant to—magic. It looks like there's no escaping them if I'm going to be practicing magic.

At the end of each day, after no sign of any Guardian, I would close the circle and explore a new part of the Citadel. None of the other chambers are as massive and glorious as the Chamber of Knowledge, but in one wing of the Citadel, I found what are clearly living quarters, with a kitchen and a proper bathing chamber connected to a series of separate smaller chambers. I made a mental note to ask the Guardians about staying there instead.

Down another corridor, I found a large room full of empty shelves. I could almost smell the thousands of books that might have filled them. Down another corridor, I found a room as large as the Chamber of Knowledge but with many rows of stone benches. Down yet another is a series of nondescript and rather empty chambers. From what I've seen so far, it appears that the Chamber of Knowledge is at the centre of the Citadel. The tunnels and corridors seem to radiate out of it like the spokes on a wheel. My mind fills with what I imagine to be the grand adventures of the wizards of old.

Today is day five of my solitude, and a small pit of despair has burrowed into me. Did something happen to the Guardians? For the first time since I arrived here, it dawns on me that I am truly alone in this ancient underground fortress. If the Guardians were unable, or unwilling, to return, would I ever find my way out? I could die here, alone and forgotten. Has that already happened? Is this some form of purgatory?

I sigh. I can't let that sort of thinking get the best of me. I decide to close the circle early. Taking one of the torches with me, I set out to explore a new tunnel. The tunnel I choose this time, however, seems darker than the others. The shadows are more foreboding.

My feet refuse to move forward. I'm paralyzed with fear. I haven't experienced anything like this with any of the other tunnels. I swallow hard. I'm overcome by an intense feeling of being watched, so I glance over my shoulder. The space behind me has gone dark as well. I wave the torch toward the Chamber of Knowledge, but all the brightness is gone. I can see nothing beyond the simple glow of the flame. It's as though I'm not even in the Citadel anymore.

For a moment, I think I should try to find my way back to my quarters, but now that I am within it, the same darkness that seemed to push me away from the entrance of the tunnel is now pulling at me, calling to me with a sweet, undeniable urging.

I take a step down the tunnel, sweeping the torch before me. The darkness envelops me, presses in on me from every direction. I put my left hand out, feeling for a wall, and continue inching forward slowly.

Three steps later, my hand touches cold stone. I shine the light of the torch toward my hand. Even though I know my hand is there, I can see nothing except the torch's glowing orb of fire. I step forward slowly, rounding a corner. As the passageway straightens, I feel the blackness stretching out behind me, and it snaps backward, making it feel like I just stepped out of a bubble. I find myself standing at the top of a narrow stone staircase. I look back over my shoulder and see a wall of impenetrable blackness behind me.

I shudder as the hair on the back of my neck stands straight on end. I slowly walk down the stairs until I find myself standing at the entrance of a low passageway built of rounded stone blocks. I reach out and touch one of the stones. It's damp to the touch, and the stone next to it is coated in moss. To my left, a torch flickers to life. It's as though this place senses my presence. Soon, an endless stream of torches stretches into the distance, lighting the way ahead among eerie shadows.

I stoop slightly as I enter the low tunnel. I feel a slight draft. It fills the passageway with a strong musty odour. I shiver involuntarily and continue deeper. Shelves roughly hewn into the stone walls line both sides. Each shelf is approximately a foot and a half high and roughly six feet long. The flickering light of the torches reveals random objects scattered here and there: a broken clay goblet, a metal medallion.

I continue forward. With every step, the air fills with the crunch of broken pottery. The sound echoes down the tunnel ahead of me. When I pass the final torch, I stop, awestruck. The tunnel opens into a room vastly larger than the Chamber of Knowledge. A moonbeam shines through a perfectly round oculus in the ceiling high above, revealing a gently sloping hill covered in lush green grass. A simple dirt path leads from the mouth of the tunnel and winds its way up the hill, through rows of long stone boxes and toward the centre of the room. At the top of the hill stands a large white stone box. It gleams in the moonlight.

I begin ascending the slope toward the large box. It's like my feet are on autopilot, leading me up the path. As I pass by the other boxes, I reach out and touch one. I cast the torchlight over its surface. It's rough and clearly hand-carved, but there's nothing else to indicate what it's for. Simply storage?

At the top of the hill, the path widens and deposits me onto a small grassy plateau with the white box at its centre. I gasp and step back several feet. Carved into the top of the box is a perfect representation of a man with a strong jawline, intense eyes, and square shoulders. His billowing robes are painted black with illegible gold script flowing up the sleeves and the head of a red dragon on his chest. He holds before him a staff topped with a dragon, radiating with power. Moonlight bathes his entire body.

Then the realization hits me. This is a tomb. This box is a casket. I look down the hillside. These are all caskets. I hold the torch high and channel my energy into it. Its flame roars higher, and light cascades down the side of the hill. Hundreds of caskets form a patchwork quilt of order and reverence. I think back to the shelves in the tunnel I just walked through, envisioning them instead as a network of catacombs where the corpses of wizards might once have lain peacefully at rest. I look down at the grass. I can only imagine how many wizards who came before me now lie buried beneath me.

In a daze, I take a step forward, but my foot comes down on uneven ground. I stumble, falling against the casket beside me. With a sickening sound the stone top shifts just enough for me to see black, billowing cloth with gold script within. My heart plummets as I imagine a bony hand underneath the cloth silently reaching up to slide the top open and grab my arm. Uncontrollable fear fills me until my bones feel as cold as ice and my breaths come deep and fast.

My mind is paralyzed by fear, but I'm dimly aware of my feet gaining a will of their own and sending me careening back the way I came, through the maze of caskets, through a catacomb so old that its inhabitants long ago turned to dust, and through the gates of darkness that tried to warn me away.

I don't stop until I'm safely back in my quarters, where I eventually succumb to sleep and am overrun by dreams of long-dead wizards chasing me through the halls of the Citadel.

When I wake, I almost jump out of my skin. All the torches are lit, the fire is roaring, and Caitlin is leaning against the wall, her arms crossed. She's staring at me.

I sit up and cross my legs. "How long have you been standing there?"

"Long enough to know you were having bad dreams."

"Wait . . . Were you watching them? Were you there?"

"Relax. I noticed you were tossing and turning. I've been here only a few minutes."

I rub the sleep out of my eyes. "Do you? Ever?" I ask while eyeing her warily.

"Do I what? Watch you sleep?" She waves her hand dismissively. "I have far more important things to do these days. I'm busy searching for other wizards, Aiden. I don't have time to eavesdrop on your thoughts, conscious or otherwise."

"Oh, okay. Well, good morning, I guess." I'm not sure I believe her, but at least it's an answer.

She sighs heavily and pushes herself off from the wall. "I'm glad you didn't try to kill me this time."

I scowl. The fog of sleep is still thick in my brain. "You seem determined to make me try," I say jokingly.

She passes me a mug. "You were shivering in your sleep when I came in, so I covered you up, stoked the fire, and made you some tea. I'm surprised I didn't wake you. You're a deep sleeper."

"I guess I am. Or maybe all of this magic stuff requires it." I sip the tea while the mug warms my chilly hands. I look over at the fire pit. Caitlin managed to place the grill over it and boil water in a steel kettle all while I lay there dreaming.

"Do you remember what you were dreaming about?"

The memory of looking into the casket of that nameless wizard makes me shiver, and I realize I can still feel the moonbeam tickling my skin and hear the faint call of the blackness surrounding the catacombs.

Caitlin looks at me with concern. "Is everything okay?"

I set the mug down on the stone floor. I force a smile before walking over to the basin to wash my face with ice-cold water. Something makes me hold back from telling her about my discovery of the tomb. "The constant solitude finally got to me yesterday, is all, and I started going a bit loopy."

I continue to wash the sleepiness from my face. "What day is it?" I ask.

"It's Saturday morning."

A couple of minutes go by, and the only sound is the splashing water. I feel Caitlin watching me.

"I guess I should come back when you're ready," she says.

I turn from the basin and reach for a towel. "No. It's okay. Believe me. I could use the company."

"Well, I have some news that should make you feel better. I spoke with the Guardians last night, and they've agreed to allow me to bring you somewhere you can use your wristband today . . . Somewhere safe. Maybe you can give James a call . . . or maybe your mother."

It's reassuring to know that she's thinking of me, and that the Guardians haven't forgotten about me. And she's right. As long as James will talk to me, it'll definitely raise my spirits, and I would feel much better knowing my mother is still doing okay.

I look down at the tiny device resting near my bed. I've had a wristband since I was ten, but for some reason, it feels foreign to me now. Maybe it's because the black scorch marks on it remind me of when it reacted to my magic and scarred my wrist. I press my thumb to its backplate, half expecting it to go up in smoke. The screen comes to life. Some of the pixels are dead, but otherwise the wristband seems okay.

"Hello, Aiden," the professional-sounding female voice says. "How can I help you today?"

A moment later, a much more mechanical voice speaks: "Warning: no signal."

"Enter silent mode." I know a lot of people do it, but I just can't bring myself to talk to my wrist all day long. I'd rather use the interactive motion features.

I look up at Caitlin. "No signal."

"Let's see what we can do about that."

"Are we actually going to go outside?" The thought of lungs filled with fresh air comes to me. Then the image of moonlight bathing the casket of the wizard fills my mind, and I push it away.

She smiles. "No, sorry. That's too dangerous. There are, however, places in the Citadel that are closer to the surface than others. I had your account modified to have worldwide coverage, so once we get a signal, it should work fine."

"Thank you. I'll eat breakfast later. Let me get dressed, and I'll be ready to go."

We make our way down one of the tunnels I've not yet explored. This tunnel branches off in several directions, and after the third right and the fourth left, I am completely lost. Caitlin walks quickly and purposefully, always staying a few feet ahead of me. It's a good thing I know how hard she worked to get me to the Citadel, because I'd otherwise think she was trying to lose me.

Our journey so far has been silent, but when we turn down yet another tunnel, I chuckle softly.

She glances over her shoulder at me without breaking her stride. "What's so funny?"

"I was just thinking how you're really living up to your title as Seeker with all of this twisting and turning. If I tried this on my own, you'd have to send out a search party."

She smiles and slows slightly to allow me to walk alongside her. She glances at me again, and I feel some of her aloofness fade. "I'll take that as a compliment."

We walk several more seconds in silence, and then she slows even more. "I've been exploring these tunnels for a long time. In many respects, Lannóg Eolas is as much my home as it is yours."

She doesn't say anything further, but I don't break the silence. I get the sense that she isn't finished speaking. Sure enough, after a few more seconds, she speaks again, her voice much quieter.

"The Guardians didn't just wait for you to show up, Aiden. They've been actively searching for you their entire lives. When I was seventeen, I ran away from my dysfunctional family when my dad was stationed in London. Sean's father, Patrick, was the one who found me. At the time, I was living on the streets, trying to prove to the world that I didn't need anyone. But the fact is, I was at the end of my rope. Patrick was still the Guardian of Alteration then. He was so nice. Looking at him, you just knew he was warm-hearted and kind. I felt ashamed that I'd planned to use him for a warm meal and an opportunity to steal as much as I could without getting caught."

"Wow." It's all I can think of to say.

She laughs quietly. "I was a little deviant back then. He brought me to a restaurant and paid for my meal. A hamburger. A *real* hamburger! I'd barely taken a bite when he told me he'd been drawn down that alley by my latent magical power."

"He sensed your magic?"

"Yeah. That's when I almost bolted. I was ready to drop that damn hamburger right there. There have been times when I felt it might have been better if I had, but I really needed some cash, and I thought I'd found myself an easy mark."

I chuckle. "I guess it was more than you bargained for."

"You could definitely say that. He brought me here and promised me that if I practiced hard, the Citadel would awaken and become a home like nothing I've ever had." She glances over at me and shrugs. "I didn't know where I was exactly, but it was shelter, and it was only a short walk from downtown London. He also told me there'd always be food. For some reason, it already felt like home, so I stayed. Over time, I actually started to believe that maybe I was the wizard he was searching for. They put me through test after test to try to prove I was like you, but I failed them all." She smiles wryly. "Until I showed them I could sense magic."

"What does that mean exactly?"

"It turns out I'm somewhere between a Guardian and a wizard. I have magic of my own, but my talent is so focused that the only thing it's good for is finding others like me—or, perhaps more accurately, others like you. Like I said earlier, I'm magic-sensitive. When someone with magic is nearby, it's almost like I can smell it. The Guardians called me Seeker and gave my life purpose . . . meaning. They loved me the way my mother never did and my father, as absent as he was, never could." She glances at me with sad eyes.

I can't imagine what it would have been like if I'd gotten here only to learn that the Guardians were wrong about me. I don't think I could have gone back to my normal life. I feel some of the anger I've been directing at her start to fade. "I'm sorry. That must have been difficult to accept."

She nods. "It took me years. To be honest, I wasn't sure I was actually over it until I saw you that night in the club. I've seen two people torch out in the past ten years, and that was more than enough for me to fully understand just how dangerous it would be to ignore the magic welling up inside you. I had to help them find you for your own sake."

"What do you mean, torched out?" As soon as I ask it, I'm afraid of the answer.

Caitlin stops me there in the tunnel. Her expression is dead serious in the flickering light. "It's what happens when people don't embrace their power before it embraces them. It's not a pretty sight. I've searched the world over for anyone with anything resembling the kind of strength you have. I got close twice before, but they couldn't embrace their power even as it overwhelmed them."

"So they torched out . . ."

She nods, and her eyes grow distant. I get the distinct sense that she's lost in a vivid memory.

"They both died of massive acute brain aneurysms. They were very messy."

She takes my hand, and her eyes find mine again. "I wasn't going to lose you that same way."

I squeeze her hand. I can feel myself beginning to forgive her. "So there were others like me?" I'm not sure if knowing I'm not the only one with this kind of power gives me comfort or crushes my ego.

"None who have passed the tests," she says without hesitation, which makes me wonder how many people have died while the Guardians searched for me.

"Thank you for saving me, and for keeping an eye out on James and Keegan . . . and my mother."

Caitlin smiles. "Of course. It's all part of my duties to you and the Guardians." She resumes walking down the tunnel. "I'll need to return to my other duties, though."

I catch up to her. "What do you mean?"

"Now that you're here, actively using magic, nature's magic is flowing stronger throughout the world. There'll be others whose powers will awaken, and they'll need my help and guidance."

I say nothing for a long time as I think about what's at stake. "It doesn't sound like you'll be able to do it all yourself."

"That's just it. I'm sincerely hoping I'll find some who will become Seekers like me." She pauses, holding up a hand. "We're here. Just through this opening."

We step into a small chamber that doesn't seem all that different from my quarters other than the fact that the air smells fresher. We place our torches into sconces on the wall, and I hold up the wristband. Sure enough, I've got a signal—just barely.

Scanning the screen, I find that James has left me twenty-six voicemails and nineteen texts. The first few texts are fairly innocuous inquiries into how I was doing and whether I'd found a job yet. They then get progressively more annoyed before they cycle from questioning to worried to angry and back to worried again. His voicemails carry a worried tone until they turn to pissed off. The final six messages are depressing daily checks to see if I'm still alive.

I ponder how I'm going to handle this. How do I tell my best friend that I'm alive and training as a wizard in a subterranean citadel below Ireland? There's no way to couch that in easy terms.

"I don't know how James is going to respond."

"Perhaps you should start with your mother," Caitlin says. "Give yourself a bit more time."

I sigh. "Good idea."

I check the time. It's 11:15 a.m. here, which means it's 6:15 a.m. in Toronto. It's a good thing both my mother and James are early risers.

My mother answers on the second ring. "Aiden?"

She sounds as though she can't believe it's actually me. Not for the first time, I wish I could convince her to get a wristband with video capability. She has always steadfastly refused, claiming she doesn't want people seeing how bad she looks.

"Hi, Mom!" I'm surprised by the emotion in my voice.

"How are you, baby? Your lovely friend Caitlin has been bringing me meals and your letters. I can't believe you won a trip to Ireland! How wonderful! I would have forgotten my wristband too. Did it finally get to you? Is that why you're calling me now?"

I'm five thousand kilometres away from home in the middle of a life-changing experience, and I have to lie to my mother. I feel tears spring to my eyes as I glance over the wristband at Caitlin. She studiously avoids looking at me.

"That's right, Mom. I had her send it by surface mail. You know how expensive these things are. It just arrived."

"Wonderful. She's a lovely girl, Aiden. Full of stories. You know she told me she's been to Spain!"

"Spain?"

"Oh, yes. I've always wanted to go to Spain," she says longingly.

I laugh. "Maybe we can go when I get back, eh, Mom?" I wipe away a tear that runs down my cheek.

"Only if one of us wins the lottery, I think."

I laugh again. "True, true. Has Suzanne been by?"

"Oh, yes. She came by Sunday and made a lovely dinner."

My sister cooked? I keep the surprise out of my voice. "That's wonderful, Mom. And you have enough medication and everything?"

"Yes, dear. Caitlin mentioned you were very concerned I might have run out, but you must have got the dates confused because I still had enough for another week."

"That's good. That's one less thing to worry about."

"Anyway, honey, I know it must be costing you a fortune to call me from there, so I'll let you go." The sadness in her voice causes guilt to well up within me. "You make sure you visit me the moment you're back in Toronto! I want to hear all about your trip. Ireland!"

"We can talk longer, Mom," I say quickly, not wanting to hang up. "I have a pretty good plan."

"Aiden..."

I can almost see her rolling her eyes. "Yes?"

"There's no such thing as a good plan. I know you can't afford this. You hang up and enjoy your trip now. Mamma loves you, sweetheart."

I squeeze my eyes shut. "Thanks, Mom. I love you too."

The sound of her television unmuting briefly fills the air before she disconnects.

Caitlin smirks. "It sounds like I have a fan."

"Thank you so much for visiting her. It means a lot." Any reservations I had about her character have vanished.

She doesn't say anything. She simply bows her head in acknowledgement.

I stare at the wristband for a long moment while watching the seconds tick by on the screen. I finally flick my wrist, and James's face appears. I press the little phone icon. He answers halfway through first the ring, and his face appears above the wristband.

He glowers at me. "*Aiden?*"

I cringe at the anger in his voice. "Hey, James. How's it going?"

"Don't 'hey, James' me, man! Where the *fuck* have you been for the past month and a half? I need some answers, asshole."

I swallow hard. "Well, it's kind of a long story, but it basically involves me getting hit by a car—well, almost hit by a car, anyway—and then being abducted to Ireland."

A long, heavy silence is the only response I get.

"Oh, and maybe some, uh, magic?" I turn my back when Caitlin grimaces at me. "It's hard for me to remember, really. I was unconscious for a while, and I've kind of been trapped in a cave for another few weeks since coming to."

"Did you say magic? In a cave? Are you *high*? And what do you mean you're in Ireland? There are pictures of you all over the news. Do you know that? You know you could have called me if you were in any kind of trouble.

You could have at least answered your damn phone! I've been calling you non-stop! Danielle and I have searched *everywhere* for you! I even went out on a limb and asked Keegan to try to do some of his voodoo shit to see if he could find you. You know I don't believe in that crap, so I've obviously gotten really desperate here. All he could say was you were 'drifting in the blackness,' whatever that means."

He's silent for a few seconds, and I see him squinting at something he sees behind me. "Where are you? Are you really in *cave*?"

"I know it's hard to believe, but . . . well . . . I really am in Ireland . . . in a cave. Do you want to visit?"

"Visit? *Ireland?*" His voice is incredulous. "I thought you said you were abducted," he says bluntly.

His lawyer's mind is seizing on an inconsistency in my story. I'll have to tread more carefully. I turn around and look at Caitlin again, and she shakes her head at the mess I'm making.

"Okay," I say, "maybe I wasn't abducted per se . . ."

James shakes his head disbelief.

"It's very complicated," I say, "and difficult to explain over the phone, but . . . let's just say everything is related. My headaches, the church, the car accident at Union Station—"

James starts to speak, but I put my hand up to stop him.

"In a way you were right," I continue. "The headaches were from stress. It just wasn't the stress I was expecting, and it wasn't anything I could have prepared for. James, I spent three weeks in a coma."

James's eyes go wide. "Are you serious?"

"The people here helped me recover, and they're still helping me now, but I need you here, James. I need my best friend to help me get through this."

James stares at me, through me. I can sense his skepticism warring with his humanity. "Just like that? Drop everything and visit you in Ireland?"

"I know it sounds crazy, but yes."

His face scrunches up, and for one horrifying moment I think he's going hang up on me. Then he sighs. "Aiden, man, I hate you for making me this worried about you that I'm actually half thinking of agreeing to this."

I smile at him. "I'd really appreciate it if you did."

He chews on his bottom lip. "Fine. But I think you're losing your mind.

I'm doing this only to make sure you're okay, and if you are, you've got some explaining to do. I'll book myself a spot on the next flight."

"Actually, the people who have been taking care of me have offered to pick you up. They can get you here faster and cheaper than flying."

James is shaking his head before I finish speaking. "Aiden . . . I want to believe you haven't completely lost it, so I'm not even going to bother to ask you what in hell is faster and cheaper than *flying*. I'll be on a flight to . . . Dublin? Does that work?"

Caitlin nods in the background.

"Yes," I say. "I'll have someone meet you there."

"Who's meeting me?" James asks. "How will they know who I am?"

Caitlin steps up beside me, and James's eyes go wide at the sight of her. She smiles, and she looks stunning even in the torchlight. I try not to gawk as she talks to James.

"Caitlin here." She gives a little wave. "My darling James, I will meet you at the Oak Cafe Bar in Terminal Two."

James blinks and then practically stutters before he speaks again. "I just booked the flight. I'll see you in Dublin at five in the morning."

The hologram blinks out.

"Well," I say, "overall, I think that went pretty well."

Chapter Twelve

Before Caitlin left to meet James at Dublin Airport, she assured me that she would hide the fact that she had been secretly keeping an eye on him and Keegan in Toronto for the past month. I waited for them in the Chamber of Knowledge, anxious to see my best friend again.

When they arrived, Caitlin wasted no time leaving, saying she had to go collect firewood and run some other errands. I think she wanted to avoid any potential drama between James and me.

James stands with me, silent and slack-jawed, beside the massive table engraved with the wondrous map. We watch the water cascade out of the open quartz river mouth. We gaze out at the stone circle below us and the Guardians sitting around it in silent meditation. The Chamber of Knowledge is looking particularly radiant today: the quartz rivulets on the table sparkle; the dark red crystals at the top of each grand, soaring column gleam in the torchlight; and the water is clear, crisp, and perfect. Slowly, his hand reaches out to tug on my robe.

"Aiden?"

"Yes, James?"

His voice is soft and reverent. "I know this place, right? This is the place from that vision with Keegan?"

"It's kinda scary, eh?"

"It's absolutely terrifying!" He peers over the edge at the lower chamber once more, staring at the Guardians.

James leans in close to me. "And who are those people?"

"They're the Guardians of Knowledge," I say simply.

He looks at me when I don't elaborate. "Don't give me any of that 'you don't need to know' bull like they'd say in a movie. We all saw the vision—you, me, Keegan... We're meant to know what all of this is."

I smile. "Come. I'll tell you everything in my quarters, where we'll have some privacy."

We walk down the spiral staircase, and James reaches out to touch the water cascading down beside us. He holds his hand before him and takes in the scent. "It's so fresh!"

"Beautiful, isn't it?"

James looks at the water longingly. "Can you... you know... drink it...?"

"Yes, give it a try."

James cups his hands and briefly holds them under the water. He then draws his hands to his lips and drinks. He swallows the water in a big gulp, his eyes closed.

"Well, what do you think?"

He looks at me and grins widely. "Wow." He laughs. "It tastes... nothing like the water at home."

"It's basically mineral water, except, you know, natural instead of bottled for rich people."

James laughs.

We continue down the stairs and find ourselves in the shadow of one of the grand sarsen stones. James says nothing as I lead him past the meditating Guardians toward my quarters. I tried to convince them they didn't need to be here, but they insisted on being on hand in case James took the revelations as poorly as I did.

When we enter my quarters, James roams the place, taking everything in.

I gesture at the white stone bench. "Have a seat. Can I get you something to drink? More water? Tea?"

"I think we're going to need something substantially stronger than either of those." He nudges my hay mattress with his foot. "Is that seriously what you've been sleeping on?"

"It's more comfortable than it looks. It gets pretty damp in here, and the hay holds the heat nicely."

James walks over to the bench and takes a seat, shifting uncomfortably. "Well, at least it's not as hard as this thing..."

I chuckle quietly. "I'll make us some tea." I grab the steel kettle and fill it with water. "I'm afraid we don't have any alcohol here, or at least I don't think we do. There's still so much I don't know about this place."

He watches without comment as I toss a couple of logs into the fire pit. I aim my hand at the pit, and the logs burst into flames.

"Holy shit!" James almost falls off the bench. "How the hell did you do that?"

I pull the grill over the fire and place the kettle on it. As we wait for the water to boil, I can feel his eyes burning into the back of my head, but I'm grateful that he decides not to press me. When the kettle whistles, I fill two mugs with hot water and tea. I sit then beside him and pass him his cup.

"So, where should I start?" I ask.

The way James looks at me makes me believe he's second-guessing coming to visit me. "How about starting with what you just did to the fire?"

I smile, but he remains stone-faced. Fair enough, I suppose. If our roles were reversed, I'd probably want an explanation too.

"It turns out that the headaches I've been complaining about, the dreams I've been having, and all of our wristbands dying that night are all a result of my being the first wizard to walk the Earth in about three thousand years. I was getting the headaches because I wasn't using the magic inside my blood, and it was building and building with no outlet." I shudder.

"You were in pretty rough shape for a while . . . but magic . . . ?"

"The Guardians said the pressure would have killed me, that I was actually very close to that happening. When I was almost hit by the car, it snapped me into instinct mode, and the magic escaped."

James sips his tea and stares into the fire. I know that look. He's not buying my story, and he's losing patience.

"James, I know this goes against everything you know to be true, but I'm asking you to suspend your disbelief for a while and just . . . listen to me."

He takes another sip of his tea. He's quiet for a long time, and then he looks at me. "Go on. That plane ticket was expensive. I'll listen."

I'm not sure if he's joking, so I smile instead of laugh. He doesn't return it. He's looking at me with his serious lawyer's eyes.

I set my mug down on the bench. I rise and pace the room a bit before speaking. "The world isn't the place we think it is, James. Three thousand years ago, a man named Nuada, the last wizard this world has seen, created the Guardians to safeguard the knowledge of magic until someone came along who could use it. When he died, the powers of the Earth tipped out of balance and have continued tipping ever since."

"Leading to the shitstorm the world is facing right now."

"That's one way to put it. Magic, it seems, is part of nature. We need magic to return the world to balance. The way I understand it, it has been lying dormant for all of these centuries, waiting for a time when the power of religion dies away enough for it to make a resurgence." I pause for a moment. "Apparently that time is now, and I'm the one with the ability to use it. The more I use it, the stronger it gets . . . and people's blood will start calling for it."

James continues sipping his tea as he mulls over my words. He then leans forward and stares into the fire for another couple of minutes.

I sit down beside him again and return to my own tea. I'm dying to know what he's thinking.

James finally turns to me and says, "Ever since that day at Keegan's shop, he and I have been getting headaches as well." His voice falls to a whisper. "The same type that you were having."

I stare into my tea. "Evelyn, the eldest of the Guardians, thinks that you completed a circuit when you touched Keegan and me that night, which sent my magical charge flowing into all of us. The headaches are the first sign that there is magic within you trying to manifest itself."

"Wait . . . You're saying you somehow supercharged me into being a wizard? Keegan too?"

"That's basically what I mean."

"And I can either accept it or die?" He looks at me, searching my face for the answer. He must not like what he sees, because he runs a hand through his hair and stands up. "That's a shitty choice, Aiden." He slams his mug down on the bench. "I need to go for a walk. Is there anywhere we can go?"

I know James well enough to know that he's really asking to go somewhere relatively normal. The living quarters with the kitchen I found down one of the tunnels will do nicely.

"Yeah." I set my own mug down. "I'll take you on a short tour of one of the tunnels here."

I grab a torch, and we enter the Chamber of Knowledge. James looks at the

Guardians seated around the circle, but it's not until we've started down the tunnel that he says anything.

"Tell me more about these Guardians. Are they just going to sit there until I leave?"

"Probably. They're not used to having visitors, but they wanted to be here in case we needed their help, especially given how poorly I reacted when I got here. They're teachers. Four of them teach about the various disciplines of magic. One teaches the history of magic and the world. Another teaches the fundamentals of magic and how everything fits together. The seventh is called the Speaker."

"The Speaker?"

"Yeah, she's basically the voice of Mother Nature."

"Mother Nature . . ."

"The one from whom all magic flows. Some of them refer to her as the Goddess."

"So my Wiccan aunt had it right all along?"

I chuckle. "In a manner of speaking. Mother Nature provided magic so that humans who could attune themselves to it would be able to harness the elements and help improve life for animals, humans, and plants. All would benefit, and the world would remain in balance."

"Why'd she take it away?"

"Her power weakened as religions grew stronger until they were finally able to overthrow her. It's taken three thousand years of working behind the scenes for her to stage a comeback."

"Hmm," James says. "Vengeful bitch, eh?"

I laugh quietly. That remark almost sounded like the James I know. There might be hope yet. "Your kind of woman! The Speaker is her voice, a direct conduit from her to the rest of the Guardians. She's how they knew I was about to 'explode.'"

I let him digest that for a moment before continuing. "The last wizard, Nuada, split his craft into ten different schools. Some of these are lost, but the ones that remain are destruction, illusion, conjuration, and alteration. The Guardians are like encyclopedias devoted to each of them.

"Aleksandar, for instance, is the Guardian of Destruction, so he'll be teaching me everything there is to know about magic such as fireballs and tornadoes and earthquakes, if that's what my strength is. It turns out that what I did to the car in Toronto was a variation of an earthquake spell."

James shoves his hands into his pockets and starts looking around. I take this as a cue to stop talking for a while, so we just wander down the tunnel. We look into a few of the empty rooms as we go. After about ten minutes, he stops and stares down the passageway. It shows no sign of ending.

"This place is huge," he says. "Does it loop back, or will we have to turn around?"

"If it loops back, I've never made it that far."

He stares for another few seconds before turning back the way we came. I follow him and try to make small talk a couple of times, but he doesn't bite, so we walk in silence until we return to my quarters.

James sits, cradling his head in his hands. "Do you really think I might be a wizard too?"

I sit beside him and place my hand on his back. "There's only one way to find out," I say quietly. "Do you want to try some magic?"

He doesn't budge, but I feel his body tense beneath my hand.

"It will help relieve your headaches."

It takes a few seconds, but then he looks at me like I'm crazy. He swallows hard, and I see a resolve growing in his eyes. "What do I do?" he asks quietly.

"Magic is all about intent. It's about using your will to influence the state of something outside of yourself. I find it really helps me to use my hands as focus points, but you could probably use anything. I'm guessing that's why so many depictions of wizards include wands and staffs. They're focus aids. Focus all of your attention on the fire. Notice how the flames ripple in the drafty air? You can try to put the fire out all you want, but you'll never do it if you focus on the flames, because that's not the actual source of the fire. Move your focus down the flames until you see the coals beneath the wood."

I watch as James concentrates on the coals. After a while, the flames reach higher. He's definitely starting to figure it out.

"Good," I say. "The coals need oxygen to burn, so I want you to focus on starving them of it. Smother them completely until the fire goes out."

For a long moment, nothing happens. Then James pushes off the bench. "Screw it! It's not going to happen today, Aiden, but thanks for letting me try."

David appears at the entrance to my quarters. "Hello there." He smiles, but his eyes look serious. "There's no need to be disheartened, my boy. It took Aiden weeks to do more than cause a small amount of smoke. The fire responded to your attention when you focused on it, which means our suspicions are correct. Different wizards will show different aptitudes, at least untrained. I believe it would be prudent to begin including you in our daily lessons."

James doesn't answer right away. He stares into the fire for a moment, and then he smiles at us. It's a genuine, heartfelt smile. "I've spent my entire life not believing in God or anything that I can't see with my own two eyes. But I've seen this. I've felt this. And as crazy as it sounds, it feels real. It'll take me some time to fully accept it all, but there's no other reason for these headaches."

"No other reason?" I ask. I find this a curious thing for James to say.

"I've been to the doctor, of course. Everything checked out. She said it was probably stress." He winks at me.

I laugh. "Tell me about it."

"Our friend Keegan will also have to join us," James says to David. "He must be affected too."

David bows his head. "Of course. Are you prepared to leave the life you had behind and begin a new one? Once you begin your training, it won't be safe for you to return to your normal life, should you so choose, until your training is finished. Your wristband won't work here, and contact with your loved ones will be short and carefully monitored."

"Can my fiancée, Danielle, visit me?"

David inclines his head in agreement but raises a hand. "She is welcome here, of course, but once your studies start, you, Keegan, and Aiden will be isolated until you can demonstrate an ability to use your magic in a controlled fashion. After that point, she is once again welcome."

James looks at me with just a hint of a smirk. "I wonder if a 'Bachelor of Magic' will be as challenging as a 'Bachelor of Laws?'"

David smiles. "You and Caitlin shall go together to bring Danielle and Keegan here. Unfortunately, it's not yet safe for Aiden to leave."

James looks at me, his eyes wide. "I can't believe this is happening!" He laughs. "Magic! I'm going to learn magic!"

It's difficult not to laugh along with him.

Chapter Thirteen

Caitlin returns with James, Keegan, and Danielle. The men each carry a large duffel bag containing their belongings. They chat and laugh as they enter the Chamber of Knowledge. Danielle follows cautiously in stunned silence. I notice she has no luggage of any kind, which means that James is abiding by the rules. If she were going to stay, she would have arrived with a wagon's worth of clothes.

Upon entering the Chamber of Knowledge, Danielle and Keegan gaze in open amazement at the high vaulted ceilings, the circle of standing stones, the ancient stone table, the waterfall—all of it. Their amazement turns to hesitation when the Guardians file in and stand before us. Their hoods are down, so they're not as intimidating as they could be, but even on a good day, they're still rather enigmatic.

James, in a show of bravado, sweeps Danielle into a hug. "Pretty amazing, isn't it, babe? This will be my home for the next while. I wish you could stay with us."

Danielle looks at him and smiles sweetly. "Honey, I don't even camp in trailers. The thought of spending a few months in a cave practically gives me hives. Look at how much effort it took you to convince me to come by for just an hour."

James returns her smile. "You'd never let me do this if you didn't at least see it."

"True." Almost overtly, she begins caressing her rosary beads. She gives the Guardians a dubious look. "This," she says with a sweeping gesture that manages to include both the Guardians and the Chamber of Knowledge, "is pretty much a slap in the face of everything I believe in."

James grimaces and looks at me. I shrug awkwardly. The truth is, she's right. It will be impossible to reconcile what James, Keegan, and I are going to learn here with Danielle's Catholic upbringing. Part of me is surprised she hasn't been struck down by lightning simply for setting foot in this place.

She looks around and runs a finger slowly along the triskelion on the throne closest to her. "It is lovely, though. It looks so old!" Her dark amber eyes settle on me, and a huge grin spreads across her face. Forgetting her unease, she rushes forward and envelops me in a hug. "Aiden! We were so worried about you! I thought for sure you'd be in terrible condition from living underground and after the accident and everything, but you actually look pretty great!" She reaches out and plucks at the fabric of my robe. "And the robe suits you somehow." She laughs.

I grin. "I think I wear it well! I'm sure James and Keegan will have identical robes provided to them in our quarters. If they're lucky, they will look as good on them!"

Danielle and I laugh. James's face lights up, but Keegan's seems to go ashen at the prospect.

I turn to James and give him a tight hug. "Thanks for coming back." I then give Keegan a hug every bit as tight. "Thanks for trusting James enough to come!"

Keegan smiles. "I know we'd just met, but it was pretty intense. We shared an amazing experience. When James told me what happened to you and offered me a chance to better tap into my powers . . . well, how could I resist?"

Evelyn approaches slowly, using her staff as a support. I notice Danielle gripping her rosary a little tighter as she gets closer. Evelyn smiles. It's the type of smile a grandmother would dole out to her most loved grandchildren. It even seems to make Danielle relax a bit.

"It's been many centuries since these halls have felt this much life, but look! Even the Chamber of Knowledge is happy!"

She's right. The remainder of the centuries-old dust is falling away from the walls, revealing a brilliant white stone that almost seems to emit its own light.

"In times long past," Evelyn continues, "these caverns were the home of many different wizard families who lived together in harmony. Perhaps they shall be once again!"

"Maybe they shall!" David says. "But for now, I think we should let these lads get changed and settled in. Danielle, when you're ready, Caitlin will take you home. Once James gets a handle on his ability to use magic, you will be welcome to return."

"Thank you," Danielle says. Then, as she peers at the stone circle, she says a bit quieter, "How do you know we're actually in Ireland?"

I'm about to answer, but Sean steps forward. He smiles disarmingly. "We can go only by our histories."

At first, I find his generic answer odd, given that they weren't shy in telling me we were beneath Skellig Michael. Then I realize he's being far more prudent than I would have thought to be. Danielle is a devout member of the Catholic Church, one of the world's largest bastions of faith and a primary seat of El's power. I wonder if the Guardians would have agreed to let her visit if they'd known beforehand how religious she was. I glance at them. They appear quite stoic, but they might very well be deeply concerned about having her in our midst.

Danielle nods. "Okay. Well, I came more or less to make sure James hadn't completely lost his senses. When he came running to tell me he'd found Aiden in Ireland and that I had to come with him, I thought he'd finally lost it. When he called the university to put his studies on hold and then packed his bags, I knew he'd lost it for sure. Now I don't know what to think, to be honest."

"I know what you mean," James says. "I thought that about Aiden too at first."

David taps his staff lightly, and we all turn to him. "Perhaps the four of you would like to chat privately over dinner?"

"Oh!" I exclaim, looking at Danielle. "I wasn't even thinking. I'm sorry. Dinner won't be fancy, but if you'd like to see where James will be spending his free time, I can show you our quarters."

I can only imagine that what she really wants to do is leave—and leave quickly—but she smiles and says, "That would be wonderful, Aiden."

I step past the Guardians. "Right this way."

James quickly follows me and grabs hold of my arm. He bends toward my ear. "No magic in front of her," he hisses.

Danielle and Caitlin stand side by side at the entrance to the tunnel that leads to Toronto. The rest of us mill about as we each say goodbye.

Danielle grips both of my arms and stares me straight in the eye. "You look after him, Aiden. I won't pretend to understand any of this. I'm only letting him stay because you're here." She squeezes tighter and furrows her brow. "If anything happens to him, I'll find these caverns come hell or high water and will strangle you myself—magic or no magic!"

I laugh lightly, unsure whether she's joking.

She briefly says goodbye to Keegan before turning to James. They embrace tightly, kiss passionately, and stare longingly into each other's eyes. James murmurs something to her too quiet to hear and she replies, squeezing his hands tightly. After a few moments, Danielle wipes a tear from her eye and turns to Caitlin. Together, they step through the tunnel and disappear into the darkness.

We watch them go.

James leans in close so that only Keegan and I can hear him. "If you have any notions of making this our headquarters, we're going to have to install a rail system along the tunnels so it's a whole lot easier and quicker to go back and forth. I'm not hiking a couple of hours each way every time I want to have sex! Plus, think of the money we could make offering fifteen-minute express trains to Europe!"

Keegan laughs.

I give James a punch in the arm. "You'd hike twice that distance. Come on. Let's get settled in for the night. We'll likely have a long day tomorrow."

When we arrive at our quarters, we discover two more sleeping pads set up in the room.

James looks at me. "I guess this means we're not expected to cuddle to keep warm!"

"Damn!" Keegan says with a grin.

We all laugh.

Keegan checks the place out. "Sweet digs," he says jokingly as he tries out the stone bench.

"The simplicity of it all actually grows on you," I say. "The fire will keep us warm and toasty, and it doubles as a cooking fire. We can shower and bathe in the basin there. Admittedly, the water is quite cold. One of us will have to learn a spell to heat it up."

Keegan walks over to the basin in dips his hand in the water briefly before pulling it out. "Yikes . . . You're not kidding."

I then briefly explain to them the other necessities regarding food, supplies, where to go to relieve ourselves, and so forth.

"Any other neat places to show us?" Keegan asks.

"This place is huge," I say. "We'll be able to explore for a long time." It dawns on me how happy I am to have friends here with me.

We hear the rap of a staff on stone. James and Keegan stiffen, looking to the entranceway anxiously. A moment later, Mary appears.

"Greetings, wizards," she says. Her robe billows behind her as she strides in confidently.

When I last saw Mary, her curly black hair was dusted with grey. She's cut it since then and spiked it. She also changed the grey to purple highlights.

She inclines her head slightly to James and Keegan. "My name is Mary. I specialize in the fundamentals of magic."

She holds a canvas sack out to James and Keegan. "These are practice robes for the two of you." She pauses long enough for them to grab the sack and pull the robes out. "We've decided that it would be prudent to initiate you as wizards before we begin your lessons. It will bind the three of you together even more, making all of your experiences that much more meaningful."

James and Keegan look at each other, uncertainty on their faces, before they look at me. I shrug noncommittally.

"I've never experienced one, so I don't know what to tell you," I say.

"It's nothing to worry about," Mary says. "It's a simple yet beautiful ceremony."

"Guys, I can say without hesitation that the Guardians have given me no reason to distrust them in the month I've known them."

"Is there anything we need to do to prepare?" James asks.

"Nothing except get cleaned up and into your robes," Mary says. "When you're ready, please join us in the Chamber of Knowledge. Aiden, you will have to light the torches and guide our new wizards through the ritual. We have discovered the way to dim the flames within the sconces so it will be dark."

With that, Mary leaves as quickly as she arrived.

We ready ourselves in silence. Our growing jovialness gives way to a strange mixture of mild apprehension and giddy excitement. Following my normal routine when preparing for ritual, I wash myself fully without rushing. It's something I've done daily since arriving, and I feel it helps wash away all distractions and rinse my spirit clean. James and Keegan follow suit.

As the three of us don our robes, I'm surprised to notice that Keegan has several tattoos in addition to the Eye of Providence on his calf: some strange symbols running up the back of his left leg, an eagle on his right shoulder, and a phoenix at the base of his spine. Tattoos aren't exactly popular these days, and with his sense of fashion, I would have thought he'd have eschewed them.

James turns to me while he ties his rope around his waist. "What happens now, sensei?"

I smile. I think for a moment how best to set the tone for the initiation. I go with grave. "From this moment on, we three are equal as brothers. We have shared one deep experience already and will experience many more. Come and let us be initiated together as wizards."

I step forward, embrace Keegan, and kiss him on the cheek. I then do the same with James. I watch as they also exchange the gesture.

"We will be creating a sacred circle now and entering it for the initiation. Follow me closely. Pause when I pause, and speak what I speak. Most importantly, allow yourself to fully feel the energy flowing through the space."

We step out of our quarters to find the Chamber of Knowledge pitch-black except for seven tiny candles, each held tightly in the palm of a Guardian. In the flickering light of the candles, I see that the Guardians are in full ritual mode: their hoods are up, their staffs are at the ready, and they stand evenly spaced around the circle's perimeter. Evelyn stands at the exact centre of the circle, ready to perform the actual initiation. We approach from the west and slowly walk sunwise around the circle. As we pass each torch, I pause and whisper, "*Bheith ag lonrú.*" Each torch roars to life at my command. We reach the north, where a Guardian wears the mask of a wolf. Beneath the robe, I can just make out David's customary tweed bow tie. I face him, and sense the energy of the spot churning through the four of us.

"Picture a rich forest surrounding us," I say slowly, my voice low but powerful. "With the blessing of the great wolf of the evergreens, I call upon the powers of the north."

I throw open my arms, and my two friends do likewise. The wolf opens its mouth and releases its power in a mighty howl. The energy exchange is palpable. This must be the first time David has seen the circle in full power; the amazement burns in his eyes.

We continue around the circle, pausing at each remaining cardinal point to call upon the powers of the hawk, the stallion, and the salmon. When we return to the west, we turn as one to the circle's centre.

"This is sacred time," I say. "This is sacred space. We are fully present, here and now."

I revel in the power of the earth, sea, and sky washing over me. James and Keegan stand on either side of me, their eyes wide and dancing with a combination of excitement and fear. Every torch in the circle is now lit, and the faint light dances upon the stones.

As one, we step toward the centre. We approach Evelyn and lower our heads.

"Who comes before this circle?" she asks. Her voice is ancient, commanding. It comes from her with such a force that I am quite sure it's not just her behind it.

"I do," I answer.

"I do," James says.

"I do," Keegan says.

"And for what purpose do you approach?" the Speaker asks.

An uncontrollable shudder rushes through me. I know this voice. Caitlin's voice sounded like a hundred forests singing together in my dreams, but this voice is old beyond old, full of unrestrained power, and it awakens a deep longing in my soul. *This* is the voice that made me terrified of falling asleep. *This* is the voice that woke me in a cold sweat so many times over the past six years. For the first time in my life, I know the source of that voice: the Speaker is channelling the Goddess—Mother Nature—herself.

"I speak for all of us," I say, willing my trembling body to still. "We come to you as students. We wish to be initiated as wizards, stewards of your power."

"You would work to restore the old ways of respect for the Earth and the balance and harmony amongst all things?"

Our three voices answer her in unison: "We would."

"Kneel!"

The command comes as a thunderous boom that echoes through the chamber and causes the torches to flicker. The three of us fall to our knees in instant obedience.

The ground beneath me shudders, and the world spins. When it steadies, damp earth presses against me from all directions. I dig frantically, reaching for the surface, but the earth grows heavier and threatens to crush me. I struggle for what feels like hours. An intense feeling of claustrophobia grows in the pit of my stomach, and I begin to think I'll never escape.

I hear my mother's voice in my head, her excitement at my being in Ireland. I realize that if I die here, she'll never know what happened to me. I can't die here. She needs me still. I focus, calming the beating of my heart, and reach out again. This time, a fresh, cool air strikes my fingertips and, with a huge sense of relief, I dig my way out, coughing up the black earth. As my vision clears, I see Keegan and James doing the same thing.

I clear my throat of dirt, and the sound of rushing water fills the chamber. I barely have time to look up before a giant wave of water slams into me. The force knocks me over and sends me tumbling through an overwhelming current.

I swim furiously for the surface, but the current drags me, driving me deeper into the water. I struggle to form a picture of my mother in my mind; her long brown hair, her brown eyes framed by worry lines but so full of love, and her smile that comes so easily despite all of her hardships solidify in my mind's eye. Even with her now sallow and sunken face, she's beautiful. I feel love flowing from her, and with a painful slowness, I begin to feel lighter than the water. I focus on the lightness and shoot upward, breaking the surface like a dolphin.

I land on dry, hot sand, coughing violently as I spew salt water. My eyes sting; I can't see anything, but I hear James and Keegan coughing next to me.

Before I can speak, a furious wind strikes up. It whips at my robe and tears at my skin. It's a solid wall of wind that pushes me backward. This time, I keep the image of my mother clear in my mind as I struggle forward. The wind grows stronger and continues to force me back. I struggle harder. Although I can't see it, I know there is an anchor that will hold me strong in this wind if I can only reach it.

Another step. I cannot breathe. The wind is so strong that it presses air into my lungs, causing me to suffocate. Again, I take a step. The world is going dark from a lack of oxygen. I feel the cuts on my face where sand and other debris thrash my skin. Through the blowing sand, I see a tree standing strong, calm, and beautiful in the storm. I know that if I can reach it, I will be saved.

Halting step after halting step, I stagger toward the tree, my arm outstretched. I cannot seem to get any closer. Before me, my mother shakes her head like I'm a child unable to understand a simple lesson. What am I missing?

I notice something at the base of the tree. I have to squint to see it. There, mere steps from the tree, is me. I see myself squinting and struggling headlong into the wind. I've been fighting all this time to reach a reflection.

I turn my back to the wind, and the tree stands before me. It's strong and powerful. Its wide trunk invites me to take shelter from the storm. I take two easy steps and wrap my arms around a large low-hanging branch. Keegan staggers up and clings to the branch as well. Then James appears, tears streaming down his face as he reaches for the branch. When he touches it, the tree vanishes.

We find ourselves once again kneeling before the Speaker. Around us, the torches have gone out, but streams of light swirl around the circle. The Guardians are chanting. With voices deep and energized, they utter the same refrain over and over, and it spills throughout the chamber in waves: "Fill them with strength, fill them with love, fill them with wisdom." Their hair is windswept, and their robes are soaked.

From Evelyn's place in the circle comes a voice that fills the entire chamber: "Rise."

We stand.

As Evelyn opens her arms, her whole body shifts.

Where Evelyn once was stands a tall, striking woman in a billowing green gown. Her pearl-white face is framed with red flowing hair that shines brilliantly in the light swirling around the circle. She is the epitome of strength and beauty.

"Behold, Guardians!" she speaks. "These three are to bear my power and magic out into the world. They have faced the element of earth and proven they have the strength to overcome it. They have faced the element of water and proven they have the love to overcome it. They have faced the element of air and proven they have the wisdom to overcome it. I grant them now the element of fire that they may unite all living things! Train them well."

Mother Nature stares at Keegan, and in this moment I see why so many cultures around the world revere her as the Goddess. Seeing her here, now, it is impossible to think of her as anything but. Her eyes glow a rich mossy green with an inhuman potency. "Keegan. That is a fine wizard's name. I welcome you to my fold, Wizard Keegan." She takes his hand in hers, and a fire envelops them both as she bestows a kiss upon it. A bright light radiates from her as she passes him a staff made of birch. "You are my Champion of Healing. Yours is a task that shall demand much. Take this staff that it may aid you and serve as a focus for your restorative magic."

Keegan takes the staff and steps back. The swirling fire entwines itself into a braided rope of mossy green, and it wraps itself around his white robe.

Then the Goddess turns to James, flames of royal purple dancing in her eyes. "James. This is another fine name for a wizard. I welcome you to my fold, Wizard James." She reaches out and takes his hand in hers, bestowing a kiss upon it as purple fire envelops them both. She passes him a staff of oak. "You are my Champion of the Ways. May this staff keep you rooted and aid you as you work to defend my world."

James takes his staff and steps back. A braided rope of royal purple wraps itself around him.

I feel the full strength of nature blazing into me.

"Aiden." The eyes of the Goddess now dance with brilliant red flames. Her voice is terrifyingly sweet and possessive. "Your journey to me has forever changed you. You have in many respects died and been reborn. Wizard Aiden, approach."

I step forward, and she takes my hand in hers. She bestows her kiss upon it. I see behind her a great forest of trees offering me their strength and power. It is from this forest that she draws her staffs. She presents to me one of my own.

"I gift you this staff of yew, for renewal and rebirth shall follow in the wake of the fire, death, and destruction you will bring. You are my Champion of Rebirth."

I reach out and take the staff. Fire and strength flow into me and through me, ultimately becoming a part of me. A red rope winds around my waist.

When I look into her face, the Goddess's eyes are radiant green. Her arms are outstretched to encompass us all.

"Together, you shall trumpet my name throughout the world!"

She closes her arms and lowers her chin to her chest. She becomes smaller as she hunches. The brilliance of her eyes fades until I can see familiar beady eyes. The forest recedes, and soon Evelyn stands before us.

She clears her throat. "Welcome, wizards. May your journey along this path be long and joyous!"

Keegan, James, and I look at each other and embrace as brothers.

Chapter Fourteen

The next day, I awaken before the others and sit cross-legged on my sleeping pad in silent meditation.

The ritual drained us. My body has had longer to adjust to the rigors of energy moving through it, but it's still exhausted; however, I'm excited about starting a brand new day with another Guardian.

Before retiring last night, the Guardians walked us through how our training will unfold now that the Goddess declared our strengths. Keegan will begin his studies with alteration, the school of healers and mystics. James will start with conjuration because he will specialize in defense. As for me, after spending all that time with Aleksandar working on destruction, I'm moving on to illusion to see if it will amplify what I've been learning.

James and Keegan still haven't awoken by the time I finish meditating. I quietly put on my robe. My yew staff calls to me from where I leaned it against the wall last night. I stare at it, wondering if I should take it with me today. The Goddess obviously meant it to be a part of me, so perhaps I should. I pick it up, and a shiver runs through me. Its latent power mingles with my own.

I step out of our quarters to find Sean, Jennifer, and Elizabeth already waiting for us in the Chamber of Knowledge.

Jennifer stands, beckoning me forward. "Welcome to your first day in the training of illusion." Her face lights up as she smiles.

"Thanks!" I look around. The Chamber of Knowledge is spacious, but I doubt it's large enough for three separate training sessions. "Isn't it going to get a bit cramped in here?"

She laughs lightly. "Let's go for a walk."

Jennifer rests a hand on my elbow and guides me toward the far side of the chamber to the entrance of a tunnel I haven't yet explored. She grabs a torch, and we step into the passageway, making our way through the darkness.

"This will be our first lesson in illusion," she says. "These"—she gestures grandly at the chambers we're stepping into—"are what make Lannóg Eolas a fully functioning school. We are in the Great Hall of Learning. From here, you can easily see each of the schools contained within the Citadel."

What I see takes my breath away. Stretching as far as my eye can see is a network of chambers. Each chamber has a stone circle lit dimly by torchlight. I look at Jennifer quizzically.

"This first area," she says, "is known as the Chambers of the Elements. It's a series of chambers devoted to earth, air, fire, and water. They consist of nearly indestructible rock and are dedicated to the power of destruction. I understand you are hesitant to take on that study, but remember, nothing can be created without something being destroyed. Destruction magic is where creation magic finds its source. Since it appears that the Goddess has confirmed Aleksandar's suspicions, you'll spend the majority of your time here in these chambers, learning how to harness the power of the elements themselves."

She leads me through the chambers.

"The Chamber of Fire," she says.

I notice countless scorch marks on the walls and even the floors of this chamber. The place looks like a test facility for fireworks or other explosives.

"The Chamber of Air," she says.

As we pass this chamber I see rubble scattered everywhere, as though a tornado had torn through the place. We step around the broken rocks and come to a chamber with water trickling down its walls.

"The Chamber of Water," she says. She points out small dark pools scattered throughout the stony floor.

In the final chamber, a deep fissure has rent the space in two.

"The Chamber of Earth," she says.

We carefully skirt the edge of the chasm and find ourselves standing in a tunnel running in both directions as far as the eye can see.

"We're still exploring," Jennifer says, "but we believe Lannóg Eolas was constructed in concentric circles joined together by spokes, if you will. It seems to be very reminiscent of a spider web. Each section of the Great Hall of Learning is separated from the other by one of these rings. This is so it's possible to walk between them without disturbing any training that may be happening. Through the Great Hall, we can visit or bypass as many of the schools as we want."

She leads us into the next chamber. "Here we have the Chambers of Reflection. We'll return here to study the power of illusion."

At the entrance of each chamber in this section is a carving depicting various items and people with their reflections appearing in a pool of calm water.

Jennifer points to one of the carvings. "To fully understand the power of illusion, you must fully understand both yourself and your environment. Only then can you alter how others perceive things."

As we continue walking, I think I see the golden sky of dawn ahead. The tunnel we are following appears to open up directly to the outside world. We reach the opening, and I gasp. After spending so much time inside, I find the outdoors is stunning. We stand high up a steep mountainside, overlooking an arid, craggy valley dotted with standing stones in the distance. I can barely make the stones out in the dim light of the rising sun. Before us, a steep and narrow path leads down into the valley, but it's too difficult to make out the details in the early light. To the right of it, another path wraps back inside the Citadel.

I look at Jennifer questioningly. "How is this possible?" I learned from Sean that the Citadel is deep underground. But that would mean the room I used my wristband in, the cemetery, and what I'm seeing now should all be impossible.

Jennifer looks out over the land. "With us being so deep beneath the surface, it shouldn't be."

I follow her gaze. "And yet it is."

She nods. "This is one of two such self-contained valleys we know of. This one is by far the larger. We believe the entire Citadel is woven with illusion. Each chamber appears to us as though it's right next to the others." To demonstrate her point, she turns me around so I can clearly see the Chambers of Reflection, where we were just a moment ago. "But really, the short tunnels between each chamber function the same as the tunnels we use to get here from our homes." She points to the sides of the opening we just passed through. "What do you notice, Aiden?"

I study the stone. For a moment, I don't notice it, but then I see it. It's very subtle but easy to spot if you know what you're looking for. "The stone surrounding the opening is different from the walls of this chamber."

She smiles and nods. "Not just this chamber. Stones like these frame the entrance to every chamber. They appear to be made of the same portal stones that we use to travel here from our homes all over the world. They shorten time and space, which is a form of illusion. Where we stand is actually in an entirely different part of the world than the chambers we see before us."

I look at her. The incredulity must be clear on my face. "What do you mean, a different part of the world? So where are we now?" I turn and gaze out over the valley.

Jennifer smiles. "Perhaps one day we'll know the answer. For now, our theory is that the ancient wizards joined the most sacred places around the world together into the Citadel. Each place such as this is sacred. If you were to find it in the outside world and enter it on your own, these access points to the other parts of the Citadel wouldn't exist. Only by entering through a designated entrance of the Citadel can you traverse all the chambers as an interconnected network. That is our hope, at least!"

"So if we were to enter this valley while someone from the outside were already there, would we be able to interact with them?"

Jennifer is silent for a moment. "I suspect we would, yes, but it raises interesting questions. For instance, would it cause us to fall out of sync with our reality and lose access to the rest of the Citadel? Would it join them to ours so they too could access the other chambers? Or maybe we could see them but not talk to them." She briefly falls silent again. "Or maybe there are others here already and we cannot see them. This is all new to us, so until that happens, we may never know."

She lets me stare at the rising sun for a few minutes more before she starts slowly walking down the path on the right. "We'll go this way. It bypasses the valley proper and takes us to our next destination."

We soon come to a series of chambers with an image of a chest carved above each entrance. We stop briefly to examine the carvings, and Jennifer points out the intricate details. The locking mechanisms make the chests appear more like puzzles than mere containers. The chambers themselves vary from large and airy to tight and stuffy. Each has a gorgeous sculpture within it. Next to each sculpture are two smaller sculptures showing the various stages of creation of the primary one.

Jennifer looks at me. "These are the Chambers of Inception. This is where you will learn to take what is but a glimmer in your mind's eye and form it into reality. These chambers illustrate that the quality of the work you create will be elaborate if your mind is open and free but basic if your mind is closed and rigid. However, you will also notice that the sculptures in the smaller spaces are all very emotional and raw. Tight spaces are excellent for quick, emotional conjurations."

We continue our journey, passing through a small chamber. It's enclosed on all sides, but the rising sun shines through a gaping rift running the length of it. Jennifer leads me through this chamber and slows when we reach a series of other chambers. These ones are pure and clean and orderly. They exude serenity and peace. Nothing is out of place. All of the chambers have rivulets of water winding through them. Above the entrance of each chamber is an intricately carved serpent that winds its way through various scenes. A dimly glowing orb sits in the centre of each carving.

"These are the final chambers in the Great Hall of Learning, the Chambers of the Serpent. This is where Keegan will learn the skills of an alteration specialist, including learning how to enhance his natural healing talent."

"The Serpent? That sounds kind of ominous. It doesn't put me in the frame of mind of a healer."

Jennifer smiles. "Thanks to Christianity for appropriating the image. You don't have to look very far beyond the Christian faith to see where the serpent was revered. For instance, the Rod of Asclepius from Greek mythology is a serpent entwined around the staff of the god of healing and medicine. Even today, this symbol appears on the logo of the World Health Organization, various medical associations, and thousands of other organizations worldwide.

"Like the power of healing they represent, serpents can be deadly if not fully understood, but when respected and used with full knowledge, they can be used to heal many ailments. Snakes have been symbols of rebirth, transformation, and immortality for thousands of years thanks to their process of shedding their old skin and being reborn as something new. This makes it the perfect symbol for the alteration school, which specializes in changing the current state of something."

"I had forgotten its medical affiliations," I say with a nod.

We continue walking. It takes us more than three hours to walk from end to end. When we get to the farthest point, Jennifer turns me around to look back at the chambers we journeyed through. A grin spreads across her entire face when she sees the undisguised awe on mine.

"The rebirth of magic is at hand," she says. "Think of how strong your headaches were before you met us. Now that you're actively exercising your power, they're completely gone, right?"

I nod.

"Your training also has an added bonus," she continues. "The more you practice, the more magic you are letting into the world and the more magic spreads. Already, there are dozens of people who are approaching the point of needing training before their latent power kills them. Soon there will be hundreds." She gestures expansively. "Lannóg Eolas will keep them all safe."

I look around the grand chambers. She's right. Fifty wizards could easily learn how to control their power here, maybe more if the Guardians use other means of training that I'm unaware of. Maybe there will be group training, or training outside of the Great Hall of Learning.

I think of Caitlin, and how long it took her to find me, and how much effort it took her to convince me I needed help. "And that's what Caitlin's out doing now right? Trying to find others?"

Jennifer nods. "Yes. But she won't be able to do it alone. We're going to need to find more Seekers. Soon. But we're getting ahead of ourselves. Right now we need to focus on getting the three of you trained.

And so we head back to the Chambers of Reflection. Here, in an unknown part of the world, Jennifer begins teaching me the basics of illusion magic. She says illusion is, at its core, about changing how others perceive the world.

"A good illusionist," Jennifer says with intensity, "will be able to make someone see a river that isn't there. They can make you feel as though you're trapped in a snowstorm even though it's the hottest day of the year. With illusion, you can distort reality to make yourself invisible. It's a fascinating school. I think you'll find it most useful as your strength grows."

We are standing in a chamber with a large crystal prism in the centre. Before it is a stone bench. A shaft of light beams down onto the crystal from a small hole in the ceiling.

Jennifer gestures at the bench. "Take a seat, wizard."

My curiosity piqued, I approach the bench and sit. As I do, six perfect reflections of me appear. At least, I think they're reflections at first, but I realize after a moment that they're all very different.

Jennifer speaks. Her voice is but a whisper that seems to come from miles away. "Recall when we were here earlier. I said you need to fully understand yourself before you can change how others perceive you. In this central chamber, your self is reflected back at you as the six core emotions of human existence."

I feel her hands on my head. She turns my gaze toward the first image on the left, which shows my face split open in a wide grin, joy dancing in my eyes.

"Happiness," she says.

I feel myself getting pulled into the happy reflection, and awareness of all else begins to fade.

Jennifer then breaks my fall into the reflection by forcibly turning my head to the rest of the images one by one, lingering a moment on each. "Followed by sadness, fear, anger, surprise, and disgust."

I find myself blinking rapidly as I catch mere glimpses of each image in turn.

"Tomorrow," she continues, "the other images will pull you in as happiness just tried to. You must come to fully understand one aspect of yourself before the crystal will allow you to move on to the next. You could be stuck within an aspect of yourself for hours—or it could be days. And each will be much different. For today, we are merely discussing the basics. Come, it will be less distracting if we sit off to the side."

My lesson with Jennifer on the basics of illusion lasts well into the evening, and when it ends, I'm not quite ready to return to my quarters. When Jennifer leaves me, I decide to stroll back through the Great Hall of Learning. With thoughts of the future playing through my head, I eventually sit on a large slab of stone in the small chamber that separates the Chambers of Inception from the Chambers of the Serpent. I look up through the jagged aperture. I can no longer see the sun, but it looks like I still have several hours before it sets fully.

During my time with Jennifer today, I was reminded that I could have died if I hadn't received my initial training as a wizard. But a secret organization such as the Guardians of Knowledge didn't survive for three thousand years just to train a few random guys as wizards for the good of our health. We each sealed our fate last night when we swore allegiance to Mother Nature during the initiation. My fingers play idly with the red rope tied around my waist, and I think back to what she said to me. She said renewal and rebirth would follow the fire, death, and destruction that I will bring. That sounds like a lot more than protests or other political action.

The Goddess named each of us champions, and you can't be a champion without a fight. The planet, it seems, is tired of those who believe the world was created purely for humankind to drain it of its natural resources and fill its lands and oceans with never-ending heaps of refuse. She sounds ready to fight back. What have we agreed to? Are we really ready for this? I laugh at myself, a deep sardonic laugh, because so far it hasn't mattered whether I think I'm ready.

I stare across the expanse of chambers, lost in self-doubt. After several minutes of this, I see the air ripple before me. I focus on it, and the chambers slowly begin to transform. I hear laughter fill the air. I see men and women of all ages dancing and partying and playing. They're wizards.

Magic flows through the Citadel merrily, playing light shows and booming fireworks and tricks of all kinds. Giant trees grow in groves throughout the chambers. Rivers flow freely in intricate networks, their rippling surfaces glittering in the torchlight. There are mothers and daughters, fathers and sons, lovers and friends. All move freely through the chambers, and joy is everywhere.

And then there is a thundering boom from outside. With it comes a distinct shift in the atmosphere. More booms echo from above, and debris showers the chambers. The wizards now move with fear and purpose etched into their faces. Parents stagger toward their soot-covered children. A mother's face is lined with tears as she cradles the lifeless body of her teenage daughter. One by one, the trees die. One by one, the rivers dry. The society of wizards fractures into insular groups, but then even they disappear, and the heart of the Citadel is left empty and forlorn.

The ancient and terrifying voice of the Goddess fills the air around me, echoing off the walls, causing my very soul to tremble: "Return me to my glory, Aiden, and there will be peace on Earth. That is your destiny."

I know I cannot deny this. I've just experienced a glimpse into the past. I've seen how happy and connected everyone was in the Citadel of yore. I've also lived in the present long enough to know how distant and lonely everyone is in the world.

I stare across the empty chambers once more and place my hand on the wall next to me. I feel the energy of place run through it from the stony floor to the crevice above and into the open sky. *I will return you to life*, I vow silently. *My own life is yours.*

I feel the wall shift. I pull my hand away, and a section of stone crumbles to the floor. A trickle of water springs from the gap. A tiny patch of grass sprouts where the water hits the floor. From the grass the tiny sapling of a tree appears. Joy such as I've never felt emanates from the Citadel.

I head back to my quarters with a smile on my face and with purpose firm in my soul.

Chapter Fifteen

The next few months seem to fly by. It's easy to lose track of time in these chambers, and it's easier still to forget that there's a world outside of them. It's especially the case now that the Guardians have moved into the living quarters I discovered.

Shortly after moving in, the Guardians began mapping out the Citadel with a single-minded devotion that is at times infuriating. They seem to be searching for something specific, but they won't tell us what it is. During our lessons, our instructors refuse to answer any question not directly related to our training. Those who are not currently training us are almost invisible.

The only indication that their task is yielding any results is an ever-expanding map they keep near the great table in the Chamber of Knowledge. We inspect it every day. James and Keegan are curious to learn about our surroundings, but I'm always checking it to see if they've found the catacomb I explored a while back. It seems to remain hidden from them. I wonder if it has anything to do with what they're looking for. If they weren't so hush-hush about it, I'd consider asking them, but for some reason, it feels like the experience wasn't meant to be shared—at least not yet. I haven't spoken about the catacomb or its central tomb with anyone, not even James. I know he'll want to explore it if I tell him about it, and I'm not ready for that. So I hold the secret tightly, even though I feel it calling out to me almost constantly, whispering my name seductively.

I try instead to focus on learning to control my magic, letting that take precedence over everything.

With the Guardians preoccupied with their explorations, news of the outside world is scarce. Our only news comes from Caitlin in her capacity as Seeker, and she doesn't tend to share much. She has remained an enigma, as her visits are always shrouded in secrecy. She periodically returns to the Citadel to keep our food and supplies topped up and to deliver a news summary to David, who then shares it with us. She times her comings and goings to coincide with our training sessions. I'm assuming this is so she doesn't interrupt us while we're resting in our quarters.

As our training progresses, however, we find ourselves practicing at different times. Three weeks ago, I managed to see Caitlin stride with purpose from one of the tunnels and head straight to our quarters to stock up our supplies. I thought of calling out to her as she was leaving, but something in her hurried manner stopped me. I was reminded that she isn't the same woman I had coffee with on the waterfront in Toronto, but I can't seem to shake that Caitlin, or the Caitlin who visits my mother and treats her so well. I would do both of us a disservice by holding anything against her.

Every time I saw her, I tried to find the courage to talk to her, to apologize for being so angry with her even though she literally saved my life. I always wound up having an imaginary conversation with her instead, and she'd always be gone by the time I caught myself.

Three visits ago, I returned to our quarters just as she arrived. I swallowed my nervousness and decided to talk to her. Her eyes widened slightly at seeing me, and this was her only greeting. Our conversation was brief and businesslike. I tried to talk to her longer. I was as eager to hear anything about the outside world as I was to reconnect with her, but she barely glanced at me and didn't say more than three sentences. Nonetheless, I thought maybe it would open up the door. If anything, she's become more withdrawn since. Last week, she escorted Danielle to the Citadel for her first visit since James arrived, and she didn't even look at me. But today is another day, and she and Danielle are due to arrive soon.

James and I are lounging about in our quarters, waiting for Danielle to arrive. Keegan is away. He's in the Chambers of the Serpent, studying with Sean.

I turn the page on the book I'm reading. It's Ernest Hemmingway's *In Our Time*. It's one of David's favourites, a collection of short stories that he thought would help occupy my free time here.

James shifts restlessly.

I glance up at him. "You all right?"

He nods enthusiastically, but after a few seconds, he sighs loudly. "You know, Danielle and I didn't spend more than three days apart before this. I didn't really know what to expect, but I definitely didn't think I'd miss her this much! Don't tell her I said that."

Almost like clockwork, Caitlin's and Danielle's footsteps echo into our quarters.

I put the book down beside my bed and glance at James. I laugh quietly at his excited grin. Danielle appears first, and her face breaks out into a smile when she sees us.

"Hey, babe," James says nonchalantly. He then abandons any pretext and runs over to her. He embraces her, and the two kiss passionately.

Caitlin doesn't even look at them as she strides past. She unslings her backpack and squats at the cupboard to unload another week's worth of supplies.

I shuffle up to her, feeling incredibly awkward. "How's your week been?"

"Fine."

"Any luck finding any new wizards?"

She takes a deep breath. "Aiden, you're a wizard. I flopped out at being a wizard. I'm just a Seeker. You don't need to make me feel better about my lot in life. I'm happy the way it is."

I blink at her, and she just shrugs before shoving a sack of oats into the cupboard.

I kneel down beside her and lower my voice. "What the hell does that even mean?" I don't want to interrupt James and Danielle's canoodling, but the irony of the contrast between our two interactions is almost laughable.

Caitlin stands, zips up her backpack, and slings it over her shoulder. "It means that regardless of whether you're hoping to be friends or you're hoping for something more, you should stop. I'm very happy with my life the way it is. I don't need any friends, and I've gotten through this much without any family."

She strides past me, leaving me to stare blankly at the spot she once occupied.

"Aiden!" James calls.

I close my eyes, trying to block him out. I just want to curl up on my hay mattress and forget about the world, magic, everything. I honestly don't know why I've been trying to connect with Caitlin. Maybe it's because I'm lonely, even though I have both James and Keegan here with me. I miss the wider world beyond these chambers. Caitlin is my only possible connection to that world right now.

"Aiden!"

I turn with a sigh. Danielle and James are smiling at me, and it's almost too much for me to take.

"We thought maybe you could show us your tree," James says.

"Sure." I hope I sound more enthusiastic than I feel. "You want to go now?"

"That would be great," Danielle says. "It's so barren in here. It's exciting to think there's finally some life!"

When we get to the Chamber of Knowledge, we find Caitlin standing there. I try to hide my surprise. I thought she'd be gone by now. Her eyes pierce into mine and seem to burn with curiosity.

"I'm sorry," she says, "but did I overhear something about a tree?"

Before I can say anything, James says, "Aiden managed to grow a tree. A *magic* tree! Would you like to see it too?"

Caitlin chews her lip for a moment, looking around the Chamber of Knowledge and I swear I can hear Sean's father Patrick telling her in this very spot that it would be her that would reawaken life in the Citadel. When she turns back to us, her eyes glisten with unshed tears. "I'd love to," she says, to my utter amazement.

Since Danielle is with us, we take a tunnel that runs adjacent to the Great Hall of Learning. It brings us across each ring dividing the different schools, and when we reach the fourth ring, James leads us left. No one speaks the entire way there, but when we reach the open-air crevice where I saw the sapling spring from the stone, Caitlin gasps and then grabs my hand tightly. The tree, a glorious Irish yew, managed to reach its full height, some twenty feet, in a matter of days.

She releases my hand and approaches the tree almost reverently. It's the kind of tree that looks like a giant shrub, nothing like the mighty oak or the elegant birch, but she looks at it as if it were the most beautiful thing on the planet.

"He died thinking I would be the one to awaken it," she says softly, "and my greatest regret in life was disappointing him."

She looks at the trickling stream running beside the tree, and I see a tear run down her cheek.

I step up beside her. "You didn't disappoint him, Caitlin."

She gives me a sidelong glance.

"Without you," I say, "I would have died, and none of this would have happened. In a very real way, you are directly responsible for this tree being here."

She shakes her head. "You're very sweet, but no. I wasn't strong enough to awaken anything, and you're alive because I was just doing my job."

Caitlin gives me a smile tinged with both happiness and sadness, and without another word, she puts her hands into the pockets of her leather jacket and strides back the way we came.

It's been three weeks since we visited the yew tree. Caitlin has since changed how she carries out her duties here, and so I haven't seen her. She now brings Danielle only as far as the entrance to the Chamber of Knowledge before leaving again. She also gets Danielle to bring in our food and supplies. The first time Danielle showed up at our quarters with a sack of non-perishables, she gave me such a look of pity that I haven't been able to stop wondering what Caitlin may have told her. Since then, Danielle has started visiting twice a week and has even defied all of our expectations by spending the night several times already.

This morning is the first day of a three-day break from our studies. Danielle is due to arrive at some point this afternoon. James woke up early wanting to practice a new conjuration he's been working on. Since I'm already awake and Keegan is still sleeping soundly, James and I decide to head to the garden.

It's hard to believe, but the barren crevice where the yew tree sprang to life is now a lush garden, almost as beautiful as the gardens in the vision I had that same day. Twelve other trees of various species have since sprouted in the area, and the trickle of water issuing from the gap in the wall has formed into a babbling brook that gathers into a pond in the centre of everything. Moss-covered stones and ferns line the water's edge, and vines climb the walls of the crevice. Lush shrubs, delicate white anemones, brilliant purple crane's-bills, and other flowers fill the rest of the space. Through it all, a narrow stone walkway twists and turns its way to the pond's edge, where we've moved a large flat rock to serve as a meditation bench.

Most of it is Keegan's doing. His natural skill in alteration grows daily. He transforms the barren stone with the skill of an artist. The land responds to his touch in a way it doesn't with me. James's skill in this discipline is somewhere in between. I suppose that makes sense. Keegan is the healer, and it appears I'm destined to be some sort of war wizard. James was the one who completed the link between us.

Each of us has gone through what we've affectionately dubbed "basic training": several weeks of study in each discipline. As everyone predicted, Keegan has been demonstrating an amazing aptitude for healing. A broken tree branch? He can mend it. A sick bird? He can cure it. His training in destruction, however, turned out to be purely theory-based. Try as he might, he can't seem to get a torch to light. Fire doesn't seem to be in his blood.

I, on the other hand, am unable to work a single healing spell at all. I show a smattering of skill in conjuring; I can make shadows of rough shapes appear, for example. Illusion comes to me a bit easier. Although it took me four days to break free from the aspect of sadness in the Chambers of Reflection, I must say I'm getting pretty skilled at making myself blend into my surroundings.

The first time I was able to make a lake appear in the distance, I let out a cheer that brought the others running. James showed me up by making it appear as if the lake had bubbled over and a flood of water was pouring toward us. His illusion had been so real that I plugged my nose and ducked in anticipation of being swept into the current. He and Keegan had laughed quite hard at my reaction.

Illusion and conjuration are James's disciplines of choice. During the week he spent learning how to conjure things, all kinds of creatures roamed the Citadel. There was a bear cub, a wolf, a curious sentient blob that slid along behind us, an eagle that swept gracefully through the chambers, and various other things. They responded to us, interacted with us, and loved us. His strongest "familiar" had been a dog he'd named Buddy. Buddy followed us everywhere and brought us joy for a whole two weeks. We were crestfallen when he finally dissolved into the air around us.

James's illusions are so real that when he sends one at us, we feel either elation or panic. He's turned it into a bit of a game. He now regularly inundates us with illusions of crushing waves, swarming bats, and raging infernos. I thought I'd get used to them, but they make me want to run for cover every time.

There was a time when I'd think that this is James simply being a jerk, but his illusion tricks are actually good for building the nerves I'll need to survive in the world that we appear headed for. I'm learning to swallow my fear and walk through the illusions. Keegan, on the other hand, faces them head-on and somehow absorbs the magic, causing the illusion to vanish. Or he'll hold up his hands and somehow make the illusion smash into an invisible wall and crumble.

Keegan also has an uncanny ability to detect others. Several times now, he and I would be walking toward our quarters and he'd stop and put his hand on my arm. "James is ahead and waiting to prank us." I don't know how he does it, but he's never been wrong. I've learned not to doubt him.

I tried this trick once. When James sent imaginary buffalo stampeding toward me, I threw up my hands, only instead of making the illusion careen into the wall, I literally tore up the floor of the chamber and flung countless pieces of jagged rock at the oncoming herd. The chamber was ruined, and the Guardians weren't impressed. They ended up having a special meeting before announcing that our lessons were on hold until we repaired the damage. It took the three of us two weeks to devise the magic that would put the chamber back together, and James hasn't played an illusion prank on me since.

Today, the prankster in James is nowhere to be seen. His body language is as serious as I've ever seen it. I wonder if the prospects of the coming months are bothering him. We will soon be starting our in-depth training in the school we've shown the most skill in. I'm going to be learning everything Aleksandar knows about destruction so I can learn how to avoid bringing the roof down on our heads accidentally. Keegan is teaming up with Sean to learn the depths of alteration magic, and James is partnering up with Elizabeth to learn more about conjuration.

James sits beside me on the meditation bench next to the pond, but he's a million miles away. His thick eyebrows are screwed together in thought, and his eyes are glazed over. Twice since we sat down he has run a hand through his long, unkempt blond hair. It still looks odd on him given how perfectly groomed and short he used to keep it. It's pointless to obsess about your appearance here in the Citadel. I see a range of emotions and thoughts play over his features before he finally speaks.

"I'm amazed at how easily all of this is coming to us. It's like it was within us this whole time, just waiting to be set free."

I smile. "It was."

"Well, obviously we've been given this gift for a reason, right? We have to use our gifts to help restore magic to the world. But when Danielle and I went for our walk last week, she showed me the latest headlines on her wristband."

Wristbands. It's been months now since the last of our bands stopped working. Even Danielle's wristband short-circuits if she spends too much time in the Citadel.

"What's going on out there these days?" I try not to sound too eager, but I find it difficult.

"It's been slowly eating away at me ever since. What Caitlin's been reporting to the Guardians the past couple of weeks is right, and it doesn't look good. The drought in the States has worsened, and mass riots are sweeping the country. California hasn't had rain in eight months. Crops across the Midwest have withered. The Mississippi is at its lowest level in recorded history. At the same time, ocean levels have continued to rise. They think it's now a matter of months before what's left of the San Francisco Bay Area is swallowed up. With the Christian March forming the new government in Washington, all of this takes on a new and terrifying meaning."

"That's a lot to take in," I say quietly. I now wish I didn't miss David's update this week on world affairs. I was so wrapped up in finishing the repairs on the chamber I destroyed that I missed the visit and completely forgot to ask about it.

James nods. "And that's not all. There are also reports of strange occurrences happening throughout Canada. Like, the type of occurrences that only magic could cause. It's nothing significant—not yet, at least. It's just things like kids getting in trouble at school for making things fly and stuff like that. But it's got the Christian movement all up in arms. With them in power now, that's a big deal. Caitlin is apparently exercising extreme caution in identifying and keeping tabs on future wizards. The Guardians are worried about her getting caught."

"Well, we know she can handle herself." My knowing this feels bittersweet. Yet, I can't help but worry about her too, and now I feel more trapped in the Citadel than I've ever felt. "Even so, it's frustrating that we're stuck down here."

"Yeah, we've been down here, isolated, while the world marches on without us. If we stay here much longer, it will be too late for us to change any of it. I mean, we're just three guys. We're barely adults. What do they expect from us?"

James is silent for a long time. He then looks me square in the eyes. "I guess what I'm saying is it feels like forever since the three of us shared that vision at the bookshop. Are we progressing fast enough to prevent it from coming true?"

We sit there in silence. The only sound is the babbling waters of the brook. James stares at the oak tree that now grows here. Perhaps he's thinking about the oak staff the Goddess gave him. I glance at the yew tree and think about what James has said. On the one hand, he's absolutely right. We can't stay holed up here forever. We can't create a beautiful and secure home for ourselves below Skellig Michael while the world above us shrivels up and dies. On the other hand, Mother Nature has waited this long to make her play, and we're far from ready.

I sigh and lean forward in my seat. "Yeah. Caitlin's reports get worse each time. Remember a few weeks ago when David told us that the Canadian parliament authorized a substantial increase in defense spending and ordered the military to patrol the border? So far, though, it's all just tensions. Honestly, what could we even do?"

James scoffs. "Good question. Maybe more harm than good at this point."

"I know how to light torches and tear up the ground, and Keegan can grow some trees and heal some ailments. You probably have the most useful skills if it ever boiled over into all-out war. You could make our armed forces seem ten times greater with your illusions." I stare at him for a moment before continuing, making sure I have his undivided attention. "We need to trust that the Goddess knew what she was doing when she chose now to begin our training rather than three years ago. We can't go out on our own until we know more about what makes us tick. Sure, she showed us images of destruction, but that doesn't mean we're going to be the ones marching off to war. Maybe she waited this long because it's our job to step in and restore the balance after war has already ravaged the world."

He gives me a disbelieving look, but then he says, "Okay, I can accept that. But how much longer do you think we should stay here?"

"Well, it's up to the Guardians to decide, as they know best, but we should at least stay until we're specialists in our respective schools and until we know how to control and contain our powers. We've been here for, what, the better part of a year now? Why don't we give ourselves another few months of specialty training? Then we can ask the Guardians if they think we're ready."

James nods reluctantly.

"You're right, though," I say. "It's very difficult being down here with everything going on out there."

"Why don't I ask the Guardians about teaching us how to stop frying electronics?"

"That would definitely help! Let's make that our main focus. As soon as we can demonstrate that control, maybe they'll let us start making day trips back to the city. If people are starting to develop magic, we'll need to identify them and help them. It's unsafe for them to use their power untrained, and society will start thinking they're abominations. They'll make them outcasts or will do something worse. We have to be prepared to offer them sanctuary. Caitlin will soon have no choice but to bring them here, but it's getting to a point where it'll be too much for her to handle alone."

James looks around and gestures at the garden surrounding us. "This is just a start. The Citadel will be an amazing sanctuary." He nods slowly. "I'm okay with this plan. It will be nice to hang out with Danielle without her having to remove her electronics because she's worried I'm going to short them out."

I grin. "We still have a few hours before Danielle arrives, and Keegan will probably sleep in till noon if he can. Would you like to keep walking? It's been a while since we've done any exploring of our own."

We set out, aimlessly walking down the ring separating the garden from the Chambers of the Serpent. Life is slowly starting to return here, creeping out just beyond the garden. It makes me smile inside. The Citadel hasn't been home for long, but it's formed a deep connection in my heart.

We take our first left and walk beyond the Chambers of the Serpent, farther than we've ever explored. We continue walking in silence. With so much to think about, I appreciate not having to say anything while I'm with my best friend. Having him here with me is comfort in itself.

We continue walking, passing through a chamber here, making a turn there. I'm careful to keep track of our journey, but I must admit I've lost track of time. Before I can suggest to James that we should turn back, he looks over at me.

"Have you ever wondered about the kind of power Caitlin has as a Seeker?" he asks. "The power that allows her to find wizards?"

"What do you mean?"

He doesn't answer. Instead, he pauses mid-step. I see him eyeballing one of the walls in the chamber we just entered. "Look at this!" He pushes his torch toward the far wall, revealing a tunnel.

An unlit torch marks the tunnel's opening on either side. A sun with a triskelion at its centre is carved into the stone above it. James flashes his torch into the dark opening, illuminating a crude stone staircase just barely wide enough for my shoulders to squeeze through. He advances further, but the staircase continues to rise into the darkness beyond the torchlight.

He turns to me, excitement dancing in his eyes. "This is the first chamber besides the Chamber of Knowledge that has its own passage leading away from it."

"What do you mean?"

"I mean it *leads* somewhere. It's not just a connection to another empty chamber."

I'm not sure I like where this is going. In fact, I'm positive I don't. I try to visualize the progress of the map the Guardians are making in their own explorations. Although I wouldn't say we're lost (yet), I also don't think this area appears on their map.

"So what?" I say, trying to downplay James's excitement.

"*So what?*" James turns to look at me, an incredulous look on his face. "It might lead outside somewhere."

"Somewhere . . . ?"

"To a place where there's no chance of anybody recognizing us!"

I raise my eyebrows. "James! That's *way* too dangerous! We have no idea where this tunnel leads. For all we know, it could spit us out in the middle of Washington, DC!"

"So what if it does? Do you know anyone there?"

I stare at him, my eyes wide. "Um, well, for starters, Washington is overrun by a fanatical religious group right now. It's probably the most dangerous place for us to be! And didn't we *just* decide that we should wait until we knew how to control our power?"

James shoots me an exasperated look. "It's *not* going to lead us to Washington!"

"You don't know that!"

"It's not! And we're not going to do any magic. We're just going for some fresh air. I could really use some crisp, clean air that doesn't smell like the inside of a cave."

"You knew it would be like this when you signed up, James. I was sitting right there when David warned you that you wouldn't be able to leave once you started your training."

"Yeah, but he couldn't tell us how long the training would take. What if we're stuck down here for another year?"

I try not to let my face reveal how agonizing that prospect sounds to me.

"It'll be totally safe," he says. "I promise."

He's using *that* voice—the one he uses when he knows it'll take a little extra convincing to get me on his side. It's almost always successful, but not this time.

"No way." I shake my head. "It's way too dangerous. We haven't had enough training yet. Anything could happen!"

"Or nothing could happen. Nothing's going to happen, Aiden. Come on, please?"

"No, sorry." I look away from him. I can't look at him, because the excitement on his face only confirms how badly he wants to do this. I don't want to give in.

"Pretty please with a cherry on top?"

"How many times are you going to make me say no, James?"

"Why?"

"Well, for a start, just look at how we're dressed. *Robes?* What will people think seeing us dressed like this?"

He stares at me for a moment. "Nobody will see us. We'll be careful."

I roll my eyes. "No."

"Can we at least poke our head out the mouth of the cave to see where we wind up? Maybe it's nothing . . . It won't hurt to just take a look."

"There's no way you're going to convince me on this."

"Fine. I'm going without you."

I watch as James takes a few steps up the staircase. He stops and turns around. "Are you coming, or are you really making me do this on my own?"

"James! We can't. If the Guardians find out we're risking ourselves like this, they'll be pissed!"

"They're not going to find out. Last chance."

I briefly consider giving him an ultimatum, but I think it's too late for that.

"Suit yourself," he says before disappearing up the stairs.

I stare incredulously after him. I glance over my shoulder back the way we came and then up the dark stairwell again. I can't believe he's doing this! I glance behind me one more time.

"Shit," I mumble as I rush up the stairs.

Chapter Sixteen

I reach the top of the stairs and hesitate for a moment. Not a single torch lights the tunnel ahead of me. There's no sign of James. When I call out to him, there's no answer. All I hear is the sound of my own voice echoing through the tunnel.

The tunnel seems to go on forever. I call out James's name the whole way, even though I know it's futile at this point.

Up ahead I can hear a banging sound, or maybe it's scraping. I rush ahead, knowing very well that James is up to something. I hear an ear-piercing screech as I finally round a corner. Before I can see anything, I'm nearly blinded by white light. When my eyes begin to adjust, I can just barely make out James's silhouette at the far end of the tunnel. He's yanking on a rusty iron door that looks like it's about to fall off the hinges. Sure enough, those ancient hinges are the source of the ungodly sound.

"James!" I yell angrily.

He spins, and his face lights up. "You came!"

"You could have slowed down. I called after you the whole way." His excitement makes me that much angrier that he didn't wait for me.

He beckons me forward. "I couldn't hear you. Maybe the tunnel has a magical soundproof barrier this far out. Anyway, come look at this!"

I step up to the door, resisting the urge to lecture him yet again.

My mouth drops. Through the doorway, I can see we are upon a rocky hillside. The air is fresh and crisp. Billowing white clouds fill an azure sky, and lush trees dot the landscape. Rolling hills of tall grass surround us. The sunlight bathes my skin in its golden light, and a gentle breeze ripples my hair.

The valley is the most beautiful sight I've ever seen. I can hear my grandfather once again telling me stories of verdant meadows, roaming animals, and rich forests. It's surreal.

Nestled in the middle of the valley is a small village surrounded by fields of wheat and mixed woodland. White stone buildings and thatched roofs gleam in the sun. Haggard-looking people urge cattle and other livestock toward what appears to be a central market. Here and there, people on horseback trot along the roads. Cars are notably absent. When I scan the area, I can find no road that leads to or from the village, just a single narrow footpath that disappears into the distant mountains.

James hits me on the arm. "Do you think we've gone back in time or something?"

When I can speak, my voice is nothing more than a whisper. "I don't know, James. It sure looks like it."

For a long time, we just stare at the scene before us.

"Keegan would love this," I whisper.

"You're right. He would! Wait here, and I'll go get him."

I grab James by the wrist, but he immediately pulls free.

"Aiden, it's fine . . ."

We shouldn't be here. We should be studying and practicing before Danielle arrives. I turn to say as much, but James has already gone back into the tunnel. I let him go. I can feel my willpower failing me. Seeing nature like this is a dream come true.

I step onto the rugged path that leads from the old iron door. Something else strikes me as odd, but it takes me another moment to pinpoint exactly what it is. It hits me like a jolt.

It's the silence. I'm outside in the open air, and there's no laughing, no screaming, no sirens blaring. There are no horns, no engines, no drone of electricity. There's just a gentle breeze rustling through the trees and the grass and across the rocks. It's like the shifting drafts that meander through the Citadel have followed me out into the open and filled the world with their peaceful calm. It's beautiful. It's terrifying. The only way we could experience anything remotely as serene as this in a place like Toronto would be to rent a silence booth at an exorbitant cost.

I look around, feeling my senses opening as if for the first time. My entire body tingles. I bend down and run my fingers through the long grass growing at the side of the path, and then I clamber atop a large rock.

I stand on the rock for what seems like an eternity. I hold my arms outstretched and savour the feeling of fresh air on my face. I embrace the strength of the world as it overloads my senses.

I'm still standing like that when James returns with Keegan, their eyes squinting in the sunlight. I grin at them as I turn around.

"Isn't it pristine?" James asks. "I told you it was amazing! Aiden and I think this tunnel might lead to a different time *and* place! Can we get closer to the village? Please? If we promise each other no magic?"

I can't help it. James's excitement is so innocent that I start laughing. It's quiet at first, but it eventually bubbles forth. Within seconds, all three of us are laughing long and hard. We haven't laughed this way since any of this started.

We find ourselves staring down at the village long after our laughter has died down and we've wiped the tears of joy from our eyes. Looking to each of my friends standing at my side, I can no longer deny it. My curiosity burns.

"Just a quick exploratory mission?" I ask James, smiling.

"We won't stay long! We'll just try to see if we've gone back in time." He's grinning as he says it, a hopeful, boyish grin that says everything's going to be fine. It's a grin that's gotten me into trouble several times before.

I nod, and a heartbeat later, James is tearing off down the trail toward the village. Keegan and I chase him in an attempt to keep up. It takes us about an hour to make it to the base of the rocky slope. I glance behind us periodically to make sure we can still see the path leading up to the tunnel.

We approach the village from the south, using the fields of tall wheat as cover. We slow as we near a row of old buildings whose whitewash faded long ago. Several of the buildings have windows facing us, and we don't want to risk exposing ourselves by being reckless, so we quickly find a place to hide among some stacks of hay bales well out of the way of the villagers' comings and goings.

The view from above did not hide the truth. There is not a car to be seen, and there are no signs of any tire tracks. In fact, there is no sign of any modern conveniences at all. I don't know for certain if we've gone back in time, but if we haven't, this place is certainly stuck in the past.

The buildings are of simple and sturdy construction, but years of dust and grime hide their true age. The only structure that appears well maintained is the centrepiece of the village: the church. It's massive, and its limestone walls gleam in the sun. There are two large towers on the front side, but we can't otherwise see anything interesting about it from where we're hiding.

The people themselves don't appear much better off than the buildings that surround them. They all feature stooped shoulders, shuffling gaits, and dark worn-out clothing. They lead thin livestock by ropes to and from the market, and there's not a smile to be seen.

"It sure looks like we've gone back in time," Keegan whispers as he peeks over the hay.

I nod. "And judging by how well kept the church looks, this doesn't seem the kind of place that will be particularly welcoming to the likes of us."

James and Keegan both nod.

I lean closer to them, my voice barely a whisper. "Do you think they're all right?"

James screws his face up. "I know they say not to judge a book by its cover, but..."

"Their auras are very faded," Keegan says quietly. He looks at us, his pale blue eyes radiating with a passion that speaks volumes. "There's definitely something about this village worth investigating. How does it even exist with little or no connection to anywhere else . . . ?" His voice trails off as he shifts his posture.

I follow his gaze, and hunker down a little lower. Two men are walking straight toward us. One of them looks rather angry. A string of barely recognizable French flies out of him, and he gesticulates wildly toward the hay bales. The other man looks only slightly less angry.

The three of us look at each other in panic.

"What do we do?" James hisses.

But there's nothing we can do except acknowledge that whatever it is we're doing is wrong.

"We stand up calmly and apologize to him. We're obviously in his field," I say. "How's your French?"

Without waiting for an answer, I stand up and step out into the open. Keegan and James follow right behind me.

The two men freeze instantly. The louder of the two slowly makes the sign of the cross as he looks at the other. Without uttering another word, they turn and flee into the village.

"Um," Keegan says. "What was that about?"

"No idea," James says. "But I've changed my mind. Let's get out of here before the whole village decides to show us their torches and pitchforks."

We scurry back up the trail to the iron door.

On the way back to the Citadel, we promise each other not to tell anyone about our discovery until we know more about the strange village. There are two possible reasons why the Guardians haven't mentioned this place to us: either there's something about it they don't want us to know, or they've yet to discover it for themselves. Either way, we don't want to tell them what we know. Not yet. By unspoken agreement, we'll be visiting it again sooner rather than later.

When we get back to the Chamber of Knowledge, we hear Danielle's voice drifting down from the upper platform, where she's speaking with the Guardians. James takes the spiral staircase two steps at a time. Keegan and I glance toward our quarters. Caitlin exits them with an empty backpack slung over her shoulder.

I notice she's swapped out her red leather jacket for a brown one. She unzips the jacket, exposing a large rondel dagger sheathed on her right hip. She strides past us with only a slight nod before running up the staircase to the upper platform.

Keegan slaps me on the shoulder. Only then do I realize I've been staring at her.

He leans toward my ear and whispers, "She's a Seeker, Aiden. Show a little respect!"

I shake my head, mostly to myself. "Yes, of course," I whisper.

Keegan and I join the others around the table on the upper level. Everyone is present except David. Although I can't help but think of how stunning Caitlin looks, I also keep in mind that she's here to fulfill an important duty. It's not difficult at this point, as I've never seen her so agitated about her activities as Seeker.

"What a week!" she says as she drops her empty backpack at her feet. Despite there being more than enough space at the table, she sits on the floor cross-legged and cradles her face in her hands, her long brown hair hanging loose.

"What do you have to report to us, Seeker?" Evelyn asks.

Caitlin says nothing at first. When she speaks, she doesn't look up. "Speaker, Guardians, I've made a grave mistake. For the past few months, I've been tracking a bright, very promising prospect from Montreal, a kid by the name of Francois Belanger. He can't be any older than sixteen, but I could feel his potential strength emanating from him." She finally looks up, and her eyes are haunted. "I knew he was beginning to behave differently, but I'd thought we'd have more time."

"Caitlin, please. Tell us what happened."

"This past Tuesday, I noticed that the friends he normally walks home from school with were nowhere to be found, and there was a dark cloud hanging over him. Worried, I decided to return the next day, and I found him alone again. This time, however, when he got halfway home, he randomly stopped in the middle of the sidewalk and stared at a small weed poking through a crack. Within seconds, I saw it grow. Just like that. An inch at least."

"You're kidding!" I say. "His magic manifested on its own?" I think back to her pushing me in front of a car to get the same result. In contrast, her method now seems unnecessarily extreme. I want to say something about it, but I know now is not the time.

Caitlin's eyes flick to me as if seeing me for the first time, and she nods. "It looks that way. I was so excited to see it happen." She glances to each of the Guardians. "I should have come right away to report to you, but I wanted to be sure of what I was dealing with, so I stayed in Montreal for another day."

"What else did you learn?" Aleksandar asks. "Anything?"

"On Thursday, I waited almost an hour outside his school, but he didn't come out. One of the teachers finally came out and asked whom I was waiting for. When I told her, she glanced around nervously and told me that no student by that name is enrolled at the school. Then she left so quickly that I couldn't say another word to her." She wipes a tear off her face. "I ran the entire way to his house, but I found the place empty."

"Do you know what happened to him? Where his family went?"

She shakes her head. "I looked into it. It's like they were never there."

The silence in the chamber leaves a palpable chill.

Caitlin then makes deliberate eye contact with James, Keegan, and me. "It's terrible. I keep thinking about the three of you. If kids and their families can disappear like that, what would happen to you if they ever caught you?"

A heavy silence falls. What is there to say? She's right. The outside world is changing, and it will be a very dangerous place until people understand magic. I've struggled with it for months, but Caitlin's story makes it finally sink home.

I look at her as she sits on the floor with her shoulders slumped, her hair a mess, and tears streaking down her face, and I feel compassion welling up within me. Seeker or not, she's still human. I walk over to her and kneel beside her. She doesn't budge, nor say a word.

"You did absolutely nothing wrong," I say with a decisiveness I actually didn't know I had. I place my hand on her shoulder. "Nobody could have known that he would disappear . . . and so quickly."

She looks up at me. Her face wavers between regret and resolve.

"And as for us," I continue, "we're safe here. The Guardians won't let us leave until we're able to protect ourselves from those who mean to harm us."

She smiles and squeezes my hand. "Thank you," she says.

Caitlin stands, wiping her eyes with the palm of her hand and straightening her hair crudely. She walks over to the ledge overlooking the standing stones and seems to lose herself in a moment of reflection.

I feel a hand lightly touch my shoulder. I look up. It's Aleksandar. I stand and brush my robe off. I look at him questioningly, but he's already walking toward Caitlin. Evelyn joins them, and the three of them converse quietly. The other Guardians quietly file down the stairs, presumably to return to the living quarters. I look at James and Keegan, but they both shrug.

Danielle walks over to James and hugs him tightly.

"Let's go have dinner," James says to me as he pulls away slightly from Danielle. He glances over his shoulder at the Seeker and the two Guardians. "It looks like they could use some privacy."

"I'll cook," Keegan says before descending the stairs.

James and Danielle head for the stairs but pause briefly.

"Are you joining us?" Danielle asks.

I smile, but shake my head. "Thanks for the offer, but I think I'm going to hang out here for a few more minutes."

James nods. "We'll save you some."

I can tell by the look on his face that he feels sorry for me, but I'm glad he doesn't say anything else before he and Danielle follow Keegan.

I walk around the massive table and absentmindedly trace my fingers along the mountain ranges engraved into it. I stop, my eyes focusing on the scene before me. My finger is touching the same tunnel James, Keegan, and I stepped out of today. I recognize it because in tiny exquisite detail is the same iron door and the same pathway leading down to . . . I look to where the village should be at the base of the mountain and find instead a large city.

Until now, I took for granted that this table is an actual map depicting actual places. Until now, it felt so abstracted, so arcane, so removed from our own time and place that it didn't occur to me that it was of *this* place. Dumbfounded, I sit at the head of the table where Evelyn normally sits. I can now see why she sits here. It provides an excellent view of the table and most of the Chamber of Knowledge. My eyes scan the details of the map on table. I wonder what more I can learn from it now that I've seen something featured on it with my own eyes. There are other openings in the mountains, but they seem scattered haphazardly rather than having any sort of pattern or reason. Regardless, these must be various other access points to the Citadel. I begin to wonder where each corresponding tunnel is in reference to everything else.

I glance over at the map the Guardians have been working on. They've mounted it on an easel and positioned it so they can see it while they're seated at the table. In contrast to the map of the mountain, the Guardians' map is a detailed depiction of Lannóg Eolas's interior. I look at the map closer. They've left a lot of empty space on it for the chambers they haven't discovered yet, such as the tomb I stumbled upon.

When I look again at the large city at the base of the mountain, an image of Evelyn's vision flashes in my mind. In the vision, the kingdom was ultimately reduced to nothing. I then think of the village the three of us discovered. Could it be the remains of this once vibrant city?

The Guardians meet almost daily at this table. I can't help but think they already know about the village and are simply keeping it from us. Maybe they don't think we're ready for it. I look carefully at the tabletop map, marking its features, and then look at the Guardians' map once again. If the table really is a representation of this reality, then where the village should be on the

Guardians' map is nothing but a big hole. Is it possible they haven't found it after all?

I don't know how long they've been watching me, but when I look up, I see that Caitlin, Aleksandar, and Evelyn are all staring at me. I raise an eyebrow, and Aleksandar's normally stoic face softens as the glimmer of a smile plays across his lips.

"We were just saying how you seem to belong in that spot," he says.

For a moment, I don't know what he's talking about; I'm still lost in wondering what they might know about the village. And then I think about what I must look like sitting here in my robe, focusing intently on the tabletop as though I were playing a game of chess. I suppose they're right.

"We'll see you next week," Aleksandar says to Caitlin. He then takes Evelyn's arm and guides her down the stairs.

I keep quiet while Caitlin once again looks out over the standing stones. She eventually looks over at me and offers a small smile.

"Were they able to convince you that you've done nothing wrong?" I ask.

"They convinced me that we're all learning, and that next time I should come to them when I'm unsure about something."

I frown, and this seems to spur her into action. She grabs her backpack and zips up her jacket. "Well," she says as she heads for one of the tunnels, "I better be on my way."

This is how I expected this to go, but it's not how I hoped it would. Caitlin is a Seeker, a tracker and an explorer. She wandered these caves before I did. Although I made a promise to James and Keegan, I want to share our discovery of the village with her. I also want to find out if she already knows about it.

"Caitlin—"

She stops at the entrance to the tunnel and holds up a hand. "Aiden, don't. I don't need your pity right now."

Pity? I can't help but laugh a little. "Can you sit for a moment before you go? I think we should talk."

"There's nothing for us to talk about."

"Look, I get it. I'm a wizard and you're a Seeker, so maybe we shouldn't let ourselves get too close on a personal level. I won't pretend to understand why even though you refuse to talk to me, but I get why you'd be concerned about it."

She just stands there, looking at her backpack.

"You're our Seeker," I say. "You do so much for us. I just want you to know we appreciate it."

She waves her hand dismissively and pulls her backpack on. "It's nothing. I'm just doing my duty."

I shake my head. "No." I say it forcefully enough that she looks me in the eyes. "You do way more than your duty. I want to show you something as a thank you for everything you do here."

"That's really not necessary." She looks down the tunnel she's about to walk down.

"You were a student here before the Citadel awoke," I say, and she turns to me again. "It's not the same place it was. You've seen the yew tree, but that place has since become a thriving garden." I see a longing growing in her eyes, so I try a final temptation: "Have you ever seen the Great Hall of Learning?"

"No," she says quietly.

"If you'd like to see it, I'd love to show it to you. I don't think the Guardians would object. And there's something close by I think you'll enjoy."

I'll be able to gauge by Caitlin's reaction upon seeing the tunnel whether she already knows about it.

She sets her backpack down and smiles at me. For a moment, I'm transported back to the time we spent at the coffee shop on the waterfront.

"I would like to see the Great Hall," she says, "and I have to admit I'm curious about this other thing you want to show me. What is it?"

"It'll be much easier just to show you."

Caitlin's excitement at seeing an inner part of the Citadel is infectious. When we reach the entrance to the Chambers of the Elements, from which you can see all the way across to the far end of the Chambers of the Serpent, I stop, turn, and grin at her.

"*This* is where we spend our days!" I announce. "The Guardians call it the Great Hall of Learning. This is where all the wizards you'll find will be trained."

Caitlin gasps and covers her mouth with her hands.

I laugh. "That was my reaction too—well, almost. Isn't it beautiful?"

She nods, speechless.

After several moments of just gazing at the various features, she eventually asks whether we can we go deeper. Without another word, I begin leading her forward. I watch as she traces the stone walls with her fingertips as we go. Perhaps with her unique ability to sense magic, she can feel it living and breathing. I nearly ask her about it, but I decide not to ruin the moment.

I lead her through the Chambers of the Elements before taking the passageway that leads straight to the garden. The purpose of this expedition, after all, is to see whether she knows about the village. If she doesn't, I'll show her the rest of the Great Hall on the way back.

When we step into the garden, Caitlin stops to place a hand on the wall as if to anchor herself.

"*This*," she asks in open wonder, "is the same place you showed me before with the tree?"

I laugh. I point across the garden to the distinctive evergreen with the small dark-green needles and grey-brown bark. "That's her," I say with a smile. "The one that started it all."

"Her?" Caitlin asks quietly.

"She's an Irish yew, and those are her babies." I gesture to a few saplings that have sprouted around the tree. "We think of her as the mother tree of the garden. Sean knew it was a she when she sprouted scaly green buds that grew into a kind of acorn, like the oak's."

Caitlin takes in the beauty of the garden: the trees, the bushes, the flowers, the babbling brook, the moss-covered stones, the peaceful pond, the ferns that grow at the water's edge. She bends down to examine a yellow flower with spindly blossoms.

"Gentian?" she asks.

I nod. "Keegan calls it bitterwort. He wants to use the roots for tea. We just have to wait for more to grow." I gesture at the other herbs. "He's been carefully cultivating all of these for medicinal purposes. He and Sean crafted a crane bag large enough for a small mortar and pestle and several herbs so he can learn to use them in his healing arts."

She smiles. "You three have really begun making this feel like home."

"I thought you'd like this, but there's something else I think you'll appreciate as well."

I lead her from the garden and take us down the passageway that leads to toward the village.

"As Jennifer explained it to me," I say quietly as we make our way, "the

Citadel only appears to be one solid place. In reality, it's scattered throughout the world, joined only in the places where the chambers connect. The Guardians think that portal stones similar to the ones that take us all around the world also join the chambers to each other."

"Amazing," she says softly.

"It is."

As we pass the Chambers of the Serpent, I feel a weak force pull at me from ahead. It's as though something is calling me back to the village. I glance at Caitlin. I can tell by the way she touches the stone walls with a look of longing on her face that there's no way she's been here before. I slow to a stop.

Caitlin looks at me askance. "Is everything okay?" she asks with a trace of suspicion in her voice.

I sense the Seeker in her come to life, and I try not to let it unsettle me. Once again, I'm left wondering if she can sense my thoughts as well as my magic. On the morning I woke up to find her watching me sleep, she didn't deny she could read my thoughts; she simply told me she had better things to do. I can't question her on it now, though, not when I actually do have something to hide. I play it safe. I banish any thoughts of the village from my mind and picture the waterfall in the Chamber of Knowledge.

"Hmm? Oh. Yes."

I look at her in the torchlight while I quietly wrestle with myself. A part of me wants to share this with her and to explore this strange pulling sensation, but my promise to James and Keegan echoes through my head.

"What is it?" she asks.

"In all your explorations of the Citadel, you've never been here before?" I ask finally.

She visibly relaxes. "No, this part was always off limits. Well, a lot was off limits."

I nod. "In that case, there's something I think you'll like even more than this."

We turn around and walk back toward the garden. This time, I take her through the Chambers of Inception. We stop when we reach one of the intricate puzzles comprising the locking mechanism of a chest. She reaches out and touches it reverently. I think for a moment that she's going to try to solve it, but then she draws her hand away and looks at me.

"There is strong magic in that," she says softly. "I wouldn't even know where to begin with it."

"You're right about that."

We eventually reach the vast valley that separates the Chambers of Inception from the Chambers of Reflection. I come to a stop at the top of the steep and narrow path and point at the valley below.

"Here it is! It's the central valley of the Great Hall."

We look out over the crags and large standing stones. There is no village or town there or any landmarks or other features to indicate where in the world it might be. Wherever it is, the sun has crested the outer edge, and sunlight glints off something made of metal that sticks out from behind a large crag in the distance.

Caitlin looks at me, her curiosity piqued. "Can we go see what it is?"

"I don't see why not." I'm also curious. I haven't had a chance to visit this place since Jennifer showed it to me. I don't remember seeing anything there before, but it was earlier in the day then. "Jennifer assured me that even though it's open to the sky, it's actually part of Lannóg Eolas and is totally self-contained. She was fairly confident that there's no chance of running into any outsiders."

We begin descending the path leading down into the valley. In the daylight, I can see that crude steps have been carved into the rock, which certainly makes the descent easier. It takes us about fifteen minutes to reach the bottom. I turn to look up at the small opening we came through. The climb back looks daunting.

All around us, towering outcroppings of rock jut out of the ground. The ground itself is dry and dusty. The few plants that grow between the rocks are mostly succulents and thorny bushes among tall grasses. Here and there tumbleweeds roll in the wind.

"It looks very desert-like," Caitlin says.

"It feels very desert-like," I add, wiping a bead of sweat off my forehead.

She laughs as we continue along the rough-hewn trail toward the object we saw from above.

It takes us another half an hour to find the source of our curiosity. When we do, we slow our pace considerably. Large standing stones form a circle and vibrate with energy. In the centre is a large telescope. It must be at least six feet long and twenty inches in diameter. Off to the side is a roped-off area dotted with yellow markers. Inside the rope, a man kneels, scraping at the base of one of the stones.

Caitlin and I look at each other, confusion on our faces.

"I thought no one could find this place," she whispers.

"Well, it was more of a theory, I think."

We mask our approach by following a low ridge. We pause when the man sits up, stretches his back, and wipes his brow.

"David!" Caitlin cries.

It really is David. We're both startled by her cry.

He looks over at us. "Caitlin! Aiden! What a surprise! I didn't expect to see anyone else out here today." He slowly pushes himself to his feet, using his cane as support. He straightens his bow tie, and I marvel that he's actually out in this heat in a tweed jacket.

"I was just showing Caitlin the Great Hall of Learning. I thought she would be interested to see a bit from our perspective. Jennifer showed me this place when we were learning about illusion magic, and I knew Caitlin would love it."

"Ah, I see. Well, all the better for me to have the company. And young company at that, still with the full use of their limbs!" He chuckles to himself as he turns back to the standing stone. "I'm trying to discover something about the civilization that placed these. I hope to shed some light on where this particular area is in the outer world."

"Is that why you have the telescope?" Caitlin asks.

"Telescope?" he replies distractedly. "Hmm? Oh! That old piece of rubbish?"

My eyes widen when I hear such an advanced telescope called rubbish.

"That's Sean's," David explains. "He's also been messing around with an old sextant and some charts and the like. He's trying to study the stars to find out where we are. So far he hasn't had any more luck than I have."

I take a closer look at the telescope. "It doesn't really look like rubbish."

He stares at me aghast. "It's useless! His father bought it for him, and he thinks he'll discover the secrets of the magical universe with it. No, no, no. The secrets always lie in the stones." He taps the stone next to him. "Take this marking here, for instance." He indicates a small etching he's revealed on the base of the stone. "Notice the shapes of the figures? Clearly Mesopotamian." He gazes at it for a few seconds. "Now if only I could figure out the specific civilization."

Caitlin leans forward in sudden interest. "We don't normally associate stone circles with ancient Mesopotamia."

David grins. "No . . . Most people think of the British Isles. But cultures from around the world certainly built various stone megaliths. As for stone circles, well, we've certainly discovered some in the Middle East and elsewhere. It's just that they're more common in places like Brittany and much of Ireland. That's part of what makes this one a mystery."

History was never really my strong suit. I shake my head in amazement, partly because I don't want to disappoint him. "So this is where you've been hiding," I say while leaning in close to inspect the etching.

David is already lowering himself to the ground again. "Oh yes," he says. "As the historian, my role is to watch the history of the world as it unfolds and determine how every event in the past relates to our future. It's been a fascinating experience that's taken me around the world several times. And"—he looks up with a wink and a sly glance at the telescope—"it keeps me abreast of modern technology. You'll learn all about it soon. I believe your next round of training is with me."

He turns to Caitlin, who is now crouching in the dust beside him. "Now, my dear, here's what I think . . ."

Chapter Seventeen

James, Keegan, and I crouch behind a large boulder on the outskirts of the village. The stacks of hay bales we hid among the last time we were here have vanished. Granted, it's been more than two weeks, as we've had little free time from our lessons until now. We tried coming last week, but it was nighttime in the village, and we decided not to brave the silence and deep darkness.

From our new position, we have an excellent view of the square and the church at its centre. The square is vast, far larger than is required for a village of this size. Dirt and other debris swirl across its surface, which is some sort of stone mosaic caked in years of neglect. The edges of the square are lined with market stalls.

Most of the stalls look like they haven't been used in decades, if not centuries. Grime coats their facades, and rotting boards hang loose. Any modern-day building inspector would condemn them without question. At a quick count, I'd say there are at least forty of them. Of those, only sixteen appear to have been used recently. In the middle of the active part of the market stands a tall square-roofed building. It has no signage or other markings, but it looks like a town hall.

In the very centre of the square, the church towers above everything. I stare at it in awe. It's easily the size of St. Michael's in Toronto, which makes it all the more dominant in this small village. It's also the only building I've seen here that's been kept clean and otherwise well maintained. Three dark-stained wooden doors are recessed into archways. Above the two outer arches is a decorated relief, but we're not close enough to see the details. Above the centre arch, though, stands an enormous statue of the archangel Michael. His visage takes up the entire central peak, and he stands nearly as tall as the two bell towers on either side of him. I shudder as I take in his vengeful smile and the anger, fury, and triumph that burns in his eyes as he thrusts a great sword through the head of a dragon beneath his feet. It's an imposing sight.

The two bell towers begin ringing. Their rich sound seems to echo throughout the valley. Amid the ringing, the villagers stop what they're doing and make their way to the church, entering through the centre door. They each pause to bow on their way through. When the ringing stops, we scan the village, but there is no sign of anyone. It would seem the entire village is attending the church service.

At least an hour passes, and nobody has left the church. There is still no sign of life outside the church besides the villagers' livestock.

"I'd say it's a good idea we decided not to use our magic here," Keegan says quietly. "These people are obviously very devout."

James and I nod.

"I can't take my eyes off that statue," I say.

"Yeah, it's a bit unnerving," Keegan says.

James looks away from the statue and shudders. "We should have used this time to explore the village. It would have been perfect."

"We couldn't have known they'd be in there this long," I say.

"Or that their attendance would be so dedicated!" Keegan says. "Why are we still hiding, anyway? As long as we don't practice any magic, we should be fine, shouldn't we?"

"Because the Guardians—"

"Aren't here," James says. "Aiden, you're the one who's so curious to learn more about this place." He looks at me intently. "Isn't that why we're here? To find out what the Guardians are hiding from us? You're right! It's odd that they haven't already discovered it."

"But what if they really haven't?"

"Well, if they haven't, maybe it means we were meant to discover it instead of them. Maybe there's something here we need to find."

He looks across the way to the spot where we were discovered the last time we were here. "Those two men were probably scared because they thought we were robbers or bandits or something. I mean, honestly, what kind of men spy on a village? Men with something to hide."

I think about that for a minute. He does have a point. "It would be too obvious that we don't belong if we were to just walk out now while the rest of the village is in church."

James grins. "But once the doors open and the villagers spill out, we could join the crowd and blend in."

My legs and back are sore from crouching for so long. The thought of standing and walking fills me with anticipation.

Moments later, the door to the church opens with a creak. We huddle down behind the boulder. The priest steps out first. His shoulders are stooped with age, and his face is a network of wrinkles. His face is set in a scowl, but this doesn't quite make him look unkind. His grey hair is impeccably groomed, probably waxed. His large stomach bulges, straining the clasps of his emerald-green vestments. He doesn't stay to mingle with the congregants leaving the church. Instead, he walks west past the town hall, disappearing down a well-kept path on the far side of the square.

The villagers slowly disperse, their eyes lowered and shoulders slouched. Their coarse wool clothes hang off them poorly. It makes them look like medieval peasants. The style is close enough to our robes that it makes me think we won't stand out that much. At a glance, I'd say only about a dozen of the people are under the age of fifty. There are even fewer children. The people all look thin, some sickly thin, compared to the portly priest. They look even more downtrodden than they did on our last visit, and I wouldn't have thought that was possible.

Once the villagers have returned to their regular business, both Keegan and James turn to me.

"Where are all the children?" James asks.

"I saw only a few families," Keegan says. "If we really did go back in time I thought we'd see a lot more children."

"Me too. In times like the Middle Ages they definitely had more," James says with confidence, "like five or six maybe, but even the young look old here. The way they walk—it's like pure defeat. It's as if they have nothing to live for. No wonder they aren't having more children, or any."

"I think we need to explore this more," Keegan says. "We need to see if there's something we can do to help."

"Our robes," I say finally, and I hope not to regret it. "They're not that dissimilar to their clothing, style-wise. I feel we should at least take a closer look at the church."

After a tense pause, James accepts our silence as tacit agreement. He moves to step out from behind the boulder, and we follow his lead. We head for the nearest dusty path, adopting the meek posture of the villagers. Nobody stops us, but I can feel eyes upon us, full of suspicion and distrust. The villagers watch us discreetly, seemingly afraid to stare at us openly.

As we cross in front of the church, keeping just outside of the square, I stifle a gasp. The reliefs carved into the archways depict the great battle between the angels of heaven and the fallen, led by Lucifer. The final scene shows the throne of God shining radiantly above Lucifer, whose body is posed in a perpetual fall. I have never seen such a detailed depiction of the war between good and evil displayed so prominently on a church.

A feeling of dread fills me as I feel the vengeful eyes of the archangel Michael bore into me. I turn away, trying to sink into the ground where I'll be safe from both the prying eyes of the villagers and the judging gaze of the statue.

"Can we walk faster?" I hiss. "I don't think blending in is working very well."

A man and a woman ahead of us stop and stare at me upon hearing me speak. Before I can look away, they make the sign of the cross and change course, clearly to avoid us. They disappear between a couple of buildings.

"Do we really look that scary?" Keegan asks quietly.

"Maybe they're just not used to travellers," James whispers.

"Judging by this place, probably not," I say. "Do you really think we've found a portal that brings us back in time?"

James looks at me, incredulous. "Aiden, look around you. Do you know of anywhere in the world that still uses horses as transportation?" He points out three carts in various states of disrepair attached to horses that look a bit too underfed. "Or that use those?" He indicates a streetlamp.

I look at it as we pass. Inside the glass casing is a large half-burned candle. I look at our surroundings more carefully. Sure enough, there are several of these archaic streetlamps set throughout the village.

"No," I say. "There's definitely something different about his place."

"It looks something straight out of the history holo-vids," Keegan says.

The constant feeling of being watched is unnerving, but we're committed now, and so we continue alongside the village square until we reach a narrow road made of old cobblestones.

"Do you feel that?" Keegan asks.

I nod slowly.

"So much power..." James says.

He's right. The entire road is thrumming with an energy that calls to me like a siren, rolling down from an unseen source. It takes me a moment to realize why the energy feels familiar, and then it hits me: it's the same energy that was pulling at me in the passageway when I was with Caitlin.

Keegan grabs my arm. "I didn't want to believe it, but the Guardians *are* hiding something."

"It sure looks that way," James says distantly. "How can they not know about this place?"

I take a few steps down the road, giving in to the lure of the silent call. James and Keegan remain at my side. By the time we've taken maybe ten steps, a man steps out in front of us. He wears a coarse brown wool tunic with tattered edges, and he has a black band tied around his right forearm. He appears to be in his early thirties. He clenches his left hand tightly in what appears to be an attempt to stop the blood flowing from a wound on his palm. He looks at each of us in turn. The shock on his face is clear.

"They were right," the man says in a thick French accent. He says it quietly, more to himself than to us.

"Who was right?" I ask.

He flinches as though he didn't believe we were real until the moment I spoke. He slowly brings his eyes up to meet mine—meekly, as if afraid. "The farmer and his son," he says. "They claimed there were strangers wandering the fields."

When we don't answer, he glances over his shoulder to make sure no one else is near. "It took us some time to convince them to stop telling their story."

"Why would you want to do that?" James asks.

Keegan pulls James back half a step before the man can answer. He looks at the injured hand. "What happened? To your hand?"

The man looks down at his hand, as if seeing the injury for the first time. "I slipped with the saw. It's nothing."

"May I?" Keegan asks gently, gesturing at his hand.

The man stares at him. I can almost sense his hesitation, but then he slowly extends his palm out.

Keegan steps forward and inspects the wound. "It's deep. It should be covered. To stop the bleeding." He looks up at the man. "Have you washed it?"

The man nods.

Keegan looks around. After finding nothing else, he tears a strip from the sleeve of his robe. He reaches into the crane bag tied around his waist and pulls out a couple of small satchels of dried flowers and leaves. Looking at them carefully, he selects one and looks back up at the man.

"You shouldn't feel anything, but these herbs should keep any infection away."

When the man nods, Keegan reaches into his crane bag and pulls out a small vial and his mortar and pestle. He sets them on the ground and rubs the flower gently between his palms. The dried flower disintegrates into the mortar. He opens the vial and pours a few drops of water onto the crushed flowers. Looking at the large cut, he repeats the process two more times until the mortar is nearly full. He then takes his pestle and grinds the mixture into a thick paste. When he's satisfied, he gingerly applies the paste to the man's wound. He then gently wraps the cloth around it all.

"Change the bandage tonight, and your hand should be fine," Keegan says.

The man looks from his injured hand to Keegan. "You took away the pain," he says quietly. "Thank you."

James hasn't stopped looking at the strange man. "Why did you stop the farmers from talking about us?"

"We do not get many visitors." He steps around us toward the square. He stretches out his uninjured arm and beckons us back the way we came. "It is not safe for you to be here. There are only two paths in and out of the village. One is past the home of the priest and the other is the path you used to come down the mountain. I'll get you safely back to the path up the mountain. The market should keep everybody's attention. It's open for only two hours each day."

As we approach the village square again, we can see it's mostly empty save for the far side, where it has become a bustling market. The strange man leads us along the edge, far enough away from the crowd. Something in his manner gives me a sense of urgency. I think it's certainly time for us to leave. I just hope we can do it undetected.

When we get about halfway along the square, a deafening silence fills the air. I glance toward the market and see every head turned our way. There are frightened looks on everyone's faces. The market fills with hushed whispers.

My attention is drawn to the town hall, where I see a man standing on the steps. His long auburn hair is swept back behind his ears, framing his thoughtful face and highlighting his frowning red cheeks. He wears a simple white tunic beneath a brown laced-up vest. He's the only villager we've seen besides the priest who's wearing something other than brown wool. He holds himself with an air of authority. He gazes at us from under thick eyebrows, and he continues to watch us as we pass. His gaze then flickers up to the mountain path leading to the iron door.

Our companion hisses something under his breath and picks up his pace until we reach the path that will take us back to the Citadel. He steps aside, careful not to get too close to us as we pass him. When I pass, however, he grabs hold of my arm.

"Return in two days' time," he whispers.

And then he is gone.

Chapter Eighteen

Mary sits cross-legged on the floor in the centre of the stone circle in the Chamber of Knowledge. We're seated in a semi-circle before her. Until now, she's been the most enigmatic Guardian. I've seen her often in passing, but I don't think any of us have had a conversation with her since she led us to our initiation. That was a while ago now. I've at least gotten used to the purple highlights in her curly hair.

Today, she stares at us over winged glasses perched on the end of her nose, making her appear rather serious. She looks like she'd be just as comfortable in a business suit at the head of a boardroom table as she is in the black robes of a Guardian seated in a sacred circle.

She straightens her back while maintaining an aura of calm confidence. When she looks at me, her large eyes convey trustworthiness and a depth of knowledge to a degree that I haven't seen in anyone since my grandfather passed away.

"Welcome," she says, her voice crisp but perfunctory, "to magic fundamentals."

James glances at me. His eyes say he'd rather be investigating the cobblestone road in the village.

The look isn't lost on Mary. She leans forward and cups James's chin with the palm of her hand. He freezes, and his eyes widen in shock. She slowly lifts his face toward hers.

"I know what you're thinking, James," she says. "You're thinking, 'What a waste of time. I already know everything I need to know about magic.' Aren't you, James?" She says it politely, but there's a fire in her voice and in her eyes that makes me sit a little straighter.

When James nods, she releases his face. She sits erect once again and smiles. Something in that smile causes me to shiver.

"Now turn to face Aiden." Her voice is commanding. It's not harsh and demanding like Aleksandar's, but I imagine whole armies obeying her instantly with that voice.

James turns to me.

"You can cast fire—yes, James?" Mary asks.

James nods.

"Then light a ball of fire in the palm of your hand."

James clenches his fist, focusing. When he opens it, a brilliant flame rises above his palm. He rolls his hands together, and the flame expands, curling into an arc that rolls around itself. It builds rapidly into a churning ball of white, orange, yellow, and red heat. I stare at it, losing myself in its intricacies. It's not quite as bright as mine, but it looks no less effective.

Mary seems to admire it for several moments. "Good. Now . . ." She leans forward, and her voice takes on an almost erotic longing. "Hurl it at Aiden!"

James blinks and his head spins to her. "*What?*"

"*Now!*" Mary's tone suggests that he has no choice but to obey.

Since I'm still lost in the allure of the flames, it takes several seconds for their conversation to penetrate my consciousness. It's not until the ball of fire races toward me that I fully register what's happening. Panic fills me, and my hands come up in defense. It's too late. The fire strikes me square in the chest, and with a sizzle and a puff of smoke, it dies out instantly.

I stare down at my chest in stunned amazement. I'm grateful that my robe remains undamaged, but the heat of James's magic has warmed my skin beneath the material. I glare at Mary. Before I can speak, she raises a hand.

"Calm yourself, Wizard Aiden. You were never in any danger." She looks at James, whose face is ashen. "What did you think would happen when you attacked Aiden?"

James looks at me meekly and then at Mary. "I hoped he would be able to defend himself in time."

"He clearly was not." She glances at me with something akin to disappointment in her eyes before turning her attention back to James. "Did you know your fire would have no effect?"

"No."

She leans forward. Her face is a strange mixture of contemplation and satisfaction. "Then we have learned two things. First and most important"—she pauses for effect, staring directly at me—"is that you can never trust a wizard, even if you think that wizard is your best friend."

I glance at James again, and he looks horrified.

"Second," Mary continues, "is that every wizard has a strength, and that strength can never be used against them. Aiden, your magic is steeped in fire. It runs through your blood and influences everything you do." Her eyes seem to bore deep into my soul. "Aside from when your wristband essentially exploded while attached to your wrist, do you recall ever suffering a burn in your life?"

I think back, trying to remember another time, but I can't think of one no matter how hard I try. "No."

"And if you're not foolish, you never will. For all intents and purposes, you are immune to fire—within reason."

James leans forward as well. He now looks incredibly intrigued. Mary's tactic was terrifying, but it definitely got our attention. "So since I can wield fire, does that mean I'm immune to it as well?"

"Not exactly. You can cast fire, but you have to work at it, correct?"

James nods slowly.

Mary sits upright again. "I have spent the past several months watching you all as you practice. I've been trying to gain insights into what makes you tick as wizards. For instance, you already know that illusions have no effect on Keegan. Do you know why?"

"We assumed my previous training in energy healing allowed me to see what's real and what's not," Keegan says.

She shakes her head. "Not at all." She looks back to James. "When you weave an illusion, you bend the waves of reality, so it appears to be there. Keegan, however, is a profoundly powerful healer. His strength is life itself. Since your illusions are just energy with no life force woven into them, he sees right through them."

James and I look at Keegan. He smiles innocently and gives a playful shrug.

"So what's my strength then?" James asks.

Mary locks her eyes with James's. "I don't know yet." She says it quietly, and I see James's normally unwavering self-esteem get knocked down a notch.

She reaches out and takes his hand. "You have shown strength in many areas, James, but your true strength has not yet unveiled itself. Your energy is strongest when working with illusions and conjurations, so I suspect it will have something to do with one of those."

"Or both?"

Mary shrugs. "I don't know."

"What do you mean?"

"During your initiation, the Goddess gave you all special ropes." She points to each of us in turn, indicating the ropes we have tied around our waists. "Aiden, yours is red to symbolize destruction magic; Keegan, yours is green to symbolize the magic of healing; James, I'm afraid that our knowledge of the discipline associated with purple has been lost. Regardless, there is a pool of untapped potential within you that we will work to discover." She squeezes his hand before releasing it. "We will learn what it is. Trust me. That's why we're here."

There's a brief silence. I see James toying with the rope around his waist. I myself am intrigued by yet another mystery for us to solve. I hope he feels the same way.

"Now then," Mary says, "there's another reason I had James attack Aiden with fire."

I raise my eyebrows but say nothing.

"How did you feel after the initial surprise wore off, Aiden?" she asks.

"Um . . ." I'm unsure what she's expecting to hear.

"Think about it. Replay it in your mind." She leans in close, speaking passionately and seeming to grip her words with her hands. "Feel the fire hitting your chest again. What did you feel?"

I replay James's attack over again in my mind, envisioning the ball of fire hitting my chest, rippling across my robe, absorbing into my being. "Strength," I say quietly. "I felt stronger."

A smile spreads across Mary's face. "Exactly. Your magic is not limitless. Each wizard is born with a set amount within them—a pool of magic within, if you will. We don't know exactly how it works anymore, but like blood, your life depends on it."

She stares at each of us intently, drawing us into her lesson. "James, when you cast an illusion, you're actually sending out some of your pool of magic into the world. This released magic carries your personal signature with it, and when your casting is finished, the magic you released will slowly return to you. It's drawn to the pool within you. This is why it's important to properly understand the situation you're in before using any magic. You never want to use more magic than is required. You always want to have some left within you."

"But what if we use all the magic in the pool?" James asks. "Will it still find its way back?"

"Your magic is a part of you," Mary says quietly. "If there is ever none left within you, you will die."

James, Keegan, and I look at each other. I can see on their faces that, like me, they're thinking about all the horsing around we've done with our magic. Just last week, for example, we tried to see who could cast the largest spell.

Mary draws us close knowingly, like a mother hen protecting her chicks. "You were never in danger. Like I said, I've been watching. Experimenting to discover your limits is a good thing. It will teach you how far you can go. I originally wanted to teach you these warnings before we taught you how to use your magic, but I was convinced otherwise. While we planned out your training, some of the other Guardians made very compelling arguments suggesting that you should start using your magic first to form a basis of understanding. That way, it would be easier for you to understand what I have to teach you."

"Mary?" Keegan asks. "I understand why Aiden was unharmed, but how exactly did it make him feel stronger when James attacked him with fire?"

Mary withdraws, once again becoming the teacher. "Ah, excellent question! It's because James didn't get his bit of magic back. If you're foolish enough to attack a wizard with magic of his own strength, you must be prepared to accept the consequence of your magic being absorbed and assimilated into their own. Aiden is now one fireball stronger than he was a minute ago."

We look at each other again. There is so much more to learn.

Chapter Nineteen

Two days of learning about the basics of magic has left me more exhausted than I've ever been after any of my other lessons. Mary, who we had always thought of as quiet and soft spoken, is by far the most demanding of the Guardians. Her lessons are both physically and mentally intense, but we're learning to weave together all the teachings we've had up to this point, and I feel my skill with magic has grown a hundredfold.

I roll over with a groan and slowly stretch. It's way too early to be waking when we have another full day of lessons ahead of us, but today is the day the strange man in the village told us to return. We've been burning with curiosity. What makes today so important? Since we still know very little about the village, we haven't been able to devise any reasonable theories.

I sit up and rub the sleep out of my eyes. If we're going to get to the village and back before Mary arrives for class, we'll have to leave now. James is just beginning to stir. Keegan, it appears, is already awake. His bed is empty, and he didn't even bother to make it. It's very unlike him to leave his bed a mess. It's one of his quirks.

James looks over at it. "Keegan didn't sleep in for once."

I chuckle. "I feel like I could today."

"Tell me about it."

We wash up and dress, and I make Keegan's bed because I know he'll feel out of sorts knowing that he didn't do it.

James heads out to the Chamber of Knowledge but soon pops his head back into our quarters. "He's not out here, either. He must have already headed to the garden for his morning meditation."

"Well, we should meet him there. We only have a few hours before Mary arrives."

When we get to the garden, we find that Keegan isn't there either. We also find the Halls of Learning empty after a quick look.

"Any other ideas?" I ask.

James shakes his head.

A thought hits me. "He wouldn't have gone to the valley without us, would he?"

James casts a doubtful look in that direction. "I don't think so, but where else could he be? He knew we had to start out early today. Should we check?"

"Yeah. If we don't leave soon, we'll run out of time."

We set out down the passageway toward the village. When we exit the iron door at the end of the tunnel, we're met by the first rays of the morning sun peeking over the horizon. Dew glistens on the grass of the rolling hills. It's a beautiful sight, sure, but there's still no sign of Keegan.

James looks at me and shrugs his shoulders. "We've come this far. We can't turn back now."

"You know he'll be upset."

"I know." He glances back through the tunnel. "But he also knows the way and knows what the plan is. He can meet us here, right?"

"True."

We decide to return to the boulders at the outskirts of the village, as they are perfect for scouting the place without being seen. We're about a third of the way down the mountain path when James grabs my arm and pulls me behind a shrub.

"Look!" he hisses, pointing to the valley below.

At first, all I see are the fields of ripe wheat surrounding the village, the golden spikes radiant in the early morning sun. A few seconds later, I notice villagers moving through the field closest to us. There's a team of four villagers working their scythes in rows. Their methodical consistency would rival a modern-day tractor bot. In the corner of the same field, another group of villagers gathers the cut wheat, wrapping it into bunches and loading it onto a rickety trailer. I glance around at the other fields in our vicinity. Each of them is being worked the same way. We've arrived in the middle of the harvest. That will make getting to the village unobserved significantly more difficult for us.

We continue down the side of the mountain with extra care, darting from hiding spot to hiding spot, keeping low as we go. We won't be able to use the wheat fields to mask our approach anymore; it's something we took for granted. James points out another large mound of boulders on the village's easternmost edge. It looks promising. They're close enough to our location, and a few small clusters of bushes along the way should provide adequate cover between us and the fields where the villagers are working.

It takes the better part of an hour, but we reach the boulders undetected. We crouch behind them and look over to the village square.

There is significantly less activity in the village today, which makes sense given the number of villagers out in the fields. Not far from the square, nearly a dozen young children sit attentively outside a decrepit schoolhouse, listening as their teacher points out various features of the landscape outside the village. In front of the church, the priest embraces an elderly parishioner. A kindly expression has replaced the scowl on his face. He appears to be consoling the woman about something.

We keep an eye out for our friend with the black band around his forearm, but there's no sign of him. "What do you think, James?"

"Maybe he's at the cobblestone road. We should try to get to it."

We can't see the road from our position, but I can feel the strange power pulling at me. It's obvious that there's something magical about it. I just wish we didn't have to pass near the church to get to it.

"I don't know, James. I feel that Keegan should be with us if we decide to go into the village again. Whoever this guy is, he's the one who told us to be here. I'm sure he'll show up."

We stare out at the village for several more minutes.

"Do you see the emptiness in everyone?" James asks a while later. "It's like something within these villagers is missing. And why does their livestock all look underfed or sickly with all those fields? Even the trees in the village look slightly wilted." He looks out across the valley and then peers again at the village. "Outside the village, everything looks lush and green, but in here it's all dusty and dying."

I follow his gaze, nodding in agreement. "You're right." My eyes settle on the priest. "Except for him. There's something different about the priest. He seems like an outsider." I fall silent, my gaze shifting from villager to villager. "You know, I've never been able to see auras like you and Keegan can. Is that what I'm seeing now?"

James nods. "Probably. I couldn't see auras before coming to study with the Guardians, so I'm no expert. What do you see?"

"It's weird," I whisper, "but it's almost like I'm *feeling* the energy around them rather than seeing it."

James leans against a boulder. "That sounds different from what Keegan and I experience." He stares at me expectantly. "What do you see when you look at me?"

I focus on him, but all I see is James crouching beside me with a couple of grimy smudges on his face from all of our stealthy intrigue. There's nothing out of the ordinary at all. I shake my head.

"You look the same as the others," I say as my focus slides.

Then James's face goes blurry for a heartbeat as though my eyes have started watering. I blink hard, trying to clear them. In squeezing my eyelids together, I notice something within myself for the first time. It's as though there's a whole other *me* just below the surface. I hear Mary's voice telling us that the magic is a part of us—that we can't live without it. I reach deep within, tuning my consciousness to this inner magical self.

I open my eyes both within and without, and I almost fall backward. James has now jumped into crystal clarity. It's as though he's brighter, crisper, more . . . real. At the same time, rays of light shine out of his every pore so intensely it's almost blinding.

"What is it, Aiden?" James asks. His voice seems a thousand miles away. "What do you see?"

It's impossible to describe. He would need to see what I'm seeing to truly understand it. When I try to describe to him what I did, he tries it for himself. Twice, his eyes open and disappointment washes over his face. The third time, however, he opens them just a crack at first, and then he widens them quickly.

"Aiden, you're literally shining!"

His eyes flick up to mine. When our eyes meet, everything shifts. It's a world-breaking, earth-shattering shift. I feel as though I'm being sucked into him. The expression on his face says he's feeling it too.

A sense of surprise that's not mine pervades my thoughts. It's quickly followed by *What's happening?* It's in my thoughts, but it's James's voice.

There's another shift, subtler this time, and the village fades into a park.

Green grass surrounds us, and the sound of squeaky swings permeates the air. Children laugh and scream.

"Push me, Mommy!" I say in an excited voice.

The world pulls back and up, and my mother's hands press against my back, pushing me forward. Excitement fills me as I fly forward on the swing.

"Whee!" I squeal. I am overcome by giggling.

I thrust my feet out ahead of me as I go forward, and I speed up. I pull them behind me as I fly backward again and then thrust forward, each time gaining height. Butterflies fill my stomach as I go higher and higher, and the chains on the swing begin to go slack as I reach the maximum height. A jolt of adrenaline rushes through me each time they snap back into place.

"James!" my mother calls out. "Don't jump, sweetie!"

But I'm going to jump. I've seen my brother and his friends playing on the swings. All of them love to jump off, and it looks amazing. They're like superheroes flying through the air.

I continue to swoosh forward and backward, and then with one final burst of energy, I fly up. When I reach the highest point, I release, flying forward.

"James!" my mother yells, panic filling her voice.

I don't know why she's so worried. I feel like a bird, like a plane! Nothing can hurt me right now.

When I feel myself come down toward the ground, I wish I could fly farther. I fill my mind with thoughts of powerful eagles soaring high and spread my arms out like wings. I close my eyes. I'm a young bird on my first flight, and then I'm hitting the ground. I hear a crunch, and intense pain erupts in my right arm.

My mother screams. "James! James! Help!"

"I'm sorry, Mommy!" I say.

She coddles me and holds me close, tears streaming down her face from her panicked eyes. "Don't worry, baby. You're going to be okay! Why would you jump, baby?"

"Tommy jumps all the time, Mommy. I wanted to feel like a superhero too."

And then the pain becomes too intense, and all I can do is scream until my lungs hurt.

James reels back. Shock is written all over his face, and tears are streaming down his cheeks. I feel them running down mine too.

"Did you see that?" he whispers.

"See it?" I whisper back. "I felt it and lived it!"

"How the hell did you do that?"

I shake my head. "The moment our eyes met, I felt this irresistible pull, like my consciousness was merging with yours."

The shock on James's face morphs into excitement. "That's what I felt too! But why has it never happened before? Why now?"

I shake my head, unsure. "It felt like some kind of soul gaze precipitated by us both having just found that magical state within ourselves."

"A soul gaze," he says softly. "You're right. That's exactly what it felt like! It was so much more intense than anything I've felt before."

"Do the Guardians know about this ability? You'd think they would have taught us about it already if they did know. We should talk to Mary about it when we get back. She might be able to help explain what happened."

I fall silent. It doesn't take a soul gaze to tell me that James is upset. His eyes are wet with more tears threatening to spill out. I place my hand on his shoulder.

"James, why did you show me that moment?"

He's quiet for a long time. When he speaks, I can barely hear him. "I don't know why I shared that memory. I've never told anyone this before, but . . . You've met my parents. My mother is actually my stepmother." The tears flow unchecked now. "That memory you experienced is the last memory I have of my birth mother. I didn't know at the time, but she had something wrong with her heart. When she ran to get help for me, her heart gave out. She died instantly, and it's all because I was stupid and decided to jump."

After just having lived the memory, my heart breaks. I give James a long hug. "I'm so sorry."

"It's okay," he says quietly. "I think blocking it from my mind was my way of dealing with it. It's so fresh and real now."

"For me too. But I'm here for you."

He looks up at me with a sad smile. "I know you are. You and me—always here for each other."

James hugs me back. When he pulls away, he wipes his tears and clears his throat. "I need something else to focus on."

We quickly scan the village square. The priest and the old woman are still standing in front of the church.

As much as I don't want to go further into the village until Keegan arrives, I need to find a way to distract James. "We have to find that man or we'll miss our chance," I say.

"Let's try that way." James indicates a couple of nearby buildings. "We can sneak around that way and then double back when we find a way around."

"*If* we find—"

A man clears his throat behind us. We jump and spin around.

A thin man in his early thirties with a long scraggly beard stands there. His large blue eyes bounce back and forth between us. He glances to the surrounding fields and then to the church toward the priest. It's not the same man we met two days ago, but he does wear a similar black band around his right forearm. He crouches beside us.

"*Ah! Vou vêtyà!*" he says in a coarse whisper.

James and I look at each other in confusion.

"I think he's speaking French," James says, "but I took advanced French classes in law school. It's not a dialect I understand."

The man closes his eyes, as though trying to focus. When he opens them again, he speaks slowly. "You are the strangers," he whispers. It's obvious he's not asking a question, but rather saying it so it becomes more real.

I nod. "Two days ago, we met a man who was also wearing this." I point to his black armband. "He said to meet him here today."

The man sidles closer to us. His voice takes on a conspiratorial tone. "Jacques showed us his hand. He says you took away his pain."

"Our friend is skilled with bandages and the use of healing herbs," I say slowly, conscious of the fact that willingly admitting to knowing magic to someone who lives in a village such as this wouldn't be wise.

The man stares at me for a moment, as if he's unsure whether or not to believe me. He peers around the boulder at the priest, who is just leaving the village square.

"My name is Nicolas," he says, "Nicolas Possot. We must get you to

Mathieu's house. You will be safe there. Our enemies do not know of the path up the mountain, but it is better to not take chances."

"Where is Jacques?" I ask. "Will he be meeting us there?"

Nicolas turns to us. "We have not seen him since that afternoon."

He says it so matter-of-factly that it doesn't register at first. When it does, James and I look at each other in shock.

"Maybe he was worried that people saw him talk to us," James says. "Could he have gone to stay with friends or family in a nearby village?"

Nicolas gazes at the square again, a faraway look on his face. "No one leaves the village," he says, his voice hushed.

A commotion arises on the far side of the market. We look over to see a child playing in a sandpit. Above him, a wooden beam has come unravelled from its mooring and is teetering dangerously. A woman, probably his mother, is yelling at him to move, but he's too busy having fun. Others start shouting at the boy, but this only serves to confuse him.

The mother charges forward just as the beam slips free. As the beam drops to the sandpit, the woman grabs the boy and thrusts him out of harm's way. But as she gives him that saving push, the beam strikes her on the back, and she crumples beneath it.

Several villagers scramble toward the scene from all directions, but one man screams as he runs toward her; he must be the woman's husband. He grabs hold of the beam and tries to lift it, but it doesn't budge.

Nicolas grabs me by the arm. "You must help!" He pulls me forward with him.

He runs directly toward the sandpit, which takes us right past the church. James and I have already committed to helping, so I try not to think of the worst that could happen.

The priest has already reached the sandpit, where three men strain to lift the beam. There is a lot of commotion, but he still manages to see us heading his way. For no more than a heartbeat, our eyes meet. His eyes transform from concern to shock. He tells the men to continue with their efforts and then he heads back to the church.

Once we get to the sandpit, James, Nicolas, and I add our strength until the beam finally lifts away. The husband grabs his wife in his arms, sobbing and wiping the dirt off her face. The little boy watches in silence, tears streaming out of his wide eyes. The men who lifted the beam are ringed around them in silence. Slowly, more people gather. They all hold a fist to their chest.

Silence fills the square, broken only by the ragged breathing of the woman and the frantic cries of her husband. "*É fô dabor l'édâ!*"

I look over at James, who stares at the scene in shock. Having just shared with him the experience of his own childhood accident, I know why. Our "soul gaze" now seems to serve some purpose—but what?

I feel anger and guilt and sadness pull me in. The remaining emotions from our shared experience are too much. James looks at me. I see in his eyes a resolve I didn't know was there.

He rushes forward and squats next to the man and his injured wife. He puts his hand on the man's shoulder and says softly, "I can help . . ."

The man looks at James's hand with suspicion. His posture grows rigid as though he wants to flee. Before that can happen, Nicolas walks over and puts his hand on the man's other shoulder. "Bernard," he says. He speaks to the man quickly in French, pointing to both James and me. I can't understand what he's saying, but when the man looks up again, there's a slight element of hope in his eyes.

Nicolas grabs my arm with a sense of urgency. "I have convinced Bernard that you can help her. We can't do what you need to do in the open. We will take her to Mathieu's house." He glances behind us at the church. "It is not far from here, and we will be protected from those loyal to Père Georges. We must move quickly!"

James looks around. He points to a flat board lying close by and gestures at it wildly. "There!"

Nicolas, Bernard, and I scramble to the board, dragging it quickly to the woman's side. We gently shift her onto it. We try not to jostle her, but her strangled sobs give way to a muffled scream when we move her. She eventually settles, but her breathing remains raspy.

I wish I were more confident in our ability to actually help her. I'm useless when it comes to healing. Without Keegan here, whatever happens next is going to be all on James.

The four of us grab hold of the makeshift stretcher. Keeping it low to the ground, we carry it quickly and smoothly across the square to a dusty path near the cobblestone road. The couple's son runs along behind us. Nicolas leads us to one of the few two-storey buildings in the village. It's made of pale grey stone. There are only two windows, both of which are on the ground level, though they are too high to look into from the outside.

"Mathieu!" Nicolas cries as we near the door. "Mathieu!"

Just when I think we're going to have to lower the stretcher to the ground so someone can open the door, I hear the sound of several heavy locks disengaging before the large wooden door swings open with a creak.

A clean-shaven man with a hard jawline and piercing brown eyes pops his head out of the darkness. He looks to be in his late forties, and he has his long hair pulled back into a ponytail.

"Nicolas? Bernard?" He looks down as the child squirms out from between the two men and runs up to him. "Henri?" He reaches out to ruffle the boy's hair as he looks to each of us questioningly. His eyes widen when they come to rest on the unconscious woman on the stretcher. "Anaïs!" He throws the door open wider, and he runs to her side.

Mathieu is shirtless. His torso is as chiselled as his jaw, and his muscles ripple as he reaches out to take Anaïs's hands. Scars run up and down his arms and stretch around to his ribs from his back. He has the look and bearing of a man who flouts authority if he doesn't get his way.

"*Mathieu . . .*" Bernard says urgently. He looks anxious to get inside, and I don't blame him.

Mathieu looks up at Bernard and rolls his eyes at him.

I glance at Nicolas, who grimaces. "She and he are first cousins, but her husband and he do not see eye to eye. It is especially tense where Henri is concerned, as Bernard would just as soon prefer that Mathieu never sees him." He looks back toward the square. "Mathieu . . ." He tosses his head in that direction.

Mathieu's eyes narrow coldly at the train of villagers slowly heading toward us. He then gently kisses Anaïs's hand before standing aside to let us pass through the door.

Once we're inside, he shuts the door solidly behind us and re-engages the four locks. After a brief and rather angry exchange in French with Nicolas, he slams home a thick wooden beam across the door, completely barring entry.

Chapter Twenty

Although the outside of Mathieu's house is rather spartan, the inside is the opposite. Dark wood panelling lines the walls, and the two windows on the front of the house are angled slightly to allow for maximum light to enter the small foyer. There's a staircase leading to the second floor directly in front of us, but Mathieu leads us around it though an intricately carved dark wood archway and into a narrow hallway lined with towers of ancient-looking parchment and old books.

It quickly becomes obvious that the hallway is too narrow for all of us to carry the makeshift stretcher together. I carefully take over carrying it by the front, while Nicolas takes over the back. Bernard looks down the hallway with a skeptical look on his face, and he makes the sign of the cross. Anaïs squirms, and I struggle to keep the stretcher level. Her breathing is still raspy. Is it getting worse? I slowly urge the stretcher forward, and Nicolas follows my lead. Bernard murmurs something unintelligible and follows us closely into the next room.

We arrive in the kitchen. Much like the hallway, the floor is cluttered with tall stacks of old parchment and other artifacts. The lighting here is darker. The only window in the room sits high on the wall with its drapes drawn. There are otherwise two wall sconces with candles burning in them. In the corner is a woodstove that doesn't look like it sees a lot of use. A large but cluttered table sits against the far wall.

With one sweep of his arm, Mathieu clears the table of several drawings, sketches, and pots. After everything clatters to the floor, he kicks some of it aside so we won't trip on it.

Nicolas and I place Anaïs gently on the table, while James scurries about, throwing apart the drapes to allow more light in and frantically opening the cupboards. Bernard stands next to his wife and places a hand lovingly and gently on her head. He watches with distrust as James runs around the room.

Mathieu watches the flurry of activity for a while before asking something in that strange dialect of French.

Nicolas shakes his head, casting a furtive glance at Bernard and his son. Speaking lowly, he says, "They do not understand our language, Mathieu, but they seem to understand the tongue of the ancients."

I see shock flash over Mathieu's face, followed quickly by excitement. "Really?" he says, his voice betraying awe. He turns back to James. "What are you looking for, Wise One?"

James is too involved in his search to register what he's been called. "Candles!" he yells urgently over his shoulder. "We need more candles! Aiden, we need to light the candles and cast the circle! Quick! We don't have much time."

Mathieu looks at me before snapping into motion and disappearing down the hall. He returns a moment later with six candles. "Will this be enough?"

"Yes, thanks." I grab the candles and hastily position them into a circle large enough to encompass the table, James, Bernard, and myself.

Bernard watches in apparent confusion.

Since we don't have any time to waste, I dispense with the ceremony part of the circle casting and go straight for pure intention. I pick up one of the candles and hold it before me. Thinking thoughts of energy, healing, protection, and magic, I begin walking the perimeter of the circle.

The candle in my hands roars to life with a whoosh that seems to suck some of the brightness out of the room, and the flame stretches tall and powerful. If Bernard's eyes popped open any wider, they'd fly right out of his head. He shouts frantically at Henri, gesturing toward Nicolas. The boy runs to Nicolas, though it's obvious he'd rather be with either his father or uncle. Nicolas holds him tightly, keeping his eyes covered.

As I walk the circle, white energy rises up from the floor behind me, and every candle I pass bursts into flame. Bernard's head whips about fearfully, and he starts yelling at James in his incomprehensible French.

James has his eyes closed as he tries to centre himself. When Bernard's verbal onslaught continues, James turns to him and places a hand on each shoulder. Bernard falls silent, panic threatening to explode out of him.

"Your wife needs you, Bernard," James says softly. "She needs you here at her side, and she needs you to be calm."

Bernard's fearful eyes dart from James to Mathieu and Nicolas.

Mathieu steps forward. "I will translate what you've said."

It looks like there's a sour taste in his mouth, but he places a hand on Bernard's shoulder. At first, Bernard attempts to shake free, but Mathieu tightens his hold, and the two argue bitterly for several seconds. They are speaking too fast for me to follow. Bernard gestures repeatedly at James and me while making the sign of the cross.

I start to think that things could escalate out of control, but then Anaïs moans loudly, piercing the tension.

Bernard stops talking, and his shoulders slump. Without meeting my eyes, he nods briskly in my direction. Mathieu returns to Anaïs's side and gently places his hand on hers while Bernard cradles her head.

I complete the circle and look to James. He has rolled up the sleeves of his robe and is studying Anaïs intently. I imagine he's watching her energy flow while evaluating the seriousness of her injuries as Keegan would in the same situation.

"Can you help her?" I ask.

"I think so. See this section here?" He points to a spot just above the base of her spine. "It's torn to shreds. See it? I need to somehow reattach everything and mend the bones if she's ever going to walk again. That beam hit her in just the right spot and snapped her spine."

I nod emphatically, but I can't say I understand what he's talking about. I don't say anything, because I don't want to make him doubt himself.

"You've done this before, right?" Nicolas asks from his spot outside the circle.

I glance at James and notice the beads of sweat on his brow and his tense posture.

"Oh yes," I reply innocently. "Nothing to worry about. But we do need to concentrate."

I catch Mathieu's stare, and his mouth sets into a fine line. He squeezes Anaïs's hand. He knows I'm lying, but I get the sense that he's seen enough in his day to understand why.

James holds his hands out toward Anaïs, hovering them above her body. The circle grows brighter as the flow of energies within it increases.

Bernard makes the sign of the cross and begins praying reverently. Seconds later, a wave of energy splashes against the circle. He sees the circle flare up, and it terrifies him into silence.

That's probably a very good thing, because I felt the reaction of that energy pulse, and it was definitely the power of faith trying to force its way through the protective boundary of the circle. If he had maintained his frantic prayers, it would have pitted the strength of my circle against the strength of the power of faith, and I'm almost certain that would have been the end of the healing circle.

James now has his hands directly above Anaïs's spine, centred over her lumbar area. I can see waves of energy coursing between them as he works to reattach tissue to bone. I hear a rather sickening grinding sound as her bones shift within her, and I'm immediately grateful she's still unconscious.

Tears stream freely down Bernard's face as he bends over his wife, watching the transformation. He murmurs softly. I cannot understand the words, but they seem full of love. Perhaps he is finding some kind of balance between his hope and his fears.

There's a final snap, and the bone beneath Anaïs's skin shifts into what appears to be the proper position. She moans loudly, and Bernard bends down to kiss her gently on the forehead.

There's a loud pounding on the front door that makes us all jump. We then hear a muffled shout.

Mathieu raises a hand. "It will hold should Père Georges's men try to break in, and that is the only entrance they will find." He says the priest's name with unmasked disdain.

"Thank you," James says breathlessly. "Now that her spine is set, I need to focus on the rest of her back."

Anaïs's back is black and blue, and blood still seeps from an open wound. James furrows his brow as he leans in close. His hands hover over her back, moving in slow, concentric circles. Slowly, the blackness begins to fade, and the laceration disappears.

"You're doing it!" I say in a hushed but excited whisper.

He glances up at me, flashing a quick smile. "Fixing the bone and muscle tissue was the easy part. The hard part is regenerating her nervous system. It's shot all to hell, Aiden. If I can't fix it, she'll definitely never walk again. I'm not even entirely sure she'll live. They don't have much of a healthcare system here, to say the least. Is there anything at all you can do to help?"

I can feel the penetrating eyes of Mathieu and Nicolas burn into me when they hear James mention the chance of death. I do my best to ignore them, but I don't think I can hide the despondent look on my face. "When it comes to healing, I can't see or feel anything, James. I'm just here for moral support on this one."

James frowns. "Let's hope moral support is enough." He leans in close to Anaïs. "Come on, Anaïs," he says, his voice full of compassion. "You can do this. You want to get through this so you can be there for your son!"

He pours what might be the last of his energy into what he's doing, and the circle gets a little brighter. More sweat forms on his forehead, and his face transforms from focused to frustrated.

He looks up at me. "I can't get it, Aiden." Disappointment drips from his words. "I've only managed to get hold of one strand, and her life force is still seeping away. We need to stem the tide somehow."

Bernard looks on. He may not understand the words coming out of James's mouth, but the tone is more than enough for him to understand everything he needs to know. Tears fill his eyes anew.

Knowing that we are this close to success and yet also almost certainly doomed to failure because of my own inability to help is crushing me, and I feel myself tearing up. "You can do it, James. You can do it!"

"You must keep trying, Wise One," Mathieu says with determination etched into his face. "Anaïs is strong."

James's focus slips a bit when he shakes his head in defeat. "I can't," he says. "I just don't have the strength. I'm not Keegan. My strength is illusion magic, but illusions won't help this woman." He pounds his fist against the table in frustration, which jolts her, and she cries out in pain.

Bernard and Mathieu shoot looks full of daggers at James. He's quiet for several seconds. He stares down at his patient and frantically runs his hands through his hair. When he looks up at me, the loss in his eyes strikes me straight through to the core. But as he stares at me, a slight glimmer of hope crosses his face.

"Aiden, you need to come here. Right now."

Two quick steps and I'm standing at his side.

"The soul gaze from earlier," he says so quickly he almost trips over the words, "was to prepare us for this moment! Step behind me and put your hands on my shoulders. That's it. Yeah. Just like that. Now let your focus slip for just a second, like you did when we soul-gazed."

In that heartbeat, I *feel* him. It's as though there's an anchor pulling at my energy, and somewhere deep down, I realize what he's doing. He needs more power than he has, and the only other person in the room he can get it from is me.

I extend my consciousness in his direction, willingly giving him what he needs, happy to finally be able to help in some way. I feel my magic gliding down his arms, amplifying his own magic. I feel it reach his fingertips, and now that I've joined myself with him, I can see what he's seeing. All around the base of Anaïs's spine is a tangle of nerves and threads of energy that are a mangled mess. Inside her body, blood is seeping into spots where it most definitely shouldn't be.

A gentle tendril of our merged energies enters her body. I feel warmth radiating from her, and it's far too hot for a healthy human. She's in shock. She's burning up with fever and losing blood fast.

James is right. He may have healed much of her injuries, but she's still slipping. I give him total control of my energy, trusting him to use what he needs.

Our magic flows through Anaïs's blood, through her heart, stabilizing her. The blood flowing from the wound slows, and our magical focus follows the flow down into it.

With a surge of energy, we heal the wound. We then follow her blood as it pumps through her, searching for any other injuries. There are more, a bit deeper down, so we heal them as well. When the last of her injuries resolve, James guides us back to her heart, where he gently pulls our magic away from it.

Our focus slowly rises out of her and we observe the torn threads of her nervous system. James reaches in and nimbly uses his magic to pick up an end of a thread and then another. He focuses on each for a moment, and then, satisfied that they belong to each other, he brings the two ends together. I feel energy flowing out of me when the two threads join into one. He then does this for the other severed threads of her nervous system. He's very careful not to join the wrong threads.

After what seems like hours, the mending is finished. Anaïs's nervous system is once again whole, and her wounds, both inside and out, are healed. Her breathing has gone from shallow and ragged to deep and regular. With a sigh, I release the energy of the circle.

As the circle fades, Bernard looks down at his wife with relief on his face. Mathieu raises Anaïs's hand to his lips and gives it a tender kiss. He steps back when Bernard calls for his son, letting the family have a moment.

Mathieu crosses the room to stand beside Nicolas, and the two of them converse quietly in French. When they look at us again, there is a hope in both their eyes that I've not seen in any of the villagers since we started observing them. It stands in marked contrast to the incessant pounding on the front door and angry shouts from outside that continue to fill the house. I think of the black bands I've seen on Jacques and Nicolas that set them apart from the other villagers and the cold way Mathieu looked at the villagers outside his home. I now wonder what we've walked into.

James smiles at me, interrupting my thoughts. "That was the hardest thing I've ever done in my life."

"And you were amazing!"

He takes a deep breath. "You should take your energy back before I get too dependent on it."

James slowly relinquishes my power. I feel a gentle surge within me as it returns. The world seems a little bit lighter than it did a second ago. Without my power propping him up, James turns haggard almost instantly. He looks like he hasn't slept in days.

"You look as bad as I feel," he says, his eyes now red with exhaustion. "We're in serious trouble."

He tries to turn to the others, but he has to grab onto the table to keep his balance. Before he can say anything, his eyes flutter closed, his muscles go lax, and he collapses into a heap on the floor. I manage to kneel next to him before the world goes black. The sound of glass shattering in the foyer is the last thing I hear as I lose consciousness.

Chapter Twenty-One

I groan as awareness returns to me and intense pain pulsates through every muscle in my body. I open my eyes to complete darkness, and all of my senses come alive. My arms are thrust behind my back at an awkward angle, causing my shoulders to ache even more. I try to move, but I'm bound by ice-cold metal rings, one on each wrist and a large one around my neck.

I'm lying naked in a puddle of water on a stone floor. The sound of dripping water and scurrying rats fills my ears. A shiver runs up my spine as a chill fills my body. The air is musty. The smell of stale urine is so pungent I can practically taste it.

Where the hell am I?

Slowly, images of a small village return to me, along with images of a dying woman, James healing her, and then blackness.

What kind of place locks people up for saving lives?

I scrunch my face up and try to block out the pain as I reach across the floor with my foot. At the very limit of my reach, I feel something resembling another body. Please, I think, for the love of everything, be James.

"James?" I nudge the object with my foot. "James? Is that you?"

There's a muffled groan, and then I hear the sweet sound of James's voice, though it's considerably coarser than the last time I heard it.

"Aiden? What's happening?"

"I think we're in some sort of prison cell." Hazy memories keep returning to me. "The last thing I remember is the window shattering at Mathieu's house. The villagers must have broken in."

James coughs, and then groans again. "Ugh. I hurt everywhere."

There's a long silence, and then, "You don't think Mathieu and Nicolas sold us out, do you?"

"To save their own skin?" I ask thoughtfully. I picture Nicolas's innocent face and Mathieu's stern, cold eyes. "I don't think so," I say uncertainly. "I know we don't know either of them very well, but I can't see Mathieu selling out to anyone."

"Why not?"

"He seems to have positioned himself rather resolutely against the village priest. Why else would he provide a safe place that Nicolas thought would protect us against the priest and his followers?"

"It doesn't seem that safe. Look at what happened."

"That's beside the point. Also, I don't think Nicolas would do anything that Mathieu would disapprove of."

"No . . . You're probably right. Do you think they're here with us?"

I recall the hope I saw in Mathieu's eyes. "I think we represented some sort of advantage in their struggle against this Père Georges. I can't see them just letting us be taken. If they're not here with us somewhere, perhaps a worse fate has befallen them."

I cough, and the pain makes me wince. "I wonder where Keegan is. He should be here by now, or better yet, here with help from the Citadel . . ."

I begin using my feet to pile together small clumps of hay and other debris, anything that might burn.

"What are you doing?" James asks.

"Give me a second."

I twist my head around to look toward the pile I've created, and I focus on creating a spark to set it on fire. The spark races out of me, but searing pain erupts on my neck and wrists. I cry out and try to clench in pain, but every movement brings me into contact with the metal rings, which now feel as hot as molten metal.

"Aiden! What's happening?" James's voice is full of panic, and I hear him wriggle toward me.

A strangled gasp escapes my lips, and I focus on calming the energies within me. Slowly, the burning metal cools. My skin is still on fire, but I'm able to think clearly again.

I open my eyes, but the cell is still dark. "Whatever metal these rings are made of has completely intercepted my magic."

"What do you mean?"

"I don't know," I say hoarsely. My mouth is parched. "It just burned like you wouldn't believe. I couldn't concentrate because of the pain."

"But . . . how did it burn you . . . ?"

"I don't know . . . Just don't try any magic."

"Wise advice," I hear a man say. His voice is velvety, and the French accent is more refined than that of the other villagers we've met.

My head snaps up. There is the scraping sound of a key being slid into a lock and a clunk as the old tumblers engage.

An ancient wooden door held together by strips of black iron swings open. After the darkness of the cell, the flickering light of the torch is almost blinding. I squint against it and see the dark figure of Père Georges standing in the doorway. He looks down at us, pity in his eyes.

All of my previous observations about him are reinforced now that I can see him up close. He is the exact opposite of the villagers. Shiny brass buttons hold the fine fabric of his frock together. His hair is impeccably groomed. Three fingers of each hand are adorned with ornate rings. Even in this dim light, I can tell there are no calluses on his smooth hands.

Père Georges carries a small stool in with him, and he sets it in the middle of the cell. While he gets comfortable, I take stock of our surroundings. We're in a small room with crumbling stone walls and a wooden ceiling reinforced with large square beams in various states of decay. There is no furniture or any windows. In the flickering torchlight, I can see the glint of at least three sets of beady eyes staring at us from the corners of the room.

The priest holds the torch above me, and I squint my eyes against its glare. He reaches out and pulls the metal away from my neck. James gasps, but the priest just smiles sadly. It must look terrible.

"He wasn't sure the iron would work on you," Père Georges says quietly, "but he thought it might. I must admit, I didn't think you would try anything before I got here."

"Who didn't think it would work on us?" I ask. Anger at whoever is behind these devices fills my voice.

"One of your friends; one of the so-called Black Bands." He laughs lightly. "Very little gets by me, not even the shady dealings of a handful of villagers sporting black bands on their arms." He leans forward. "Oh, don't worry. He didn't tell me willingly. It took quite a lot of . . . shall we call it coaxing? But he offered up his secrets eventually." He tilts his head to the side, absentmindedly rotating one of the rings on his right hand. "Why do you look so surprised? I control everything in this godforsaken village. Did you really think no one would report strangers wandering the streets?" He sits upright again, and his lips turn up in a sneer. "Someone is always willing to trade secrets for immediate gratification."

My anger instantly turns to guilt knowing that someone was tortured because of us. Was it Mathieu? Nicolas? Jacques? Maybe all of them.

"Why are we here?" James asks.

"You tell me," Père Georges says. "I'm not the one sneaking around the village like I have something to hide."

When neither of us answers him, he laughs quietly. He then draws himself up. "I am authorized to use any and all means necessary to learn your secrets should you ever appear. The Catholic Church has known for centuries that this village holds information your master wishes to keep concealed."

"I thought people were always willing to trade secrets," James says sarcastically.

Père Georges eyes James shrewdly. "These villagers seem unwilling to offer up secrets regarding you." He leans closer to James. "Or perhaps they are unable. Perhaps your master stills their tongues to keep the secret contained."

"Who is this master you keep mentioning?" I ask, struggling to sit upright.

He looks at me, his face managing to convey that I am both hated and not worth his time. "All magic comes from Lucifer himself. It is a power designed to lure the righteous into temptation of the worst kind."

I can't help it. I laugh. "Surely, you can see how far from the truth—"

Père Georges strikes me in the face with the back of his hand, and one of his rings slices my cheek. "You would do better to remember your place, demon."

I stare at him and realize two things. First, he believes us to be actual demons. Second, I realize with growing horror that the only thing saving him from the magic churning inside me is the iron clapped around my neck and wrists. If the memory of the pain from my last attempt at magic weren't still so fresh in my mind, I would have already lashed out in anger.

Père Georges must see that in my eyes because he laughs. All traces of pity and kindness are gone. All that's left is calculated coldness. "I did not expect you to speak English. I always imagined my first interactions with demons to be in Latin or Hebrew or one of the other languages of the old world." He steeples his fingers and glares down at us. "Where are you from, demons? And how is it you found your way to this village?"

When I don't reply, he stands and saunters over to the far wall with his torch.

"Very well," he says. "I have ways of extracting the information I desire. For now, I need you to decipher something for me." He then thrusts the torch into a wall sconce.

The flickering light illuminates an ancient stone tablet embedded in the wall. Upon the tablet is an inscription. I squint at it. The inscription consists of symbols, a mix of tightly controlled lines and curves carved with knifelike precision into the tablet. I think back to a special exhibit on languages I once attended with James and Danielle at the Royal Ontario Museum in Toronto. I remember being amazed by the ancient Sanskrit texts showcased there. This text looks similar, but whatever it is, I definitely can't read it.

The priest alternates his gaze between James and me, searching for a sign that one of us understands it.

After several minutes of tense silence, Père Georges sighs. "As you wish. I'll return tomorrow to see if you've had a change of heart."

He stands, taking the torch with him. Blackness envelops us once again when the wooden door closes with a thud.

"Aiden?" James's voice is but a hoarse whisper in the dark. "Are you there?"

"Where else would I be, James?"

There's a long silence.

"I couldn't hear you breathing anymore," James whispers. "I was worried."

I answer him with more silence.

"The tablet feels important. If we could get free of these bonds, do you think my illusion magic might be able to translate it?"

I think about that for a few moments. "It's possible," I say finally. "Jennifer did say all illusion was rooted in reality. You might be able to make it look like English."

"We have to try to break free while we still have the strength."

Despair fills me. James is right, but I don't even have the energy to consider how to break free.

I sigh. "Do you think Keegan's come looking yet? They must be wondering where we are. Where are they?"

"I don't know, Aiden. I don't know. Wherever they are, I hope they're okay..."

James's voice fades into silence, and exhaustion claims me sometime later.

I awaken with a start as the wooden door opens with a loud groan and Père Georges walks in. He's wearing a red cassock today. He doesn't speak as he closes the door behind him and places the torch in the sconce by the tablet with the inscription.

He sits on his small wooden stool and pulls out a Bible. Without saying a word, he begins reading it silently.

"Father?" James asks eventually.

Père Georges lowers his Bible and looks at James with something akin to boredom. "Yes, my son?"

"Why are you keeping us here? Surely this must go against your faith."

"Have you translated the inscription yet?"

"No..."

"Your freedom..." Père Georges pauses, reconsidering his words. "Your *future* is dependent on your cooperation. I should think you'd be a bit more willing."

There's a knock at the door.

"*Entrer!*" the priest calls.

The door opens, and a villager in her early fifties enters. She keeps her eyes lowered meekly as she carries in a tray of food. I can't see it, but it smells like chicken.

"*Grant marci,*" Père Georges says with a smile full of kindness.

The woman leaves without uttering a word.

As the door closes, the priest's smile fades. "Forgive me if I don't wait until you're ready to talk before eating."

For several minutes, we listen in silence as Père Georges scrapes his fork against his plate and chews loudly. Chicken, mashed potatoes, boiled vegetables: the smell of his meal is agonizing given how hungry I am.

Père Georges takes a large swallow from a goblet before returning it to the tray. A moment later, he knocks it with his elbow, and delicious-looking water spills out onto the floor of the cell. I hear James actually whimper at the sight. The priest chuckles. He then pulls a white cloth handkerchief from a fold in his cassock and wipes the corners of his mouth.

James coughs before speaking. "Did King Solomon not write in Proverbs, 'If your enemy is hungry, give him food to eat, and if he is thirsty, give him water to drink'?"

"Quite right. So he did," Père Georges says. "Fortunately, demon, I am well versed in the scriptures. Paul the Apostle writes in his letter to the Ephesians to 'Put on the full armour of God so that you can take your stand against the devil's schemes.' I am wearing that armour and am ready to stand against your wiles. A servant of Lucifer is not my enemy, but the enemy of God." He coughs, and a bit of his chicken spittle lands on my face.

When he's finished eating, Père Georges puts the tray down and stands. He walks over to the tablet and traces his fingers along the inscription.

"My predecessor found this," he says, almost to himself. "He thought it was vitally important, and I'm inclined to agree."

He spins, and with a speed that belies both his age and his size, he crosses the space between James and him. Towering over him, he grabs the iron collar around James's neck and pulls him a few inches off the floor. He stabs his left hand toward the inscription repeatedly. "Tell me what it says!" he hisses.

James blinks and pinches his mouth closed.

The priest shakes him by the collar. "Tell me, spawn of Lucifer!"

James's eyes pop open, and Père Georges stops shaking him.

"It says," James says hoarsely, "go to hell!"

Père Georges blinks and releases the collar. He takes several steps backward in shock. Then he laughs, quietly at first, but then it builds to an almost maniacal level.

After a momentary silence, he glares at James and me. "Do you think I enjoy living out my last days in this accursed village, where they all despise me?" he snarls. "I had a parish where I was loved!"

He stares into the darkness. "When I was young, I thought chasing down demons was a worthy cause. How was I to know the Lord would wait until a year before my retirement to call on my services?"

Père Georges sighs. He eyes us carefully while he smoothens out his cassock. "Ah, very clever. Making me tell you about my life so you can exert your vile influence over me. That may have worked with Père Ferdinand, but it shall not work with me."

He grabs the torch and steps over the tray. He pauses to kick the remnants of his meal into the corner for the rats. He then opens the door and steps through it.

He stops to look at me for several seconds, genuine sadness in his eyes. "I almost forgot. Your friend passed away this morning." He shakes his head slowly. "Such a waste. Jacques was actually a very promising young man before he got mixed up with you."

The door shuts with a thud that reverberates throughout the cell. This time, the darkness is almost welcome. For several minutes, I can hear only the sound of the rats enjoying their scraps. Then James clears his throat.

"It wasn't our fault, Aiden," he says as much to himself as to me.

When the door opens the next day, Père Georges enters and walks slowly over to the tablet, holding the torch out to it. He turns to us, eyeing James first for several seconds and then me. "Which of you is going to earn his freedom today by translating this inscription?"

After a long moment of silence, I shake my head. "We can't." *And even if we could*, I think: *We wouldn't tell you.*

He seems to ponder this. "You cannot?" he asks. "Or will not?"

"Cannot," James says.

"Perhaps," the priest says with resignation, "you just need a bit of encouragement."

He steps over us and leaves the cell, shaking his head. Through the open doorway, I can hear him climb a set of stairs. Soon, the sound of multiple people descending those same stairs fills the room. Their gruff voices make me look at James with concern.

James meets my gaze with a burning intensity. "Now's our chance, Aiden. We have to try to see what it says."

Four rather large men enter. Their clothing is the first indication that maybe we haven't gone back in time as we originally thought. They're wearing tall black boots polished to a sheen, black pants, and black jackets with red stripes around the cuffs, red buttons straight up to the neck, and a golden cross emblazoned on the left breast. They're dressed like soldiers of some kind of elite unit of a holy army. They all seem to have a permanent scowl on their faces. I peer past them, but Père Georges isn't with them. Perhaps whatever is about to happen to us would offend his priestly sensibilities to witness firsthand.

One of the soldiers looks at us with disgust and snarls, "On your feet! Now!"

Between their uniforms and the man's accent, which is much closer to the priest's than it is to the villagers', I'd say these men aren't native to the village either.

James and I glance at each other, but neither of us moves.

"I said, on your feet!" the soldier repeats, louder this time. He reaches out with a hand easily the size of James's head and grabs a fistful of his hair, hauling him to his feet.

One of the soldiers storms my way, and I struggle to get to my feet before he reaches me. But standing with my hands bound behind my back is considerably harder than I thought it would be. I'm only halfway up when a second soldier grabs me by the hair and knees my stomach so hard that I careen into the wall. When I cry out and start to collapse to the floor, he yanks me to my feet again.

Blood trickles down the side of my head where I slammed into the rough stone wall, and my stomach is on fire from the knee it just took. Where the hell are we? This village is clearly French, but I can't see this form of imprisonment being sanctioned by the French government. It feels like we've stepped straight into a medieval village. But if we haven't gone back in time, the only other explanation I can think of is that we're in a part of the French countryside so remote that the priest holds ultimate authority and can get away with such lawlessness. That thought fills me with dread.

Two soldiers grab James by the arms, holding him firm, while the third detaches the heavy chain from the wall anchor. As the sound of the chain clattering to the stone floor reverberates throughout the cell, James looks me in the eye. It's the only warning I get before he starts to collapse.

I'm still chained to the wall and too far away to be of any other help, so I let out a blood-curdling scream as the guards try to catch him. They spin to me in confusion. In that moment of distraction, James reverses his fall and shoots up, slamming into the guard on the left with all of his remaining strength. It's enough to make the guard stagger. For that one brief moment he's free, James focuses on the inscription, and I see his mouth working.

The air charges with magic. I feel it dancing over my skin. James grimaces as the iron bands around his neck and wrists begin glowing red, but his lips keep moving as he tries to push through the pain. His eyes squint and his hands clench and unclench, but the symbols on the wall slowly blur and begin to change shape. The magic is far from perfect, but I catch one word shimmering on the wall just as the guard on the right slams James with his fist. It reads: Dunadin.

James drops to the ground. It feels like all the air was just sucked out of the cell. Everything feels distant.

James's illusion magic has just proven what my study of the two maps in the Chamber of Knowledge made me suspect. This village is indeed what remains of Dunadin, the kingdom where the last wizard, Nuada, made his stand. Is that why Mathieu and Nicolas looked at us with such hope? Do they think we can return the village to its former splendour? If the towers of ancient parchments and books in Mathieu's home are any indication, they know much more about the village's history than the average villager. How many others know of its magical past and despise us for it? An icy feeling settles in the pit of my stomach.

Two of the soldiers grab me by the arms and slam me into the cell wall, jarring me back to the present. My head bounces off the stone surface with a crack. Fresh blood trickles down my neck, but I manage not to lose consciousness. I don't struggle. They can clearly overpower us, and we've already learned everything we needed to know.

The other two soldiers grab James under his arms and haul him to his feet. His lip is cut, and blood runs from his nose. By the looks of it, his nose is broken, but he's awake at least.

The largest of the men presses his face almost right up against James's. "Try something like that again and you're a dead man, no matter what Père Georges says. Understand me?"

James nods once, and the man steps back.

The soldiers march us out of the cell and straight up a set of stone stairs. We stumble through a door and into the nave of the village church. The light streaming through the large windows blinds me, but as my eyes adjust, I see the pews are filled with villagers. They're chanting a prayer. They stare at us with fear and mistrust as we are marched through the middle of them, our naked bodies covered in dirt. Several of them shrink away from us as we pass them. Père Georges is nowhere to be seen.

As the soldiers drag us through the crowd, I search for Bernard and Anaïs with the dim hope that they might stand up and let everyone know the good we have done, but we're rushed past the faces too quickly for me to recognize any.

We continue our forced march down the aisle. One of the soldiers presses the point of a knife into my back. I feel the fear and anger rising from the crowd. I don't think it would take much at all to make him kill me. This whole situation seems planned, like a display. They're marching us in our disgraced condition straight through the middle of all the villagers in their house of worship.

They lead us down the front steps of the church. Partway down, the soldiers shove me hard, and I fall the rest of the way, landing in a heap at the bottom. A heartbeat later, James lands on top of me, sending the air in my lungs gushing out of me. A sharp pain stabs through my chest, and I'm almost certain that at least one of my ribs is broken.

The soldiers shout at us, ordering us to get back on our feet, but with our hands still bound behind our backs and James on top of me, that's easier said than done. James wriggles and rolls off me with a groan. I struggle to ignore the pain as I try to stand, but a boot slams into my side—then again and again.

My ribs are on fire, and the wound on the side of my head continues to bleed profusely. Soldiers grab me by the arms and haul me to my feet. They push me violently again, and I stagger forward but somehow manage not to fall.

They march us through the village square. The lack of activity on this overcast morning makes the place look particularly depressing. The few souls not in church stop and stare at us. Some of them chant the same prayer as the one we heard inside the church. Among the faces, I see Nicolas. He stares at us briefly before breaking eye contact. He looks uncomfortable, but he follows along at a discreet distance and joins in the chant.

Did he abandon Mathieu? How was the house broken into? How did we wake up naked in a cell? Now he's out here chanting in full religious fervour? I feel panic rising. Nothing makes sense.

They lead us to the far side of the square, away from the market. I hear a stifled cry from James, and I quickly look over at him. His body, like mine, is coated in dirt and blood, but he didn't cry out in pain. I see the horror on his face and then follow his gaze.

If the knife weren't pressing into my back, I would have stopped dead. Just ahead of us, one of the buildings has a mural painted on the side of it. It clearly depicts James and me working dark magic. Lucifer looms in the background, grinning. Although our likenesses are painted, someone has nailed our robes onto them, which gives the mural a disturbing realism.

Next to the building is a tall elm tree. My stomach churns and my hunger dies when I look up into its branches.

On the central bough, Anaïs dangles lifelessly from a rope wrapped around her neck. On her left, hangs Bernard, his jaw slack. The pure love for his wife that I once saw in his face is but a haunting memory. On her right, little Henri's lifeless body spins slowly in the light breeze.

My blood boils with rage. These villagers are so terrified of magic that they'd rather hang an innocent family than risk having it corrupt or contaminate them.

The colour has completely drained from James's face. He looks sad, but appears to be maintaining his calm. I don't know how he's managing it. My own face is twisted with fury. I can feel power rising within me. The iron bands around my neck and wrists burn into my skin, but the pain isn't as intense as it was when I tried to use fire magic in the cell. This time, instead of distracting me, the pain brings me focus. My power is seeking a way through the pain, attempting to break the rings off me. This family did not deserve the fate the village decreed for them.

Around us, the wind picks up violently. Sand and dirt blows in our faces. The grains of sand striking me feel like they're flaying the skin off my body, but I can only just barely feel any pain. James looks around anxiously at the sudden change of weather and then looks at me, his eyes wide.

"Aiden!" he whispers loudly. A soldier shoves him, but he ignores it. "Stop! This isn't a battle for us to fight! We don't want to give them more reason than they already have to fear us."

The soldier strikes him across the back of the knees. He falls to the ground, shouting in pain, but his eyes never leave mine. They draw me in. They're pools of love and forgiveness much deeper than I can find within myself right now. At the risk of having the iron burn into his skin even more, he lets me dip into those pools, and his voice echoes through my head.

"We can't save them now. They were dead the second Bernard let us touch her with our power. There will be another way for us to escape. We can't get more people killed."

I glare at him, and a vein in my forehead pulses with my anger. The windstorm continues to rage, but the point of the knife digs into my back again, urging me to start walking. The soldiers haul James back to his feet.

"Don't give in. The power of faith is taunting us to act, but we already have four deaths on our conscience. Let's not add to that. Remember, these people are not our enemy. They're just angry at us because we're the reason their friends were murdered."

We're guided beyond the square. Even as soldiers shove him and the iron around both our necks smolders, James continues to send me images of calm, peace, and tranquility. I look up, and through a haze of red, I see the villagers have poured out of the church and are now lining the street. They back away, their chanting silenced by the unusual windstorm. Fear fills their faces and ripples through the air around them. James is right. In this game of chess, where James and I are knights of Mother Nature, these people are but innocent pawns of the Church.

Slowly, the fire in my blood calms. The wind dies down as the rage tearing through my mind begins to numb. I glance down at my wrists. The bands have absorbed so much of my energy that they're red-hot. I've been using the pain to focus, but as the magic falls away, the pain rushes in so intense I can hardly walk.

I feel one last wave of calm from James before he looks forward, breaking our connection. I wonder how much pain he had to endure to break through his own bonds and form our magical connection. But his magic worked. I'm no longer ready to lay waste to the village. Instead, I shuffle forward numbly, wondering what exactly James has in mind when he says there will be another way.

I realize that seeing the family hanging from the tree had a different effect on James than it did on me. He no longer looks like a criminal being marched to his execution. Instead, even though he's as naked and dirty as I am, he looks like a man at peace with himself. He looks like a man who has accepted his fate and is walking of his own free will to meet it calmly. It's a remarkable transformation. When he looks over at me again, his eyes are full of pain, but they are also full of resolve. "Walk with me," they seem to say.

I'm not convinced, but I reach deep inside myself anyway, searching for whatever reserve of compassion I might have. Deep down, way deeper than I've ever reached before, I find a secret wellspring of compassion and a strength of will that I'm not sure I can call my own.

Perhaps it's a gift from James from the exchange we just had. I dig into this reserve and allow it to wash over me and through me. As it does, I feel slightly lighter and stronger, and I notice that I'm now walking straighter.

With a final effort, I bring myself to my full height. I take the pain I've just witnessed and weave it together with the pain I've just experienced, bringing it into me, making it a part of me. My shoulders set in a determination to survive no matter what these cretins throw at us. A single tear makes its way down my face.

The soldiers push us roughly along the street, but James and I have both found strength to keep us from staggering or stumbling. As our confidence increases, I notice the soldiers begin to look uneasy. I'm glad James managed to talk me down from wanting to destroy everything.

No longer do the villagers following us look at us as something to be feared and reviled; maybe, just maybe, there's hope. Our newfound peace and calmness now conflicts with the image they have of what wizards should be like. We round a corner, and up ahead the street comes to an end. There is a pyre stacked in the middle of the rounded cul-de-sac. Do they mean to burn us alive? Panic wells up within me. Mary told me that I couldn't be harmed by fire as long as I wasn't foolish. Does getting captured and burned atop a massive pyre count as being foolish? I can't see how any magic will protect me from this. Even if I do wind up surviving unscathed, the villagers will side with the priest for sure. And even if I'm immune to fire, James isn't. I would lose my best friend. How could I live with myself knowing he burned alive beside me while I remained unharmed?

I glance at James. He appears calm and unworried. How is he maintaining his composure? Then it hits me. The priest wants us dead, no doubt. But more than that, he wants that inscription translated. He won't let us die until he gets his translation. For now, that is our key to survival. But if I'm wrong, I hope the power of the fire somehow amplifies my magic enough to save us both.

We walk at knifepoint up to the pyre. Our feet are bloodied from shuffling through the streets. Our bodies are otherwise at the point of complete exhaustion. As the soldiers turn us to face the gathering villagers, James bows his head in peace. I try my best to swallow my panic and do the same. We are then forced to kneel, and a low murmur arises from the crowd.

Père Georges steps out from behind the pyre. He stares down at us with malicious glee clear on his face. I can almost see him licking his lips in excitement at getting to be the one to set the torch to Lucifer's demons. He raises his smooth hands into the air and begins chanting the same prayer we've heard since leaving the church.

He then scans the crowd, his face revealing a growing anger. The villagers are dead silent. Although no one has joined him in prayer, he doesn't stop. He gestures to the soldiers, and two of them force us onto the pyre. Roughly, they bind us to wooden stakes with our bare backs facing outward.

James and I stand there, quiet and unresponsive. Below us, the villagers stare silently.

Père Georges's voice reverberates through the square. "These two men are accused of being demons in service to Lucifer himself! Though our great God requires no proof of this accusation, behold how the iron burns their skin where it touches them."

It dawns on me now that a major reason for our nakedness is so the villagers can have proof of our magic in that respect. Our charred flesh beneath the iron bonds is visible for all to see.

"There are some amongst us who view these demons as heroes. They would bring the wrath of God on us all by welcoming this evil, but the Lord has saved us today and is willing to extend his grace to his children. These demons will be punished so we can all witness God's will. Once God decrees his will has been done, we will purge them, cleansing the Earth of their pestilence, and this will send a message to their master that their kind is not tolerated here."

He steps away from the pyre, and the crowd parts fearfully before him. He watches as the soldiers tie blindfolds over our eyes. A murmur again rises from the crowd.

As I anticipate our punishment, time seems to grind to a halt.

I hear a hiss as something flies through the air. Then I hear a sickening snap, followed by James crying out in pain. A heartbeat later, my own cry pierces the air as a lash tears into my skin. Ten times it cuts into me, and ten times my body writhes and convulses. Around us, a deafening silence overwhelms the cul-de-sac, broken only by the sound of the whip slicing through the air and striking my flesh. Tears stream down my face unchecked, but I follow James's example and don't allow myself to be overcome by emotion.

As another lash releases into my skin, the pain in my back blossoms unlike anything I've ever felt before. I lose track of the lashes at around thirty. One lash incessantly feeds into the next.

I feel an odd mixture of resentment and apprehension growing within me. Neither Keegan nor the Guardians have arrived to rescue us. Where are they? Did something happen to Keegan? Are the Guardians truly ignorant about this place? I thought they were supposed to know things. And what about Caitlin? If she knew about the village, would she have arrived by now to look for me? I now regret not showing her this place.

I keep thinking I'll eventually become numb to the pain, but each bite of the whip disavows me of that delusion. When the lashes finally stop, I hear the soldiers mutter among themselves. Relief floods through me that it's over, and I let my body go slack. What a mistake! The weight of my body tears at my shoulders, and pain courses through me again as I struggle to keep standing.

I don't know if I spend seconds like this or hours, but what little light peeks in under my blindfold eventually fades to black. Then, with blessed relief, I lose consciousness.

"Wise Ones?"

I don't know how long I've been hearing the whispered voice before it begins to penetrate my awareness. I'm not strong enough to reply or move. I settle for a low groan.

I hear movement and then feel warm hands on my face.

"Oh, Wise One. I'm so sorry I wasn't able to prevent this."

I know that voice. It's Nicolas.

"They have Mathieu," he says. "He sent me out of the house through a secret tunnel. He made me promise not to try to rescue him. He said one of us needed to survive to show you the secrets."

A cup presses up against my lips, and I feel cool water splash against them. It's not much, but it's enough to wet my parched throat.

"I'm working on a plan to save both you and Mathieu," Nicolas says quietly. Then, with much more confidence, he says, "I will rescue you."

I'm barely conscious when my hands hit the cobblestone.

A bucket of ice-cold water splashes on my face. I splutter. Pain sears through me. It's unbearable.

I crack open my eyes but see nothing except stone. I'm too weak to lift my head, but I can feel the energy of the cobblestone road call to me. It's pulling at me through the pain.

"Look at him!" I hear someone exclaim. It sounds like one of the priest's soldiers. "It's affecting him. He knows something's here!"

"I told the Révérend Père this was a good idea! He's too soft."

"He let us do this, didn't he?"

There's a grunt for a reply, and I feel fingers clutch my hair. A soldier yanks my head up.

"Open your eyes, demon!" The soldier leans in close so his lips are almost pressed against my ears. "This damn village has been hiding a treasure trove of knowledge about how to defeat you, and you're going to lead us to it."

He starts walking, dragging me across the coarse cobblestone. Through the pain, I hear singing. It's a rich song with golden music coming from somewhere just ahead of us. It calls out to me, begging me to find it.

The soldier is right. If I stay conscious, I'll lead them right to it—whatever it is.

I start to relax, letting myself pass out.

"Oh, no you don't!" the soldier yells. "The bastard's blacking out again."

I feel a kick. It's probably an attempt to jar me awake. The funny thing is, the song is so alluring that I never would have been able to pass out on my own. With that kick, however, the world goes black.

"Aiden?"

James's voice is hoarse, low, and full of pain. When it finally pulls me from my sleep, I instantly wish it hadn't. The pain is still unbearable.

I crack open an eye and see that we're once again lying on the floor of the cell under the church. This time, Père Georges has left a torch burning in the wall sconce next to the ancient tablet with the inscription. I still can't read it without the aid of James's magic, but it's obvious the priest is expecting us to try.

I look at James. I try not to turn my head because it's still throbbing. His head is lowered, and his back is covered in angry-looking wounds.

Just within reach of him is a plate filled with some sort of slop. Two rats sit on the edge of it, taking their fill of whatever it is. It's just as well, because it doesn't look very palatable.

"I'm awake," I say. "How are we doing?" I mean it as a joke, as I've been pushed nearly to the point of delirium, but it comes out sincere nonetheless.

James lifts his head, and I flinch. Half of his face is black and purple, probably from where one of the soldiers booted him. "We're in serious trouble," he says quietly.

When I awaken, the torch has burned out. It's impossible to tell how long we've been holed up in this cell. The only blessing is that the blood on my back has dried—I think. At the very least, it feels like my lashes are no longer bleeding. It feels like someone has cleaned them, probably to keep us alive longer.

"Next time you tell me we shouldn't do something, I'm going to listen," James says quietly.

Despite everything, or maybe because of everything, I chuckle quietly. It hurts, but it somehow makes our situation seem less bleak.

"Nah," I say. "Pushing me to take risks is an important part of our friendship."

He grunts, but he doesn't disagree. I hear him trying to shift into a more comfortable position, but I doubt it's even possible for either of us.

"Have you thought of a plan yet?" James asks. "You're always good at getting us out of the trouble I get us into."

"I don't have much experience at being held in a medieval dungeon."

"I'd never imagine in a million years ending up in a situation like this."

"I know what you mean." A memory of cold water splashing on my lips surfaces. "I think our only hope at this point is Nicolas."

"Nicolas? After seeing him in the streets, I thought he'd abandoned us."

"So did I, but he gave us water, didn't he? He told us Mathieu was captured too and that he was working on a plan to free us all."

James grunts. "I missed that part. But he better work quickly."

Before I can reply, I hear a thud against the door. A soft groan escapes my lips. I'm not ready for another round of punishment. I tense up when the lock clicks and the door opens. A thin trail of light spills into the room.

"Aiden? James?" comes a hushed whisper.

It takes a moment for me to recognize the voice through the cloud of fear that's filled my thoughts.

"Caitlin?" I ask shakily.

It's Aleksandar who answers. "Get up. Time is short." His gruff voice is tinged with fear.

"We can't move," James says as though it's the most natural thing in the world.

The door opens further, and a figure steps through furtively. It's Caitlin. She draws up short when she sees us. She shakes her head and calls back through the door in a harsh whisper. "I'm going to need you."

Aleksandar enters quietly. He's wearing the robe of a Guardian, but he carries a small satchel on his back. He looks down at us. "Fools!" he hisses.

He steps forward, raising his staff. "Close your eyes." His demanding voice brooks no argument.

"Guardian, no!" Caitlin hisses.

She grabs Aleksandar's staff. He pauses and gives the Seeker a sullen look. She shakes her head slowly, pushing the staff aside.

"We may yet have need of your staff's power, but now is not the time." Caitlin points to my neck. "These rings are almost vibrating with an absence of magic. They're like a void." She squats next to me and gently presses a finger to my neck just above the iron band, causing me to cry out in pain. "And look here. You tried using your magic, didn't you, Aiden?"

"The metal reacted most unpleasantly," I say.

She runs a finger along the seam of the band and then looks up at Aleksandar. "I don't recognize this type of lock. We'll have to move them with the iron intact. I just need you to break the chains that bind them to the cell."

"Oh," Aleksandar says grudgingly. "Is that all?"

Caitlin nods matter-of-factly and clambers over the slop to inspect James.

Aleksandar shakes his head and pulls out a small axe from his satchel. "*Now* you should close your eyes."

He positions the chain flat on the stone surface. He raises the axe with both hands above his head. I squeeze my eyes shut as the axe flies down, severing the chain. He then turns to James and severs the other chain with another precise strike.

"Remind me to stay on your good side, Aleksandar," I mutter under my breath.

Caitlin helps me up. She flashes me a smile before looking to Aleksandar. "You help James. I've got Aiden."

They help us to the top of the stairs and lead us through the darkened pews of the church. Scattered here and there on the floor are the priest's soldiers.

I look at Caitlin, and all she does is shrug.

When we exit the church, the early light of dawn spills across the village. Caitlin and Aleksandar waste no time in ushering us toward the path leading into the mountains and to the iron door.

As we round a building on the village outskirts, a man and his family jump in surprise when we almost stagger into them. I recognize them. They were in the crowd when we were brought to the pyre. Fear fills the eyes of the man and his wife, and their two young children cower behind them.

For a long moment, we all stare at each other. And then, remembering what

I've learned from James, I bow my head as much as I can without wincing from the pain.

"Be on your way in peace," I say through clenched teeth.

The man looks at me in shock. Perhaps he expected Lucifer's demon to set him ablaze. The next moment, he and his family scurry off.

"I see you've made quite the impression," Caitlin mutters in disbelief.

We make it to the path without running into anyone else and slowly climb our way to the iron door. At our slow pace, it takes us the better part of the morning, but there's no sign of pursuit from the village.

As we climb, I feel an energy stir within me. It's similar to the pull of the cobblestone road, though it's far less intense. James and I stop simultaneously. His eyes meet mine, and we turn to look back over the village.

"Caitlin!" I whisper in awe. "Look."

In the centre of the village square, opposite the church, what appears to be a peach tree has grown. Its brilliant blossoms are radiant even from here.

Villagers slowly approach it from all directions to stand and look at it in awe.

James grins at me, and despite our being at the very apex of physical and emotional exhaustion, we embrace each other tightly.

Chapter Twenty-Two

In the Citadel, Caitlin helps me down the narrow staircase at the entrance to the tunnel leading to Dunadin. "Let's get you to your quarters to get you cleaned up before anyone sees you. We should also get you dressed, to cover up these wounds. Danielle doesn't have to see you like this."

James sighs. "She's still here . . . ?"

"Of course she is," Aleksandar scoffs.

"She's worried about you," Caitlin says. "She's worried about both of you."

When we get near the Great Hall of Learning, a loud gasp echoes down the tunnel.

I look up. It's David, Keegan, and Danielle. David looks at us with a blank stare. Keegan is crestfallen, and Danielle is frantic. It's no wonder. Blood and filth cover our naked bodies. We're marked with cuts and bruises, and thick iron bands hang around our necks and wrists. The only saving grace is that they can't see the lash marks on our backs—at least not yet.

"James!" Danielle cries out.

Keegan runs toward us, but Aleksandar blocks his path.

"This iron bound to them burns them when they use magic," Aleksandar says, "so you cannot heal them with your abilities."

Keegan nods and steps aside. His shoulders slump in his powerlessness to help us.

Aleksandar strides past him to speak to David. His face is sullen and more than a bit frightening. "They risked ruining three thousand years of work—of hope—for whatever fool's errand they went on. They nearly got themselves killed! And for what?"

Ouch. That verbal slap from my mentor reminds me that emotional pain has a level of its own outside of physical pain.

Danielle rushes to James but stops short. She looks like she wants to wrap her arms around him and never let go, but she can't seem to find a way in that isn't wounded. She settles for gently pulling his hand up to her face and pressing it against her cheek. Tears stream down her face.

Caitlin places her hands on Danielle's shoulders. "They need to wash up, and Keegan will need to apply his salves," she says quietly. "The Guardians will then need to speak to them in private. I'll take you to the garden. I'll bring James to you the moment he's available."

Danielle nods and wipes the tears from her face. She squeezes James's hand tightly. She then follows Caitlin down the tunnel toward the garden.

James stares at his hand for a moment. The weight of the iron band overcomes him, and he lowers his arm shakily.

David steps forward, his cane echoing on the stone. He stops beside Keegan and places a hand on his shoulder. "Go to them. You cannot use your magic to help them now, but their wounds will need tending to. You are the most qualified. We await you in the Chamber of Knowledge, where we will discuss how to deal with those iron bands."

Keegan nods but doesn't move. When David and Aleksandar disappear down the passageway, he stares down after them into the darkness. After a long moment, he turns to us. His eyes betray his dejection.

"How could you guys leave without me?" His voice is nothing more than a whisper, full of pain. "We were supposed to learn about the village together."

My heart drops, and a lump forms in my throat.

He's right. We're supposed to be in this together. James and I knew Keegan wasn't in the village. We should have turned back the moment we got to the iron door and didn't find him there. I hang my head in silence while James stares off into space.

Several moments pass like this before Keegan steps up and puts his arm around me. At his touch, I shrink away in pain. He looks at my back and gasps.

"Oh my God," he says so quietly that I can barely hear him. He then looks over at James. "What happened?" There's still pain in his voice, but it is now tinged with compassion, and I can see tears welling up in his eyes.

"It was terrible," James says in a haunted voice. "Terrible. We wouldn't leave you here on purpose, Keegan. When we woke up, you were gone. When we couldn't find you, we thought maybe you'd gone ahead." His voice drops to a whisper. "We thought you would meet us at the village."

"By the time we realized you weren't coming," I say quietly, "it was already too late."

"Where were you, Keegan?"

Keegan looks like he's about to say something, but he stops himself. Instead, he gestures down the passageway. "Come. Let's get your wounds cleaned and dressed. We'll have plenty of time to talk then."

When we reach our quarters, Keegan guides us into the basin, taking care to help us navigate the uneven terrain. James and I stand waist-deep in the water while Keegan carefully washes our wounds with the gentle touch of a healer. He also washes our bodies clean of dirt. The pain is unbearable. James and I both strangle our cries as fresh fire tears through our wounds when they reopen anew.

"Once these are clean," Keegan says, "I'll apply a salve that will prevent infection."

"If only we could get these things off," James says as he pulls at one of the bands on his wrists. He winces. The skin underneath is still raw.

Without looking up, Keegan continues speaking. "David woke me early because Evelyn had fallen ill."

"Is she okay?" James asks.

"Yes, she's fine now, but none of their medicines were working. That's why they came to me. I don't know what was wrong, but she was so weak it took half the day to heal her. When I emerged from her chambers, Mary told me you didn't show up for our lesson and she hadn't been able to find you. I knew instantly you'd left without me. I made up some excuse and told her I needed to rest. Then I ran as fast as I could to the village. I couldn't find you anywhere, but I noticed a terrifying chill pervading the whole village."

"Is that why you went for help?" I ask expectantly.

"Yes."

Keegan crosses the room and grabs a mortar and pestle full of dark green leafs. He slowly and purposefully grinds them into a pulp. "Comfrey," he says as he slowly pours some oil into the mortar. "It grows everywhere in Britain. It has amazing healing properties. I'm also adding some tea tree oil to help prevent infection."

When he's managed to grind the mixture into a fine pulp, he starts applying the salve to my back and to the large bruised section of my chest.

"It feels better already," I say through clenched teeth.

He smiles. "It'll take some time, but trust me. This is the next best thing to magic right now."

"Yeah." I wince when Keegan touches a particularly deep cut. "We could use some magic right now." The salve burns mildly, but it seems to numb the pain a bit.

Keegan pauses. "I'm worried about the wounds beneath these iron bands. I don't want them to fester, but there's not enough of a gap to apply the salve without digging into your skin."

"And you are not doing that," I say, pulling away.

"By the look of things," Keegan says, "it's good I didn't try to help you on my own."

"So what happened after you couldn't find us?" I ask.

"Well, the Guardians put out a call to Caitlin when Mary informed everyone that you didn't show up and were nowhere to be found. I wasn't sure what was happening at first, so I feigned ignorance. Caitlin arrived the next morning and immediately started searching the tunnels for you." He shakes his head slowly. "She must have been down every last tunnel in the Citadel, but she didn't find the village. It's like it was hidden from the others until I led them up those stairs and down the tunnel."

"Wow," says James. "Interesting. Maybe only wizards can see it."

"What did they say when they found out about it?" I ask.

"You should have heard the rebuke I took when they realized I knew where you'd gone," Keegan says. "I wouldn't have led them to you if they'd given me any other choice!"

"But why?"

"Our promise."

Although I appreciate his loyalty, I can't help but think of the danger it may have put us in. "Keegan, you must have known something was off."

"I did. But I thought you guys would be able to handle it. I didn't know the risks."

"That's true," I admit. "You couldn't have known the dangers we faced."

"I had no idea, so I feigned ignorance for almost two whole days before they convinced me that something terrible must be happening to you."

"Well, they were right when it comes down to it." I'm silent for a few seconds before meeting his eyes. "How long have we been gone?"

"Four days," Keegan says absently, and then he pulls back. "I think you're as cleaned and dressed as you're going to get for now. I'll bring you some clothes."

James and I dry off slowly, careful not to rub our salve-coated wounds with our towels. We stand next to the fire pit. The warmth is welcoming. Keegan hands us some clothes, but they're our street clothes from our previous lives, not the robes we've grown accustomed to. It feels odd pulling on a T-shirt and a pair of jeans.

As we dress in silence, Caitlin strides in, saying, "I brought you these," and I nearly jump out of my skin. I'm instantly transported back to the dark cell beneath the village church, and I stagger backward onto the stone bench.

"Aiden! It's me!" I hear through the fog of terror. Footsteps approach quickly. "It's Caitlin. I'm so sorry. I didn't mean to startle you."

There's a light touch on my arm, but I pull away, drawing deeper into myself. The touch recedes, and I feel Caitlin sit beside me. She speaks softly, but I can't understand the words. Regardless, the sound of her voice draws me out of my memories.

When my eyes open, I see her beside me. She's speaking quietly of her last visit with my mother and how happy my mother was to hear that I'd be visiting soon. I must not have been out of it for long, because James isn't even finished dressing yet.

Keegan squats down in front of me. "Aiden, are you okay?" He looks into my eyes with such compassion that my heart breaks anew that we hurt him by breaking our promise to him.

I nod. "I'm fine, thanks. Just a little relapse." My voice is far shakier than expected.

He stares at me for a few more seconds. Then, seeming to believe me, he takes one of the robes that Caitlin brought with her and offers it to James.

James, still shirtless, gives the robe one look and says, "This looks more breathable." He forces a grin.

Caitlin springs up off the bench. "James, you look exhausted. Have a seat."

He shuffles over and plunks down next to me.

Keegan hands me the other robe. I just sit there with it folded neatly in my lap.

Caitlin once again inspects the iron bands clamped on us. "We still have to deal with these things."

"It's probably not wise for them to move around with them still on," Keegan says. "The jostling will aggravate the injuries."

"I'll go see if the Guardians have thought of a way to get them off. In the meantime, Keegan, why don't you see about getting some food and water into these poor wizards."

It feels like hours have passed before Caitlin returns, and when she does, her face is set in an entirely unpleasant expression. She's carrying her backpack with her, and she looks distracted.

"What's wrong?" Keegan asks.

She frowns. "It appears we have two choices, and I don't like either of them."

"What are they?" I ask. "Anything is better than sitting here with this damned iron pulling on my skin."

She looks at me askance. "You'll probably change your mind in a moment."

Caitlin drops her bag to the floor and smoothly lowers herself until she's sitting cross-legged. "Option one: I experiment with my different lock-picking tools until I find something that works on these convoluted mechanisms." She opens her bag and pulls out a small toolkit. She unrolls the kit along the floor, revealing close to twenty picks of various sizes and shapes along with a few small hooks and a pair of tweezers. "Option two: Aleksandar uses his axe to crack them open."

I stare at her, appalled.

James coughs gently beside me. "I don't know about Aiden, but I think I'll be choosing the first option."

"Um, yes!" I blurt. "How the hell is option two even an option?"

Caitlin smiles, but it seems distant. "It's slightly more complicated than that. Given their obvious age, how they are used, and the intricate nature of the mechanism itself, we think it's entirely possible they're booby-trapped."

"Booby-trapped?" Keegan asks quietly.

Caitlin nods. "Yes. Most likely to prevent people from breaking out of them. I have to choose the correct tools, and I might have only one chance to get it right, or else it could kill you."

I blink and look at James. "These aren't very good choices..."

He shakes his head. "It almost makes me want to just keep mine on."

"That's definitely not an option," Caitlin says bluntly.

"What about mounting a raid on the village to get the key? Or someone could sneak in. You're a Seeker. Can't you do it?"

"I already considered it. How likely would it be for me to find the right key? Trying the wrong key would be a bad idea. This isn't a haphazard trial-and-error kind of thing. Safely opening these locks will be a delicate matter."

Keegan puts a hand on mine. "Aiden, your wounds will get infected and may eventually turn septic. We can't wait much longer."

I look at Caitlin's array of tools. "I'm assuming this isn't your first time..."

"I once broke into the inner offices of the Louvre," she says quietly. "I'll tell you the story one day."

I chew on my bottom lip. There's really no choice. "Give it a go," I say quietly. "If we don't get these off, we'll probably die anyway." I swallow. "Just promise me you won't tell my mother the truth about how I died."

There's fear in Caitlin's eyes, but beneath the fear I see determination, and that's enough to give me some comfort.

She stands, picking up her tools from the floor. "James, may I share the bench with Aiden?"

"Of course." James shuffles over to his bed, and he sits down on it with Keegan's help.

Caitlin leans in close to my neck and inspects the opening of the lock. She chooses two picks from her set, eyeing them carefully. She then carefully inserts one into the mechanism, subtly testing it as she does. She shakes her head. "Too big." She smiles in a way that's meant to be disarming.

She tests the second pick. "This one."

She then takes another tool from her kit. "Pick," she says, holding up the pick. She raises the other tool. "Tensioner."

I freeze. I have little knowledge of picking locks, but the words *pick* and *tensioner* in a situation where my neck is literally on the line have me on edge.

"I'm going to need you to be absolutely still and calm while I work," Caitlin says. "I don't want you to move or even talk. Inside the lock is a series of pins. I need to adjust each one perfectly to mimic the pattern of the key before I attempt to turn the tumbler. Any movement from you at all will make it difficult for me to feel the positioning of the pins to release the mechanism. Any sound from you at all will make it difficult for me to hear the response of the pins in the tumbler." Her head quirks and she looks at Keegan. "Actually, Keegan, you may be able to help. Can your magic create a bubble around us to insulate us from sound? You will have to be very careful to not let the magic touch the metal rings."

Keegan considers it for a moment. "I can't create a bubble *around* us without it passing through Aiden and James, but I can probably create a cushion of air in front of the entrance to our quarters that would effectively keep sound from coming or going."

Caitlin smiles. "That would be wonderful." She turns to me again. "Are you ready?"

I nod and swallow.

Caitlin applies a small amount of tension to the lock and then slides the pick into the hole. She taps on the pins in tiny increments. I clench my eyes as she works. I can't feel her work on the mechanism, as her movements are too subtle, but I can hear the gentle tapping on the pins.

"It's old and complicated," she says mostly to herself, "but it's not as difficult as I thought it would be."

I'm relieved by her words, but I can still feel sweat gather on my forehead.

"Shit!" she says, a few seconds later. "A pin slipped. Starting again."

About fifteen minutes pass. James and Keegan are absolutely silent, and the only sound aside from the water running into the basin is Caitlin's tiny pick working its magic.

I briefly crack open an eye. Caitlin's eyes are closed, and a slight sheen of sweat has formed on her face.

Ten more minutes pass, and she finally whispers, "I have it." She slowly turns the tumbler, and with a satisfying clunk, the metal band releases from my neck and falls to the floor.

Underneath, much of the skin on my neck has either torn away or is otherwise blistered. Keegan takes a step forward, but he stops when Caitlin raises her hand.

"Let me get the wrist bands off first," she says. "I need to maintain my concentration."

Caitlin has an easier time with the bands on my wrists. I cry out each time the metal falls away, tearing a piece of skin as it does. Once both are off, an overwhelming sense of freedom rushes in. It's so intense that it briefly washes away the pain.

I wrap my arms around Caitlin, tears streaming down my face. "Thank you so much!" I whisper hoarsely.

"You're quite welcome."

I pull back, wiping the tears from my eyes. I look over at James. "Your turn."

Caitlin lets out a long breath. "I just need a minute to recompose myself." She wipes her forehead. "That was tense."

I smile through the pain and try to stand, but Keegan rushes to my side.

"Careful, Aiden. You're probably disoriented. Let's get you to your bed while Caitlin works on James."

I slowly make my way to my bed, where Keegan helps me down slowly.

He shakes his head when he sees the torn and blistered skin where the iron bands once were. "I've never seen such horrifying wounds. I can't imagine how they feel."

"You don't want to," I say quietly.

"I'll be right back. I'm just going to gather some more potent herbs. These wounds need very tender care."

I let my eyes drift closed, but I open them again lazily when I feel Keegan kneel beside me moments later. His hands hover over my body as he whispers quietly. I feel the telltale tingling as his magic flows through me and my wounds begin to heal. My ribs still throb with pain, but the rest of my body begins to feels better.

Keegan's hands stop and come to rest on my chest. I can feel the heat from his magic radiating off them and into me as his whispering flows over my body.

"Your ribs are bruised," he says quietly. "I could probably heal them, but it would take a lot of energy. They should cause you only mild discomfort at this point."

I nod. I can live with that compared to the pain I've endured until recently.

A few seconds later, Keegan stops whispering. He stares at me with some confusion. "The injuries from the metal aren't responding to my magic. I've tried several times, but nothing seems to happen." His brow furrows as he focuses. "It's strange. I can't even see them with my magic. It's like they're not actually there."

"Oh, they're there," I say. "Trust me."

"All of this from just one attempt to use magic?"

"There was more than one," I say quietly, haunted by the memory.

For a moment I think he's going to ask what drove me to keep trying to use magic at such a price. He instead lightly touches the wound on my neck.

"Can you feel that?" he asks.

When I recoil from his touch, he pulls away quickly.

"I'll take that as a definitive yes," he says. "Does it hurt when no one touches it?"

I think about it for a second. "I'm conscious that the burns are there, but they don't really hurt anymore."

I stare down at my wrists. The two angry bands of blisters and torn skin are slightly faded but still very much evident. I can feel the heat still radiating from both my wrists and my neck. I can't imagine going through the rest of my life with these scars.

"Will they ever heal?" I ask quietly.

"I think so," Keegan says while staring at my neck. "They don't seem to be getting any worse—"

A scream pierces the air. It's such a horrifying scream that I don't even recognize its source at first. When it hits me, I look up in panic.

"James!" I shout.

I press my hand against my ribs as I struggle to sit up and try to ignore the pain. Keegan is already at James's side.

James, his neck free of the iron band, stares at his left wrist as blood spurts from underneath the band that still clings to him. His face is twisted in agony, and his mouth is open in a scream that won't stop. Caitlin fumbles among her lock picks. Her hands are covered in James's blood.

"What happened?" Keegan yells.

"I missed a pin," Caitlin stammers. "I was sure I had them all, but I must have missed one."

"What do we do?"

"I dropped the pick! It became slippery in my hands . . . I think it's on the floor."

Keegan glances at the red wetness of her hands. "Aiden, can you find it? I'll help Caitlin wash up." He grabs Caitlin by the arm and guides her to the basin.

I clamber beside the bench, searching frantically for the pick, driven by the sound of James's screaming.

The screams fade away, replaced by the despairing sound of James crying.

"Make it stop!" he hisses.

I look up at him. "James! What happened?"

"It's cutting, Aiden," he sobs. "There's a blade inside, and it keeps cutting into me." He cries out again.

"Caitlin, we have to get it off!" I yell.

"I know that!" She and Keegan urgently wash the blood off her hands under the running water. "I can't *do* that without that pick! Shit! Shit! *Shit!*"

"Found it!" I say.

The others race to my side.

Keegan's eyes settle on James's wrist. "Oh my God," he whispers.

Caitlin snatches the pick from me and sits on the blood-soaked bench.

"Caitlin..." Keegan mutters.

"What?" She grits her teeth. "I need to work."

"We need to stop the bleeding."

She gives him a look. "With what, Keegan? If you cover it, I won't be able to work. Whatever this thing is doing to him, we don't want it to cut his damn hand off!"

"Oh, God..." James moans. The blood still trickles freely from his wrist.

"Sorry, James." She turns back to the iron band. "Our only choice here is for me to get this thing off you. We'll then need to move quickly to stop the bleeding while I work on your other wrist."

James stares at her. His face has gone white.

"Hold him still," Caitlin says to Keegan. Her voice is completely emotionless.

Since the trap has already sprung, she works quickly.

"That's the one," she whispers. "The second last pin is jammed in this lock. I missed it."

There's a click, and the iron band falls to the floor. Beneath it, James's wrist is sliced open, and bone glistens from the gash.

Caitlin riffles through her bag and pulls out some gauze and a bandage roll. She expertly bandages James's wrist. "That will slow the bleeding," she says.

"But you saw that, Keegan. I need to get this last one off so you can use your magic. Otherwise, we'll need to get him to a hospital."

"To a hospital? He won't last that long," I say quietly, instantly regretting my indiscretion as Caitlin shoots me a withering look.

James lets out another series of sobs. Blood has already seeped through the thick bandage around his wrist.

Caitlin doesn't look away from the final band. "James," she says, her voice charged with emotion. "James, I am so incredibly sorry, but I need to get this final band off so Keegan can heal you, and I can't do that while you're trembling. Keegan's going to give you something to focus on besides the pain, okay?"

She moves closer, focusing on the lock. She raises her pick to the opening, but pauses.

She shoots a look over at Keegan. "Say something to him, wizard!"

Caitlin is the kind of person you want with you when everything's falling apart. She seems to thrive under the pressure; it seems to focus her on the task at hand. She closes her eyes and opens them again. She sets her lips in a fine line while her fingers start moving nimbly. Within minutes, the final iron band falls to the floor.

Keegan's magic immediately fills the air. His lips move softly, and his voice almost sounds like music. The energy swirling around his hands dances along with his words, and slowly the tears flowing down James's face dry up. I lose track of time as Keegan's hands move around James's wrists and then slowly start to travel over the rest of his body. Before my eyes, the wounds on his chest fade and disappear.

When Keegan finishes, he gingerly unwraps the gauze from James's wrist. When he looks up at us, tears fill his eyes. His healing powers didn't touch the burns James suffered by using magic with the bands on, but the slices from the mechanical trap have almost healed completely.

"James," he says, sniffling, "can you flex your fingers, please?"

For a second or two, there's no movement, and then James's index finger twitches. Moments later, his hand slowly closes.

Keegan envelops him in a hug.

Almost two hours pass before James and I feel recovered enough to face the Guardians. Thanks to Keegan's sound insulator, it appears no one heard the commotion. When Caitlin escorts us to the Chamber of Knowledge, we find the Guardians sitting at the table on the upper level. Evelyn sits at the head as usual. The six others sit on either side of her, forming a kind of semicircle. The expressions on their faces range from grim to sullen. The torches around the grand table are lit, and they cast eerie shadows. This looks more like an inquisition than a welcoming committee. As we approach, I can tell by the way they look at me that they can see the raw skin on my neck through the open part of my robe. I resist the urge to close my robe tightly around me. Keegan made poultices that he believes will help speed the healing, but we decided that the Guardians should see the full extent of the wounds first.

The four of us take seats opposite the Guardians. We look across the table and wait for one of them to speak. They sit there in stony silence. The table, it seems, is ours.

I lean forward and rest my elbows on the stone tabletop. "We've discovered Dunadin."

Several of the Guardians gasp.

Aleksandar, however, remains nonplussed. "It would appear that they got the better of you."

James continues where I left off. "We were exploring the caverns a couple of weeks ago when we found a tunnel we've never seen before. Curiosity got the better of us, and we decided to see where it went." He looks around the table, and then his eyes settle on the map the Guardians have been creating. "We couldn't see the tunnel on this map, but we assumed you were hiding it from us because it was so easy to find. At the other end, we discovered a village."

I place my hands on the table and look at the map engraved on its surface. I point at the kingdom in the centre of the valley. "That is now a small village containing powerful magic," I say. "We don't know what it is because we weren't able to find it. Whatever it is, we can feel its pull from within the Citadel, by the mouth of the tunnel. The closer we get, the stronger the pull."

David looks over at Caitlin. "You said you felt this as well when you returned, did you not?"

"I did. It was different from what I feel when a wizard is close. It's more primal and more powerful."

David leans back and gestures for us to continue.

"On our first visit," I say, "we met a man named Jacques, who told us to return in two days' time. When we returned, we discovered he'd been captured by the vengeful village priest. They call him Père Georges."

"Pardon me . . ." Aleksandar cuts in. "I did not hear a single person in that village using a language other than a very old dialect of French. I don't believe either of you have fluency in that. How did you communicate with them?"

James shrugs. "Both Jacques and Père Georges speak English fairly well. Beyond that, it seems that knowing English is confined to a group the priest referred to as the Black Bands. At any rate, on this next visit, there was a terrible accident and we were asked for help."

"Why?"

We turn to Keegan, and he looks back at us sheepishly. "I didn't use any magic before then. It was just some herbs and a bandage. If they already expected us to be wizards, perhaps the accident itself was the test?"

The Guardians confer among themselves for a moment before turning their attention back to us.

David shakes his head slowly. "We find it very disconcerting that these villagers actively sought your help. If they know what you are, that puts you in incredible danger."

I nod. "It seems there are two factions in the village, the Black Bands and the Catholic Church. We don't believe Père Georges is from the village at all. He and his men believe the village is hiding something from the Church." I shudder. "He referred to us several times as demons, and he knows there's magic somewhere in the village. They don't know how to find it, though. His only clue is an ancient stone tablet with an inscription that he wanted us to translate. He said one of his predecessors found it."

David turns to Elizabeth, the Citadel's expert on the power of faith. She seems to digest the information I've given her.

"When Aleksandar told me you were being held in a cell beneath the church, I was worried," she says. "Now you say this priest had at least one predecessor who actively hunted for magic in Dunadin. This makes it that much more terrifying that you were there at all, let alone by yourselves. If the Church knows this village is Dunadin, the original seat of the world's magic, we may not have much time before they launch a full offensive." She looks at me expectantly. "Were you able to decipher the inscription?"

"Only part of it." I look at the bright red rings of burned skin on James's wrists. "James was able to cast an illusion spell that translated some of it to English. That's how we learned the village is Dunadin."

"The inscription must be written in the language of the ancient wizards," David says. I can hear the longing in his voice.

Sean speaks up next. "I take it you used magic to help after this accident..."

James glances at me before speaking. "It was a woman, Anaïs. She would have died had we not helped her. I set her spine and rebuilt her nervous system."

"You did *what*?" Keegan looks flabbergasted.

Sean, however, looks impressed. "Tell me how you did this."

"I needed Aiden's help in the end," James says. "He loaned me his power to give me the strength to do it."

The Guardians whisper among themselves. That a wizard can loan out his power to another wizard seems to astound them.

Finally, Aleksandar looks to us. His expression has softened somewhat. "What happened then?"

"The energy we needed to heal Anaïs had drained us both so completely that we passed out. When we came to, we'd been stripped, bound in that god-awful iron, and locked up in the cell. We were then paraded through the village and beaten viciously. They even marched us past the tree where they'd hung Anaïs along with her husband and young son."

Gasps erupt around the table.

Tears begin welling up in my eyes at the memory. "I wanted to destroy them." I try to keep my anger at bay here in the Chamber of Knowledge. I place my hands in my lap and clench my fists. "I could barely control my rage at the injustice, and I could feel the magic pulse through me..."

"Go on." Aleksandar searches my face, eager to hear more.

"Honestly, my mind had abandoned all reason. It was pure instinct." I hang my head and relax my hands. "That instinct was violent. If it hadn't been for the iron bands..."

"Yes, those bands," David says. "The knowledge of the weaknesses of wizards has been lost. We will have to be more vigilant regarding what can cause you harm."

"Père Georges already had reason to suspect the iron would contain our magic," James says.

Elizabeth's eyes go wide. "How would the Church have such knowledge? Over the millennia, we've come to learn they know very little about magic and wizards. What they do know is mostly sparse."

I shake my head. "Père Georges didn't know it would work. He got the information from Jacques, the first villager we met. The priest had him tortured. Jacques was one of the Black Bands."

"What can you tell us about the Black Bands?" Aleksandar asks.

"Père Georges suggested there's only a handful of them in the village. We met three members: Jacques, Nicolas, and Mathieu. Jacques is dead, and Mathieu, who is the apparently their leader, was captured. They seem to know a bit about magic and wizards, and it's clear they oppose what the Church is doing in the village. They could speak to us in English, and we were referred to as Wise Ones. It seems to me like the Black Bands resent how the Church has treated the village and want to return it to the ways of old."

After a brief silence, James picks up the narrative. "Anyway, when we saw what they did to Anaïs and her family, I saw the sky darken and the wind pick up. I could feel Aiden was imminently close to releasing his power despite the iron bands on him. That's when I realized something. It's exactly what Père Georges wanted."

"How did you know this?" Elizabeth asks.

"We felt the power of faith bounce up against our circle while we were performing the healing. It was like it was testing the strength of our boundaries before trying to break through. It couldn't, but that was no reason for it to stop plotting against us."

"So you suspected the priest had something planned?"

"Yes. It looks to me like Père Georges tried to manipulate us into acting without thinking. If Aiden had succumbed to his rage, who knows the damage he could have caused? The whole village would have turned against us. The priest probably would have crushed what was left of the Black Bands."

Evelyn finally speaks. "That has ever been the greatest risk a wizard faces according to the ancient tomes. Their emotions run deep and strong, and they can sometimes override their ability to think rationally. It's what led to the destruction of Dunadin by Nuada."

James nods excitedly. "Exactly! The realization hit me that if we rained fire and brimstone, or whatever the hell Aiden was going to do if he unleashed his power, we would be justifying everything the Church has taught these villagers. The priest literally painted us as demon spawns of Lucifer. I knew we couldn't let that happen. We needed to show them another way . . . so they could see we're nothing to fear."

"So what did you do?" Aleksandar asks.

"Aiden and I did what we call a soul gaze. I helped calm him down and bring his emotional impulses under control." He glances over at Jennifer and answers her unasked question. "Just before the accident, we stumbled upon a new technique that allows us to join with one another, sharing memories. It's what first gave me the idea that I might be able to borrow his power too."

"Perhaps this is more than a coincidental discovery?" Mary asks.

James nods. "It's possible Mother Nature chose that moment to reveal it to us. If we hadn't discovered it when we did, we wouldn't here today."

"We'll have to experiment with it to learn exactly how it works. It sounds extremely powerful."

I nod and lean forward. "That's when the real torture started. We suffered a public lashing in front of the entire village. I get the sense that Père Georges doesn't have as firm a grip on the village as he'd like. I think he was trying to exert fear and control. He kept saying the village was hiding something from him."

"Do you think that's true?" David asks.

I'm silent a moment before continuing. "I don't know. What I do know is the people of that village are the most downtrodden and miserable people I have ever seen. If anything, the Black Bands are an indication that the people want something more. Mathieu had a house full of old texts, but we didn't have a chance to find out what they are. I'm pretty sure they're in the hands of the Church now."

"Hmm . . ." David scratches his chin. "Curious . . ."

I look to each of the Guardians. "If we can rescue Mathieu and find Nicolas, I think we could help these people take their village back."

My statement sets off a muddle of questions. I put my hands up. Amazingly, the room falls silent, and I sense a subtle shift in the balance of power at the table.

"I don't know *how* we can help them." I glance at Aleksandar and Caitlin.

"You saw the peach tree that bloomed while we were leaving. I believe that happened because Mother Nature felt magic return to the land there, and because villagers responded to that magic! It's the same as what happened here with the garden. It was enough to bring the villagers running from their homes to witness it. If we can show them how magic will heal the land, and if they'll join us, we'll have allies in the not-so-distant future."

"Keegan's abilities could help bring life to the village again," James says. "The passageway to the village is clearly marked and established—at least to us. There's no reason why we shouldn't use it, right?"

David leans forward in his throne. "From what we know of the ancient histories," he says, "the Kingdom of Dunadin served the wizards of the Citadel. For as long as there were wizards residing here, the kingdom flourished. It is my understanding that the Citadel brought life to Dunadin, and Dunadin brought life to the Citadel. Perhaps it is no accident that you boys discovered that tunnel. Perhaps it is one more piece of the puzzle laid out by the Goddess."

Aleksandar scowls. I can't help but think he is loath to forgo meting out a punishment, but when he speaks, there is no trace of anger. "Well, it appears that we'll have to start incorporating lessons in diplomacy into your studies so you'll know how to deal with politicians." His gaze seems to burn into me. "And you, Aiden . . . We'll need to teach you how to control your impulses. We can't have one of our primary wizards succumbing to every whim he has to destroy things!"

Evelyn clears her throat. "Let us not forget this Père Georges, who appears to rule the village with an iron fist. Wizards James and Aiden, this first test of yours outside the Citadel came to you at a great cost. We do not know how long the scars from it will last. It is true that the trials you have experienced will serve to strengthen you on the rest of your journey, but if the Church already has this Mathieu fellow you speak of and the texts he's been collecting, then it is far too dangerous to allow you to return." She points a bony finger at my neck. "At this point, they already seem to know more about how to hurt you than we do. We need some time to ponder how best to handle the priest and his men."

"He truly was convinced we were demons sent by Lucifer," I say. "His belief was so intense we actually thought we had walked through time back to the Middle Ages."

Elizabeth stands and walks along the table to where I am seated. She takes my hand in hers. Her eyes reach deep into my soul, exuding calm. "It's not as simple as good versus evil, Wizard Aiden. You were chosen for this duty because you hold firm a belief that humankind needs to respect Mother Nature in order to save the Earth. The Church views the Earth as a mere stepping stone on the way to heaven. They certainly believe that it should be treated with respect as one of God's creations, but that is secondary to the goal of entering heaven. Our goal, however, is to transform the very Earth to a kind of heaven."

She releases my hand and turns to gaze out over the standing stones below. "Who is right? We have all chosen our sides, and the battle we fight is ancient. It predates us all. We must remember that Père Georges is not coming from a place of evil, just as we are not evil in essence. He is merely deeply committed to a cause he views as just." She turns back to us at the table and crosses her arms. "We will probably never find a way to convince him that we are not demons of Lucifer, so we are going to have to find a way to drive him from the village."

Chapter Twenty-Three

Aleksandar, Sean, and Elizabeth take us below to the stone circle while the remaining Guardians and the Seeker stay to deliberate on the next course of action. We descend the spiral staircase in silence, each lost in an ocean of thoughts.

I leave the others by the standing stones when Aleksandar beckons me to follow him. He leads me to the entrance of the Great Hall of Learning. He slows to a stop and faces me. He then looks me deep in the eyes.

"Good," he says. "I was hoping your excursion didn't made you cocky. I still see that special mix of humility and confidence in you that will make you a successful leader."

"Cocky? I don't think there's anything we could have done differently to make me *less* cocky! You saw the shape we returned in. Look at my neck!" I pull the top of my robe open to punctuate my point. "Never before have I experienced something that made me come face to face with my mortality."

"And yet you triumphed! Surviving a situation like that can sometimes make one . . . egotistical. I know that you were gravely injured, but you made it back to us. Also, Keegan has made quick work of most of your wounds."

"You're worried about me losing touch, losing grounding—"

"I was merely curious how your experience affected you. Did it make you feel immortal? Godlike? Do you still place the same worth on life as you did before you left? This may be the first time in my life that I've trained a wizard, but I've served in the military since before I became a man. I've seen many boys make the brutal journey to manhood at the end of a rifle."

I slowly begin to grasp the point he's trying to make, and I shake my head.

"The fact that I'm mostly healed now doesn't make what I endured any less real. It doesn't change the fact that I came close to dying. This is imprinted on my psyche."

Aleksandar nods, mostly to himself. "As it would."

"The healing of my physical body didn't change the experiences or undo the emotional pain. If I'd ignored James in the heat of the moment, if I'd embraced my desire for destruction, I might have revelled in it. But I didn't. Resisting using my magic for retribution, despite feeling both physical and emotional anguish, has given me a new perspective on the value of life." I look down at the angry red blisters ringing my wrists. "I also get to live with a constant reminder of what can happen if I lose control."

Aleksandar places a hand on my shoulder. "I see. That in itself is valuable. Perhaps once wizards reach a certain stage of their training, we need to send them on a"—he stares blankly for a moment, as though searching for the right words—"a rite of passage where they must face a difficult challenge while being forbidden from using their newfound power."

"Yes, I think that would go a long way toward striking a balance between one's magic and one's humanity. Wizards are capable of using magic, but they should be secure in the knowledge that they don't have to. Honestly, though, is it even possible to replicate such a situation? James and I were imprisoned in iron bands that had dire consequences if we used magic." I laugh sarcastically. "Hell, even with those consequences, I still wanted to use it."

"A valid point. We shall have to think on this. In the meantime, your training in destruction magic will begin in earnest. I expect you to be well rested, so I recommend a nap."

"You want to start *tonight*?"

"We would have started last night had you been here. Also, Mary wishes me to inform you that you will have to find time out of your own schedule to take her final introductory class." He nods his head as an acknowledgment that our discussion is over. "Meet me in the Chamber of Air." He turns and strides off.

I watch as he disappears down the tunnel. Moments later, Keegan joins me on my left and James on my right.

"Does your first lesson start tonight too?" Keegan asks.

I glance toward our quarters. "I guess we should rest."

"Danielle's still at the garden," James says.

"So maybe Keegan and I will rest here to give you two some alone time."

James flashes me a goofy smile that's been all too rare these days. "That might be best for all involved." He winks.

I stifle a laugh, as it risks hurting my ribs. When James ambles off down the tunnel toward the garden, I notice he has a slight limp that wasn't there before.

I see movement at the edge my vision. I look up to see Caitlin standing with her arms crossed at the ledge above the standing stones. Although I can't tell for sure, it feels like she's staring at me. Her face is a neutral mask, but I feel the disappointment emanating from her. I can only imagine what she's been thinking given how James and I allowed ourselves to get into such a compromising situation. I keep watching her. I feel that all the effort I've put into winning her over was blown out the window by one irresponsible act.

"She's an enigma, that one," Keegan says quietly. "I can see why you care for her."

I glance at him. "Is it that obvious?"

He smiles. "It's my job to read people. But yes. If you're trying to hide it, you're doing a terrible job."

I give a quick chuckle, placing a hand on my sore ribs.

Once Keegan and I have gotten a fire going in our quarters and we're relaxing on our beds, I pick up the conversation again.

"I feel we made a really strong bond when we first met at the coffee shop—even before that! At your shop, when we saw her there. But here she's so . . . cold all the time. I just want to understand her."

"You could start by not being so rash and irresponsible," Caitlin says from the shadows of the entranceway.

Keegan and I both jump. She's leaning casually against the tunnel wall.

"Where's James?" she asks.

"He already left to go to the garden to see Danielle," Keegan says.

Caitlin pushes off the wall, scooping up her bag in one fluid motion. She then sits down cross-legged next to the fire pit. "I'd planned on walking with him there to check on Danielle. I'll just wait here."

I try to read her face, but the flames in the fire pit cast a flickering light on her. She must feel my eyes on her, however, as she looks over at me. Her eyes are shrewd and penetrating.

"How long have you been putting yourself in danger like that, Aiden?"

"It's not like that. It's a sleepy village completely isolated from the rest of the world." I sigh as her body tenses at my evasion. "We discovered it by mistake last month."

Her body tenses at the revelation. "A *month*? Are you out of your mind?"

"I almost told you the day I showed you that valley where we saw David working, but something stopped me."

"Your own ego stopped you." A hint of bitterness has crept into her voice. "You knew I would stop you from going, and you couldn't have that." She looks over at Keegan, frustration clear on her face. "I understand Aiden and James running off to have a good time, but I can't for the life of me figure out how they roped you in."

Keegan shrugs. "We've been here a long time, Caitlin. The promise of fresh air and a bit of excitement..."

She frowns and looks down at the floor. "You know, I was in a hotel room in Salamanca, Spain, when David showed up to tell me you and James were missing. There's a young woman there who could be joining you here within a matter of months if her abilities don't get exposed before then. I was supposed to be scouting her so I could start planning an intervention, but instead I spent all that time hiking through Lannóg Eolas, exploring every nook and cranny, terrified I'd find you dead in a pit or beneath a rock slide." Her hands squeeze into tight fists. "David frantically searched Toronto to see if you and James had gotten tired of your training and risked going there for a break. He almost exposed us to your mother, trying to determine if you were hiding there."

"Caitlin," I mutter, "I didn't know..."

She shakes her head and kicks at a stone surrounding the fire pit, causing sparks to fly. "I got back from my search just as Keegan finally fessed up about the village." She looks over at him, but he just stares at the wall opposite him. "I was furious. I'd wasted days worrying, and you knew where they were the whole time!"

"Caitlin..." I can't seem to find the right words to say.

She glares at me, anger flaring in her eyes. "When I saw your injuries, I was even more furious at your recklessness."

She leans forward and reaches out to grab hold of my arm. I pull away, thinking she might want to murder me, but then she stops when she sees the red band of blisters around my wrist. She looks up at the one around my neck.

"Do they hurt?" she asks gently.

I nod my head slowly.

She looks like she wants to say something, but she remains silent.

"I promise you we weren't reckless, Caitlin. Believe me, we were cautious. It was a week before we even approached any of the villagers, and when we did, all we did was apply some healing herbs and a bandage."

"What about the accident?"

"When they asked us to help save that woman's life, how could we refuse? We were brutally punished for trying to be good human beings and for being different from everyone else. And they punished innocent people simply for interacting with us."

Caitlin stands up and gazes down into the fire pit. "You both have to realize that this is all bigger than you and me." She tosses her head in the direction of the Chamber of Knowledge. "It's bigger than them. The forces at play here are the very forces that formed the modern world!" Her voice drops low. "And they want to kill you."

Keegan and I glance at each other as we consider the gravity of her words.

"My job, along with finding others like you, is to keep you alive," she says. "I know the Citadel is an exciting and mysterious place. Remember, I once lived here just like you. But please, please tell the Guardians or me when you want to go off exploring. Let us help keep you safe until you have the knowledge and strength to better defend yourselves."

She kicks her foot against a stone of the fire pit again. When she shakes her head in disappointment, Keegan looks at me like a puppy that's just been rebuked. I feel the same way.

"Caitlin," Keegan says. He waits until she looks at him. "You said 'forces.' Are there more entities than just the Catholic Church that are actively seeking us?"

She turns back to the fire pit and mutters something to herself.

"Caitlin?" he says, leaning forward.

She looks at him again. "The Church is an agent of the power of faith, but you've heard the Guardians also speak of the power of science. They have a militant arm as well, a group called the Technicians. They belong to the upper echelons of the global scientific community and ultimately control it."

"They sound powerful," I say.

Caitlin shakes her head in a way that reassures me a bit. "They want nothing to do with us at the moment. I'm not sure they even know we exist. The Church considers magic evil. Science doesn't believe in magic, so as far as we know, they're not pursuing us because we're just a fairy tale to them."

"Well, that's a relief," Keegan says. "I'd hate to see what today's technology could do to us."

"Let's focus on one thing at a time, shall we? You guys learn the basics of magic. The Guardians and I will worry about everything else."

I contemplate what Aleksandar might have in store for me tonight in the Chamber of Air. Am I going to learn about tornadoes and hurricanes? It all seems rather strange in contrast to faith and science.

Almost as if on cue, Caitlin says, "Well, I should leave you to your rest."

She picks up her bag and crosses into the shadows again, and then she's gone without another word.

As Keegan and I settle down for a much-needed nap, I'm left wondering if her concern for my safety has more to it than her duty as a Seeker.

When Keegan and I shuffle into the Chamber of Knowledge after a relaxing nap in our chambers, we find Aleksandar there pacing impatiently.

Keegan takes one look at him and whispers to me, "Good luck!" He then scurries off to find Sean.

Aleksandar strides up to me and continues walking past me toward the Great Hall of Learning. I scramble to catch up with him.

"You didn't give me a time to meet you in the Chamber of Air," I say breathlessly.

"I had hoped you would figure out that evening starts at sunset."

"It's pretty hard to know when sunset is down here."

He grunts. "You're the wizard." Then he stops and looks at me pointedly. He looks rather irritated. "You forgot to bring your staff."

"Um, I'm sorry?"

He scowls at me, making me feel like a child. "You have five minutes to prepare yourself properly. Don't be late, and no running. A wizard should always be exactly where he needs to be when he needs to be there."

When Aleksandar gives commands like that, there's no option but to obey. When I arrive at Chamber of Air with my staff, I find him standing there with his back to me. I look around the chamber in an attempt to guess what he has planned for me, but all I see are a bunch of boulders and smaller rocks strewn about the place. The Chamber of Air is what they call this place. What's so special about it?

"You're late," he says.

He spins, hurling a large rock at my head.

I duck out of the way, and it barely misses me. I glare at him, stunned. "What the fuck? Have you lost your mind?"

He takes an aggressive step toward me, his face contorted in fury. His voice booms through the chamber. "I've told you before. Watch your language in my presence!"

Another rock flies my direction. I step aside, and it bounces off the wall.

"Are you going to continue to be late for everything for the rest of your life?"

This time, the rock strikes a glancing blow on my right shoulder. Pain radiates down my arm to the tips of my fingers.

I grab my arm, cradling it. "Aleksandar! Will you stop with this tantrum?"

His eyes flare. "Silence!" His voice booms throughout the chamber. "It doesn't matter how many times I instruct you on something . . . You just don't get it!"

Three more rocks fly in my direction. Each time his throw misses, he gets angrier. The fourth rock strikes me across my left arm. When I cry out in pain, he actually grins sadistically.

"You're nothing but a wimp, *boy!*"

Something twinges inside me that I've tried to keep buried for many years. It's a mixture of pain and anger and a deep feeling of emotional betrayal. Another rock strikes me, this time on my left thigh. I feel myself fall to my knees, but I can no longer feel the pain. Aleksandar starts to laugh.

All at once, his laughter changes slightly in tone. When I look up, my father is standing above me. I scramble backward in shock, and he starts kicking me on the floor while trying not to spill his beer. He tries to kick at me again but misses, and his beer sloshes on the floor, on me. His laughter dies instantly.

"You spilled my fucking beer, you spoiled little prick!"

He lunges forward and lashes out at me, striking me across the face. While

I'm stunned, he grabs hold of my hair and forces my head toward the pool of spilled beer.

"Lick it up, boy! Beer can't be wasted by some pansy-ass shithead like you!"

He presses my face into the puddle. The boozy scent makes me gag.

"I said lick it!"

I can feel the anger in me burning. I know how this memory ends. It ends with me humiliating myself, licking at the beer on the floor while my father laughs like the drunken asshole he is.

But not now—this time, I have a card up my sleeve that he doesn't know about. I'm no longer just a nerdy runt, powerless to defend myself. This time, when he kicks me in the ribs, I roar. The muscles of my legs pulsate as they thrust me off the floor. I bring my hands up in front of me, fingers spread, gripping the very air itself like claws. I lift my head up high. My eyes are closed as I bask in my power. It coalesces around my hands, gathering the energy of the air around me. I can still hear my father laughing. I can even smell the beer on his breath.

The air starts to swirl around my hands, gathering pressure. I feel it whisper to me when it's ready. I smile.

"Hey!" I shout. The frenzy in my voice empowers me further.

The laughter stops.

"*Shut . . . the fuck . . . up!*"

With the last word, I unleash the energy that has built up around my hands, thrusting it toward my father. A magical ball of supercharged air flies from my hands and strikes him square in the chest. It sends him sprawling into the wall—the wall of the cavern.

The sound of Aleksandar's stocky body hitting the wall reaches me. The illusion vanishes. His eyes go wide with shock. I look around. The stones that he threw at me were caught up in the force of my anger and were crushed into pebbles and dust.

I run to him, fearing that maybe I've maimed him. I crouch down beside him.

"Aleksandar! Are you hurt? I'm going to go get Sean and Keegan. Wait right here!"

All he does is stare at me, and then he begins to convulse.

I panic, but before I can scramble to my feet, he pulls me back down by the robe. I look down at him, confused. What the hell is he doing?

And then I see that he's laughing. A deep, heartfelt laugh shakes his body. He's completely lost his mind.

"I'll be fine, Aiden. I've taken stronger kicks than that, although, granted, that was one solid blow." He groans as he tries to sit up. "Well done!"

I'm so confused. "I don't get it. I just threw you against a wall! Why aren't you pissed off at me?"

His eyes glint. "Language!" Then he reaches his hand toward me. "Help me up, Aiden."

I help him to his feet. He uses the wall to steady himself. He stands there for a minute, breathing slowly and calmly.

"That," he says with a wince, "is going to hurt for a while."

He stands there for another minute before he speaks again. "Do you know what just happened?"

I hold out my arms and look down at the red blisters on my wrists. They're a painful testament to my failure in this lesson. "I almost killed you because I lost control."

I try to speak calmly. I try not to look away from him, to own up to my actions. For the very first time, I see just how great my power is and how the responsibility for the damage caused by my losing control rests squarely with me.

Aleksandar stands upright and tentatively tries to stretch. "Well, that, yes, but I drove you to lose control. The key to the mastery of destruction magic is that you must let go of control in order to truly gain it."

I look at him blankly, and he chuckles coarsely.

"What I mean is that destruction magic is instinctive. To be successful at it, you must act, not think. You struggle to control yourself right now because you lack the knowledge of what you're capable of. It's easy to hamper yourself if you're always so controlling that you're afraid to try anything new."

"So what do I do?"

"You must learn to overcome your boundaries and what you think is real or fake. Then and only then will we start to teach you how to control what you know is possible. I'll show you how to control magic that reveals itself to you and how to make it work without being goaded into it. It is a subtle distinction, to be sure."

"Like what happened in the village."

"In the village, you allowed an enemy to drive your reason from you; this time, however, I provoked you into losing control to teach you an important lesson. This must never happen again. When you lose control, you give it to someone else. No, wizard, you must always be in charge of the magic flowing through your veins."

"So how will we make this work?"

Aleksandar considers this for a moment. "I have the foundational knowledge of how your magic works. When I'm within these walls, I have access to a lesser form of the same magic. You have the power but lack the foundation. Our job here is to combine our two talents until you have both." He points to two large boulders nearby. "Come. Let's sit."

I watch Aleksandar as he ambles over to a boulder and slowly takes a seat. He winces when he does so. Despite what he told me, I still feel bad for using my magic on him.

"I still don't see how letting me throw you into a wall helps us."

Aleksandar gestures to the boulder next to him. When I'm settled on my rocky seat, he continues the explanation.

"It let me see how you use magic. As Guardians, we are able to see the currents of magic itself even though we are relatively powerless to affect them. In many ways, it's similar to how Caitlin's talents work, but less focused. For instance, we knew around the same time as she did that there was a strong disturbance in the flow of natural energies centred in Toronto. Without her, though, we wouldn't have been able to pinpoint its source in time to save you." He looks at me closely. "Does that make some sense?"

I ponder it for a moment before nodding.

He smiles and then leans toward me. "What we just did here was push you into using your power instinctively. You opened yourself to me. You allowed me to see how your magic flows in its natural, unrestrained state."

"So does that mean you understand my magic now?"

"I understand it better than I did before. It's enough to start the process of helping you access it without having to resort to physical or emotional attacks."

I sigh. "That would be great."

"You have an amazing amount of power, Aiden, and you've denied it for so long that now it's like dipping a ladle into a giant pot of borscht that's boiling over. It *wants* to be used!"

Aleksandar reaches over and grabs my arm. "Think back, Aiden. Think back to when the rocks were striking you, and you didn't know how to stop them. You took control of the air around us to protect yourself. I want you to think of the precise moment when you hurled your magic at me. Tell me what you felt."

"Anger."

He laughs. "Anger is good for destruction magic, but perhaps try to remember what happened when the magic first started building in you, right up until it exploded from your hands. If we can isolate how it made your body *feel*, you will stand a much better chance of doing it without the external stimulus."

"But I've already been doing magic. I've been lighting torches and candles and things."

"Absolutely! But with that magic, you're taking something that already exists—the wick, for example—and causing it to catch on fire. What we're talking about now is progressing to the point of creating wind where there was nothing but air before."

"I see." I think back to the moment when I was angriest. I recall the feeling of power that rose within me, swirling around me as the rocks struck. Was there anything there that I used as a foundation to build on? I must have a confused look on my face, because Aleksandar chuckles again.

"What is magic, Wizard Aiden?"

"It's the act of using my will to influence the world around me."

"And how exactly did you influence the world around you just now?"

"I raised a wind."

I pause to think about it again. The more I think about it, the more I realize that making magic with nothing solid to alter is really no different at all from making magic with a candle in front of me.

"But the wind," I say finally, "is every bit as real as the flame, even though it's not visible."

Aleksandar smiles. "Exactly! Just because we're dealing with magic doesn't mean your science teachers in school were wrong. Everything in this world is matter, and matter cannot be created or destroyed."

"But it can be altered."

Aleksandar simply gestures at the space between us. "Try again."

I focus on the air before me, imagining all the tiny molecules that make it real. I focus my will on forcing the molecules to move faster.

Slowly, very slowly, the slightest of breezes picks up. It's more of a draft, but it's certainly not one of the natural drafts of the Citadel. It's hardly enough to move a feather but probably enough to cause the flame of a candle to flicker slightly.

"You must *believe*, Aiden."

"I do believe."

Out of the corner of my eye, I see Aleksandar shake his head. He leans in close enough so his lips are almost touching my ear.

"You are not wholly committing yourself," he whispers. "You are being hindered by doubt, however tiny, that what you are trying to accomplish is actually possible. Remember, as a wizard, you have the ability to influence the elements. You just have to believe in yourself."

"I do believe in myself, but it's hard."

Aleksandar takes my hands in his and gazes into my eyes. "You have spent your entire life believing that such a thing is impossible only to find out that it is not only possible but also that *you* can do it. Repeat after me: I am the Wizard Aiden, and whatever I desire shall be."

I repeat the words, and then I repeat them again and again, but tonight the most I'm able to do is raise a breeze that stirs the dust on the ground.

After what seems like hours, Aleksandar pats my back in encouragement. "I think we've tried enough for now. It's late. I will meet you here at dawn tomorrow."

He doesn't wait for an acknowledgment. He gets up and limps toward the exit.

"Thank you for helping me," I call out after him. "I know it must be difficult."

He pauses and turns. "It's what I've spent my entire life training for, Aiden. To be honest, I didn't think it would happen in my lifetime. If it's a challenge, it's an excellent one!"

Chapter Twenty-Four

My senses come awake before I do, and though my eyes are still closed, I know something is terribly wrong.

Half a second later, I hear scuffling as the others awaken in their beds.

I struggle to a sitting position, trying to force my tired brain to alertness. I look around for the source of the disturbance, but there's nothing out of the ordinary.

Keegan is already out of bed. He's staring at the wall opposite us as if he can see through it. James is still lying in bed, but Danielle is sitting straight up beside him. Her eyes are wide, and her back is rigid. There is a definite feeling of wrongness permeating the air.

"Aiden?" Danielle says. She looks around, frightened. "Do you feel that?"

"Yeah, I do. Keegan, what is it? Do you know?"

Keegan walks across the room and places his hand on the wall. He seems to gaze and listen far beyond our quarters, seeking the source of the disturbance. The rest of us watch him in silence as the strange feeling of dread builds.

The walls tremble, and Keegan cries out in pain. He then lets out a long mournful moan.

James leaps out of his bed and pulls him back away from the wall. When his contact with the wall breaks, Keegan stops moaning. Chills run down my spine as James holds him tightly.

"Keegan," he says, "what's wrong?"

With a haunted look in his eyes, Keegan looks up. "They're breaking into the Citadel."

"Who?" I blurt. "*Who's* breaking in? *How?*"

"Many people. It's like a collective. I don't think they know with certainty that we're here, but they're trying very hard to look for us, and it's hurting the magic that binds the Citadel together."

The tremor happens again, and a low thrum follows it.

"Who are they?" James growls. He grabs Danielle by the hand and pulls her to her feet. "We're going to check the Chamber of Knowledge. Everywhere leads there." He rushes past us with Danielle in tow.

Keegan scans the walls. He then places his hands on my shoulders and turns me toward the exit. "Let's go with them. James is right. All the tunnels here seem to converge on the Chamber of Knowledge, so it's there we might find some answers."

We find James and Danielle standing halfway to the stone circle. They're alone. Whatever the disturbance is, it doesn't seem to have awoken the Guardians yet. When we rush up to them, James puts his hand up.

"Stop for a second," he says quietly. He cocks his head as if listening to something.

"Do you hear a choir?" Danielle's voice is distant.

We stand there in the shadows of the ancient stone circle, frozen in place and listening intently.

And then I hear it. It drifts gently on the subtle drafts of the Citadel. It's choral music. I shiver as memories of St. Michael's Cathedral flood in. I turn to Danielle and James.

"Back at St. Michael's," I say, "when Cardinal Gallagher stared at me so intensely . . . I dreamed I was standing in this very chamber and that the music of his choir was trying to penetrate the Citadel. It wasn't nearly as intense as this though."

The voices of the choir swell, and a steady drone fills the air. It's as if the Citadel itself is crying out against the assault.

"They *do* know we're here . . ." I mutter.

At the same time, James says, "Père Georges must have contacted the Church and told them what happened."

The groaning of the ancient stone walls continues. It grows louder as the music of the choir grows louder.

"Why wouldn't they just send their soldiers instead of, um, singing us out?" James asks.

"They probably don't know where *here* is," Danielle says.

I look at her, and she shrugs her shoulders at me. I'm impressed. I didn't think of that.

The chamber shakes, sending a shower of stones down upon us.

"James, Aiden," Keegan says, "we're going to need our staffs and robes. We need to mount a defense before they bring the walls down."

We rush back to our quarters and quickly change into our robes before grabbing our staffs and a torch each. When I start to light my torch with magic, James grabs my arm.

"We don't know how much magic we're going to need for this," he says. "Remember Mary's training. There's no sense wasting it on that right now."

We light our torches with the fire still burning in the fire pit. I look over at Danielle. She just stares at us. I can see both fear and excitement on her face.

"You should probably stay with us, babe," James says to her. "No matter what happens, you'll be safe within the stone circle. Its energies act as a shield and will hold them out. And the closer we all are, the less we'll have to work to keep you safe."

"If you thought I had any intention of staying here on my own," she says with a nervous chuckle, "you've lost your mind."

"Should one of us check on the Guardians?" I ask.

"There's no time," Keegan answers.

As if on cue, the Citadel shakes again, and a large stalactite crashes onto Keegan's bed and explodes. When the cloud of dust dissipates enough for us to see each other, we run back to the Chamber of Knowledge.

"Look!" Keegan shouts, pointing at the grand columns that support the chamber.

Near the top of each column, the dark red crystals are pulsating, casting a red undulating light throughout the room. They must be part of an ancient warning system. It adds a distinct sense of urgency to our actions.

We run to the stone circle, and James urges Danielle forward.

"Quick," he says to her. "To the centre."

She pulls to a stop and glares at him. "You want me to stand in that death-trap after a chunk of the ceiling just crushed Keegan's bed?" She gapes at the ancient sarsen stones and doesn't budge.

James looks up at the massive stones and winces. "I *really* wish you hadn't said that."

I try to help. "Look, Danielle, we don't have time to explain why they used these stones to create the circle, but this is where we hold all of our rituals. It's where our magic is strongest, and it's where we'll be able to mount the best defense."

She seems to search my face for something. A half-truth? A white lie? I'm not sure if she found anything, but she eventually decides to creep along with us to the centre of the circle. She eyeballs the stones the whole way like any one of them could tumble onto her at any second.

James, Keegan, and I use our torches to light the torches of the circle.

I look to the other two. "Ready?" I hope I look more sure of myself than they do, but I doubt it.

"Ready," James says.

Keegan holds out an open hand and looks down at it. "I'm a healer. I'm not sure how my magic will help us now."

Another shower of pebbles fall around us.

"We need everyone we have, Keegan." James sounds exasperated. It's uncharacteristically harsh for him. He must be worried about Danielle.

I clasp Keegan's shoulder and give it a squeeze. "Keegan, yes, you're a healer. That means your whole life revolves around keeping others protected, saving them when they're in trouble. We know you won't be much help in a fight, but you *can* help with our defenses. We need the strength of your will to help provide protection. We'll take care of the rest."

Keegan nods and steps to the edge of the circle.

James looks over at Danielle. They exchange glances before they pull each other into a hug.

"We could use your help too, babe, if you're willing," James says. "From what we learned in the village, we might be able to use your energy to boost our own if you're willing to offer it."

"What do you mean? My energy?"

"What we are about to do relies on intention and will, and our power will amplify that and turn it into something that can help us. If you focus on creating a wall of protective energy around this place, we should be able to harness some of your intention and use it to help keep us all safe."

Danielle narrows her eyes at him. "You know I've been a Catholic my entire life, right?" She looks around the chamber, and her voice drops to almost a whisper. "How the hell did I wind up *here*? Dating a wizard is one thing, but you're asking me to fight the authority at the head of my faith. I love you, James, but that's a lot to ask from me."

James takes her hands in his. "When this is over, we'll have to have a talk about the difference between your beliefs and your trust in a religious organization that would do the kinds of things Aiden and I saw in the village. But right this moment, the ceiling is falling on our heads. Regardless of where your allegiances lie, you're with us now. We need to stop this."

Danielle closes her eyes and then draws herself up. She takes a deep breath. "I'll help in any way I can." She sounds uncertain but sincere.

"There's one more thing, Danielle." I'm hesitant, but I know this must be said. "I don't know what's going to happen here, but—" I look up at the ceiling as a big piece of rock falls just outside the circle. "You're probably going to feel the need to pray." I think back to Mathieu's house, when we were healing Anaïs, when Bernard's prayers for his wife threatened to disrupt the circle. "Any prayer inside or near the circle could destabilize it. It could get us all killed."

She stares at me in utter disbelief. She shakes her head. Then, with far too much sincerity, she says, "I hate you right now, Aiden."

James leans in to give her a kiss, but she turns her head away.

"Just do whatever it is you need to do so I can get out of here alive," she says flatly.

He frowns and settles for giving her a peck on the cheek. "I love you, Danielle," he says in a voice full of emotion.

Danielle retreats further into the middle of the circle and crosses her arms. She looks anxiously between the standing stones and the rocky ceiling.

James turns from her and closes his eyes. He takes a deep breath, forcing himself to focus on our immediate danger, and then looks at me. "Well, brother, it's your show!"

I wish we had more time. Danielle doesn't deserve this. But if we don't act now, it might be too late.

"Let's go!"

With purpose and efficiency, we perform the opening of the circle, imbuing it with all the protective energies we can muster. Danielle remains amazingly calm as each torch flares and the area we trace out burns with the energy of our intention. She turns and looks away as we circle around. It's almost as if she refuses to acknowledge what's happening around her. Maybe it's in keeping her distance that she can maintain her fortitude.

As we complete the circle and the air thrums with its energy, I see Danielle's eyes widen slightly. I follow her gaze and try not to grin. Tiny tendrils of energy flow from her feet to the edge of the circle. She's decided to help protect us after all.

The sound of the choir grows even louder. It's a Gregorian chant. There's a crash on the upper level of the chamber as something collapses.

"We have to protect the Citadel!" I shout. "Let's expand the circle."

Keegan looks at me askance. "You can't possibly think we can protect ourselves and the Citadel at the same time . . ."

James replies for me. "No circle will protect us if the Citadel comes down on top of us. We need to make it large enough to at least protect the Guardians' quarters until they make it out here."

We stand near the circle's centre, the three of us, with arms outstretched, back to back to back, and we concentrate on expanding our sphere of protection. With a painstaking slowness, the glowing green edge of our circle expands outward.

The circle reaches the closest wall and moves through it. Where it touches the wall, the trembling stone calms, and a feeling of peace returns to that part of the chamber. I feel the energy flowing out of me and into the circle as we push it toward the far walls of the chamber. Once we secure the entirety of the Chamber of Knowledge, we'll push it out even further down the tunnels.

The choir grows louder again. Within the circle, all remains calm; however, at the edge of the chamber, a section of rock shears off the wall and falls to the floor with a mighty crash. Seconds later, the bright white power of El touches the edge of our circle. It sparks and rears back. It somehow exudes shock and anger as it hovers just outside the circle. Then, with righteous indignation, it slams into the circle like a warship at ramming speed.

Sparks of mixed energy erupt as the power of faith strikes. Again and again, it rains its anger down, but our circle stays strong. It then rears back once again, pausing, studying our defenses. It circles us, searching for a weakness.

I hear a whimper to my right and glance over at Danielle. Tears stream openly down her face. She looks over at James in horror.

"He's calling to me, James," she says in disbelief. "I can hear the voice of God in my head." Her hands rush up to her face, and the rippling tendrils of energy she's feeding the circle wither and die.

"What's the voice saying, Danielle?" James asks with worry in his voice.

She falls to her knees and begins sobbing. "He says that if I open myself to him and put my faith in him, he will protect me."

"But we will all die," Keegan says.

Danielle nods, covers her face, and falls silent.

James looks between Danielle and me, biting his lower lip. "She'll pick the side of God," he whispers, crestfallen. "It's all she's ever known. We don't have much time."

"Form a link!" I shout. I place my staff on the floor in front of me. I reach back to take James's and Keegan's hands. They do likewise, and we form a circle of wizards within the circle.

I tentatively focus on the air in front of the choir's energy. I then envision a pathway from our circle to the source of the choir, thrusting the circle outward at that point. An arc of energy shoots out from us. It travels down the pathway and casts the choir's white energy in the green glow of a grassy field.

The power of faith pulls back quickly, tightening into a ball, and the singing vanishes. Suspense hangs in the air as we stand within our circle, staring out at faith's ball of energy. The air around our circle begins to thicken, and the ball of light expands into white billowing clouds that roll up against the boundaries of our circle. A low hum starts in the distance, rising in volume as it gets closer. The distinct sound of male voices, deep in prayer, fills the chamber.

The sound splashes against the circle, and the entire Citadel seems to groan, straining from the force of this new onslaught. The boundaries of our circle retreat, falling back until they merge with the stone circle around us. Danielle casts a fearful glance at the flickering glow of the circle, and I see her lips moving soundlessly. Keegan, James, and I stand firm, forming a united front against this new power even as it digs deep into our defenses. The stone around us rumbles, and every torch goes out. The chamber plunges into darkness save for the dim pulsating light of the dark red crystals.

As wave after wave of the chanting rushes against our defenses, I rack my brain for something that could help us. A plan slowly starts to take form.

"Keegan? James?" I say through the darkness. "I'm going to try something here. I need you guys to keep this smaller circle together."

"Don't do anything stupid, Aiden," James says through clenched teeth.

"That's why I'm doing it instead of letting you."

I give him a sidelong glance and flash a nervous grin. He smirks back at me.

I slowly cede my part of the wizard's circle to the other two, making sure that their share of the power grows to fill mine as I withdraw. They won't be able to sustain the whole circle at this strength for long, but I don't need long. When just a tiny part of me is still linked to the circle, I stab my staff into the floor in front of me.

I channel the energy flowing through the circle, pulling some of it into the staff. I grasp the staff firmly before me with both hands. I then reach down through it into the rocky foundation itself, calling on the spirit of Lannóg Eolas to release some of its energy to me. I feel the energy of rock flowing up into me, but I reach deeper still until I sense water flowing underneath. I draw the energy of the water up into the staff, merging its smooth flowing energy with the solid enduring strength of the rock.

I cast my consciousness into the staff and feel the power of the water swirling through the power of the rock. I weave a thread of circle-charged air, joining them all together into a charge of earth, air, and water. I knit the three elements together with the harmonious fire of my will. The energy builds until it cycles through the staff to me and back through me to the staff. It blends, becoming my own, gaining power with every passing second.

The rolling clouds of faith seem to sense the energy building. Faster and faster they churn outside our wall of energy, seeking a way to bring the circle down. As the energy grows both within and without the circle, I see Aleksandar appear at the mouth of a tunnel. Beyond him, Jennifer escorts Evelyn. The rest of the Guardians then file into view.

They take in the scene. Our circle blazes bright green against white billowing clouds. In the centre stand James and Keegan, who exert the very extent of their power to hold the circle together. At the circle's edge, I stand with the power of land, sea, and sky twisting and twining through my staff and me.

United, the Guardians march toward the circle. For a moment, I think they might try to cross its boundaries. In our training, we've learned that crossing a circle's boundaries at the wrong time can have dire consequences for both the participants and the onlookers. I sincerely doubt this is a good time to try.

They instead take up positions around the circle, fearlessness etched into their faces even as the bright clouds of El's power roll over them.

As one, they raise their staffs high, ablaze with the power of the wizards of old. The power of faith falls back from the edges of the circle. Aleksandar looks over at me with a nod.

I step closer to the edge of the circle, stopping just short of it. I thrust my staff into the rocky floor, and I throw my consciousness out after the clouds. As the force of my power strikes, the chanting grows more intense.

Using the power of the circle and the elemental power that flows through me, I cast my power deeper into the enemy. Like a spear, my energetic self flies up through the clouds and dances through the pockets of chanting and prayer. Farther and farther I go, and louder and louder the prayer gets until it pounds against my being, beating me back.

The bright billowing clouds surround me. Have I been swallowed up?

Before I can think about it any further, the clouds part, and I find myself floating in an expansive night sky. A massive stone building appears in the distance. It sits on a hill surrounded by an ancient city. As I transform back into a corporeal being, I find myself in front of the building's decorative facade. I stare up in awe at its eight columns and large dome. Before me stands St. Peter's Basilica. I have arrived at the Vatican.

I quickly take stock of my surroundings. At this hour, tourists still flood the square, but the doors and windows of the famous church are shuttered. I sense the presence of guards just inside the door.

I take a deep breath before thrusting my magic out once more. The locks securing the entrance shatter, and the wide doors fly open before my power. Three guards, alerted by the intrusion, rush past me, unseeing, toward the front steps. I don't take any chances. The first guard to try doubling back is still reaching for his stun gun when my wave of magic hits them all, rolling them down the stairs. I take off into the church at a quick pace.

After using my magic to jam the front doors closed, I begin seeking the source of the prayers. I rush through the gilded church lined with statues and paintings. I follow the sound of the voices to a pair of double doors, and throw them open with sheer force of will. The doors crash against the walls and practically fly off the hinges. The prayers abruptly fall silent.

I step through the doors and into the Sistine Chapel itself, trying not to let its majesty distract me. Easily a hundred feet long and almost half as wide, the three-storey chapel has a high vaulted ceiling, and every surface is decorated. The first level has beautifully painted drapes. Running from end to end of the second level are vivid and lifelike frescoes of different scenes from the lives of Jesus and Moses. On the third level, twelve arched windows blaze with the light of bright spotlights. My eyes travel up to the ceiling, where Michelangelo's *Creation of Adam* shines down on me. It's one of the most beautiful sights I've ever seen, and I try my very best not to lose myself in its intricacies.

I take another few steps, conscious of the *Last Judgement* fresco looming over me. Before me, a sea of cardinals in their full red ceremonial robes and matching scarlet-red silk birettas gawk at me to see who has disrupted their gathering. At the base of the *Last Judgement*, standing tall and strong before the altar table, his arms outstretched, stands Pope Gregory XVII in his full papal attire. His steely blue eyes meet mine. His hard-edged countenance is framed by a shock of white hair. I'm surprised to see Cardinal Gallagher, the Archbishop of Boston, standing there to his right. He's still entranced in focused prayer. His feet are spread and his head is thrown back as though he alone carries the weight of the world.

Between the cardinals and me stand the members of the choir of the Cathedral of the Holy Cross, all the way from Boston. Their eyes are ablaze with holy fire, and their sublime Gregorian chant rings out through the chamber.

I pause for a moment. I look at the Pope, and he holds my gaze unflinchingly. I reach within myself, grasping hold of the power of water, and I swirl their prayers into a giant ball, spinning it faster and faster, making it smaller and smaller, until it fits in the palm of my hand. I take it and hold it in my hand before them.

The choir stops.

I don't say a word, for I left my voice back in the Citadel. Instead, I weave the power of earth into the ball of prayer in my hand, filling it and hardening it until it's a solid stone orb. I let the orb fall to the floor and it shatters into a thousand pieces. Everyone gathered in the chapel gasps in horror.

The passion in the eyes of the choir dims. Cardinal Gallagher lets out a mournful cry and sags forward. The Pope reaches out, placing a hand on his shoulder. Gallagher lifts his head, finally looking at me, and I see recognition flare in his eyes.

When Pope Gregory's gaze meets mine once again, his eyes are filled with fury. "You shall pay for that, spawn of Lucifer."

I could answer his threat in many ways, but with Aleksandar's last lesson still fresh in my mind, I choose the simplest and most effective response. I bow my head and quietly walk out of the building.

I lift my eyes to the night sky, and my consciousness floats upward once again. Darkness surrounds me in the absence of the bright clouds, but I soon sense the familiar stone of the Citadel as I find my way back.

The energy of the circle still burns brightly as the Guardians surround it and Keegan and James stand shoulder to shoulder, channelling their power into it.

I see my body standing strong, supported by my staff, and there is a slight glow surrounding me. I float toward it, and my consciousness tingles as it passes through the circle's boundary and settles back into my body.

I open my eyes. My grip on the staff is stronger than ever even as my legs go weak. I feel the air surrounding our circle. It's clean and pure and free of intrusions, and the red crystals have gone dark again.

"We are safe," I say in a hoarse voice. I then sink to my knees, unable to hold myself up any longer.

The two other wizards unwind the circle so the Guardians can enter.

James, Danielle, and Keegan all run to my side.

Keegan places his hands on my chest. I can feel them burn with magical energy. I look up into his concerned face.

He gasps. "Your eyes, Aiden. They're like the ocean."

"The ocean?" I murmur.

"I mean, it's like an actual ocean current is flowing through them."

"Whoa..." James says.

Danielle, however, gasps and makes a subtle sign of the cross.

"I can still feel the power of water flowing through me," I say quietly.

"They're beautiful," Keegan says with a blush.

For just a heartbeat, I see a flare of loneliness in his eyes. A moment later, he stands, helping me to my feet.

"I think you're otherwise okay," he says.

James and Keegan hold me steady as the Guardians wander over as if they knew the whole time that everything would be okay.

Everyone takes turns inspecting my eyes, but no one else comments on them.

Evelyn, David, and Aleksandar step forward into our inner circle. I see them look over at Danielle with concern, but James has his arms wrapped around her protectively, so they turn to Keegan and me instead.

"Well done," David says.

Aleksandar nods and grunts his assent.

"Well, we're happy to do our part, but we're wizards," Keegan says. "What about you guys? How did you do that?"

"We are not the first to defend Lannóg Eolas from El's attacks," Evelyn says. She pauses as though to choose her next words carefully. When she speaks again, her voice is slower, quieter. "It is assumed throughout the world that the Vatican is the seat of the Catholic Church. This is not entirely true. It is certainly the centre of the Church, but it is also supported by every denomination of Christianity and holds strong alliances with all the Abrahamic faiths.

"When St. Peter assumed the mantle of leadership of the Church, he learned the truth behind the story of David and Goliath—that Goliath was not a literal giant of the army of the Philistines, Israel's most dangerous foe, but rather a symbolic representation of the most powerful wizard of the time, Nuada, faith's greatest foe. David, full of desire to build a great temple to God, earned his kingship by finally defeating Nuada."

I look over at Danielle. I can feel her eyes burning into me like furious daggers, full of accusation that I've gotten the love of her life wrapped up in something so heretical.

Evelyn grips her staff tightly before continuing. "When St. Peter learned of this, he came to believe that magic was so nefarious that it likely still survived, so he created a secret army of highly trained priests. These priests met in a small shrine in Rome that eventually became St. Peter's Basilica. These priests were tasked with hunting for the last Citadel of the Wizards."

"They've never found us in the physical world," Aleksandar continues. "Although that's not for lack of trying. In the Middle Ages, teams of Christians under the guise of missionaries and Knights Templar would set out to find us. When they eventually gave up on that, they discovered that the power of prayer allowed them to ride out into the ethereal world on the waves of choral music and hunt us that way."

"If I may . . ." David clears his throat. "The ironic thing is that one of their oldest monasteries was founded right above where we stand right now."

"Skellig Michael?" Keegan asks.

David glances at Danielle and seems to wilt a bit. He probably wishes to take back what he just said. He nods slowly and changes the subject. "Anyway, the fact is they've never found us in the physical world, but music is much more powerful than most people believe it to be. It succeeded where all of their grand holy crusades failed, and they've been using it periodically ever since. We think it takes a great deal of effort for them to organize it though, because they don't do it very often."

"I suspect they will be in the near future," I say grimly.

"What makes you say that?" David asks.

"My consciousness travelled all the way to the Vatican. When I manifested in the Sistine Chapel, I saw the Archbishop of Boston, who was visiting St. Michael's in Toronto the day we went. I saw him next to the Pope, and he definitely recognized me."

"Cardinal Gallagher?" Danielle asks, her voice barely a whisper.

"The very same."

Aleksandar furrows his brow and looks over at David. "It would seem Cardinal Gallagher is more of a problem than we thought."

David nods. "I will contact Caitlin and let her know she was right."

When he turns to leave, Evelyn puts a hand on his arm. "Tell Caitlin that for now she must divert her attention toward counterintelligence. We need to know what the Cardinal is doing, as well as any activity on the part of the Church that could threaten the Citadel."

David leaves quickly without another word.

Aleksandar turns his attention back to us. "You hit them back with a fairly substantial bit of magic, and with what you told us just now of this Cardinal, we may be in more danger than we were before. There are ancient wards we can activate to help defend us against their intrusions. Now that they know we're a growing danger to them and not just a dying order of reclusive librarians, they'll no doubt redouble their efforts to find us."

"Let us discuss this further," Evelyn says. "Aleksandar, if you will assist me, please."

The Guardians begin heading for the spiral staircase leading to the upper level to confer about how best to defend the Citadel.

James goes to say something to Danielle, but she beats him to it.

"I have to leave," she says firmly.

"But..." James stammers. "But I thought you could stay until tomorrow..."

She shakes her head. "It's not that, James." She turns to me. "Aiden, you were right. I wanted very, very much to pray—to pray for my life, to pray for yours. I did as you asked and ignored that urge, but it was the hardest thing I've ever done in my life. It felt like I was betraying both my faith *and* myself."

James takes her by the hand. "Danielle..."

She looks at him and traces a finger along his jaw. "I need some time alone to digest everything that's happened. I have to figure out how to come to terms with it."

"But you can't go just yet. You have to wait for Caitlin."

"I'll ask Jennifer to take me back. She knows the way to Toronto."

James sighs. "But Danielle—"

"Can you please ask Caitlin to bring me my things?" She gives his hand a squeeze before running off to find Jennifer.

Chapter Twenty-Five

James is idly collecting Danielle's belongings into a neat stack beside his bed while Keegan and I clean up the rocks that fell during the attack this morning. We're doing it the hard way—manually carrying the chunks of rock—because we want to preserve our magic in case another attack is imminent.

James sighs for probably the sixteenth time in the past hour and looks up at us. "Do you think she wants *all* of her things, or just her handbag?"

"Just her handbag," Keegan says.

"She isn't gone, James," I say. "She'll be back as soon as she reconciles her faith with you being a wizard."

He looks up at us, a forlorn expression on his face. "What if that never happens?"

I look at Keegan and shrug. "Well," I say slowly, "then you'll probably hate me as much as she does. But it's not going to come to that."

I squat to pick up another large chunk. Beneath it is what's left of Keegan's pillow. It's a good thing we awoke when we did. I carry the rock down the tunnel to the Chamber of Knowledge, dropping it on a pile we're making just outside our quarters. I wipe the sweat off my forehead and lean against the wall. What James needs is a distraction. We all need a distraction. Continuing our lessons would help, but Caitlin arrived earlier today with a report. She didn't stay long, and ever since she left, the Guardians have been locked in a debate about what to do next.

I look up from the rock pile to see Aleksandar and Elizabeth heading toward me with their staffs in hand. Elizabeth's fire-red hair billows down her back in waves. It's the first time I've seen it without a ponytail. It's stunning.

She calls past me down the tunnel leading to our quarters. "Wizards!" She taps her staff on the floor three times, and it echoes everywhere.

A moment later, James and Keegan emerge.

My curiosity gets the better of me. "What have you decided?"

"We have some questions that need answering," Aleksandar says.

"What about?"

"The village. These Black Bands. Did you say the leader was collecting ancient manuscripts?"

I nod slowly. "The manuscripts were in Mathieu's home when it was raided."

"So you believe these to be in the hands of the Church?"

"Yes. Père Georges said he had Mathieu in custody. But Nicolas, who managed to avoid capture, said he was going to rescue him."

"And you say they referred to you as Wise Ones?"

"Yes," James says. "It felt a bit odd."

Aleksandar frowns and glances at Elizabeth. "Given everything that has happened this morning, we can't put our trust in this Nicolas. Whatever those manuscripts are, they obviously gave the priest an advantage in dealing with you." He points to the ring of blisters around my neck. "If he manages to get the manuscripts to the Vatican, there's no telling the damage they could do to the Citadel with their next attack. This is assuming they don't have them there already."

Elizabeth nods. "We've sent Caitlin to trail Cardinal Gallagher and determine exactly what his position within the Church is. But we can't afford to wait for her to return, so the five of us are going on an excursion."

I exchange glances with James and Keegan. *The Guardians are finally taking us to the outside world?*

"*Really?*" Keegan asks.

"Your training is far from finished," Aleksandar says, "but you have all shown great progress in your lessons, and you showed great resolve and fortitude during the attack. You are also proving yourselves ready by cleaning up this mess without the use of magic."

"What's this about?" I ask. "Where are we going?"

"Caitlin was able to find some information out about Père Georges," Elizabeth says. "Before joining the Catholic Church, François Georges attended Université de la Sorbonne Nouvelle in Paris, where he met his wife, Claire. He tried to very hard to clear his social media past, but there are always ways to dig. The evidence points to him being a very liberal-minded freethinker who loved his wife deeply. Tragically, she died in a flood while they were on a humanitarian mission to Thailand. The young François spiralled into a life of alcohol and drug abuse."

She looks at us intensely. "This is where it gets interesting. He was rescued from that life by a Father Blyton, who later became a certain Pope Gregory XVII. François then devoted himself to God. He turned his life around and entered the seminary when he was thirty-three. It took him eleven years to become a priest, but once he did, he moved to different parishes every two years, always moving to progressively more challenging and larger communities."

"Despite the terrible things he's capable of," I say, "he does seem to have a way with his parishioners."

"Yes, but much later, when he was sixty-two, he suddenly requested a transfer to a quiet parish in Saint-Ouen-sur-Seine, where he became priest of Notre-Dame-du-Rosaire. For the next ten years, little was heard of him, but all the parishioners Caitlin spoke to remembered him fondly."

"And then something happened," Aleksandar says gravely. "Père Georges picked up and left his life as he knew it."

"We know very little else at the moment," Elizabeth says, shaking her head.

"As much as we'd like to reclaim these artifacts in a peaceful manner," Aleksandar says, "we would stand a much better chance of doing that if we understood what made Père Georges pick up and leave Paris. Unfortunately, we probably don't have the time for that."

"So what do we do?" I ask.

"You can show us the lay of the land while it's still daylight. Then we'll go in under the cover of night. Make sure you bring your staffs with you in case things don't go the way we hope. I've got water, some snacks to tide us over, and a few supplies in my satchel."

It's raining when we step out onto the mountain path just outside the door to the Citadel. The clouds hang low and thick, making it impossible to see even the fields outside the village. I move to begin making my way down, but

Aleksandar stops me. I look up at him, and he has a finger to his lips.

"The Church doesn't know this is the way we come," I whisper.

He places his lips to my ear. "Even if the Church didn't know of it before, they've now been able to interrogate at least two members of this Black Band you speak of. We must assume they know everything."

He beckons Elizabeth to his side. The two of them crouch low and step off the rocky path into the tall grass beside it. They move quickly and stealthily through the grass to one of the many shrubs dotting the area. They scout the top of the path in silence before returning to us.

Aleksandar motions for everyone to gather close, and speaks quietly. "We don't know what those manuscripts contain, and we don't know what your villager friends know. More importantly, Père Georges is likely interrogating all of them by now. Our assuming they don't know something could be a fatal error."

"Good point," James says. "But it's safe, right?"

He was the most eager of us all to go on this trip. I was right about his needing a distraction.

"So far," Elizabeth says. "We'll descend slowly until we can see the village below the clouds. Once we know there's no one watching for us, we'll pick up the pace."

We're halfway down the mountain when Elizabeth frantically motions us back, and we press ourselves against the mountainside. In the silence, I can hear footsteps crunching on the rocks. I peek down the path, ignoring the urgent motions of the Guardians.

Just down from us I can barely make out a thin bush. I see movement on the other side of it, and for just a moment, memories of the time James and I spent in the cell beneath the church fill my mind. Through the haze, I think I see the hulking form of one of the priest's men. A second later, however, that image fades to reveal a thin man, walking up and down the path, nervously twisting his beard between his fingers. He pauses and looks in my direction. Did he hear us? I recede behind the rocky wall to avoid revealing our position. Then I see his face.

"Nicolas!" I hiss as I poke my head out from behind the rock.

He starts at the sound of my voice. "Wise One? Is that you?"

"Yes!" I say, a bit louder this time.

I start to step out, but he throws both of his hands up for me to stop.

"No!" he hisses, confirming Aleksandar's fears. "Stay hidden."

He glances down the path, and then he rushes toward us. He rounds the edge of the rock where we're hidden, and hunkers down beside me. He takes in the others calmly and then looks up at me.

"Word of your escape from the church has spread throughout the village. No one has ever escaped Père George's clutches before, but more men loyal to him showed up this morning. I was forced to flee the village. They haven't found me yet, but they're scouring the outskirts for access to Lannóg Eolas."

"You know of Lannóg Eolas?" I ask incredulously.

A small smile pulls at the corners of his lips. "I was one of Mathieu's best students. The Hall of Mysteries contains many secrets, but Mathieu was happiest to discover the name of the home of the Wise Ones." His smile fades. "I was the only one he could share this with before he was captured."

I turn to Aleksandar and Elizabeth and give them a knowing look. They were right. If the Black Bands know this much, how much else do they know? But the Guardians simply stare back at me with confusion written across their faces.

"Didn't you hear that?" I ask.

"If you spoke English, we might have," Aleksandar says quietly as he shoots an uneasy look at Nicolas.

I blink. "What do you mean?"

James and Keegan look just as confused as I feel.

Aleksandar leans toward Elizabeth and whispers something to her. She nods, and he turns to Nicolas, bowing his head in greeting.

"I am Aleksandar," he says, "Guardian of Knowledge."

Nicolas turns to me. "Why does he not speak as you do?" he asks. "You are from the same place, yet you speak the tongue of the ancients, and he speaks . . . something else."

"The tongue of the ancients?" James asks, puzzled.

This isn't the first time we've heard Nicolas mention this, but we had no idea what he was talking about before.

James looks at me, and then we both look at the Guardians.

"What does he mean?" he asks them.

Elizabeth raises an eyebrow. "What is it he said again?"

James, Keegan, and I share a puzzled look.

"He wants to know why we speak this so-called tongue of the ancients and you don't," Keegan says.

"Keegan," Aleksandar says, "would you please ask him where he learned to speak this tongue of the ancients?"

Keegan glances at everyone before asking Nicolas the question.

"I learned it from Mathieu," Nicolas says, a note of pride in his voice. "Mathieu has spent his entire life devoted to the Hall of Mysteries and the mysteries contained within. In order to study the ancient manuscripts, he had to first learn how to read them, as they are written in your language."

Keegan repeats Nicolas's answer to the Guardians.

"David will be ecstatic," Aleksandar says to Elizabeth.

"Indeed," she says. "This is all very curious."

"What's going on?" I ask.

Aleksandar scoffs. "How would they learn to speak English—a language that in its present form has been around for less than six hundred years—from manuscripts that are *three thousand* years old?"

When no one says anything, he rolls his eyes. "Nicolas isn't speaking English. When you speak to him, the words coming out of your mouth aren't English. We suspect his teacher, Mathieu, actually did discover the language of the ancient wizards."

"Is that even possible?" I ask in shock.

"If I didn't hear it for myself," Elizabeth answers, "I would have said no, but the magic flowing through you must recognize the ancient words and is translating it for you."

Nicolas looks between us intently. "What did they say?" he asks me.

I mull over my answer for a few seconds. "They say they can't understand you, either." I motion to Keegan and James. "The three of us are still learning." I then motion to the Guardians. "These are two of our teachers."

Nicolas nods and says, "Ah," as if it all makes sense to him, and then, as if it's the most commonplace thing in the world, he says, "These ones are Guardians of Nuada."

James, Keegan, and I gawk at each other.

"What is it?" Elizabeth asks.

"He knows you who are," I say, "Guardians, I mean! He just called you

Guardians of Nuada!"

Aleksandar's face has become a sullen mask. "If he knows that, then it is imperative that we recover that information from the Church."

"Do you know where Mathieu is?" I ask Nicolas. At this point, I have become the official interpreter between the Guardians and the Black Bands.

"He was moved to Père Georges's manse. I can take you there."

"And the Hall of Mysteries?" James asks. "Can you take us there as well?"

Nicolas cocks his head slightly. "The Hall of Mysteries is vast." He gestures widely, encompassing the entire valley with one sweep. "They are far larger than the village. But I can take you to the room containing the manuscripts once we rescue Mathieu." He pauses, and a heartfelt smile spreads across his face. "He will be ecstatic to return there with the Wise Ones themselves!"

It's a perilous climb down the mountain in the rain. We are about ten minutes from the bottom when Keegan puts a hand on my shoulder.

"There are people below," he whispers.

While the rest of us fall back, Aleksandar drops to the ground and army crawls to the edge of the ridge. He peers over it for several long minutes before crawling his way back to us.

"There are two men and a woman, all dressed in black," he says. "They're making their way up toward us."

My heart drops. "In black? With red buttons and a golden cross on their breasts?"

"Yes. You know them?"

James shudders. "Those are Père Georges's soldiers." His voice is haunted, and I can feel his pain.

"We have maybe five minutes before they get here, if we're lucky."

"James," Elizabeth says, "you will have to cast an illusion to make it seem as if we're not here."

"But what will happen once they make it the rest of the way up the mountain?" I ask.

"Then we hope the natural defenses of Lannóg Eolas will protect it. Surely this is not the first time an agent of the Church has climbed the mountain. If your information is correct, they've not discovered it yet."

"We are open to better ideas," Aleksandar says quietly, "but we're running out of time."

James points at a small pile rocks. "Quick, throw a couple of those rocks on the far side of them!"

Keegan and I each grab a rock. We crawl along with James until we reach the ridge.

Peeking over, I see the path winding down toward the fields in the distance. Halfway up, I see the three soldiers marching their way up the incline. To the left is a small wood that grows from the valley below up to the side of the mountain. I recall passing it each time we've come to and from the village. It made me miss seeing trees. I also recall thinking it would make a good hiding spot near the base of the mountain should we ever need it.

"There?" I ask, nodding in a direction of the trees. James nods, and Keegan and I throw.

The rocks sail silently through the air. At the same moment they strike the foliage of the trees, I see vague images that look like Keegan and me near the edge of the wood. An air of sudden stillness descends upon the path, followed by the hushed whispers of the soldiers below. The soldiers spin just in time to see the image of Keegan's head disappear behind the trees.

A cry goes up from the three soldiers. They rush down the path and charge into the woods.

"That looked exactly like us!" Keegan whispers.

James grins. "Thanks . . ."

"We need to go quickly now," Aleksandar says, starting down the path again. "It might not take very long for them to realize they're chasing nothing."

We slow when we get to the bottom of the path. We decide to approach the village from the west, where a large but somewhat sparse forest grows out past the fields. It provides us with just enough coverage. From the edge of the trees, we peer out at the village across a small field while the setting sun illuminates the rooftops and the square in a deepening glow. On the far side of the village I can see the large boulders that once provided us with a hiding spot, but on this side there is nothing but wide open, freshly harvested fields. We hunker down here, faces peering out of the trees.

Aleksandar and Elizabeth squat down beside me.

"What are we looking at?" Aleksandar asks. His voice has grown hoarse from whispering so much.

I look out over the village. "You see the church in the middle of the square? Most of rickety shacks all around are market stalls, though we've only seen the ones on this side in use. That taller building?" I point to the place where I once made eye contact with the man on the steps. "I think that's the town hall. I saw some official-looking man there, but I'm not sure who he is. Maybe the mayor? And there, northeast of the church—that's the cobblestone road we told you about. That's where we feel the powerful magic."

"Is that the entrance to the Hall of Mysteries?" James asks Nicolas.

Nicolas nods. "The road leads into the forest on the far side of the village, but it quickly becomes overgrown as it disappears into the trees. It leads to the entrance of an old mine. It's well hidden by thick overgrowth."

"I'm curious," I say. "Why haven't the priest and his men tried following the road to this mine?"

"For the same reason they've never discovered the entrance to Lannóg Eolas. Mathieu believes a powerful magic guards it from the Church."

When I tell the Guardians what Nicolas said, Aleksandar gazes longingly along the cobblestone road. "And Père Georges's home?" he asks.

When I ask Nicolas about it, he points to a well-kept lane on the northwest corner of the village square. Much like the cobblestone road, the lane disappears into some trees, but these appear to have been planted for privacy. We can just barely make out a large roof with brown shingles.

Aleksandar smiles. "When the sun sets, that's where we go."

We move through the field in a slow train, hunched as low as possible to limit our exposure to whoever might look our way. With only the small sliver of a waning moon casting its light on the valley, we have a cover of darkness more complete than anything we could have hoped for. I keep one hand on James in front of me, and I can feel Keegan's hand on my back. Nicolas is in the lead, with Aleksandar behind him. Elizabeth brings up the rear.

Large black shapes loom in the darkness, and they form into the shapes of houses and market buildings as we draw near the village. The streetlamps provide dim illumination, and I can see flickering candlelight through a few of the windows, but it otherwise seems that most of the villagers are asleep.

We change direction and head north along the edge of the field. Dark silhouettes of large trees rise up around us, and the ground beneath our feet becomes spongy. We've come to a grassy lawn.

Nicolas whispers to me past Aleksandar's hulking dark form.

I immediately whisper to Aleksandar, "He says the lane to the priest's manse is about forty feet ahead."

I can barely make out the Guardian's nodding head.

We move slowly from tree to tree along the lawn. The trees are large enough that very little moonlight filters through their leaves. After a few minutes of this, I see the familiar glow of electric light. We stop at the end of the tree line and stand in a row of disbelieving faces.

Compared to the rest of the village, Père Georges's manse is opulent. The source of the light is a few bright spotlights that illuminate the area around the building. A tall iron fence surrounds the perimeter. Vines climb the fence, and rows of perfectly manicured cedar shrubs line the front lawn. The house itself stands as a beacon of light against the darkness. It's at least four times the size of Mathieu's place. It's a two-storey yellow brick house that would best be described as a stately home. Lights blaze through four bay windows on the front side and two large windows on the side facing us. A small set of stone stairs leads up to a gabled front entrance.

We all look at Nicolas questioningly.

He returns our look with indignation on his features. "As you have seen, we are a farming community," he says bitterly. "Père Georges collects our harvest, as has every priest before him. From that supply, each family in the village gets a dividend of wheat that has to last the year. Those who hold jobs in the village, such as the schoolmaster, get a bit more as payment. Mathieu has told us that the yield of our harvest would otherwise allow us to live comfortable lives, but as you can see, all of that comfort is reserved for the so-called Révérend Père."

"He must sell the rest and keep the proceeds for himself," James says. "How is the grass so green here while the village itself is so dry and dusty?"

"All of the water of the valley's basin is diverted to the fields to ensure a good harvest," Nicolas says. "The manse, however, sits on the town's only natural spring, so Père Georges has almost total control of the water supply for the village itself."

"What do you mean?" I ask. "He just hoards it?" I can feel the anger building inside me, but I try my best to keep it under control. I try instead to understand the situation as best I can.

"Well, each week, he selects one villager to maintain the manse's landscaping. He does it on a rotating schedule. As payment, he offers full access to water for that week instead of the basic rations normally available. This, of course, is provided he is satisfied with your work. If he's ever unhappy with something, he'll send you home early, and you won't get another chance for months, if at all."

"But can't you just use some of the water meant for the fields?" Keegan asks, incredulous.

Nicolas looks aghast. "And risk a bad harvest? The whole village would suffer as a result." A faraway look enters his eyes. "When I was a child," he says quietly, "someone did just that. They were executed in the village square."

I shudder at the memory of my own experience at the hands of Père Georges.

"That's horrible," James says. I see the haunted look in his eyes.

Nicolas shrugs. "Père Georges is much better than Père Ferdinand was. At least Père Georges shows love and compassion in his dealings with his parishioners." He shakes his head. "It is our way of life here—or it *was*, I should say. We hope your arrival here marks the beginning of change for the better."

"What's that?" Elizabeth asks, pointing to a dark object near the entrance of the manse.

I squint. It appears to be a small covered trailer.

Nicolas follows what she's pointing at, and his eyes light up. "The lost manuscripts!" he exclaims excitedly. He turns to us. "These are the manuscripts the priest's men stole from Mathieu's home."

"It's the manuscripts," I tell the Guardians.

"They must be preparing to take them to the Vatican for study," Elizabeth says. "We have to get them before it's too late." She looks around. "Keegan, how many people are nearby right now?"

Keegan squats and places his palm on the ground, focusing. "Only one, but they're not in the manse. They're patrolling the grounds on the far side right now."

"With the six of us working together, we should be able to pull the trailer into the forest and hide it. It won't stay hidden if anyone looks for it, but let's hope the forest will be the last place they look. It could buy us some time to return for it."

A minute later, we wait in silence as one of the priest's soldiers marches past. She swings the beam of her flashlight left and right. She moves with discipline and efficiency. If anything, these holy soldiers are well trained. Strapped to the soldier's waist is a handgun.

"This one is armed," James says. "There's no way we're pulling that trailer with an armed soldier marching the grounds."

Aleksandar reaches into his satchel and pulls out a length of rope. "I don't want to have to kill her. If someone can distract her, I'll incapacitate her. We'll decide what to do with her after."

When the soldier disappears around the house, Aleksandar crouches low and sprints across the yard with the rope in one hand and his staff in the other. He stops near the trailer and presses into the shadows behind it.

After a few more minutes, the soldier rounds the house again. When she approaches the trailer, I squeeze James's arm. He nods. A moment later, a shape roughly the size of a human appears down the lane toward the village square.

The soldier flicks her flashlight left and right, and for a brief second the shape glows grey in the passing beam. She flicks the beam back just as the shape takes off down the lane. She gasps and raises her wrist to her mouth. "Gibbs!" she barks into a wristband. "I've got a runner! Coming your way!"

She then draws her gun and launches into a sprint. When she rushes past the trailer, Aleksandar brings his staff down on her head with a crack, and she drops like a stone.

Aleksandar runs to her side and presses a finger to the side of her neck. He looks up at us as we arrive.

"She's alive," he says, "but she called someone, so we'll have to be quick."

He expertly ties her hands together behind her back and drags her across the lane to the iron fence, where he secures her with the rope and places a length of duct tape across her mouth. When he returns, he carefully places her gun into his satchel.

We quickly take up stations around the trailer. The lane leads through the iron fence and then forks into two directions. One direction runs toward the village while the other runs past the manse and to the edge of the forest. We're grateful that the way leading to the forest is mostly downhill, as we don't know how much time we have.

With two of us pulling and four of us pushing, we move the trailer down the lane and eventually veer off into the forest. We struggle to get the trailer through the undergrowth and over several rocks and logs until we settle it into a small gully. We then scramble to grab loose brush and scatter it across the trailer to camouflage it as much as possible. It's probably less perfect than what Elizabeth had in mind, but no one will likely find it until the sun rises. Even then, it won't jump out at them.

To finish the job, James casts a subtle illusion over the whole area, making the trailer appear to be a thorny bush. He could have hidden it in plain sight, but if anyone were to walk up to it and touch it, the illusion would collapse. There's also no telling how long it'll take us to return and how much more magic James will need to use in the meantime. At least this way it's naturally hidden in case the illusion does end up unravelling.

We run through the trees back to the lane. While the others run toward the manse, I pause, looking back. I close my eyes, feeling my magic flow through the staff. I call up a gentle wind. It's just strong enough to scatter the leaves and loose soil at the lane's edge to cover up the signs of the trailer's passage.

When I catch up with the others, I find them standing at the door to the manse.

"There's no sign of this Gibbs fellow," Aleksandar says, "but we're going to have to be quick because he'll come looking for her before long."

He tries the door, but it's locked. To the left of the door handle, a palm print reader flashes red.

"We don't have time to do this nicely," he says to me.

"Clear the steps," I say to everyone.

Everybody stands clear, and I face the door. I begin to feel the air around me energize, swirling around me. I call to it, urging it to do my bidding, and it gets heavier, faster, stronger. I glance behind me. The others' robes billow violently as the wind howls past them. They shield their faces from flying debris as they struggle to keep watching.

I focus, gathering the tumultuous wind into a concentrated ball of power at the tip of my staff. Utter silence falls around me as the air calms. I thrust my staff toward the door with a cry, and the power of the wind jumps from the tip of my staff with the force of a hurricane.

The sound of crunching, snapping wood fills the air as the door explodes inward, shattering off its hinges.

I lower my staff. For a heartbeat or two, an apprehensive silence settles upon the house before the high-pitched scream of an alarm pierces it.

I gesture the others forward, and they rush up the stairs and into the foyer. Nicolas looks torn between panicking about the strange noise and gawping at me like I'm some kind of god, but I can't spare the time to explain either to him right now. I grab him by the shoulders.

"It's an alarm!" I shout over the noise. "Like a bell! Ignore it. Where will we find Mathieu?"

"I-I-I don't know," he stammers. "None of us has ever been inside this place."

I shake my head at Aleksandar, and he steps farther into the house. We follow him to a large central hall with a soaring two-storey ceiling, an ornate staircase rising to the second floor to the right, and several doorways with fancy white trim lining the wall to our left.

Pictures and paintings lie scattered on the floor among broken frames and shattered glass. The force of the wind must have knocked them off the wall. We pick our way through the debris, toward the first doorway to the left. We peek through the opening into a living room with a leather sofa, a reclining armchair, an elegant-looking coffee table, a fireplace with a marble mantle, and a very large holo-screen.

We continue to the next doorway and find an office. Dark wood panelling lines the walls, and there is a faux fireplace against the back wall. Two large gilded gold statuettes of Jesus hanging from the cross are mounted on the wall on either side of the fireplace mantle. A large mahogany desk and plush black leather chair sit on the left side of the room. In front of the desk are two armchairs. Upon the desk a Bible sits open. I glance at the pages. It's turned to the Gospel of Matthew, but a thin film of dust covers the words. Also on the desk are a village registry dated thirty years ago and an old rotary phone. These are also covered in dust.

"It would be a pretty safe bet to say that Père Georges has never used this office," Keegan says.

"He must have one somewhere else," James says. "If not here, in the church maybe?"

"Somewhere, yes," Elizabeth says, "but where's Mathieu?"

"Should we try the basement?" I ask.

After a frantic search, we can't find the basement anywhere. Five minutes later, we've searched the kitchen, the dining room, the master bedroom, the guest bedroom, and three washrooms. We regroup in the office.

"We're running out of time!" Aleksandar shouts over the alarm.

"Maybe they've moved him," James says.

Nicolas shakes his head. "He was brought here just this morning."

"Would they have brought him to the Vatican?"

This time, it's Elizabeth who shakes her head. "No, I don't think so. It would make more sense to keep him here until they've extracted everything they can from him."

There's a loud click from somewhere in the room, and the whir of machinery fills the air, just barely audible over the sound of the alarm. I look around, and see a very surprised Keegan standing next to the fireplace. His hand is on one of the statuettes of Jesus, except it's now tilted forty-five degrees.

The faux fireplace then recedes, and that whole section of wall retracts to the right, revealing a deeper section within the office. It's twice as big, and everything about it is modern. A sleek desk of black glass sits by a floor-to-ceiling window. One of those fancy holographic keyboards hovers above it. Beside it is another door. On this side of the office, the walls are black quartz, and the floor is gorgeously redone old hardwood.

On the far wall is a giant gleaming screen divided into twelve equal sections, each showing a video feed of a location somewhere in the village. The feeds show what appear to be the courthouse, the town hall, and the church, the latter of which shows Père Georges and three other men dressed in priestly robes engaged in conversation. Other feeds show several houses, including Mathieu's house, which now looks rather empty without the stacks of manuscripts. Two of the feeds show views of outside the manse, and one shows a view of the path leading up the mountain. The final feed, on the bottom right corner of the screen, is dark. The details are difficult to make out.

Nicolas stares at the screen as he slowly approaches it. He points at each video feed in stunned amazement.

"Magic?" he asks.

"Technology," Keegan says, shaking his head.

"These are all places here in the village . . . But what is this here?" Nicolas peers at the darkened feed and squints at it, pressing his face up close. "Oh!" he shouts, and he repeatedly stabs the screen with his finger.

I step closer and squint at the feed myself. "What is it, Nicolas?"

"It's Mathieu!"

Sure enough, I can just barely make out Mathieu's form in the darkened room. He sits in a chair facing the screen. His arms, chest, and legs are strapped to the chair with thick bindings. His head has drooped to his chest, and it's difficult to tell whether he's still alive.

"Where is he?" Nicolas says. "Where could he be?" He can't stop staring at the screen.

I look around the room. "There!" I shout. "The door!"

Aleksandar gives a quick nod as he walks over to the door. It's locked. He steps back and gives it a hard kick, and the door flies open, revealing a walk-in closet.

There sits Mathieu.

He doesn't seem to be fully aware of us, but he lolls his head from side to side. Aleksandar works quickly to undo his bindings.

Nicolas stands by the door. "Mathieu . . ."

Keegan files past him to take a closer look. "He's been badly beaten, but he seems stable enough. We should be able to move him. I'll be able to help him once we get him someplace safe."

Aleksandar kneels as he prepares to lift Mathieu onto his shoulders.

"We have to go! Now!" Elizabeth hisses.

I look over at her. She points to a feed showing two black-clad figures approaching the manse stealthily. They raise their assault rifles, readying them.

Aleksandar hoists Mathieu onto his shoulders in a fireman's carry, and brings him out of the closet. He glances at the screen. "We cannot go out the front door," he says. "Aiden, keep them out! James, we need an exit!" He nods his head toward the window. "Keegan, Elizabeth, with me!"

"Nicolas," I shout, "stay with Keegan!"

We each take up our positions, and a moment later I can hear the sound of footsteps running up the stairs toward the front door—or what's left of it.

I lunge for the Jesus statuette and straighten it. The wall slides back into position with a whine. There's a shout, and I look up to the wide eyes of one of the soldiers. His rifle comes up, and just as the wall settles into position, the sound of bullets reverberates through the room. I stumble backward, tripping over my own feet. I nearly crash into the desk as panic fills me. Gunfire rings out over the sound of the blaring alarm, and bullets start ripping through the quartz walls of the office. I push off from the desk and stumble forward, crashing down to my knees. Cursing, I grab my staff and thrust it toward the Jesus statuette. It feels sacrilegious, but it's all I can think of. Magic flows out of me, through the staff, and it fuses the statuette in place, seizing up the wall mechanism. It's not a perfect solution, but the soldiers are essentially locked out.

I hear shattering glass. I look behind me, and I see James with his staff raised high before the blasted window. He steps aside as Aleksandar files past him, carrying Mathieu through the opening. Nicolas and Keegan are close behind. James darts out the window, and Elizabeth calls to me. I can't see her, as the room has now filled with smoke and dust. I focus on the sound of her voice and clamber back to my feet. I stagger forward and out the window. I find myself on a stone path that winds around the house.

I pause to look around. The others are making their way toward the trees ahead. James must have cut through the iron fence with his magic. Just ahead of me, Elizabeth breaks into a run toward the fence, but she glances back to make sure I'm following.

A loud blast punctures my ears, and they begin ringing. I look back into the office as a cloud of smoke billows forth from the window and envelops me. The soldiers have broken through.

Resolve settles within me and I spin to face them. I plant my feet in a solid stance while trying to ignore the ringing in my ears. I raise my staff before me in my right hand. I sweep my left hand upward in an arc, gathering air, solidifying it in front of me. The two soldiers rush in, assault rifles raised, and their muzzles start flashing brightly as bullets erupt from them.

My energy rushes through the air between us, and I feel each bullet as it strikes the wall of solid air I'm holding before me like a shield. The soldiers, realizing the futility of their gunfire, start to circle around, looking for a way around my barrier of air. But I don't give them the chance. I use that moment of disruption to my advantage.

I stab my staff forward, summoning the elemental fire coursing through my blood. I feel the power respond to my call, and it rushes up from the depths of my being. It races down my arm to the tip of my staff, and a ball of fire erupts from it. The soldiers jump back from it, and they stagger as the fire explodes at their feet. Again I stab, and a second ball of fire races through the air toward them. This time, my aim is perfect. It strikes them at chest level and throws them both back through the hole they blasted into the office. The fire catches on the hardwood floor, and flames reach up, melting the large screen and spreading into the rest of the manse.

I hear a haunting scream. My legs weaken. A dark thought creeps into my mind. Those men aren't going to make it out.

I feel Elizabeth's hands on my arms as she pulls me toward the trees.

"Oh, Aiden," I hear her mutter.

We run for the trees, her hands urging me forward. When the sound of the alarm dies, I glance back to see the manse ablaze. The sight of it drives me onward.

Chapter Twenty-Six

The cold, damp soil of the forest floor soaks through my robe, chilling my knees. Tears run down my face. The ringing in my ears has faded, but that soldier's dying scream is burned into my mind.

James and Aleksandar kneel beside me, both their hands on my back. I clench my eyes tightly. I can see his face. He was about my age. Maybe he had a wife. A young child. There must be someone who will wonder why he isn't coming home. I hear the voice of the female guard echoing through my head. "Gibbs!" Was he Gibbs?

I shake my head. My guilt-ridden conscience is running away from me. Yet, I can't help but think that someone, somewhere, loved him, even if it's his lonely mother who's waiting for him to come home, just as my own mother is waiting for me. And now he won't be going home, nor will the other soldier who was with him.

James and Aleksandar say nothing. What is there to say? That they deserved it? That it was either them or us? That they forced my hand? I've said all those things to myself already.

Calloused hands grab either side of my face. I open my eyes to see Mathieu kneeling before me. Sadness is written on his features.

"Wizard Keegan tells me this is the first time you have killed a man." His voice is filled with compassion.

I nod and close my eyes again. I don't want to talk.

"I wish I could tell you it gets easier," he continues. "If you're like me, it doesn't. It also doesn't help to dwell on the act. They're dead. Nothing can change that. But I remember every death by my hands. I carry them with me. I see their deaths as giving purpose to my life. Those soldiers died because they belong to a group that wants to oppress my people and murder all of yours. But the person they were still deserves to be remembered. Take who they were within you. Use them to reinforce your purpose and make you stronger."

I swallow. I focus on building a picture of the two soldiers. I don't know if I'm comfortable going through life with the images of the people I've killed forever sitting on a mantelpiece in my head. But Mathieu's words at least give me something besides myself to focus on. They remind me that the reason we're here is much bigger than me. I can see why men like Nicolas and Jacques would follow him. He has an inspirational way of speaking.

I wipe my eyes with the backs of my hands. "Thank you, Mathieu," I say quietly. "How are you feeling?"

He smiles, offering me a hand up, which I take willingly. "I'm feeling fine, thank you. Wizard Keegan is very skilled at his art. Thank you so much for helping Nicolas rescue me."

He looks through the trees toward the manse. It is entirely enveloped in flames now. The fire casts an eerie glow. "If we move deeper into the forest, there's a narrow trail that will take us across to the Hall of Mysteries. The fire will alert the village, and it won't be long before Père Georges and his men realize what's happened, but we will be safe there."

"But Mathieu," Nicolas says. "The manuscripts! They're all—"

"Safe where they are for now, if I understood Wizard Keegan correctly."

James translates quietly to the Guardians.

Elizabeth steps forward, her hand raised. "It is imperative that the manuscripts not make it to the Vatican. James, ask him if we can guarantee their safety where they are now."

Mathieu listens to James and then studies Elizabeth for a moment before speaking. "It is impossible to fully guarantee their safety where they are, but they are safer than they were a short while ago." He pauses for a moment, as if considering something. "If I'm not mistaken, there are thirteen men of the Church in the village currently, including Père Georges. When they find out about the fire, they will come here and will assume we have taken the manuscripts somewhere else in the village."

"Why would they assume we've stayed in the village?" I ask. "Any sane person would flee this place."

Mathieu looks up, his eyes haunted, and he emphasizes every word. "Because no villager has *ever* left the village." He shakes his head slowly. "We would never think of taking the manuscripts anywhere else." His eyes drift in the direction where we stowed the trailer. "Down that way lies another path. It is the pass Père Georges, his predecessors, and now the Golden Crosses use to enter the village, but it's protected by some sort of magic."

There's a period of silence after James finishes translating his words.

Mathieu looks to us again. "In my younger days, Père Ferdinand would occasionally invite more Golden Crosses to the village. They always made life even more difficult for the villagers, so one day I started hunting them down and eliminating them. I tried keeping their numbers always limited to four, and eventually they came to be superstitious about having more than that. I once even tried to retrace their steps down that pass. A terrible heaviness descended upon me, making it difficult to go forward, but I forged ahead, pushing through it. I stopped when I came to the killing ground." He shudders.

"The what?" I ask quietly.

"A section of the trail leading away from the village. In that moment, I realized that this is what happened to all of those who've tried to escape the village before me." His voice falls to a hoarse whisper. "There is no escape."

For a long time, no one says anything, and then a steely resolve enters Mathieu's eyes again.

"Did you hide the signs of the trailer's passing?"

"I did," I say quietly with a nod.

"Then the manuscripts will be safe until we can find the means to carry them to your Citadel."

"What about you? Are there more Black Bands to worry about?"

Mathieu turns to Nicolas and grips his arm. "Of course! Nicolas, I must ask you to run and tell the others that it's not safe to remain at home anymore. Our friend Père Georges will doubtless stop at nothing to strike back at us now that we've made this move against him. He will target the Black Bands in his search for the manuscripts. Tell them to stick to the trees. Stay hidden."

Nicolas looks crestfallen at having to leave us, but he bows slightly and disappears.

Mathieu turns to us. "Come. I will take you to the Hall of Mysteries."

He then sets out, walking briskly deeper into the forest. We're left with no choice but to follow.

Aleksandar leans in close and whispers, "I don't entirely trust this man."

For some reason, I couldn't agree with him more.

Mathieu's narrow trail is hardly a trail at all. In the glow of the burning manse, I can just barely see James ahead of me through the thick foliage. When the darkness of the forest overtakes the light of the flames, we group up, using touch and sound to stick together.

A journey that might have taken us twenty minutes during the day has taken us more than an hour. But we're getting close. I can feel the irresistible pull tugging at me, drawing me ever forward.

We round a long rocky ridge and come to a stop. We hear voices ahead. They seem to be headed in our direction.

"What's this?" James hisses to me.

Mathieu pushes us back further into the trees. "They're unlikely to be Black Bands," he whispers. "We only recently sent Nicolas to find them."

"They must be Père Georges's men," I say. "We must hide."

As they near, flashlights beam in our direction.

Aleksandar presses in close. "They're speaking English."

I squeeze James's arm. "It's the Church. We can't let them see us."

A familiar tingling flows through me and the air between us. A beam of light glimmers off James's face, and I see the concentration etched there as he holds his illusion strong in front of us.

A figure draws close. I can just make out the gold cross on her chest. I hold my breath. It's the soldier Aleksandar tied to the fence back at the manse. She walks straight for us with her flashlight flicking left and right. Occasionally, she cocks an ear, listening.

As she draws close, I see James's lips moving silently, and there's a subtle shift in the air.

I can no longer see James. Instead, a solid rock sits next to me. I glance to my left, and a fir tree now stands where Aleksandar once was. James has created six separate illusions for us instead a single large one to screen us.

The soldier heads directly for the fir tree. She steps up to it, shining her flashlight around it. She sidesteps the trunk, using her forearm to brush the branches away. It's the ultimate test of James's powers; it's an illusion that not only looks real but also feels real.

The beams of the flashlight disappear into the trees, and darkness descends upon us once again.

"We should go quickly," James whispers. "I'm not sure I can be that convincing a second time!"

"Mathieu?" I whisper.

Mathieu's face presses in close to mine, his finger pressed up against his lips.

A second later, I hear the crunching of a boot shifting on the forest floor several metres away. It stops. Then a light flares to life, and the crunching recedes in the opposite direction.

Mathieu watches the light fade before turning back to me. "Let's go," he whispers urgently. "They shouldn't have found this place."

We move fast. The fear of the so-called Golden Crosses behind us overcomes our fear of stumbling in the dark. The magnetic pull of the Hall of Mysteries grows greater as we draw closer.

The transition is almost shocking when it comes. We've been in such thick forest for so long that stepping into the grove of sparsely spaced trees makes the place feel expansive. I feel the cobblestone road beneath my feat. It's uneven and ancient. At the same time, hauntingly beautiful music fills my soul. It's a wordless song, just the rich sound of a woman's powerful soprano riding through the air and beckoning to me, reaching deep within me.

"Do you hear that?" Keegan asks.

"Yes. It's beautiful," James says.

The Guardians draw closer to each other.

"It's very faint," Elizabeth says, "but I do hear something."

The forest opens to a tiny clearing. The razor-thin moon shines down faintly on the thick undergrowth circled by the trees. Mathieu rushes ahead. He pulls some of the foliage aside, revealing a round wooden door in the ground. He twists an ancient black metal handle, and it groans in protest. When he lifts the door open, we peer down into a dark hole. Near the top edge, we can barely make out a skinny wooden ladder.

Aleksandar insists on going first. Moments after he reaches the bottom, the flickering of torchlight reaches our eyes. He then looks up at us and waves us down.

We descend the ladder one by one. Mathieu comes last, closing the door above him. When I get to the bottom, I find the others standing there in stunned amazement. I step forward, and my mouth falls open.

We stand in what looks to be a massive chamber of a glorious palace. Gleaming white stone walls support a beautiful vaulted ceiling painted with vast murals depicting the stories of the lives of the wizards. In one, a wedding takes place. In another, children frolic on the green grass while animal familiars keep watch. Another mural depicts an epic battle. On yet another, a brilliant red dragon flies from the parapets of what appears to be Lannóg Eolas. Fire spews from its mouth in an awe-inspiring display of raw power.

Along the walls are shelves and shelves filled with thick books and parchments.

I look at Mathieu, who stands there with an expression of pride on his face.

"What is all this?" I ask, wonder filling my voice.

"The ancient lore and stories of your forefathers," he says quietly, almost reverently.

"Aleksandar, it looks like the Guardians weren't the only method Nuada used to preserve the knowledge of the wizards."

The Guardian shakes his head as he reaches for a parchment. "This will help us discover much of the knowledge that has been lost with the passage of time."

"I'd appreciate it if he didn't touch anything quite yet," Mathieu says. "There are gloves we can provide that will prevent the oils of his skin from ruining the parchment."

I stop Aleksandar from touching anything, and then we continue deeper into the vast room. My awe grows as I take in painting after painting. Then I stop dead, enthralled by a large and particularly vibrant painting just past a large bookshelf.

"What is it, Aiden?" Keegan asks.

"I know that place," I say softly.

It's a painting of a great funeral procession marching down the Citadel's catacomb toward the great tomb I discovered filled with countless caskets. At the top of the same slope, in the centre, a casket lies open, dark and inviting. My eyes trace back to the procession, and I peer closer at the man they carry on a gilded golden bier. His jaw is strong and his shoulders square, making him look vigorous even in death. He is dressed in a robe of black and gold. A large staff with the head of a dragon rests diagonally across his body.

I shiver. This is the funeral of the wizard whose tomb I stood beside in Lannóg Eolas.

"You've been there?" Aleksandar asks, shocked.

I nod. "That casket was sealed," I say, pointing to it, "but the lid shifted as I stood beside it. I've been doing my best to forget about it."

In the painting, ghosts of long-dead wizards stand beside their caskets, watching the procession approach. There is a strange sort of glow emanating from the top of the slope, and it rises endlessly into the air.

"It looks like the artist has chosen to depict this place as the source of all the power within Lannóg Eolas," Keegan says quietly.

The Guardians inspect the painting. "We are taught that the magic of our staffs comes from the magic of Lannóg Eolas and the ancient wizards who once lived there. We have been seeking this chamber to guarantee its safety. You shall take us there when we return."

"Whoa! What's *that*?" James asks. He's standing at the entrance to another room several metres away.

We stride toward him, eager to see what he's discovered. At the very centre of the room, on a slightly elevated platform, is the source of the song that calls to us all. It's a large crystal pyramid about thirty feet tall, and it literally thrums with power.

I approach it, my eyes wide, my hand reaching out. Heat radiates off it. It's not a scorching heat; it's more welcoming. I stop to stare at it, into it. Keegan and James also stare into it from the other two sides, their arms outstretched toward it.

Mathieu is at my side. "It's beautiful, isn't it?" His voice is a soft whisper in my ear. "The base of the pyramid describes its creation and its purpose. It protects Dunadin from the outside world, encasing it in a magical barrier that, for whatever reason, only the Church can penetrate through that one path."

My fingers drift closer.

"It's so beautiful," Keegan whispers.

"Yes, it is," Mathieu agrees. "Now . . ." His lips are right next to my ear. "I need you to destroy it."

"What!" I pull back, breaking free of its enticing grip. "Why?"

Before I can turn to face him, Mathieu presses the tip of a knife against my back. I freeze.

"Because this device enslaves my people!" he shouts, venom dripping from his words. I feel the blade dig into my skin. "I have spent my life trying to free us from the servitude of the Church only to discover that your kind had done so much worse. The magic of this *thing* holds us captive here, suffocating our spirit! That ends now."

He points to a small engraving on the base of the pyramid. "According to this, it takes three wizards to destroy it. Now—"

"Mathieu de Fretel!" comes Nicolas's voice from the ladder.

Mathieu grabs me from behind and presses the knife to my throat. He turns to Nicolas and snarls, "*What?*" And then he focuses. "*Nicolas?*" he asks incredulously.

Our attention shifts from Mathieu to Nicolas. Standing there at the base of the ladder is Nicolas in a black uniform with a gold cross on his chest. Behind him, six other soldiers fan out to flank us, rifles at the ready.

Nicolas smiles. "His Holiness Pope Gregory thanks you for your service, Mathieu," he says coldly. "Without you, it would have taken many more years to call forth these demons."

"You deceived me?" Mathieu asks, shocked.

"Your ego is so big, Mathieu, that it didn't take much effort. The hardest part was staying in character for so long. Père Georges felt it imperative that I not make contact with anyone else once I ingratiated myself to you. Now, kindly step away from the demons."

"No!" Mathieu yells. "I will not see my life's work to free my people undone by the likes of—"

It happens so fast I don't even see it. One moment there's a screaming madman with a knife to my throat; the next moment I'm staggering backwards as warm blood sprays the side of my face, and Mathieu de Fretel drops dead at my feet. I stare at his lifeless body in stunned silence, and then I look up at Nicolas. He has a charcoal-grey pistol pointed at us and a cruel smile on his face. Smoke curls out of the barrel.

He shrugs. "I've listened to his arrogant, self-absorbed voice every day for the past ten years. Lucky for you, Père Georges was quite firm in his statement that no harm shall come to you before we've had a chance to study you firsthand." He gestures with the pistol. "Now if you'll be so kind as to come this way. Your destruction of the manse has set us back, but with *five* hostages now"—he smirks at the Guardians—"His Holiness Gregory and His Excellency Gallagher will both be most pleased."

I glance around the room, but there are really no options. There are weapons trained on everyone, and while I might be able to defend myself, I definitely can't save us all. I lower my staff and step toward him.

"Wise decision, demon," Nicolas says.

But something's happening. It's something he doesn't see right away, and something I didn't expect. As I step away from the pyramid, the singing grows louder and the pulling sensation grows stronger. It's as if I am wading through molasses.

"What are you doing?" Nicolas screams.

I turn to see the crystal of the pyramid pulling away like taffy. Each side of the pyramid is attached to James, Keegan, and me.

I stop, amazed, but the crystal continues flowing out of the pyramid, and it pools at my feet and rushes up my legs. As it does, the floor trembles.

"Stop that now, or they're dead! All of them!" Nicolas swings his pistol around to the Guardians.

The trembling grows stronger. With an ear-splitting crack, the floor opens up and thrusts upward, swallowing four of the Golden Crosses. Aleksandar uses the distraction to dive, knocking Elizabeth over just as Nicolas's pistol goes off.

Nicolas retrains his aim at them just as James and Keegan appear at my side. Keegan's staff swings out, and I feel his protective shield envelop us. It expands rapidly to embrace the Guardians.

James glances at me, and together we thrust our staffs into the floor. I feel the power of earth flowing through my body, channelling into my staff, through the palace floor, twisting and twining with James's energy. Together, our energies race through the ancient stone tiles, exploding them as our power reaches out to Nicolas and the remaining Golden Crosses. With an even louder crack, the floor shakes again, and the hole opens wider, engulfing the two soldiers. Nicolas teeters precariously on the edge for a heartbeat, panic in his eyes, and then he too falls in.

I raise my staff out of the floor, which trembles again as the hole shifts and seals itself into a jagged ridge.

James, Keegan, and I run to the Guardians.

"Aleksandar, are you okay?" I shout.

He glares at me, seemingly irritated that I'd be concerned about him. "I'm fine," he grumbles, but he accepts my arm as he clambers to his feet, favouring his left hip.

I look over at Elizabeth, who casually dusts herself off.

The Guardians approach the dissolving crystal pyramid. Elizabeth traces her fingers along the engraving that Mathieu referenced.

"Mathieu was wrong," she says quietly. "The engraving doesn't say it takes three wizards to destroy the barrier. It says it will protect the village dutifully until the Protectors of Dunadin arrive to reclaim their place."

Sure enough, the engraving shows the wizards standing together in unity with a pyramid joining all three and a sphere emanating from it all.

"So . . . we are the barrier now?" Keegan asks, looking at James and me.

Elizabeth nods. "You three are now responsible for the safety of the village, this valley."

As she says it, I realize she's right. Deep within my soul, I can feel a glowing energy. The golden song that once emanated from the pyramid now sings within me.

She turns to us. "If Nicolas was working for Père Georges this whole time, then they know where the manuscripts are hidden. We must get them."

"But by that same token, they'll also know of this place," James says. "Should we split up? How are we going to find our way back through the forest to the hiding spot?"

Aleksandar shakes his head. "No. We stay together, and we all go for the manuscripts. They are already loaded on a trailer, ready to be taken to the Vatican. They are our priority." He looks at me. "When we get to the surface, you'll have to seal this place. We cannot risk anything else being removed."

We climb the ladder one at a time and emerge onto the cobblestone road. I'm surprised to find that the sun has risen. Once everyone has stepped away from the door to the Hall of Mysteries, I fuse the metal handle, locking the door until we can return.

I look down the cobblestone road. It takes me a moment before I realize that it's not just trees I'm looking at. Scattered among the trees along the road is a group of about twenty elderly villagers, their telltale dirty faces and worn tunics far worse than usual. They stare at the smoldering metal on the door with wide eyes.

A man in a white tunic and brown vest steps forward. It's the same man who stared at us from the steps of the town hall the day Jacques led us across the square. Eyes every bit as intense as they were that day stare at me from beneath thick brows.

Since I don't know what else to do and since no one else is doing anything, I step forward with an outstretched hand to greet him.

He stares at my hand for a moment, uncertainty written on his features. Then, as one, he and the other villagers drop to their knees, heads bowed.

He speaks first, his voice soft and respectful, but also full of resolve. "Wise Ones," he says in heavily accented English, "as mayor, I speak on behalf of this village. I have seen the Hall of Mysteries from which you have just emerged, seen the stories told of a time when our forefathers came to the gods in the mountains and petitioned them for help. According to these legends, with your help, our humble village was once raised up to become the centre of the known world. But our forefathers betrayed you."

I glance over at the Guardians. They seem curious to hear more.

"We can never hope to atone for the sins of the past," the mayor continues, "but we come to you now out of desperation to plead for your help. An earthquake has struck the village with such might that the church, the schoolhouse, and many homes were destroyed. We also lost our granary and most of our livestock to a rockslide that rolled down the mountains, and our only remaining well has collapsed in on itself."

As he speaks, I cannot help but recall how the floor of the Hall of Mysteries opened up to swallow the Golden Crosses. Mother Nature saved us there, but at what cost? I look at the villagers gathered here. I've seen some of them receive council from Père Georges during our reconnaissance of the village, but there is no sign of Golden Crosses or Black Bands in this group.

"Where is Père Georges?" I ask him.

"He and the other men from afar were in the church when it collapsed. There is a team of men trying to rescue them, but school had also just started for the day." His voice cracks with emotion. "Our children are trapped, and we fear there are not enough able-bodied men to rescue them in time."

He pauses long enough to gesture to a basket of fresh vegetables that a villager carries. "As payment, we have brought the last of our harvest. We can also offer you what remains of our livestock. Please, we beg you, Wise Ones."

I search the tired and desperate faces of the gathered crowd in silence for several moments. James and Keegan are in a similar state of shock as I am. The Guardians remain silent, though I can sense the tension in Aleksandar's body. I don't think he likes this one bit.

But I know what I must do. I wouldn't be able to live with myself knowing that I turned my back on these people. My eyes meet Keegan's, and he smiles knowingly. He reaches out and takes James by the hand. Together, they step forward and stand beside me in unity.

I look down at the mayor. "What is your name, my friend?"

"Jean du Roux, my lord."

"Then stand, Jean du Roux. There are gods in these mountains and underground palaces, I am sure, but they are not us. We have been taught this history that you speak of, but like you, we are not those ones of old. We are the first wizards in three thousand years to call the mountains that surround you our home, and we are still in training. The earthquake that has caused such ruin in your village came as a result of our defending this place against the forces of the Church, so we accept a great measure of the responsibility. We cannot in good conscience accept your generous offering, but we will dine together as equals after we have helped rescue your people."

Jean looks up at me with both surprise and uncertainty on his features. I reach out my hand, offering to help him to his feet. After a moment, he accepts it. When he stands, he refuses to look into my eyes, but he does manage to glance up at them every so often.

"I realized the power you can wield when I learned that you healed my dear sister, Anaïs," Jean says.

This time, it's me who is surprised.

Jean smiles softly. "To one such as myself, I do not know if there is a difference between a god and a wizard, but I will gladly dine at your table if you will help us."

"Lead the way, my friend."

Chapter Twenty-Seven

We walk with Jean as he leads the procession down the cobblestone road and out of the forest. As we emerge from the trees into the village, I feel a horrible sense of loss and no small measure of guilt that we had a role in this. The devastation is unbelievable.

The village is small to begin with, but it looks like half the homes are now rubble. A round tower just to the left of the road lies in ruins. I see Jean look at it sadly as we pass. When I peer through the broken walls, I see mounds of threshed grain there. It's the village granary. It now sits open to the elements. A flock of birds has already descended on it.

We reach the end of the road, and the village square opens up before us. My eyes sweep the area, and again I'm overwhelmed by the loss. The wooden market shacks are torn apart and flattened, and the massive church, which was once the magnificent centrepiece of the square, is now a broken ruin. The roof has collapsed entirely, and the front and left walls are piles of rubble. Four men coated in dust sift through the destruction, carefully removing the rubble, searching for the priest and the other men.

The once grand statue of the archangel Michael has fallen and now lies in the dust before the church. His tall, muscular body is snapped in three places. His sword, with his arm still attached to it, fell on the peach tree, sheering off half the tree's crown. His legs and torso are partially buried beneath the rubble of the front wall of the church, and his head ended up rolling almost as far as where we stand. The vengeful smile and the fury mixed with triumph radiating out of his eyes look almost pitiful down there in the dust.

My eyes linger on the remains of the peach tree. The blossoming tree seemed to me an excellent symbol of a new beginning for the village—a new hope. And from the way the villagers flocked to it in awe on the day it spontaneously sprouted, they seemed to see it in the same light. Seeing it now, dying, as half of it lies severed beneath the ruins of the church, adds to the already crushing sense of defeat that permeates the air of the village.

Jean watches me take in the scene before us, and then he slowly steps up next to me. "The most devout of us believe the damage was God's punishment for our thinking of welcoming you."

Again, I feel the guilt creep in, but Jean starts walking again, urging us along with him.

"We must get to the schoolhouse," he says.

I walk alongside him. He has spoken for his village and the villagers, but I want to know more about what he thinks. "And what do you believe?" My voice is distant.

For a long time, he doesn't answer my question. Conflicting emotions are written all over his face, but when he finally speaks, it's clear it's from his heart. "I believe that I saw more kindness from you in a day than I'd seen in that supposed man of God in a lifetime. You are a stranger to Dunadin." Sorrow fills his eyes as he gets lost in a memory. "Yet you took my sister, Anaïs, who was certain to die, and returned her to life. You healed her injuries so she would be there for her family, for her husband and young son. You walk with peace in your steps, and with the joy of life on your faces."

"It is not always so," I insist.

He gives me a knowing look. "No, I suppose not. When you saw what Père Georges did to my sister and her family, you were consumed by an anger that had me worried this village would burn to the ground and the entire valley would be consumed by flames. I saw it in your eyes. I think we all did. It added to your humanity."

I know for certain now that Père Georges knew what he was doing when he tried to demonize James and me in the eyes of the villagers. Jean and I exchange glances, and I hope he sees the sorrow I feel for what we now face.

"This village has had a rough life for a long time now," he continues, "and Père Georges never lifted a finger to make it easier for us unless it was self-serving. And then you come along. You were willing to die rather than destroy us. Now that you're back, perhaps you will bring a bit more life back to us."

I look around the village. I still can't fathom the destruction. "I wish I could tell you that our friendship will keep you safe, but I can't. The reality is, the closer you get to us, the more danger you'll be in."

"Perhaps it is a risk we will have to take. We have suffered for so long."

I shake my head. "It's not that simple. The Church has long suppressed the powers of nature that we serve, and now that they know we're active again, they will strike at us. If they find out you're in league with us, they will seek to destroy us both."

I gesture out at the empty fields surrounding the village, a sobering reminder that the harvest is over and winter is on its way. "Their attack on our home almost brought the walls down around us, and now their need to stop us has destroyed your homes and has put your entire harvest at risk just when you'll need food and shelter the most. I feel I cannot apologize enough."

We walk in silence for a while longer. Jean has the look of someone who is taking his time to absorb a lot of new information. He finally sighs and comes to a stop. The others draw close to us.

"No need to apologize, Wise One. I suppose I positioned myself as an enemy of the Church from the moment I became mayor. You see, when my father read to me the secret oaths of office, he did so from within the Hall of Mysteries itself."

We all look at him in shock.

"Secret oaths?" Elizabeth says.

He nods. "In the Hall of Mysteries, my father showed me the myths and legends of our past, and he taught me that the mayor of Dunadin has two responsibilities. One is to protect the people, but the other is above all else. The mayor must protect the Hall of Mysteries from the Church. For many years, I didn't know why, for Père Ferdinand was a bitter old man who never expressed any interest in it. But when Père Ferdinand died of a sudden illness, Père Georges arrived."

"We were told that there are substantial differences between the two priests," I say.

"Yes, this is true. Père Georges is everything Père Ferdinand wasn't. He's kind to the children, caring to the elderly and infirm, and intensely interested in unearthing what he views as the village's secret. I didn't catch on right away, but as months turned to years, he grew more aggressive with his questioning.

That's when I realized that this so-called secret we're harbouring is *my* secret."

"So what did you do?"

"Well, for the longest time, I couldn't understand why he wouldn't just walk into the Hall of Mysteries. I mean, it's right here under his nose! It's the strange device in the centre of the hall that somehow prevents the priest from finding it."

"That appeared to be the case, but this device is no more. It waited for the presence of wizards to ensure the safety of the valley. That responsibility now falls onto us."

"I suppose this is why I was so excited when I first heard the rumours that strangers had found the village. That day I saw you in the village square was the first time in my entire life that our legends and myths were verified."

"Did you find all of this out on your own? Or did you have help from the Black Bands?"

"Ah, yes, the Black Bands! I struggled to learn about the device, so I enlisted the help of my cousin Mathieu de Fretel, who created the group as a means to secretly study whatever they could learn . . ." He trails off and looks at me, perhaps seeing the sadness on my face. "Was it something I said, Wise One . . . ?"

I shake my head. "Jean, I am terribly sorry. I didn't put two and two together when you told us Anaïs was your sister. Mathieu died in the Hall of Mysteries. Nicolas murdered him."

Jean's face goes blank, and tears well up in his eyes. "Nicolas . . . ? Nicolas was Mathieu's best student!"

"He was a servant of Père Georges," I say flatly.

Jean lowers his head in a moment of respect. When he raises it again, he glares at the ruins of the church. "If the Révérend Père survives, he will face justice . . ." he says bitterly. He looks at me again, squaring his shoulders. "What's done is done. There will be time for grief later. Right now, we must rescue the children."

He begins walking again, faster this time, wrapped in a blanket of silence.

We round a corner and are just about to step down a small path when someone calls out.

"Aleksandar! Elizabeth!"

We look around in surprise, trying to see who it is. It's Jean who spots them first. He points to the edge of the square. It's Sean, Jennifer, and Mary.

Jean stands there, fidgeting with his tunic, and I sense his anxiousness to get to the schoolhouse.

When the Guardians approach, they eye Jean warily before embracing Elizabeth and Aleksandar.

"We felt the tremors of an earthquake," Mary says. "When you didn't return this morning, Evelyn felt we should check on you." She looks around at the devastation. "David has gone to fetch Caitlin in case she is needed. They should arrive later today."

Aleksandar grips Mary's arm as one might a long-lost companion. "I'm glad you are here. We may need your help."

With those words, we start down the path and soon come face to face with the remains of the schoolhouse. I try my best to take in the chaos. Ten men struggle to carry large pieces of rubble away from the site. They work frantically but are careful in removing each piece as they go along. Several elderly men and women load smaller pieces into wheelbarrows to help clear the area.

Elizabeth clears her throat. "Do you know how many people are still trapped?" she asks Jean.

"Here? The children were in school when the earthquake struck. Fifteen of them, plus their teacher, Delia Burgon." His eyes quickly scan the site. "They're all still trapped. These men are the youngest and strongest among us."

"What is the status of the rest of the village?" Aleksandar asks. His military training seems to be kicking in.

"Among those trapped in their homes and the church, we guess there are about sixty. We are realists. We know that most of the missing are probably dead, but the village needs every person it has. This is why we came to you." His shoulders slump as he watches the rescuers work. "When I knew you returned, I dared to hope that maybe things would change. But with Mathieu dead, and the children . . ."

"Well," I say, "let's see if we can give you some of that hope back, Jean."

I stride toward the collapsed schoolhouse, with James and Keegan in tow. I don't know where to begin.

"Can you sense anything, Keegan?"

"Pain," Keegan whispers quietly. "Much pain." He lowers himself down. He closes his eyes and presses his hands firmly to the ground. I see his energy field shimmer as he flexes it and quests outward. "But there is definitely life underneath."

He's quiet for another moment, and when he opens his eyes, they are haunted. "I think I count sixteen heartbeats. Several are faint."

"Sixteen?" Jean asks in a whisper.

Keegan nods. I can't tell if Jean is excited or upset.

"Then it might not be too late." When Jean looks at me, there are tears in his eyes. "There is still hope."

James leans in close to me. "How are we going to do this? With all of those kids under there, we can't just try. We need a plan. I'm not strong enough in any of the more physical forms of magic yet. At this point, all I can think of is sending calming illusions to stop the children from panicking."

I think of the emergency services in Toronto, who often give out toys to comfort children who've experienced trauma. "That's a good start. Try cute and friendly animals or something." I then think of Caitlin and her telepathic ability. I wish she were here to speak with them, set them at ease. I take in the site again. "Air isn't my strong suit," I say, "but I can't think of anything else that would work. I don't want to manipulate the stone or earth in case it does more harm than good. If I can generate enough of an air current under each stone to lift it out, we could—"

"Fling them at us?" Aleksandar asks scornfully. "And what happens when one of the stones you move causes others to fall?"

"Then I will hold them up until I can move them too."

"Or we can work as a team instead of having a lone hero ride to the rescue," Elizabeth scoffs.

"If you have a better idea, we're all ears," James says.

"Actually, we do," Aleksandar says. "Right now, the villagers are doing the job themselves. From what I've observed, I'd say they've done this kind of work enough to know what stones might shift if they pull the wrong one."

"Earthquakes are rare here," Jean says, "but we're accustomed to doing all of our building and razing ourselves."

"Keegan," Elizabeth says, "if we could convince these men to lift the heavier stones by themselves, heavier than they think possible, could you lend each enough strength and possibly heal any pulls or strains fast enough that there's no lasting damage?"

Keegan looks at the men, considering her question. He nods slowly. "Yes, I should be able to do that."

"Aiden," Aleksandar says, "your magic would be more useful for this if it weren't so volatile. We cannot risk an accident here. However, you should keep an eye on everything. If something looks like it's about to collapse, prop it up until one of the men can get there. No heroics. Sound good?"

I look at James and Keegan. "What do you think?"

"I think that's an amazing plan," James says. "Keegan's got the heavy lifting, Aiden's the spotter, and I'm on fuzzy animal detail."

Keegan looks a bit uneasy but otherwise determined. "Let's do it."

I turn to Jean. "Well, are you okay with this plan?"

"I understood little of it, but you sound confident that it will work. What do you need of me?"

"We're going to give your men some extra strength to make it possible for them to carry even the heaviest stones on their own. This will expedite the process. Can you explain that to them?"

He blinks at me for a moment. "And you wonder why we think you are gods . . . Yes, I can explain it to them."

Jean steps forward and starts speaking to the men in French. Most of them nod quietly and continue working. One of them shouts something and gesticulates angrily before storming off. With his departure, the air becomes uneasy.

Jean stares stonily after him. "Pierre is a very devout man. He is not yet comfortable with having magic influence him directly. It would probably be best to proceed before the rest have too much time to think about it."

I nod to James, and he begins concentrating on creating illusions of whatever small, cuddly critters come to mind.

"Keegan," I say, "I'm ready when you're ready."

Keegan kneels on the dusty ground, closes his eyes, and begins concentrating. We watch with bated breath as the men continue to work, their steps lumbering and unstable, both from the burden of the heavy stones and from their deepening fatigue. Slowly, their heavy steps give way to powerful strides. One by one, they give a shout of glee as they seem to sweep the stones away and cast them aside almost effortlessly. They begin to chat excitedly among themselves as they work, occasionally shouting at one another regarding their unbelievable feats of strength.

Now I know why the Guardians suggested I watch carefully. With their newfound strength, the men have cast away much of the caution they were previously working with. One man eventually reaches for the largest piece of rubble he can find. He squats and wraps his arms around it. I see his limbs quiver, and a bead of sweat runs down his forehead. But the stone starts to move. He stands, slowly at first, and then he gains confidence and steps almost casually away from the rubble and tosses the stone to the ground.

The others, having seen what's now possible, quickly form a relay line. The largest and strongest man among them picks the stones out of the rubble and passes them along.

"That is Gérald," Jean says. "He wins the award for farthest hammer throw every year."

Small wonder, I think. His bulging muscles are evident even beneath his loose tunic. Within his bushy beard, his teeth are bared in a snarl at the challenge, but his beady eyes barely squint with even the largest stones. The other men, however, grimace as they pass the heavy stones from man to man until they're tossed aside.

I glance over at Keegan. His face is flush with concentration, and he trembles slightly.

Elizabeth follows my gaze and steps forward. She kneels beside him and wraps her arms around his shoulders. "Breathe, Wizard Keegan," she whispers into his ear.

Keegan's face has practically turned purple. He furrows his brow as he struggles to let out a breath without losing his concentration. A harsh huff issues from his lips, and he sucks in a deep breath. This causes much of the alarming colour to fade from his face.

The big man lifting the stones directly from the wreckage lets out a shout. He hoists a stone into the air, and a cry escapes from below. In a flash, Jean bolts forward and grabs the child whose arm has just appeared. He pulls the child out and carries him to safety.

The Guardians watch quietly as Jean lays the child down and rises to wait for the next. Sean and Mary bend down and begin to tend to the wounded child while Aleksandar and Jennifer rush to Jean's side to lend a hand when more children appear. I keep a careful eye on the operation, holding my staff at the ready.

Soon, we pull three more children from the rubble. After that, we find Delia, the teacher. Her leg is shattered, but she otherwise seems okay.

As the men continue to work, Jean begins to look more and more uneasy. Only now do I realize that it's entirely possible he may have children of his own trapped underneath.

I spare a glance at Keegan. Sweat now cascades down his face. He is bent in half, supported only by Elizabeth's embrace. His entire body trembles with the effort of giving each of these men the strength to carry the rubble.

I wish I could help in some other way. All I can do is try to keep my focus, and I do so by concentrating on the elements around me. And it's a good thing, too, as I'm fully prepared when I hear a man yelp. It's Gérald. My attention zeros in on him. He's holding a giant boulder, but he's lost his footing and is slipping. Time seems to grind to a halt. A loud snap echoes through the air as the man's leg shatters under the weight of the boulder. Only then do I see that he's revealed the face of a child right beneath him. There's no time to think.

As the boulder begins to drop, everyone gasps. My senses focus on the boulder about to crush the child who has had time for just one breath of fresh air. I immediately think of the potential shockwaves the falling boulder might cause, putting even more children at risk. If I let this boulder fall, our rescue of these children could come to a sudden and deeply devastating end. My eyes close, and an image of the boulder flares to life in my mind's eye.

Every minute detail forms in my mind as I become the air beneath the boulder. I can see tiny flecks of dust breaking off and scattering on the earth. I can hear the faint whoosh as the boulder pushes the air out of the way as it falls. I can feel the coarse texture of its surface catching the air.

I focus on the movement of that air around the stone. The air particles beneath the stone vibrate more violently and resist the downward pressure the stone exerts. The weightless air quickly becomes a cushioned pad of resistance that pushes back on the stone. For just a moment, the boulder seems to hover in thin air.

I try to give the air beneath the boulder a gentle push, but it responds instantly to my touch, and the stone hurtles toward the wall of a nearby building.

Gérald, still clutching the stone, hurtles with it. He screams in horror as he's swept up in my magic. If he hits the ground like this, he'll die. I shift my consciousness, and now I'm no longer air, but earth. I am earth so solid and dense that I was carved into a stone hundreds of years ago and was part of a schoolhouse until today.

I feel the air rushing past me and feel the weight of the man attached to me. In my current form, I know I'm going to kill him. Tight, so tight, are the walls that hold me together. They are confining, and I long to be free.

Thinking of the freedom I had as air, I fragment myself into thousands of tiny pieces. I then fragment each of those pieces into millions of tinier pieces. By the time I hit the wall, I am nothing but a blast of sand.

The shock of hitting the wall jolts my consciousness back into my body, and I fly backward, falling so hard that I cry out in pain. For several moments, my senses are so acute that I can hear the wind rush through the feathers of a hawk high above. Then my normal senses rush back in, filling with the laboured breathing of the rescuers.

The relay line breaks down as the men look from me to their friend lying at the base of the wall across the way. For a moment, I think they're all going to abandon the search and run to aid him, but then they look up at Jean and the children they've already rescued.

Seven of them regroup and restart the rescue, beginning with reaching into the rubble and pulling out the child who was nearly crushed. Another picks his way over the rubble to where I slammed the poor man into the wall.

When the men pull the girl out, Jean runs forward, tears flowing freely. "*Eloise! Ma pouvra petyouta!*" He embraces her and caresses her hair.

I sit up and stare at them blankly, blinking occasionally. We have, it seems, reunited father and daughter.

Jennifer appears in front of me. "Are you okay?"

"Yes, I'm fine," I say. In truth, my body feels like it just got hit by a wall.

By the way she looks at me, I can tell she sees through my lie, but given the situation, she doesn't question it.

I nod in the direction of the man lying at the base of the wall. "Will you help me over there?"

"There's nothing you can do for him," Jennifer says as sadness creeps into her eyes. "You need to stay focused on keeping these children safe. If you hadn't been so alert, Jean's daughter would be dead right now. I'm sure that man would count saving the life of a little girl worth dying for."

I don't say anything. I instead stare at the man on his knees, rocking gently back and forth while he clutches at the shirt of the man I inadvertently killed. I stare at the lifeless body, letting the scene sink in. I tried to save him from being crushed against the wall, but my unwieldy strength killed him anyway.

I feel a hand on my shoulder. I look up to see Mary staring down at me. "I know it doesn't feel like it," Mary says gently, "but you did what had to be done, Aiden. We sometimes cannot save those we want to. Today, the universe asked for the death of a small child and possibly more. You prevented that, but you had to pass the death on to someone else instead."

"I refuse to accept that," I mutter. "Why did he have to die?"

"This is the ending of the Anthropocene era, the ending of the age when humanity runs rampant over the planet. You, James, and Keegan must become leaders in the dawn of this new age of magic. You must help to guide us all through the tumult that will follow. This man's death is one of the unfortunate prices of power." Mary places a hand under my chin and stares deep into my soul. "There will be time enough to grieve and doubt after this crisis is over. Right now, you are here as an emissary of the wizards to help a village in need. You must be strong. Stand."

She extends her hand in a gesture that I know is merely symbolic. If I were to actually try to use her to lift myself up, I would pull her over. Regardless, I take her hand and stand slowly, my muscles screaming in protest.

"There must be something else I can do besides watch," I say.

"What you just did was incredibly dangerous to yourself. All three of you are in danger of using too much of your power. If you do too much more, you risk serious injury—perhaps even death. No, I would not recommend any other way of helping other than what you are doing right now."

I look over at Keegan, who's still trembling, but there is nothing I can do to help him. My magic and his don't mix. I look over at James, who's focused intensely on maintaining who knows how many separate illusions to keep the remaining children calm. That network of illusions is likely so tightly bound that to try to boost it in any way might cause it all to unravel.

"I shall help rescue the children as they become free," I say with confidence.

Mary reaches out and squeezes my arm. The simple gesture indicates to me that all will be okay. With a half-forced smile, I head out into the rubble to take over for Jean, who is still comforting his daughter, Eloise.

At first, the men eye me with suspicion. I should be thankful they don't beat me savagely, given what they just saw me do to their friend. By the time I carry the third child out of harm's way, however, they grudgingly accept that I'm truly there to help.

A couple of hours later, we have fourteen children free, but we're having trouble finding the last one. Almost all the rubble is cleared away now, and there is still no sign of her—a girl called Amélie. Keegan is too taxed to seek her out with his magic, and James and I fail to do so, so a few of us shout her name as the men carry away the rest of the rubble. Soon, a cry goes up from a man named Luis. Instead of passing the next stone along, he gently places it aside. He then squats down and gently lifts the girl out of the rubble. As he stands, the child's arm flops down.

The other rescuers converge on his spot as he stares down at Amélie's lifeless face, their right fists raised to their hearts. It's the same gesture I observed when they thought Anaïs was dying after the accident. It feels like a mixture of honour, respect and grief. Reverently, the villagers line up and carry her to the schoolhouse playground. They set her down, and one man brushes the hair out of her eyes. The man who found her cries softly. An elderly woman leaves, presumably to find the girl's parents.

Mary looks over at Jean. "Who is that poor child?"

"The cobbler's daughter. Antoine lost his wife to a severe fever two years ago. Amélie was his life."

One of the men calls over to us in French. I don't understand his words, but I hear a sliver of hope in his voice. He gazes at me, then James, then Keegan. James looks impassive, and Keegan looks like he's ready to pass out as he lies there in the dust after exerting himself so much.

Jean turns to us. "Can you . . . ?"

His question fades into silence when he sees me close my eyes, but I know what he is asking. When I open them again, they are filled with tears.

Mary slowly shakes her head. "The power of death is too much for even these ones."

We all stand in silence for several minutes. Exhaustion and sadness are plain on everyone's faces.

"That was intense, Aiden." James's voice is soft and quiet. "You should come sit with Keegan. He needs us."

I turn away from the sombre scene before me and gasp. Keegan is now lying there on the ground, curled into the fetal position. Tears streak his face, and his breath is coming in ragged gasps. Shockingly, his hair has gone from a rich brown to pure white. The rest of the Guardians gather at his side.

I look at Mary, and she smiles at me sadly.

"He exceeded his own strength long ago," she says. "Guardians, perhaps we can help." She strides toward them. "This may not work, but if Keegan is able to draw so much pain into himself as he has just done, he should also be able to draw our health and strength into himself as well."

The Guardians each kneel down beside Keegan and place a hand on him.

"Yes," Mary says with a nod. "Touching him will make the transfer easier for him."

James and I move closer. I now notice the subtle ripple of energy that flows from Keegan. Something else is wrong besides him being drained.

"James, look at the magic coming from him," I say.

"What do you mean? I just spent so long envisioning a colony of furry animals that I can't see much of anything right now except whiskers and bushy tails, to be honest, and I'm trying to see as little of that as possible."

Although I appreciate that James can manage to find the humour in any situation—even when there's precious little to smile about—I know this is serious.

"Mary hopes he can draw on the Guardians," I say, "but the energy isn't flowing into him; it's flowing out of him."

"Flowing out?" Mary asks quietly.

"Keegan normally heals others by drawing out their ills," Sean explains. "He draws their pain and strain into himself. Something's different here."

I take Mary by the arm and direct her to one of the arcs of energy. "Here. Stand here and allow your focus to drift into the universe. What way do you feel yourself being pulled?"

She stands quietly with her eyes closed. Slowly, she starts to rock toward the men surrounding Amélie's lifeless body.

Her eyes open. "You're right," she says softly. "He is sending his own energy into these men, healing their ills remotely."

I kneel down in the dust at his side. "Keegan?"

He doesn't reply, but I see his jaw twitch. *Can he hear me?*

"We have finished rescuing the children," I say. "The men don't need your healing anymore."

For a long moment, there is no response at all. He then clenches his eyes tighter. "Too much damage," he gasps. Pain ripples across his face. "Have to heal them."

Sean looks up at the men across the way. "Those were extremely heavy stones they were moving. If the damage was too much for him to draw within himself and he had to send his magic into them, maybe they actually do still need his healing."

I glance at the men. They look crestfallen and exhausted, as they should, but I can't tell just by looking at them whether there's more going on than that.

An idea strikes me. "You're his closest friend, James. Maybe you can convince him of the danger."

James looks at Keegan's tense body and doesn't give it a second thought. He leans in close to Keegan's face once Sean has stepped aside. "Keegan," he whispers, "I know they're still injured and you can't stop healing them yet, but if you give them everything they need all at once, it's going to kill you. There must be a way you can tap into our energy to give you a hand, to strengthen you enough so you can keep helping them . . ."

Nothing happens at first, but Keegan's eyelids eventually begin to flutter rapidly. And then a faint tendril of energy reaches out, questing its way toward us. It finds a group of friends willing to give it everything they have. It takes several moments, but the tendril grows stronger, and Keegan's breathing begins to slow.

Jean watches us from the playground. He speaks to the men, and they all make their way over to us a moment later.

"The act of saving these children has deeply injured your men," Sean explains. "They cannot feel it because this one is masking the pain while he heals the damage to their muscles, tendons, and bones. We don't know how much longer he'll be able to continue."

One of the men takes a look at Keegan and then sits beside him and closes his eyes. The Guardians slowly back away, making room. The other men sit beside Keegan as well. Soon, the energy flowing into the men grows stronger, and Keegan's breathing slows to almost normal.

"Of course," James says, smacking his forehead. "Healing all those men at once would drain anyone, and he kept it up even as they moved farther away. Now that they're closer, he doesn't have to reach as far to heal them."

There's a commotion behind us as several villagers begin to arrive.

"Antoine is here. The cobbler," Jean says quietly.

The cobbler runs to his daughter's body lying peacefully on the playground. He begins wailing hysterically, and he falls down upon her. Other villagers surround him in solidarity and try to comfort him, but there will be no comfort for him today, or any day soon.

Seeing that Keegan is now stable, Jean excuses himself and walks toward the gathered children, where another group of villagers comfort them and tend to them. Several of them look seriously injured. Most, if not all, will carry scars from this day for the rest of their lives.

Jean's own Eloise is with them. I can see an elderly woman tending to her. The girl has her father's auburn hair. She sits on the ground with her left arm wrapped around her knees, and her right arm at her side, bent at a terrible angle. Tears flow freely from her when Jean crouches beside her and comforts her with a hug.

The woman says something, and Jean nods. Eloise stares straight ahead with a stoic strength as the woman takes her arm and sets the bone with a snap that makes me wince in commiseration. As the woman wraps Eloise's arm in a splint, Jean pulls his daughter in close, squeezing her tightly.

I walk over to them. "How's she doing?"

Jean looks up, tears welling in his eyes. "She's going to be sore for a long time, but she'll be fine. Thank you for your help, Wizard Aiden. Will Wizard Keegan will be okay?"

"Yes, I think so. He is already much better than he was. I'm afraid that Amélie won't be, though, nor will Gérald."

Jean gazes across the way to where the villagers have laid the man and girl beside each other. More people gather around them in silence, their fists raised. I see the sadness in Jean's face mixed with relief at the fate of his own daughter.

"It is true," he says, "but today we saved fourteen children and their teacher, and we had thought them all lost forever. Your help will not be forgotten. If you'll pardon me, though, I need time alone with my daughter. She needs me."

I smile at him. "I'm glad she's going to be okay."

I walk over to Aleksandar and Elizabeth, who I find chatting together as they look in the direction of the village square. They look exhausted but concerned.

"All appears stable here," Aleksandar says to me, his voice tired. "We need to return to the church and check on Père Georges."

"And come up with a plan to recover the manuscripts from the forest," Elizabeth adds.

My eyes go wide. With all that has happened, I almost forgot the very reason we came to Dunadin in the first place. "Of course!"

Chapter Twenty-Eight

Aleksandar, Elizabeth, James, and I approach the church cautiously. The bustle of activity we saw when we last passed it has now stopped. Only two men remain to carefully clear away the rubble.

As we step around the remains of the archangel Michael and the fallen stone of the crumbled church, we come across the bodies of three members of the Golden Cross lying side by side on the village square. Their eyes are closed, and their arms are crossed over their chests peacefully.

James looks at them as we skirt around them. "This doesn't look good for the dear old Révérend Père."

When we draw near, one of the men clearing the rubble stops. His hair is white and wispy, and the many wrinkles on his deeply tanned forehead are deep. His rough hands look like they've seen a lot of hard labour. He pulls a handkerchief out of his back pocket and wipes a layer of dust off his face. He looks at us with suspicion.

"Père Georges?" Aleksandar asks simply.

The man stares at us for a moment. He then raises his arm and points in the direction of the manse.

"He must have escaped," James says.

"Nicolas would no doubt have told him where we hid the manuscripts. We must go!" Elizabeth says.

I can see the wooded lane leading to the priest's manse from here. I glance around the village square, looking for a way we could possibly sneak to it relatively unseen. However, the collapsed market stalls, the crumbled church, and the flattened homes that lie in the dust make me realize that the time for us to be circumspect has long past.

"This way," I say.

We're about five feet down the lane when I first feel it—that uneasy feeling of being watched. I slow down and put my hand out to alert the others.

"I feel it too," James says quietly.

We inch forward, glancing left and right between the trees.

"If Mathieu was correct," Aleksandar whispers, "there should be only one Golden Cross unaccounted for."

"I'd hoped he would be with Père Georges," Elizabeth replies, "but I fear that might not be the case."

We continue forward. I can feel the hairs on the back of my neck standing on end. The sound of leaves blowing and trees creaking occasionally makes me spin in fright, but nobody assails us. By the time we reach the iron fence surrounding the still smoldering remains of the manse, I've convinced myself that the feeling of being watched was only my insecurities.

We move past what's left of the manse toward the forest where we hid the manuscripts. Before heading into the trees, we pause to look around.

"Well, no sign of anyone," Aleksandar says.

"Where could Père Georges be?" I ask.

"He could be anywhere by now," Elizabeth says. "We need to get to the trailer."

We head into the forest, taking extra care to be alert for any sound or movement. I can sense us all becoming uneasy as we get closer to our hiding spot.

We are about halfway to the trailer when the unmistakable sound of a twig snapping echoes from the path behind us.

"Shit!" says James.

I spin. My magic comes to life, responding to my needs. The magic builds within me, the air around my hands heating rapidly as the power of fire responds to my call. I feel James solidifying the air around us into a barrier.

"I wouldn't do anything rash if I were you!" It's a firm voice with just a trace of a Boston accent. "Cease calling upon the power of Lucifer immediately!"

The magic continues to cascade around us as Cardinal Gallagher steps from the trees and onto the path. He's wearing the red robes of his office, but he's exchanged his biretta for a simpler zucchetto. It's not the sight of him that makes us release our magic so quickly; it's whom he's holding in a vice-like grip with his left arm. Her normally impeccable brown hair is dishevelled and frizzy, and her panic-stricken amber eyes are glued to the gun aimed at her head.

"Danielle!" James cries.

He starts forward but freezes when the Cardinal jabs the barrel of his gun against her temple. Danielle shuts her eyes and begins sobbing uncontrollably.

"Take one more step, demon, and she dies," Gallagher growls, his eyes flaring. Fury drips from his words. "I imagine you're returning for your precious manuscripts. When Père Georges told me they disappeared, I knew they couldn't have gotten far. I knew you'd be back for them. They're too important to let them fall into our hands." He smiles, but it only serves to make him look even more sinister. "We're going to become very close friends, especially since the earthquake has unfortunately destroyed the only passage through these mountains. And as a kind gesture of our new friendship, you're going to give me some answers. We can start with how you managed to find your way to this village without setting off our alarms."

"Probably the same way you did," I say.

His eyes flick to me. "Doubtful. Let's try again. And if you fail to answer truthfully this time . . ." He glances at Danielle, and his pistol clicks when he pulls the hammer back on it.

"I'll murder you with my bare hands!" James growls.

"And she'll still be dead," Gallagher says flatly.

Elizabeth places a hand on James's shoulder. She then takes a step forward to address the Cardinal. "There's a path that leads up into the mountains on the south side of the village. We come from those mountains."

"Impossible," Gallagher says. "I've had every inch of these mountains searched."

Elizabeth bows her head slightly. "The way has long been disguised by magic."

"So you admit to cavorting with Lucifer and using the power of the devil?" he sneers. He looks at Danielle and gently caresses the side of her face with the black metal of the pistol. "Things would have been much better for you, my dear, if you had just told me how to find them."

A small, lithe form flits through the trees behind Danielle and the Cardinal. At first, I think it's my eyes playing tricks on me, but then Caitlin's face appears from behind a trunk of an old oak tree. She's dressed all in black, and she holds a finger to her lips.

"*Don't panic. I'm going to stop him,*" comes her voice in my head.

I keep my face impassive and try to nonchalantly glance at James and the Guardians to see if anyone else heard her. No one else even seems to be aware she's there.

The Cardinal presses the muzzle of the gun to Danielle's temple again. "I should have pursued you in Toronto, Aiden. If I'd known your master was so close to acting, I would have never let you escape the cathedral." He glances behind us, toward our hiding spot. "No matter. Any minute now, my men will return with some special bracelets that Père Georges tells me you are intimately familiar with."

I shudder and barely hold back a wave of nausea. I can almost feel the iron bands on me already. If he thinks I'm going to let him put those on me again . . . I look at Danielle and realize I don't have a choice. I can't be responsible for her death. I glance at James, but his tear-filled eyes are locked on his fiancée.

Gallagher chuckles quietly, aware of the power his words hold over us. "They were a marvellous discovery, I must say. Since he sent us those reports, we've reached out to some . . . friends to see if they can help us develop a more modern version. They will be extremely useful for what's to come."

Gallagher traces circles on Danielle's temple with the muzzle of his gun. He lightly taps the trigger with his finger. One wrong move and she could die. Behind him, however, Caitlin approaches as silent as a cat.

He looks behind us again. "They're taking too long. They should be here already. You demons are stopping them, aren't you? Maybe I should just kill her now . . ."

"*Keep him calm,*" Caitlin's voice whispers into my consciousness.

"No!" James screams.

Just as I reach out to try to stop him, I feel James's magic exploding. In the same moment, Caitlin springs toward Gallagher, her hand rushing for his. Gallagher's finger touches the trigger, squeezing it, just as Caitlin's hand strikes. With a deafening bang, the gun goes off, just wide of Danielle's face.

In one smooth motion, the Seeker grabs the Cardinal by the wrist, and she yanks him off balance. She pivots, spinning him. His scarlet robes swirl around him, and his eyes go wide in surprise. The gun goes off again and again, and I hear bullets flying dangerously through trees. As he spins, he falls. Caitlin lands astride him as they hit the ground. I see her rondel dagger flash just before she thrusts down, piercing his throat and pinning him.

Cardinal Gallagher stiffens. He gurgles once before his body goes limp.

Danielle's eyes are as wide as saucers as she stares down at him.

James rushes forward and wraps his arms around her. "Baby, baby," he whispers as he turns her away from the scene. He kisses her gently on her forehead.

She looks up at us. Her face is blank. "He was going to kill me," she whispers.

James and Elizabeth take Danielle aside to give her a chance to recover.

In the meantime, Caitlin, Aleksandar, and I make our way through the trees until we come to the gulley where we stashed the trailer. The trailer sits just outside it. The men from the Church must have pulled it out. Aleksandar, who's carrying Gallagher's body, walks up to the trailer and dumps the corpse unceremoniously next to it.

"Where's David?" I ask.

Caitlin gives a sharp whistle twice, and David steps out of the trailer.

"Oh, thank the Goddess you're all right, Seeker," he says as he climbs down. "All of you. And the others?"

"They're fine," I say, "relatively speaking . . ."

"What happened to you two?" Aleksandar asks David.

"We had to kill the two soldiers that Gallagher brought with him," the Seeker says matter-of-factly. "We thought it best to have David wait here."

"How did you find us?" Aleksandar asks. "How did you find the trailer?"

"When we saw the state of the village, we had no idea where to start, but we spotted two men leaving the church, and they headed in this direction. One we assumed was Père Georges based on the frock he was wearing. The other I recognized as a member of the same elite guard that's been following Gallagher around since you asked me to look into him. We tailed them to these woods, where they met with the Cardinal and exchanged a few words. Gallagher ordered his men to find the trailer while he and Père Georges headed back toward the village."

"Did you hear what they said?"

Caitlin frowns. "Just barely. They said something about a hall and something about a safe house?"

"They must mean the Hall of Mysteries," Aleksandar says.

"And Mathieu's house," I say.

"What would they want with that place now? They've cleaned it out."

"Perhaps, perhaps not. Maybe they believe they missed something. Maybe they still think the entrance to the Hall of Mysteries is in the village."

"Why would they? Nicolas was one of them and he knew exactly where it was."

"Yes, but you heard him: he wasn't allowed to contact anyone while he was pretending to be Mathieu's assistant. Maybe he didn't get a chance to tell anyone else about it. Or maybe the magic guarding it wouldn't let him reveal it."

Aleksandar scratches his chin. "It's possible."

"At this point, the only thing in the village Père Georges seems to be interested in besides us and the manuscripts is Mathieu's house. That must be where he's gone."

Aleksandar nods. "When the others are ready, that's where we shall go as well."

"What about the manuscripts?"

Aleksandar turns to Caitlin. "Did they get any of them, Seeker?"

"No. I figured the trailer was more important than either Gallagher or Georges, so I followed the Cardinal's men. They had just managed to pull the trailer out of the gulley when David and I showed up to stop them." She looks into the gulley, and only now do I notice she's dragged two bodies there. "I'm sorry you had to see that, David. The Cardinal and his men are responsible for the deaths of twelve prospects I've been following. He's been one step ahead of me this whole time."

She crouches beside Gallagher's corpse and begins digging through his robes. A moment later, she rises, smiling.

"I *knew* we'd find something like this," she says.

She holds up a thin black rope with a small gemstone attached to the end of it. It hums weakly, but I can sense a familiar power.

Caitlin hands the stone to Aleksandar. "I overheard Gallagher ask someone about this when I was tailing him in Germany. It apparently provides safe passage through the mountain range to this village."

Aleksandar looks at it closely and then reaches into his satchel. He pulls out an identical gemstone and rolls it between his thumb and forefinger. "Do you remember David explaining how these are necessary to enter Lannóg Eolas?" he asks me.

I nod, although in truth I'd completely forgotten.

Aleksandar stows the gemstone away in his satchel. "It is both interesting and terrifying that the Church uses the same stones to gain access to the village. That means our entire network is open to them should they discover it."

Our heads turn to the sound of people approaching us through the woods. It's James, Danielle, and Elizabeth slowly making their way toward us.

"Danielle . . . ?" David whispers.

Caitlin nods. "Yes, she's been through an ordeal, to say the least."

When they arrive, Danielle takes one look at the red robes of the corpse, stained with black dirt, and then averts her gaze to a faraway spot through the trees.

James goes to speak, but Danielle beats him to it.

"Wait . . ."

He looks over at her, but she remains impassive. She continues to stare through the trees.

"Let me speak."

"Go ahead," James says quietly. "We're listening."

"When we were attacked," Danielle says shakily, "in the Citadel, it wasn't the voice of God I heard. It was Cardinal Gallagher's." She glances down at the red robes again. Once more, she looks away. "He somehow spoke directly to me, impersonating God and playing to my insecurities."

"I'm sorry, Danielle," I say. "I'm sorry you got caught up in all of that."

She crosses over to me and takes both of my hands. "No, Aiden, I'm sorry I trusted my faith over you—over the three of you."

I nod and then bow my head.

"Gallagher returned to my church last Sunday," she continues. "He said the Pope himself wanted to meet me. I've never had a chance to meet the Pope!" She laughs sardonically and wipes away a tear. "I was so excited at first, but it didn't last long. Gallagher verbally and physically abused me the entire way here. He is—or *was*—no man of God."

When she fades into silence, I pull her into a hug.

"I understand completely," I say. "No need to apologize."

She sniffles. "I've decided to throw my lot in with the ones I love, if you'll have me. I was thinking about it before this happened, but now I'm sure of it."

I squeeze her tighter. "Of course. We're happy to have you."

When we part, Danielle slides into James's arms.

Aleksandar clears his throat. "We'd better get to Mathieu's house. Elizabeth, perhaps you should stay here with the trailer. It should be safe for the time being."

We don't make it as far as Mathieu's house.

As we pass through the shadow of what's left of the peach tree, Caitlin stops me in my tracks. She nods toward a man sitting on the outstretched arm of the archangel Michael.

Père Georges's bulk is unmistakable in a village where everyone else is underfed. He runs a hand through his bedraggled grey hair. He glances around the village with a faraway expression on his face.

We quickly look around. There doesn't appear to be anyone with him.

We approach slowly, hesitantly. We step over the white marble sword of the fallen angel, and Père Georges focuses on us with piercing blue eyes full of pain. He coughs hard, and when his hand comes away from his mouth, it is speckled with blood. He looks at it, sighing, and he rubs it off on his frock.

"Life would have been so very different had my wife not died all those years ago," he says distantly.

I look to the others and try to gauge their responses. Everyone looks as uncertain as I feel. We edge closer without saying a word.

Père Georges looks up at me. "I treated these villagers as if they were my children," he says almost admiringly. "I did so even though I constantly wished I could renege on my promise to His Holiness to answer his call whenever it came. I wanted nothing more than to return to Paris, to my church, to my memories of Claire." His eyes stare off into nothing, and I sense he's losing himself in his memories. "I am an old man now," he says with a sigh. "I had hoped to see, for just one last time, that fateful corner of the world where I last held her. Instead, I faithfully gave the last of what I had to give to driving you from hiding."

He coughs again. It's a deep hacking cough that racks his body. He winces in pain, and in that moment, I can't help but feel sorry for him.

"We can heal you," I say quietly. "You can see that corner of the world again."

Père Georges looks up at me again and straightens his back. "Word has spread that you rescued all but one of the children?"

I nod.

He nods in return, and he seems momentarily satisfied. "Perhaps there is hope for you yet, demons. If on Judgement Day, the Lord judges by good deeds alone, then perhaps we shall see each other once again."

Père Georges closes his eyes as his words fade, and with a thud, his lifeless form falls ungracefully from the archangel's arm into the dust.

Chapter Twenty-Nine

We stand before the only two-storey house in the village left intact. I can see torchlight dancing on the walls through the shattered remains of Mathieu's front windows. The door hangs ajar, but there is no sound coming from within.

Caitlin cocks her ear to the doorway, listening intently for several seconds. She then casts a glance at us over her shoulder.

"Are you're sure there's only one left?" she asks Aleksandar.

"If Mathieu is to be believed, there were thirteen originally. We've found eleven of them and Père Georges. That leaves one, and this is the only place of any significance that we haven't checked."

She nods once. "I'll check it out."

The Seeker quietly slips through the door, her dagger at the ready. She carries herself like a cat hunting its prey.

A silence fills the air, and several minutes pass. All we can do for now is stare at the doorway and wait.

A quiet thud comes from within.

A few more minutes go by. The silence is thick and heavy.

"Should we see if she needs any help?" James whispers.

Aleksandar shakes his head. "She is more than capable."

Suddenly the sound of a struggle erupts from just inside the doorway. Seconds later, a large man dressed in a black tunic tumbles out. He hits the ground beside us with a thump. We back away until the dust clears. When it does, we find the man staring up at the sky with lifeless eyes. Only then do I notice the puncture wound through the gold cross on his chest.

Caitlin pops her head out though the doorway. "Aleksandar, there were two." She brushes a stray wisp of hair from her face.

"Is it secure?" Aleksandar asks.

She kicks the door open the rest of the way. She stands there in the doorway while she wipes her dagger with a rag and sheathes it on her hip.

"For now," she says.

The torches in the foyer cast an eerie light on the stairs and the hallway. Once cluttered with stacks of papers and books, the hallway now looks bare.

We move into the kitchen. The books that once covered every surface are also gone except for a few volumes. A portable holo-tablet sits next to them.

"I guess they didn't take everything after all," I say.

David immediately crosses over to the holo-tablet and taps the screen. It glows. "Heh," he says, looking to Caitlin. "Still unlocked."

Caitlin smirks. "It sometimes pays to work fast."

David quickly scrolls through a bunch of information on the screen. The rest of us crowd around him, curious, but the text scrolls by too fast for us to read.

"Hmm," he says.

"What is it, David?" Aleksandar asks.

"They had no idea where to start with these texts."

"Well, that's good."

Jean is the first to arrive at the house. He carries his daughter with him.

"This is Eloise," he says, his voice full of love. He ruffles her tousled auburn hair a little. She glares at him in return, and he chuckles. "She doesn't speak English."

He sets Eloise down and looks around the kitchen. The light in his eyes dims. "I didn't really want to bring her here just yet. She loved Mathieu. He and Anaïs were her only family besides me. But our own home collapsed in the earthquake, so we have no choice."

James purses his lips. He steps away from Danielle and kneels before Eloise. Reaching into the folds of his robe, he pulls out a beautiful and delicate purple bellflower.

The girl's eyes go wide. When James offers it to her, a radiant smile transforms her tiny face.

"*C'est à moi?*" she asks, her voice barely a whisper.

"*Oui,*" James says with a smile.

She reaches out and takes the flower from him. She cradles it in the palm of her hand like it's the most beautiful thing she's ever seen. James looks like he's trying not to laugh.

"*Grant marci!*" she says sweetly.

I feel in that instant that James has just gained a friend for life.

"Where did you get that?" Danielle asks quietly when James returns to her side.

"I found it in the forest outside the village. It was supposed to be for you, but I figured you wouldn't mind." He winks at her.

Jean looks over at the table. "What have you found?" he asks, eyeing the stack of books. "Mathieu told me next to nothing. We figured it was safest for all of us if we cut contact. We met only once in the past year."

"These books are ancient," Aleksandar says. "And they're written in a language far older than we can recognize. Look at this ancient script." He carefully opens one of the books and points to the text. It's the same flowing Sanskrit-like script that was on the tablet in the basement of the church. He looks at James and me. "I'm assuming it will turn out to be the language of the ancients that Nicolas and Mathieu spoke. If so, we will need your assistance with translating it." He turns back to Jean. "Between these and the manuscripts in the trailer near the manse, we may learn some extremely useful information."

Jean nods. "I suppose the villagers will be grateful to be rid of that manse."

"I suppose so. Elizabeth is out that way. We will go to her when the rest show up."

As if on cue, voices drift through the open windows at the front of the house.

Jennifer enters and looks at us with a smile. "Mary has gone to get Elizabeth, but we brought you someone we thought you might want to see." She stands aside and Sean enters with Keegan, who limps into the kitchen and settles down on a chair. His face, usually full of colour, is gaunt, and he seems to grimace slightly with every movement. His white hair makes him look like a ghost. I'm somewhat relieved, however, that he's able to walk unaided.

James, Danielle, and I go to him and each give him quick hugs in turn.

"Good to see you up and about, bud!" James says.

"Thanks, guys," Keegan says, forcing a smile. "There was a time when I didn't think I was going to make it. I'm glad you were there for me."

Jean clears his throat behind us, and we turn to look at him.

"Wizard Keegan," he says, tears filling his eyes, "I am sorry to interrupt, but I must say that what you did for us today shall never be forgotten. We owe you a debt of gratitude that we can never repay."

Keegan reaches out and squeezes his arm. "Thank you, Jean," he says quietly. His eyes sweep over all of us, settling on Eloise. "More than ever, I feel we were pulled here at this particular moment to help you." He then focuses on James and me. "They're going to need all the help we can offer to rebuild the village."

Both James and I nod in agreement.

"We're here to help," James says.

Jean looks at us and shakes his head slowly. "Your help would be very much appreciated." He bows deeply. "Outside the Hall of Mysteries, we spoke of dining together. Would you join us as guests of honour for dinner tomorrow? So many of us lost our homes today, so we will have our meal together in the town square."

James answers for us with a heartfelt smile. "We thank you for your offer. We gladly accept. However, the night might grow cold and damp, and you have many injured amongst the young and the elderly. We would be delighted to host a feast in our home, Lannóg Eolas. We do not have much, but we can offer shelter to the entire village for the night."

Jean considers our offer for a moment. "You are too kind. I accept on behalf of the villagers. Many thanks. Some may be hesitant, but I believe the promise of a warm meal and protection from the elements will sway them." He smiles, clasping each of our hands in turn. "I will let them know. I will also send out hunters to bring you what game we can find. It's the least we can do in honour of our new friendship."

Jean takes Eloise by the hand and says something to her in French. The girl smiles up at him and nods.

"We will go speak with the other villagers." Jean smiles at us, and he and Eloise saunter out of the house.

Aleksandar stares wide-eyed at James. "*Dinner?*" he exclaims. "You've invited the whole God-fearing village to the *Citadel*?" The big man storms off, leaving the house as well.

"I'll go calm him down," David says, and he strolls off after him.

James looks at Jennifer. "What's with him, anyway?"

Jennifer smiles up at him. "You must understand, James, that we have lived in secret our entire lives. Our parents lived in secret. Our parents' parents lived in secret. It goes all the way back to the beginning of our family trees. Those who let slip their secrets would go missing shortly thereafter."

"Is that still the case?" I ask. "Even now?"

"Our duty has always been to await your arrival and then teach you everything we know. But when your whole life has consisted of keeping secrets from even the closest family and most trusted friends, it can be hard to change. Before the power within you began to grow, most of us didn't even know each other's identities."

Danielle tilts her head at Jennifer. This glimpse into the inner workings of the Guardians seems to have piqued her interest. "What do you mean? How can such a small group meet over the years and not ever learn about each other?"

"We enter the Citadel through a tunnel close to our homes. Mine is in my basement, under the stairs and behind a secret wall. I believe my great-great-grandfather built the house over the tunnel when he got too tired of making the long walk in the winter. It's very Narnia-like." She smiles. "I suspect that C. S. Lewis either was a Guardian himself or perhaps once accidentally saw a relative disappear into one such tunnel. You know how dark those tunnels are now with torches. Imagine how dark they were before the torches came to life."

A haunted look crosses Jennifer's face. When she continues, her voice is much quieter. "We would enter the tunnel with a lit candle to guide our way because modern conveniences such as flashlights wouldn't work any better than wristbands. Something about these tunnels disrupts electrical energy fields. So, yes, we would walk down the tunnel from our homes to the central chambers in the Citadel, but the candle would always go out whenever we arrived. No warning. No breeze. The candle would just be extinguished."

She looks lost in a memory. "That single moment the candle would go out terrified me each and every time. My spine would always tingle with my next steps in the darkness. It was exactly ten steps to my seat at the table, and each step was always full of trepidation. But then I would sit, and a calmness would come over me, telling me that I was safe and everything would be fine."

"What about the others?"

"The others would show up shortly after. Or sometimes they'd already be there. We all showed up around the same time, though I don't know how. And when the last person sat, the sound of a giant gong would reverberate through the air, signalling the beginning of the gathering."

When Jennifer has finished speaking, Sean says, "It's an interesting experience sitting at a table with six others who you cannot see and know only by voice. It's strangely intimate. My father said that even when Caitlin arrived and began to explore the Citadel, our own torches remained dark. It was not yet time for us to speak our secrets. Even amongst ourselves, we couldn't speak any of our secrets. My knowledge was exclusively for me to impart to wizards, not other Guardians. Instead, we would take turns telling stories."

Together, we all laugh at the thought of the keepers of the world's greatest secrets spending their days together telling stories. It's good to hear people laugh again.

Jennifer smiles at everyone. "You find it strange, but imagination is at the heart of all magic. You cannot begin to use magic if you cannot escape from the box of reality. Our storytelling binds our magic to Lannóg Eolas, weaving our lives into the very air of the Citadel and binding us all closer together as a group.

"What were some of the stories about?" I ask with a grin.

"My favourite story was told by Aleksandar's father, Stefan. You should ask Aleksandar about it one day. It may help crack his shell a little. Aleksandar has been a Guardian for forty-two years—longer than anyone save David and Evelyn. For him to suddenly give up the secrecy he has shrouded himself in is not easy. I understand that his great-grandmother was Jewish and living in Germany at the time of the Holocaust. I believe that likely helped make their family even more reticent to share with strangers."

"I didn't know about any of that," I say quietly.

"We can never know what journey another has taken through life, what things they have suffered, what they are suffering right now," Jennifer says. "That's why it is best to never judge others too harshly." She looks at me intently. "We should return to the Citadel to prepare for our guests."

Aleksandar's heavy footsteps echo throughout the Chamber of Knowledge as he paces, ranting to Evelyn about our plan. "I can't *believe* it. Here! They're coming *here!*"

Although he has gotten over the initial shock, Aleksandar has many concerns about the villagers being invited to the Citadel this evening.

"Even if I agreed to share our most sacred location with the world—which I most certainly did *not*—we are in no condition to host anyone! Look at this place! As the home of the world's only wizards, this place should be fit to entertain kings! It shouldn't be so dank and dusty . . . There's no proper lighting, no proper seating . . . And what are we going to do for tables . . . ? Where are they all going to *sleep?*"

"We'll also need silverware and bone china," David mocks.

Aleksandar spins around and glares at him. "*What?*" he growls.

"Honestly, Aleksandar, these people are simple villagers . . . simple *impoverished* villagers. They just lost a child and several others to an earthquake that was more or less caused by us. The last thing we need is for them to think we're some sort of royalty."

James looks around the chamber. "It *could* do with a thorough cleaning, though. I doubt we need china or anything like that, but a sprucing up would definitely help."

"And some better lighting," Jennifer adds cheerfully.

Aleksandar throws his hands up. "Finally! Someone with some sense."

"Both of those are probably my department," I say. "It'll take more than elbow grease to get this place ready in time, but a nice windstorm would clear the chambers of both the dust and dampness, and I'll even take care of all of this debris caused by the Church's attack on the Citadel. Also, since the people of Dunadin seem to be pinning their hopes of their future on us, the so-called Wizards of the Mountain, it would probably be a good idea to have at least a bit of fancy magic on display. Fire with no discernable source would likely do the trick."

"Or it could absolutely terrify them," James says. "Sure, definitely clean the place because, as both you and Danielle know very well, I hate cleaning. But I can craft an illusion to look as though the sun is shining down into the chamber from a rich blue sky above our heads."

"Wow, you can do that?" Danielle asks.

"Sure can, babe. Watch."

James swirls his hand, and the air above us spins. It spins slowly at first, but it gets faster as it takes on a strange solidity, almost like gel. The rough stone ceiling of the Chamber of Knowledge seems to disappear. In its place appears a clear blue sky. White fluffy clouds drift out from the distance and float overhead. The faint sound of birdsong echoes through the air. The chamber itself is now as bright as day.

Danielle gasps, and even the Guardians look impressed.

"That's pretty good," I say. "Can you set up picnic tables?"

James shakes his head. "I can make people *see* what isn't there simply enough, but illusions will use a lot of my energy if people interact with them too much. Unless . . ." He looks around the chamber again. "Some of these larger stones lying around could be useful. Keegan, do you think you could alter them into tables and chairs?"

Keegan glances at the boulders scattered throughout the chamber. "In a few more days I might be able to, but I'm still far too weak right now. Sorry."

"Oh, no worries," James says. "You should definitely rest. I can make-do with making the boulders appear to be wooden tables and chairs. If I set the illusions right, no one will actually touch anything but stone."

Jennifer smiles. "That should work," she says. "You should be able to embed or fuse the illusion into the rock."

"Well, Aleksandar?" I try to read his face, but it tends to range only from stony to stormy on the best of days. "I know it's not exactly real, but if they *think* we're better off than we are, would that work? For now?"

Aleksandar gestures around at the chamber and throws his hands up in despair. "If we're going to actually go through with this, anything we can do to make this place look better than it does is better than doing nothing."

"Well, in that case, everyone please move to the garden so I can clean the chambers without hitting any of you with stray pebbles! The garden is the only place that doesn't need to be cleaned. I'll prevent my magic for entering there."

James releases his illusion, and it dissipates. "I'll save this for when everyone's set to arrive. It's easy enough to restore."

When everyone has cleared out, I channel my intention down into my hands. I swirl my hands in front of me, embracing the element of air and calling it to me.

All around me, the air picks up speed until it's a growing vortex. When it reaches a crescendo, I envision it racing from my outstretched hands in long, steady bursts. These bursts spin up and around the chamber before they begin racing down the corridors and through the other chambers. They sweep away layers of dust, cobwebs, pebbles, and other debris. They continue to whip around until they dry out pockets of persistent dampness. I feel very much like the conductor of an orchestra leading a powerful wind section to play its music to the very heights of a massive concert hall.

Several minutes later, I stop to take a look. I gaze around the Chamber of Knowledge in wonder at my own magic. I start down the corridor to the Great Hall of Learning. No cobwebs or anything there. That's excellent. But then I scowl when I see the piles of dust scattered everywhere. All I've done is move it from one place to the next. I stare at one particularly large pile of dust that looks more like a miniature sand dune before flicking my hand toward it. It erupts into a billow of dust that gets all over everything.

I look around, thinking of an alternative. I think about how dry it looks in here now. Wait. *That's* the answer! Water.

I think of the water that cascades down the spiral staircase in the Chamber of Knowledge. That should be enough for what I need, and it has the drainage I need as well.

I walk back to the chamber and approach the water that pools just to the right of the stairs.

"Come, little water. It's time to do what you do best!"

I crouch, suck in some air, and gently blow across the surface of the water. The water leaps up joyously at the touch of my breath, eager to do my bidding.

I reach out again with my hands, using them as the physical manifestation of my will to guide the water throughout the chambers. It slowly rises out of its bed, seeping across the floor.

I focus my will and feel the flow of water grow in strength. It swirls and stretches across the Chamber of Knowledge until it finally reaches toward the other corridors.

Soon, the water is a couple of inches deep across the floors, everywhere except where I'm standing. My one little spot is still dry and safe. I swirl my hands around, churning my will before me. The water responds instantly, bubbling up and roiling like a rough sea, washing centuries of dust and grime off the floors.

When every surface in the chambers has been washed, I raise my arms up with a flourish, twisting them above my head. The water I have spread through Lannóg Eolas rushes back to me, churning in a mighty waterspout. I send it to the base of the waterfall and, with a downward thrust of my hands, the dirty water spirals back into the pool and drains away. I grin in satisfaction and rub my hands together. Another job well done.

I look around the chamber. The water has cleansed everything thoroughly, including the grand columns that stretch up to the vaulted ceiling. Upon them, I can now see fine engravings similar to what I saw in my dreams, and what we saw in the Hall of Mysteries. The dark red crystals of the columns sparkle.

Next, using the power of air, I move the large fallen stones into four rows of tables. I then arrange many smaller stones to serve as chairs.

Everything glistens wet and clean. I consider using a windstorm to dry everything out again, but the chambers could use some heat anyway. I focus on a spot just above my hand and clench my fist, envisioning my desire. A fireball erupts, crackling with heat. I stare at the energy flowing into and out of the fireball, trying to think a way of keeping it going. I soon find it: a conduit of energy that loops from me to it and back again. I create a conduit of fire and change it into a circuit. Just one tiny tendril of energy links me to it. I then set it down on the floor and walk several feet away from it. The ball of fire continues to crackle as though on its own accord. I extinguish the fire with a snap of my fingers.

I look down the various corridors between the Chamber of Knowledge and the tunnel that leads to the village. I know James didn't want any grand displays of fire, but surely a little one can't hurt. I smirk.

As I traverse the tunnel leading to Dunadin, the fire inside me builds in anticipation. When I get to the iron door at the end, I stare at it, focusing intently. I bring my hands up before me. I focus my will into my palms and direct it to either side of the door. I clench my fists. With a whoosh, two balls of orange fire roar to life. Using my newly discovered method, I tie their energy into circuits and repeat the process all the way back to the Chamber of Knowledge.

I turn to look at my work. It's a beautiful trail of "fire gates" burning brightly, each connected to me by a tiny tendril of energy. I close my eyes. Without any effort at all, I can feel each and every gate—how strong they are, how much light they're producing, how hot they are. I focus. I can feel the fire itself, but I can also sense the area immediately surrounding each gate. I find this an interesting observation that could prove useful.

I slowly spin in a circle, admiring the spotless chamber and the corridor of light. I thought that scattering pieces of my burning will throughout the Citadel would have made me feel weaker, but quite the contrary: I feel so *alive*!

I approach the garden with a giddy smile.

The Guardians and the Seeker are gathered near the yew tree, speaking quietly and seriously. Keegan, James, and Danielle are chatting near the bench by the pond. They laugh at something James says, but their laughter dies when they see me approach. Those standing by the yew tree also stop and look.

"Ladies and gentlemen," I say, "the Chamber of Knowledge is ready for James's grand illusion!"

No one speaks.

I shrug. "What's wrong?"

"You should *see* the energies coming out of you right now," James says. "You're alive with power!"

"What are you talking about?"

Keegan looks awestruck. "Exactly what he said, Aiden. You even look taller. There's so much power coming out of—and into—you. What's going on?"

"I feel amazing. More alive than I've ever felt before."

James looks past me, but no one can see my handiwork from here. "What did you do?"

"I just lit some, uh, things to light the way for our guests."

"Things . . . What *things*?"

"Well, just these small flames I created. They're self-sustaining . . . mostly."

Everyone exits the garden without another word. They all stare at the trail of fire gates leading toward the Chamber of Knowledge.

"These must be what's affecting you," says Keegan. "The fire energy is rolling around itself and building a charge, and it has nowhere to go except back into you."

"Does that mean it's making me stronger?" I ask, thinking about it.

"Very intriguing," Mary says slowly. "I don't think it would make you stronger. Wizards have a fixed strength. But it might let you call more magic at once, which would seem as though you're stronger. Can you get the energy back?"

"Oh, yes. The moment I call for it, the energy returns. These things are attached to me."

When we reach the Chamber of Knowledge, I give James a friendly punch on the shoulder. "You're up."

James closes his eyes. A perfect sun blossoms in the ceiling of the chamber, followed at once by a clear blue sky. A few seconds later, the sky begins creeping to the floor while at the same time the rocky floor transforms into a lush field of green beneath our feet. The field rushes out to meet the sky at the horizon. Before long, the chamber looks a hundred times larger than it really is.

Stretching from the tunnel where my fire gates burn, a marble roadway winds through the grass to where I arranged the large stones into rows. Below the rows comes a terrace of fine interlocking stone. In the blink of an eye, the rows are now beautifully crafted wooden tables with matching chairs. Each table is decorated with fine linen place mats, crystal wine flutes, and two large candles.

It's so beautiful that everyone is speechless.

"James," Keegan says finally, "if any sort of records exist for the most beautiful illusion, I think you just shattered them. This is gorgeous."

"Thanks, Keegan. I don't think I'll be able to make it look just like this again, though. The tables and chairs will hold since they're based on actual objects, but the wine flutes and place mats don't actually exist, so we can't use them. I might be able to fool one or two villagers into thinking they were holding a glass, but the illusion would shatter the moment we pour wine into one."

"We can use the goblets and plates from the kitchens in our quarters. There are more than enough," Elizabeth says.

"I hate to ruin the mood," Caitlin says, "but just what exactly are you planning on serving tonight? I'm assuming we'll be using the kitchens in the Guardians' quarters, but even if I were to leave for provisions now, I won't make it back on time."

"We've been so busy trying to make the place look pretty that we forgot about the food," Keegan mumbles. "We have some basic supplies in our cupboard, and there are some root vegetables in our garden. I could make roasted squash, turnips, carrots, and such."

"Jean mentioned that the villagers would try to hunt some game to bring," James says. "I think between us we should have more than enough to feed everyone."

I chuckle. "Does anyone know how to prepare and cook game meat? Or are we going to ask our guests to do it for us?"

Danielle raises her hand. "My father is an avid hunter. I used to help cook what he brought home. I'll volunteer to cook the meat if someone else handles the vegetables."

"I will help," David says. "The wizards should spend their time mingling with the guests."

"I'll help too," Jennifer says.

James pulls Danielle into a tight embrace. He kisses her long and deep. "I'll make you three a deal on behalf of Keegan and Aiden. You can make the dinner. But when it's ready, we will serve it. The villagers are in flux right now. They already believe us to be gods. I don't think we should encourage the idea that we need to be waited on. We want to set ourselves apart from the experience they've had with the Church. Our bringing them their food will help us seem more down to earth."

Aleksandar nods but doesn't say anything. It's finally something he seems on board with. It really is a brilliant idea. It would be too easy for us to get full of ourselves and to think of ourselves as deserving the praise and service that the villagers would invariably want to provide.

"Does anyone know how to play any instruments?" Evelyn asks quietly. "It would be so nice to hear some music during dinner."

"Do we even have any instruments?" I ask.

"We've found a flute, a drum, and what I believe to be a lute," David says. "They're ancient. I would say the lute is probably several hundred years out of tune, but we may be able to remedy that."

"Surely they're merely artifacts now. They would probably fall apart if anyone tried to play them."

"On the contrary. They appear to be enchanted, because they're in remarkably good condition."

"Well," Caitlin says quietly, "I learned how to play the violin when I was a young child and practiced every day until I left home. With a little practice, I might be able to figure out the lute. They're both fingerboard instruments."

"That would be lovely," say Evelyn.

"Come, Caitlin," David says. "I'll show you where the lute is. Perhaps I can help you figure it out.

Moments after Caitlin and David have left, I feel a subtle shift in the fire gate next to the iron door in the mountainside in Dunadin. It's no more than a twinge, but it's enough.

I glance at James and Keegan. "They're here!"

We rush to our quarters to get dressed. When we cross the threshold, we slow to a crawl and peer around. Something has changed. The hairs on the back of my neck are standing on end, and the air tingles with electricity.

James notices them first. He reaches out to tug on my sleeve. "Look!" He points.

Brand new robes hang where our plain white robes once did.

My robe is pure black with a red dragon emblazoned on the chest. Gold Sanskrit-like script runs down the arms and flows into the cuffs, giving the impression of words constantly flowing down my arms. The sleeves are large and ornate.

James's robe is a rich dark purple with various elemental symbols rolling down his sleeves in silver. A powerful-looking owl with wings outstretched adorns the chest. Keegan's is a deep forest green with a white tree of life growing on the chest.

We say nothing as we quietly put them on. James and I stare at each other in silence for several seconds. Our robes fit perfectly on us.

Keegan looks at us, and his eyebrows shoot up. He whistles. "Wow . . ."

"Beautiful, aren't we?" I ask.

He shrugs, suddenly nonchalant. "You're okay." He pretends to brush some dust off his own immaculate new robe.

James and I chuckle.

I reach out and take hold of my staff. As my fingers close around it, the head comes to life. The wood transforms into the same dragon emblazoned on my chest. The writing on my sleeves starts to glow, and the dragon on my robe takes on an unsettling realness. A chill runs through me when I realize that this is the same outfit and the same staff that are carved on the casket of the wizard in the tomb and depicted on the walls in the Hall of Mysteries. Who was that wizard?

Suddenly, the Goddess is standing right there in our quarters. She is shrouded in darkness, half obscured by a swirling mist. Vines wrap around her body and make her look strangely seductive. She approaches me, gliding through the vines that entwine themselves around her as she moves.

A single finger runs down my chest, sending shivers up my spine. She gracefully traces her finger up to my chin. She tips my head up appraisingly. I gaze into her azure eyes.

"You look exactly how I need you to look, Wizard Aiden," she says. "A man who is proud of his strengths, proud of his station. A man who understands that he is the first I have chosen in three thousand years to do my bidding and who will, along with Wizard James and Wizard Keegan, restore humanity to its true purpose in this world. Yet you carry yourself with a humility that makes others naturally trust you. You are perfect, my darling. I could not have wished for better wizards to be born into this world."

In a flash, she is gone.

I glance down. I take a moment to think whether or not that really just happened. The dragon on my chest no longer looks ready to breathe fire, but the script on my sleeves still glows. I glance at my staff. The newly formed dragon is still there. Its eyes glow with power waiting to be unleashed. I draw myself up straighter and commit myself to owning this robe, this staff. Oddly, I do feel as if they truly belong to me.

"Thank you," I whisper.

I look over at James and Keegan. They both appear as sure of themselves as I now am, and their faces look filled with the same sense of purpose that I now feel. The head of Keegan's staff has transformed into a beautiful deer that exudes peace, while the head of James's staff is now shaped like a wise owl, its eyes all-seeing.

The anxious voices of villagers begin to fill our quarters from down the tunnel. Now and then, I can hear the Guardians conversing with them.

"Well, gentlemen," I say. "I believe it will be somewhat hard to blend in now, but shall we?"

James nods and smiles. Keegan takes a deep breath but smiles as well.

I roll my shoulders and feel the robe conform perfectly to my body, just as though it were a pliable suit of armour. It looks like cloth, but something tells me it's so much more. This is my official robe, and instinctively I know it will try to protect me against anything that might threaten me.

I walk forward with my staff in hand.

I step out into the Chamber of Knowledge. Keegan and James follow me closely on either side. I can feel us project peace and power so strongly that I can almost touch it. The chamber falls silent. There are no less than seventy people in the chamber, and they all watch us while we follow the path running through the grass. People step out of the way with a bow as we pass them.

We walk toward Jean. He was deep in conversation with Evelyn and Aleksandar when we entered. He now stares at us in awe.

"You say you are not gods," he says, "but before today I have seen you just as you are now. You are pictured with crystal clarity in the Hall of Mysteries. That is an ancient place. If you are not gods, then what are you?"

"Perhaps," James says, "the gods inspired the artist to paint this moment in time so that you would recognize us when we arrived."

Out of the corner of my eye, I see Aleksandar almost smile in approval—almost.

"We have never claimed that we do not *serve* gods," Keegan says, "only that we are not gods ourselves."

Jean looks like he's going to ask another question, but instead he keeps quiet.

James glances at me and blinks a few times. I clench my teeth. I know he wants me to say something now, but he also knows I hate speaking in front of crowds. Regardless, all eyes are on me. Everyone's waiting for me to speak.

I clear my throat. "My friends from Dunadin." My attempt to project my voice scratches my throat. "We welcome you!"

I gesture around the room, and two tiny flames burst to life on each tabletop as my magic lights the candles. James, instinctively on the same page as me, makes an almost undetectable gesture, and the brilliant blue sky fades to a deepening sunset. There is a collection of gasps, and more than one villager subtly makes the sign of the cross.

Perhaps sensing my unease, James takes over. "We have provided a seat for everyone at the tables, and we hope you will appreciate the setting. Over the course of the next few days, we shall help you rebuild your homes, the schoolhouse, the farms, the market, but for now, let us eat as friends. You are all welcome to spend the night here. Tomorrow, we will begin with a fresh start. We will rebuild your village anew!"

Once James has finished speaking, the villagers shuffle anxiously toward their seats. I watch as they sit, and I feel uneasy again. It takes me a moment to figure it out, but once I do, I wonder why I didn't notice it right away. Regardless of whether it's a family or a group of friends sitting at a particular table, no one makes eye contact. The silence in the chamber is palpable.

Jean seems to read my unease. He steps close to me and speaks quietly. "Even in the best of times, we are a quiet and very private people, Wizard Aiden. In our village, where our homes are close and everything is familiar, we are open and frank. But these people are in an unfamiliar place for the first time. This is an experience far greater than seeing even the Hall of Mysteries. They are terrified of doing something that might make you rethink your offer of help. Give them time, and they will relax."

"How many have seen the Hall of Mysteries? I thought only a select few have."

Jean shakes his head. "Mathieu studied its contents, but we have a coming-of-age ritual where we secretly introduce young villagers to the Hall of Mysteries. Based on the murals, we believe it is only one part of the ancient palaces that once filled the land. We see it as a part of our history."

I nod thoughtfully. "There's something I don't understand, Jean. If every villager eventually sees the hall, why wasn't the Church able to find it?"

He tilts his head slightly. "What do you mean?"

"You've said yourself that some among you are very religious. If they believe in the teachings of the Church, why wouldn't they tell Père Georges about your secret?"

Jean is silent for a very long time as he thinks about this. "To be honest, I don't know the answer to your question. If the Church is truly as scared of you as it seems to be, and if Père Georges had discovered the way to this place"—he gestures grandly at the Chamber of Knowledge—"there would have been many more than just one priest here when you arrived at the village that first time."

"That's a good point, especially considering the resources they had at their disposal."

"I'm trying to think of a reason why no villager has told any priests about our secret. Perhaps by some magic we are subconsciously prevented from mentioning it if a priestly type is within earshot."

I think of the crystal pyramid that once provided a barrier of protection for Dunadin.

"That's a possibility," I say quietly.

Dinner was what I would call a great success.

Toward the end of the night, the villagers move in to the Guardians' quarters, where they have fire pits to keep them warm and enough space to lay their bedrolls. It's a tight squeeze to fit everyone, but they seem to appreciate the warmth and shelter. The Guardians have decided to share Evelyn's quarters.

Once the villagers have retired for the night, the rest of us gather around the table in the Chamber of Knowledge. The torchlight reflects off everyone's faces. The Guardians begin to show their worry and concern.

I take my place between James and Keegan and look at the Guardians expectantly.

Aleksandar speaks first. "What, Wizard Aiden, is your opinion on the status of Dunadin?"

"As we've already seen, besides the now destroyed passage that the Church used, there are no outside roads that lead here besides our own. There is no postal service, no phone lines. Despite all of this, there's no guarantee that another priest or even a whole army won't find their way through the mountains before long!"

Mary speaks after a long silence. "I believe we can count on the villagers to not expose us. We could also limit our engagement with them so that we limit the chances of being discovered."

Jennifer leans forward. "Too many people have been involved. And we don't have the complete trust of all the villagers yet. I'd give good money that some of them would spill everything to the first priest they saw. We can be sure the whole Church would descend upon us after that happens. Cardinal Gallagher also seems to be the Pope's right hand, so we must assume the Church knew where he was. We have to leave the Citadel. And the sooner the better."

Chaos erupts at Jennifer's suggestion. I've never seen the Guardians openly disagreeing with each other like this, but now contradictory opinions are being voiced—and with much passion.

"It is not so simple," Evelyn says as loud as she can manage. At her voice, the chaos dies instantly, and all heads turn to her. "We can leave, but this place has been the seat of the power of the wizards since the dawn of time. It is charged and embedded with energies that the Church could use against us. And then there's this Hall of Mysteries, and who know what else below Dunadin? Once the Church learns that their team in Dunadin has been eliminated, they'll send enough people to the village that they would surely uncover everything regardless of the magical wards that protect them. We don't yet know what kind of information is in these so-called mysteries."

"So if leaving isn't the answer," Jennifer says, "and staying will lead to a confrontation, are you saying our only choice is a fight?"

Caitlin leans forward. "We're not ready to face the entire Church head-on in a fight. If it came down to that, they would destroy us in no time. At the very least, we'd be on the run for the rest of our lives."

It's easy to read everyone's silence as agreement.

This time, it's David who speaks. "I believe it's time for the next stage of training."

"Next stage?" James asks.

The other Guardians simply nod.

"You have come far in these few months, but you still have very limited control over your power," David says. "Look at what happened when Aiden tried to keep that rock from falling in the village."

"Well," I say, "what do you have in mind?"

"A quest." It's Evelyn who says this, and even the Guardians look a bit surprised. "Beyond the Guardians' quarters is a dark tunnel. You will walk down it for a full day until you find a large lake covered in mist. You will find a boat on the shore. In the boat, you will find the Goddess. You will board the boat in silence, and she will take you to the start of your quest to prove your abilities as wizards."

"A quest?" James asks. His voice sounds small in the chamber.

As one, the Guardians stand, wrapping themselves in resolution. "Wizards," Evelyn says in the resolute voice of the Speaker, "it is time for you to embark on the Journey of Proving."

Acknowledgements

First and foremost, I need to thank my partner, Chris Johnstone, for putting up with me as I burned the midnight candle at my desk, cancelled plans in order to write, and forced him to read yet another revision. He also receives a very heartfelt thank you for making my vision of the Citadel of the Wizards come to life by drawing the map found on the following pages. A very special thanks also goes to my grandmother, Ivy Dyer, for her steadfast belief in me and constant urging to continue writing.

This book would not be possible without my muse and writing partner Melissa Arnold, my sister Michelle Byer who kept me going by demanding to read each chapter as I finished it, or my early readers who provided such critical, if hard to swallow, feedback: Krys Aker (a.k.a. Grace), Michael Ahrens, Teresa Aker, Emily Bartlett, Ryan Becker, Kristine Cyr, Vanessa Di Maria, Cole Gorman, Dylan Inksetter, Noorin Murji, Donald Taylor, and especially my mom, Dorothea Byer.

A big thanks goes to the DicoFranPro project and Professeur Manuel Meune of the Université de Montréal for their help with translating phrases from English to the Savoyard dialect of the Francoprovençal language found in the remote part of the French Alps, which part of the novel is set in.

I would also like to thank my publishing, editing, and design teams at FriesenPress, and my editor Dan Varrette, who challenged me to make tough decisions and worked so closely with me to finesse the novel into its final form.

Lastly, there are two teachers whose encouragement has been a constant presence in my thoughts despite the years that have passed: Mrs. O'Leary and Ms. VanAlstyne.

Without the belief of all of you, none of this would have happened.

CPSIA information can be obtained
at www.ICGtesting.com
Printed in the USA
BVHW072102130820
586223BV00004B/298